IT'S A MAN'S WORLD

Polly works as an independent consultant for several UK media businesses, including the publishers of leading men's titles. She also writes freelance for various magazines.

Polly started her career as an investment banker and used her experiences to write her first novel, *Golden Handcuffs*, which earned critical acclaim in the *Observer, The Times, Independent, Guardian, Daily Express, Daily Mail* and *Evening Standard*. *It's A Man's World* is Polly's sixth novel, her other titles being: *Poles Apart, The Day I Died, The Fame Factor* and *Defying Gravity*. She has a degree in Engineering from Cambridge University and lives in West London with her boyfriend.

For more information about Polly please visit www.pollycourtney.com

By the same author:

The Day I Died
The Fame Factor

POLLY COURTNEY

It's A Man's World

AVON

AVON

A division of HarperCollins*Publishers*
77–85 Fulham Palace Road,
London W6 8JB

www.harpercollins.co.uk

A Paperback Original 2011

1

First published in Great Britain by
HarperCollins*Publishers* 2011

A catalogue record for this book is
available from the British Library

ISBN-13: 978-1-84756-148-0

Set in Minion by Palimpsest Book Production Limited,
Falkirk, Stirlingshire

Printed and bound in Great Britain by
Clays Ltd, St Ives plc

MIX
Paper from
responsible sources
FSC® **C007454**
www.fsc.org

FSC is a non-profit international organisation established to promote the responsible management of the world's forests. Products carrying the FSC label are independently certified to assure consumers that they come from forests that are managed to meet the social, economic and ecological needs of present and future generations.

Find out more about HarperCollins and the environment at
www.harpercollins.co.uk/green

Many people helped to inspire, shape and publish this book. Firstly, I'd like to thank the members of OBJECT for their tireless work in challenging our 'sex object culture'. Good luck with your campaigns and thank you for opening my eyes. Thanks also to those at Bauer Media who helped, wittingly or unwittingly, to provide a relevant backdrop to the story. A big thank you to my dear friend Caroline, who read every page in record time and put me straight when I went off course. Of course, I thank Sammia and everyone at Avon for turning my words into a published book and lastly, I thank Chris, for putting up with my hermit impression. I couldn't have done it without you.

To Caroline – because we all need a Leonie in our lives.

1

'Ah, Alexa. Thanks for coming to see me.' Terry Peterson leaned forward and waved at the seat opposite.

Alexa pressed the door shut behind her, relishing the wall of cold air that separated Peterson's office from the rest of the building. As the folds of soft, cool leather engulfed her, she wondered whether Peterson really believed that there had been any element of choice about today's meeting. To turn down an invitation from the chief executive of Senate Media UK, particularly an ambiguous, last-minute 'catch up', was to propel oneself straight to the top of the redundancy list.

'I've been thinking about your role,' said Peterson, leaning forward and blinking a couple of times at Alexa.

She nodded, forcing a smile despite the stomach-churning sensation that his ominous words had provoked. Alexa was on a two-year contract at *Hers*, Senate's leading title for the over-fifties, of which there were still three months left to run.

'Sorry,' he chuckled. 'Poor choice of words. Don't look so worried.'

Alexa smiled harder and joined in with a laugh of her own. Despite his fifty-seven years, Peterson had a good head of hair and piercing blue eyes that crinkled attractively at the edges as he smiled, which he did *all the time*. The chief executive wore his smile like a mask.

'As you know, I'm very pleased with your achievements at *Hers*.'

Alexa nodded again, more confidently. Peterson *was* pleased with the re-launch of *Hers*; she knew that much. Who wouldn't be pleased with a three-fold increase in gross revenue and a twenty percent reduction in costs? The magazine had been on the brink of collapse when Alexa, then a management consultant at TDS Consulting, had been seconded to establish a new business plan for the title. At Peterson's request and at vast expense, Alexa had been transferred from TDS and brought in-house at Senate Media to oversee the execution of this trans-formation – a transformation that was just beginning to bear fruit. The magazine was cash positive for the first time in a decade and Alexa had made it happen.

'I think you proved a lot of people wrong – not least the Americans.'

Alexa returned his smile. Being part of a US-owned company meant that everyone in the UK offices, including Terry Peterson, answered to the board of Senate Media Inc., or 'the Americans', as they were known.

Alexa knew what the Americans had thought of Peterson's initial suggestion that a twenty-nine-year-old management consultant should take charge of their fifty-plus title. She knew, because Peterson's PA had inadvertently forwarded her an email containing the full conversation between the UK and US board. Alexa sometimes wondered whether she would have made quite so much progress at *Hers* had she not caught sight of that email.

'I'm thinking,' said Peterson, his eyes still twinkling, 'you might be able to help us out on something else.'

Alexa felt a combination of apprehension and relief. Peterson's smile was suspiciously intense.

'Another title,' he clarified. 'It's the same set of problems we had at *Hers*, really: declining circulation, collapsing advertising industry, increasing competition from the internet . . .'

Alexa looked at him, trying to guess which magazine they were talking about. Frankly, it could have been any Senate title, or any UK magazine for that matter. The whole publishing industry was falling apart.

'I'm referring, of course, to *Banter*.'

Alexa swallowed. She looked up to the wall behind Peterson's head, where a set of black frames immortalised the front cover of every title ever published by Senate Media UK. *Banter* was there, top right, next to *Teenz*, an American import that had a limited life expectancy. Alexa glanced at the cover and then looked away, gazing at the bustle of Soho in the mid-afternoon heat. She tried to collect her thoughts. Even looking at the cover felt wrong. There was such a concentration of flesh and cleavage, it was overwhelming. Breasts spilled off the page, a smattering of strategically placed headlines obscuring nipples and other bodily parts that would tip the magazine into the category of porn – if it wasn't already there.

Porn, mused Alexa, increasingly aware that Peterson was expecting some kind of a response. That was the answer, up there on the wall, amid the airbrushed buttocks and cleavages. *Banter* was a form of soft porn. It was dirty, sexist, degrading to women and, frankly, an embarrassment to UK society. What would her mother say if she found out she was working for *Banter*?

Alexa pursed her lips, angry with herself for letting her mother's opinion interfere with her decision-making. She was turning thirty next year.

'I . . .'

Alexa cursed inwardly. The image of her disapproving mother was distracting. But there was something else, deep inside her, knocking her thoughts off course. It was small, only partially formed, but Alexa knew instantly what it was.

'I'm not familiar with the lads' mag market,' she said.

'Just as you weren't familiar with the over-fifties market,' Peterson returned, pointedly.

The feeling swelled inside her. Alexa tried to suppress it. She recognised it from the first time she had sat in this room with the chief executive – the time he had asked her to take on the *Hers* re-launch. It was the buzz of the challenge. She could do little to quash it, this amorphous sensation at the back of her mind. *Banter* was one of Senate Media's flagship brands. It was a household name. Licensed in seventeen countries and filled with the dirtiest smut that could be legally sold in supermarkets around the world – and some that couldn't – the magazine had been a controversial hit for Senate since its launch nearly seven years ago. Unfortunately, though, this was one challenge she would have to turn down.

'As I said,' Peterson went on, uninterested in Alexa's protest, 'the project isn't dissimilar to the one you've undertaken at *Hers*. The only difference is the severity.'

'The severity of . . . what?' Alexa knew that what she really ought to be doing was telling Peterson, politely, that she wasn't interested in the role. But she was curious.

'*Banter*'s circulation fell by a third this year. The audience isn't buying magazines any more – or if they are, they're buying a competitor's.' He shook his head. 'And then there's the legal costs.'

Alexa nodded. No explanation was required. Lawsuits against *Banter* were legendary. Nearly every week, *Banter* was served a writ by some celebrity objecting to a crude or racist joke in the magazine.

'The truth of the matter – and please, don't mention this outside these four walls – is that the Americans are looking to shut it down by the end of the year.'

'*What?*' Alexa stared. She hadn't meant to speak, not until she had formulated her polite rejection of Peterson's offer. But *shut it down? Banter* was one of Senate's biggest brands.

Terry nodded, his smile wavering a little. 'They're looking to cut costs.'

'Right.' Alexa tried to hide her morbid fascination. She would have liked to see a copy of *Banter*'s financials, just to find out where they were going so badly wrong.

Peterson suddenly straightened up in his chair, looking at Alexa with a strangely breezy expression.

'However! It's not all doom and gloom. I've secured us a lifeline. If we can turn things around by the end of the financial year then we're home and dry.'

We, noted Alexa. She hadn't agreed to anything.

'Mind you,' he went on, 'I had to agree to some fairly hefty year-end targets in order to get the Americans to agree.'

Alexa did some quick mental arithmetic. It was early July. *Banter* had until the end of April to hit its year-end targets. That was less than ten months. Re-launching *Hers* had taken over a year and that was just a magazine with a few online tools. Reviving *Banter* would involve websites, tablet editions, mobile apps . . . Alexa stopped herself. She was already thinking about the solutions. This wasn't a project she would be working on.

'Look,' she said, meeting his eye. 'I'm sure this would be a great opportunity for someone, but I'm not sure I'm the right person for the job.'

'Ah.' Peterson leaned forward, squinting jovially. 'I know what you're thinking. You're young, you're female and you're worried that the staff won't treat you with respect.'

Alexa hesitated. That wasn't what she had been thinking at all.

'I've come up with a solution that I think you'll like.'

'No, the thing is—'

'Hear me out.' The chief executive raised a warning finger. Alexa was reminded yet again that the smile was a veneer. 'I think we should give you the title of *managing director*. That way, we won't be treading on any toes but you'll get the respect you deserve.'

Alexa frowned. Quite apart from the fact that she didn't want to be discussing the politics of an office in which she had no plans to work, she couldn't think of a single magazine that had a managing director at its helm. Magazines were run by *editors*.

'How does that work?' she asked, despite herself.

'Derek Piggott has been acting editor for the past nine months,' Peterson explained, so I suggest that we promote him to deputy editor and—'

'*Promote?* Isn't that a *demotion?*'

'Well, strictly speaking. But I suggest we don't make him *editor* in case he tries to pull rank. I've known Derek for years. He's a good man, just a little . . . well, I'm sure you'll be fine.'

Alexa wondered for a moment what Peterson meant, then stopped herself and leaned forward in the chair.

'I'm sorry, but I think you need to look elsewhere for your managing director,' she said, as clearly as she possibly could without risk of sounding condescending.

'Alexa, I think you're the right person for the job. I called you here today because I wanted to ask *you* to undertake the project.'

And because you need to fill the position as quickly as possible, thought Alexa, wondering how much of Peterson's persuasion was down to his faith in her ability and how much was due to desperation.

'You have the experience from your work at *Hers* and you understand digital . . . wireless . . . solutions.'

Alexa managed to refrain from laughing. Terry Peterson was not known for his technological know-how. Having worked in the magazine industry since the late eighties, he was very much a man of paper and ink. If the rumours were to be believed, his morning ritual involved his PA printing out the contents of his inbox, then Peterson replying to each email on pieces of paper for the PA to type up and send. Perhaps, thought Alexa, the chief executive's aversion to new technology might be a factor in the decline in so many Senate brands.

'*That's* where the money is, these days,' Peterson went on, his confidence sounding a little shaky. 'You understand that. You did it for *Hers*. You can do it for *Banter.*'

Alexa nodded warily. There were so many reasons for not

taking on the project. It involved undisclosed targets that even the CEO was describing as 'hefty', the timeframe seemed ludicrously short and what with this Derek character and Peterson's *managing director* proposal, it sounded like a political minefield. But most of all, thought Alexa, seeing the image of her mother flash through her mind again, there was the fact that *Banter* was a porn magazine.

She held Peterson's gaze, trying again to come up with a firm but polite rejection. As she opened her mouth to speak, she saw that Peterson's expression had changed. He was smiling more intensely than ever, like a hypnotist defying his charge to disobey.

'We'll add twenty percent to your day rate.'

Alexa closed her mouth. After several more seconds of thought, she finally formulated her reply.

'I'll think about it,' she said.

2

Alexa sipped her drink, glancing periodically towards the door. She swilled the bitter cocktail around her mouth, challenging her taste buds to ascertain how exactly a Japanese margarita differed from an ordinary one and to establish which ingredient was responsible for the fifteen-pound price tag.

Only Kate would choose a place like this, thought Alexa, giving up on the challenge and accepting that tonight was going to be an expensive night. These days, hanging out in the expensive part of Mayfair was just about the only way to ensnare her high-flying friend, who seemed to spend a disproportionate amount of time in her Berkeley Square offices.

Alexa tipped back her final mouthful and asked the barman for a glass of water. As she did so, the door swung open to reveal a windswept, mousy-looking blonde who seemed perplexed by the waiter's desire to take her coat. Alexa waved Leonie over.

'Bit posh, isn't it?' Leonie screwed up her nose and nodded in the direction of the cloakroom, where men in green jackets swished soundlessly about their business. 'Don't they have pubs around here?'

Alexa smiled. 'You know Kate.'

Leonie rolled her eyes. She squinted at Alexa's glass and a look of relief crossed her face. 'Is that tap water?'

'Purest spring water from the Japanese Alps,' replied Alexa, smiling. 'Of course it's tap water.'

Leonie motioned to the barman for another and gulped down her glassful in one, pulling a face as an ice cube toppled onto her nose.

Alexa laughed. She and Leonie had been friends since high school, their surnames – Harris and Hatton – dictating that they should sit next to one another in class. Establishing themselves as lab partners for science lessons, they both went on to study biology in their degrees, albeit at different universities. After uni, their paths diverged again, Leonie opting to teach Biology in a south London comprehensive and Alexa following the more lucrative path into the world of management consulting. It was while working at TDS Consulting that Alexa had met Kate – who, coincidentally, had been at uni with Leonie in Edinburgh.

'How's school?'

Leonie's eyes flitted up to the ceiling. 'Exhausting. Most of my kids have exams, so I'm looking after the younger ones. It's all videos and field trips and lessons outside. Yesterday, I had two lads climbing out of the second-floor window and abseiling down a drainpipe, trying to distract the girls in the classroom below.'

'Sounds like the end of term.' Alexa smiled.

'Piers broke up weeks ago, lucky bastard. He hangs around the flat like a little lost puppy, waiting for me to get home every night. Although I shouldn't complain; he cooks dinner.'

Alexa laughed, in awe, as ever, of her friend's perfect relationship. Piers and Leonie had met at a kids' camp in Camberwell, just after leaving school. Predictions that the holiday romance would fizzle once they went off to universities at opposite ends of the country had been proved wrong; nearly twelve years later, they were back with the kids in south London – although in Piers' case, it was a very different bunch of kids. He had landed on his feet at King Charles' Boys' School in Dulwich, recently being promoted to Head of Science and enjoying a significant pay rise with apparently very little extra work. Leonie, meanwhile, was dealing with over-crowded classrooms, drug-addicted kids, bullies and pupils who spat in her face at Langdale Comprehensive. Still, she seemed to enjoy the challenge.

Alexa nodded at the empty glass. 'D'you want a proper drink?'

'I think I need one.' Leonie drew the menu towards her. She studied it for a couple of seconds, then slowly pushed it away. 'Um . . . actually, no. I might just . . . leave it for a bit.'

Alexa looked at her friend. She knew what the problem was. 'I'll pay.'

'We could . . . share?'

Alexa laughed. She could just imagine the barman's face when they asked for a cocktail with two straws. Then she realised that Leonie was being serious.

'My round,' she said firmly. 'What're you having?'

Reluctantly, Leonie pointed at one of the martinis on the list. 'Thanks,' she said quietly.

Alexa ordered the drinks, grateful that Kate wasn't here to witness the moment. Public sector teaching salaries were an embarrassment, particularly compared to the rates that could be commanded in their field of work.

Leonie grasped the slender stem and gently tapped her glass against Alexa's.

'So,' she said. 'What's the summit in aid of?'

'Well, I—'

'Hi!' screamed a voice from the doorway. A swoosh of short, raven-black hair could be seen from inside a cloud of suit jackets, laptop bags and rucksacks, all of which were shed in rapid succession and dumped on the bewildered-looking doorman. Kate had arrived.

'Hey, guys!' Kate leaned forward and threw her arms around the two of them. Alexa smiled as her shoulders were squeezed, aware of the dirty looks they were attracting from other customers. That was the thing about Kate. She had no shame.

'Sorry I'm so late. Bastard project. All the partners have

buggered off, leaving me to "just quickly update the pack". I think tonight might be another all-nighter.'

Alexa pulled a face. 'You're going back to the office after this?'

Kate nodded, waving to catch the barman's eye.

All-nighter. Alexa thought back to her early years at TDS, when, as a fresh-faced graduate, working through the night had been a regular occurrence. She shuddered, remembering how it felt to be trapped in that stale, airless office at three o'clock in the morning, feeling your brain grinding to a halt, filling your bloodstream with caffeine and taurine in an effort to ward off the inevitable exhaustion. Never again. Alexa had done her time. However tempting the salary, she would not be going back to work at a 'big five' firm like TDS.

Kate drew the sugar-coated cocktail towards her. 'One can't hurt, can it? Might help me be a bit more creative with my strategy.' She grinned and wolfed down about five pounds' worth of drink. Alexa watched, marvelling at her friend's stamina. She was showing no sign of slowing down as she neared the end of her twenties.

Sipping her drink, Alexa became aware of Leonie's eyes on hers. She was still waiting for an answer to her earlier question. Alexa took a deep breath and looked at her friend.

'I've been offered a new job.'

Kate stopped drinking, mid-sip, and lowered her glass to the bar.

Leonie leaned in excitedly. 'Where?'

'Within Senate. It's . . .' Alexa found herself struggling to say the name out loud. 'It's . . . you know the lads' mag, *Banter*?'

'Oh my God!' Kate gasped. 'Of course we know it! Are they asking you to be editor of *Banter*?'

Alexa hesitated. 'Sort of. It's similar to what I've been doing at *Hers*. Finding new revenue streams, new channels, that kind of thing.'

'Oh. Wow.' Kate rocked forward on her bar stool, looking respectfully into Alexa's eyes. 'Lex, that is amazing.'

11

'Well done, mate.' Leonie raised her glass. There was hesitation in her voice.

'But . . .' Alexa squirmed, avoiding Kate's open-mouthed stare and Leonie's wary expression. 'I don't think I'll take it.'

'What!' yelped Kate.

Leonie just looked at her, waiting.

Alexa sighed. She had been half expecting this set of responses. For Kate, the most important thing in life was career progression. Her beliefs were based on a kind of post-feminist mantra that went along the lines of: *women should feel the same pressure to succeed in the workplace as men.* She intended to become a partner at TDS before she hit thirty next year and, as far as Alexa could tell, there wasn't much standing in her way. Leonie, however, was naturally cautious and saw life through the lens of a secondary school teacher – always thinking about the bigger picture.

'Have you ever looked at a copy of *Banter*?' asked Alexa, by way of explanation.

Leonie replied with a loaded nod.

'What's wrong with girls showing a bit of ass?' Kate was clearly outraged that Alexa might be considering turning down such an opportunity. 'That's what men want! It makes money! *Banter* is one of the UK's biggest brands.'

'Yeah. For all sorts of reasons,' Leonie said pointedly.

Alexa ignored this comment and turned to Kate. 'It doesn't make as much money as you might think. I looked at their financials. Even stripping out the cost of lawsuits, they only make a few pence profit per copy.'

Kate looked at her, smiling a little. 'So, you're already looking at their financial model, then? You want to take this on, don't you?'

Alexa shrugged helplessly. *No*, she wanted to say. No, she didn't want to take on the role because it was inappropriate and unethical. But there was something inside her that wouldn't let her rule it out. Peterson had given her two weeks to decide and she had already used up one of them, yo-yoing between the arguments for and against.

Leonie cleared her throat. 'I can see why you wouldn't.'

'What?' cried Kate, staring accusingly at Leonie. 'Sorry, but what's wrong with working for *Banter*? We're not prudes, are we? There's nothing wrong with lads' mags. Hey,' she nudged Alexa in the ribs and lowered her voice to a conspiratorial whisper, 'it's less shameful than saying you work for Tedious Consulting.'

Alexa smiled lamely. Kate was wrong. It was far, far worse to tell someone that you worked in the soft porn industry than one of the soulless but highly respected consultancy firms like TDS – especially when that someone was your mother.

'Have you told your mum?' asked Leonie, right on cue. She knew Alexa's mother from their school days.

Alexa raised one corner of her mouth in a wry smile. 'What do you think?'

Leonie matched her expression. 'I think she'd disown you if you told her.'

Alexa sighed. Leonie was probably right. A sudden, unwanted image flashed across her mind of the two of them, aged nine, scrambling up the stairs of Leonie's parents' house, wearing various lacy garments sourced from Leonie's mother's wardrobe and their own interpretation of pop star makeup. Her mother, arriving early to pick up Alexa, had turned purple with rage at the sight of them. It was only the presence of Leonie's mother, hovering nervously in the doorway, that had saved them from the initial outburst of rage. As it was, Alexa had suffered alone, on the journey home, and the mental scars would probably stay with her forever. Alexa knew exactly how her mother felt. She was a Class A prude and nothing would ever change that.

'Who cares what your mum thinks?' Kate screwed up her nose. 'She's probably about fifty years behind the times! Fuck that. You don't need to pander to her way of thinking.'

Alexa and Leonie looked at one another.

'You haven't met Lex's mum, have you?' asked Leonie, politely.

Kate looked nonplussed, then quickly brightened again. 'What about Matt?' she asked. 'What does he think?'

Alexa allowed herself a little smile. Six months had passed and still it felt new and exciting – or rather, it still felt unreal. For once, things were working out on the man front.

'His first question was whether he'd get free copies of *Banter*.' Kate hooted. 'Typical! That is *so* Matt!'

Alexa smiled. She didn't mind that Kate took the credit for setting her up with Matt, or that she pretended to know him when in fact he had simply been one of the hundreds of guests at her New Year's Eve party. She didn't mind, because frankly she *was* grateful – to Kate or to fate – for getting them together.

'Then he kind of went a bit . . . weird.' Alexa squirmed as she remembered the way Matt's expression had changed. It was as though he had flipped from being excited to lukewarm, in an instant.

'What sort of weird?' asked Leonie.

'Well . . .' Alexa hesitated, unable to think of a better description. 'I think he just has some reservations.'

'What?' Kate screwed up her nose. 'Matt's not a raving feminist, is he?'

'No. I think it might be more . . .' Alexa hesitated, unsure as to whether her theory stood up. 'I think it could be the male-dominated environment.'

Kate's expression intensified. 'He wouldn't be jealous, would he?'

'He's too good-looking to be the jealous type,' said Leonie.

Alexa shook her head, thinking of Matt's piercing blue eyes and his fine blond hair. 'I think he's probably just worried. He said he's seen what lads can be like. He said something about a "lions' den".'

Kate rolled her eyes. 'Like he'd know, from his experience in a city law firm!'

Leonie flashed Alexa a warning look. 'He's probably had some experience on the rugby pitch.'

'Oh . . .' Kate waved a hand. 'That's bollocks. Totally different. This is the workplace. You can handle it, Lex.'

'So, is it *all* men, on the team?' Leonie persisted.

'Apart from one.'

The first thing Alexa had done following her meeting with Peterson had been to grab a copy of *Banter* and tear out the credits page. There were twenty-four men on the staff and one woman – an editor's PA/editorial assistant named Sienna Pageant.

'One girl, eh? I bet she has a laugh,' remarked Kate.

Alexa nodded, wondering, not for the first time, what type of person Sienna Pageant might be. She glanced at Leonie, who didn't need to voice her concerns; they were written all over her face.

'Well,' said Kate, as though her mind was made up. 'Damo says there's a girl in his office who—'

'Hang on, who's Damo?'

'Oh. He's a guy I'm kinda seeing,' Kate replied casually.

Leonie looked at Alexa, then back at Kate, shaking her head in wonder. 'Where do you get them from?'

'How do you have *time* for them?' added Alexa.

Leonie raised her eyebrows at this. 'Er . . . pot, meet kettle? Where do *you* get time for men?'

Alexa frowned in mock offence. 'I've had the same one for months. Kate gets a new one every week.'

'Hey!' Kate shoved her playfully. 'Only once a fortnight. Damo works in the office above me. We were working late one night . . .' A grin crept across her pale face. She flicked back a lock of black hair in a half-hearted attempt to look bashful.

'Unbelievable.' Leonie was still shaking her head, still smiling. 'Do you nip upstairs in the middle of the night, while you're waiting for the printer?' asked Alexa. 'Is that what you're going back for tonight?'

'Can we meet him?' Leonie raised an eyebrow.

'Not yet.' Kate looked slightly ruffled. 'It might not last.'

Alexa rolled her eyes. Kate's relationships didn't generally last – simply because she lost interest and moved on to the next one. Kate treated her men as she treated her projects: she worked through them quickly, always lining up the next one as each came to an end. Nobody seemed to mind when things didn't work out – there was never any great expectation from either party and Kate never went for the overly sensitive type.

'Anyway, Damo was saying that there's a girl in his office who sits there and *cries*. I just can't believe any woman would let herself do that. You have to have some self-respect, I mean . . . at least she could have the decency to take herself off to the ladies.'

'Why does she cry?' asked Leonie.

Kate shrugged. 'I guess she can't handle the banter. She's the only woman there – that's what made me think of it.'

Alexa nodded, feeling grateful that she would never have to encounter her ball-breaker friend in the workplace. She thought back to the problem in hand. What were the *Banter* offices like? Would she handle the banter? This would no doubt be banter of a vicious kind – banter fuelled by an excess of testosterone and highly-sexed males. It would be a stark change from the all-female offices of *Hers*, where conversation rarely ventured far from the core topics of recipes, home furnishings and anti-wrinkle creams. The harshest criticism Alexa had taken from colleagues at *Hers* was a back-handed compliment from Deirdre a couple of months ago about the way that she dressed. Deirdre, eliciting support from the young, ditsy secretary, Annabel, had been of the firm opinion that Alexa should be bolder in her choice of clothes, displaying more of her 'lovely young figure' to the world. It was unlikely that conversations at *Banter* would be so tame.

16

'This is an *amazing* opportunity, Lex.'

Alexa half-smiled. She could feel Leonie's wary gaze upon her again.

'We're talking about one of the nation's biggest brands.'

'Mmm.'

'And you have the opportunity to make it even bigger.'

'Mmm.'

'I bet they're offering you an awesome day rate, right?'

'Twenty percent on top of what I get now.'

'See? And you're already on mega-bucks!'

Alexa cringed, not daring to look at Leonie.

'So.' Kate pressed her face right up to Alexa's and looked her in the eye. 'Are you going to agree to take the job yet, or do I need to get a round in?'

Alexa gave a reluctant smile. 'Go, Kate. Your lover's waiting by the photocopiers.'

3

Alexa rounded the corner and waited impatiently to cross the road, squinting in the half-darkness at the lone figure at the top of the marble steps. He looked like a movie star, leaning casually against the floodlit pillar, the glow illuminating his blond hair and casting shadows across his chiselled jaw.

'Hi,' she called breathlessly, hitching the black silk dress a little higher as she darted across the road and mounted the steps, two by two. Kate's kitten heels were wearing holes in her ankles, but she put the pain to the back of her mind. 'Sorry I'm late.'

Matt didn't reply immediately. He just pulled away from the pillar and stood for a moment, appraising her heaving chest and flushed cheeks, smiling.

'It was worth the wait,' he said eventually, pulling her towards him and kissing her hard on the lips.

Alexa felt something inside her lurch. His suit was a perfect fit across the shoulders and the crisp, white shirt set off his tan. She looped an arm around his and stepped onto the dark red carpet.

'I think we're supposed to have gone through to the ballroom,' he said, 'but let's grab a drink on the way.'

He led them into a giant, echoing hallway flanked by two spiral staircases. A solitary waiter stood in the corner, holding a circular tray of champagne flutes – evidently the last remaining member of a troop of serving staff. Alexa cursed her poor time management. If she had just put down her work at six-thirty, as planned, she could have arrived on time and enjoyed her allotted quota of pre-dinner bubbly. There was always just one more feature to work on, one more financial report to check.

'Shall we?' Matt paused by the entrance to a vacuous ballroom. It sparkled with chandeliers, expensive watches and diamond earrings. Alexa took a deep breath, glancing down at her own attire. It was probably a good thing that Kate had insisted on taking her shopping, she thought. The dress was racier than anything she would have dared to buy on her own and, out of context, the jewellery had seemed over the top – but judging by what she could see here, it was exactly right for the occasion. Cut from black imitation silk, the dress clung to her waist and hips, its neckline plunging to reveal a cleavage she usually kept hidden away.

Suddenly, Alexa found herself being whisked to the centre of the room at a disconcerting pace. She gripped Matt's forearm, ignoring the pain in her feet and focusing on keeping her champagne glass upright. Through the blur, she spotted the reason for the urgency. On the stage at the far end of the hall, an ancient-looking man was tapping a microphone, indicating the start of a speech.

'Ladies . . . and gentlemen!' The shaky voice was amplified across the room. 'May I first say how grateful I am . . .'

Alexa crept into her chair and quietly tucked herself in. On her left was a middle-aged man with a ring of greying hair around a largely bald head, who was nodding gently as though enthralled in the speech. Matt took his place on her right, next to Dickie, a friend and colleague at his law firm, Fothergills.

Alexa was nursing her ankle under the table when she caught sight of a frantic waving gesture from three seats along. It was Dickie's girlfriend, whose name Alexa had already forgotten from the previous black tie event. Clarissa? Loretta? Alexa's memory was hazy. Conversation had involved skiing, horses, red wine . . . but she couldn't for the life of her recall the girl's name.

The speech droned on. Alexa tuned in and out, her heart still recovering from the rushed entrance, her mind still working on Dickie's girlfriend's name. She wasn't entirely clear on the purpose of the evening, but then, she never was. Law must have been one of the few remaining industries in which career progression was partially dependent on attendance at elaborate dinners throughout the year.

She looked around the room. In the far corner, by the speaker, an all-female string quartet sat, looking very bored. Around the edges, waiters stood, staring straight ahead like foot soldiers on parade. The guests, of which there must have been four or five hundred, varied in their composure. Some were pretending to listen, others surreptitiously poured themselves glasses of wine and a small number of people, mainly older gentlemen, were nodding off.

It quickly transpired that Dickie's girlfriend was very drunk. Her eyes were rolling around in their sockets and every time the speaker paused for breath – sometimes after a joke's punchline, often not – she would let out a loud, throaty chuckle as though the man had said something exceedingly funny.

'I always look back to something that someone once told me . . .'

'Mwahahahaha!' cried the girl.

'. . . that if you want to know the difference between a good lawyer and a *great* lawyer . . .'

'Mwahahahaha!' she cried again. People were starting to stare.

'. . . then it is this. A good lawyer knows the law. A great lawyer knows the judge.'

'Mwahahahahahahaha!' yelled the girl, this time accompanied by a polite murmur of appreciation from around the room.

Alexa sipped her champagne, trying not to catch the girl's eye in case the hysterics became contagious. *Fenella*. That was it.

Fenella's interjections were clearly not winning her any favour with the balding man on her left. Dickie was making a half-hearted attempt to shut her up, but short of physically restraining or removing her, there was little he could do.

Eventually, the speaker stepped down, amid a trickle of light applause. Predictably, Fenella clapped and whooped like a winner at the races. Alexa smiled as Dickie tried to explain that wolf-whistling was not an appropriate form of celebration.

Matt laid a hand on Alexa's thigh under the table, pressing his lips to her ear. *'The guy next to you is Dickie's boss,'* he whispered.

'Oh dear,' replied Alexa, softly.

'He's also my boss,' added Matt, with a meaningful look.

'Right.' Alexa nodded, understanding what was expected of her. Matt didn't want a Fenella on his hands tonight.

Matt smiled, leaning back as a waiter swooped over to pour the wine. *'Oh,'* he said, his mouth returning to her ear. *'There's one thing you should know about David Wint—'*

'DAVID WINTERBOTTOM,' boomed the voice on her left.

Alexa jumped. The balding man was offering his hand.

'Nice to meet you,' she said, wondering what Matt had been about to say.

'The pleasure,' he declared theatrically, 'is all mine.'

Alexa smiled politely as he grasped her hand in his and drew it slowly to his lips. He spoke in a way that might have been appropriate for very young children or foreigners: slowly and very loudly. She nudged Matt with her knee under the table, but he was already embroiled in a conversation about litigation with Dickie. Fenella, she noticed, was mumbling incoherently into her glass.

The starters were placed on the table with military precision by the waiting staff, offering Alexa a brief but welcome reprieve from Winterbottom's ogling stare. He seemed to be looking at her as though she were some form of exquisite art, not a conscious person.

'So!' The stare returned as Alexa tucked into her caramelised onion tart. She didn't actually like onion, but she decided that tasting small quantities was preferable to making conversation with Matt's lecherous boss. 'What do you do, then?'

'I . . .' Alexa avoided the man's gaze, which was now firmly focused on her breasts. 'I work in media.'

'Ah.' Winterbottom nodded knowingly. 'I could have guessed.'

'Could you?'

'Yuh.' He nodded again, glancing appraisingly at the silk dress as though sizing her up. 'Yuh, definitely a creative type. What d'you do? Graphics?'

Alexa frowned. She wondered whether her role could be classified as 'creative'. Some of her financial forecasts could probably qualify as such, but strictly speaking her profession was management or business. 'No, I look at new markets for magazines.'

'New markets, eh? Farmers' markets? Are you a communities journalist?'

Alexa pushed away the remains of her tart. 'No,' she replied, through gritted teeth. Had Winterbottom not been Matt's boss, she would have put him straight in no uncertain terms.

'Let me guess,' said Winterbottom. 'Are you . . . oh, I know. Is it a local magazine?'

'No.' Alexa heard the resentment in her voice and reined herself in again. 'No. I'm not a journalist.'

'Then why did you say you were?'

Alexa kept calm, watching as he scooped out the filling from his starter and stuffed it into his mouth in one go. A small strand of onion flicked up from the fork, leaving a trail of chutney across his left cheek.

'I said I worked in media. I look at new markets for magazines – new *revenue streams*.'

'Oh.' The man looked confused. 'So, you work in finance?'

'Sort of.' Alexa nodded. It was probably the closest they were going to get to her actual job description.

22

The waiters whisked away their plates, topping up glasses as they went. Alexa took a large gulp of red wine, leaning sideways and trying to catch Matt's attention.

'No, no, *no*,' insisted Dickie, apparently oblivious to his girlfriend's sleepy head on his shoulder. 'Regulation works better than litigation, every time. Prevention is better than cure!'

'I disagree,' argued Matt, launching into a complicated explanation for why.

Alexa turned back to her wine. It was always the same. Matt promised not to talk shop with his colleagues, then when the time came, the word 'litigation' reared its head and they were off. It was no wonder Fenella had drunk herself into a stupor.

'So!' It was the same slow, booming tone that had rung out before.

Reluctantly, Alexa turned to face Winterbottom.

'You never told me which *title*,' he said, patronisingly.

'Oh.' Alexa nodded. She thought for a moment. Part of her wanted to shock him by telling him about *Banter*, but she didn't know whether that would reflect badly on Matt. 'It's a women's magazine called *Hers*.'

'A *women's* magazine,' he nodded, smiling. 'Of course.'

Alexa managed to keep her cool. Inside, she wanted to grab the man's tightly-stretched collar and shake him off his chair, wiping that smug, condescending smile off his face.

'I trebled its gross revenue and shaved twenty percent off the costs last year,' she said.

'*Did* you?' He looked at her, wide-eyed, glancing overtly at her breasts. 'And how much revenue does a *women's* magazine bring in, these days?'

Alexa exhaled. The fire was burning inside her. This man was intolerable.

As it happened, just as the collar-grabbing fantasy started to take hold in her mind, Alexa's thoughts were interrupted by the arrival of her main course. Matt looked over and must have registered her expression because he suddenly wanted to know her opinion on joint liability in American asbestos cases.

Alexa's shoulders remained tilted towards Dickie and Matt for the entirety of her next two courses: succulent veal followed by peach melba with raspberry coulis. She wasn't enjoying the conversation exactly, or even following it, but she was doing a reasonable job of saying 'mmm' at appropriate intervals and the wine was slipping down nicely. Dickie and Matt didn't seem to mind; they were lost in a world of corporate constitutions and shareholder rights.

Dessert wine was followed by cheese and port which was followed by a random selection of red and white wine scavenged by Dickie from nearby tables. Alexa was pleased when conversation eventually moved on to random trivia such as the fact that there were apparently more chickens in China than people. At some point in the proceedings, Fenella perked up enough to work her way through a large slab of Brie, but ten minutes later was looking decidedly queasy. It was agreed, through smeary wine glasses, that the time had come to go home.

Leaning against the cold, exterior wall, Alexa watched as Matt helped Dickie ease Fenella into a cab. She lifted her hair off her shoulders, tying it into a knot and enjoying the cool night air on her face.

'You never told me,' said a voice, languid and loud, right next to her ear.

She sighed, turning to face Winterbottom and feeling her spirits sink.

'Told you what?' she asked, reluctantly. Fenella was refusing to get in the cab. Her limbs were protruding from the open door and she seemed to be yelling something about a club.

'How much money a *women's magazine* makes.'

Alexa drew a lungful of air. She knew exactly what the man was getting at. The implication was that women's magazines generated such small revenues that they weren't worth the bother.

The implication throughout the whole evening had been that women's magazines, women's jobs, women's efforts in general, were a waste of time.

The rage mixed with the wine and port in her belly and, for a brief moment, Alexa wondered whether she might throw it all up on the obnoxious man. She held it in though, glancing sideways at the cab, where Dickie and Matt were attempting to trap Fenella in a pincer movement.

'About thirty to forty million,' she said, pushing away from the wall and feeling instantly dizzy. She steadied herself and looked into Winterbottom's eyes. 'The same as the equivalent men's magazine.' She started to turn away, but kept her eyes fixed on his face. 'And by the way,' she said, 'that's irrespective of whether it's run by a man or a woman.'

She glared at him for a second, watching his jowls flap with the hesitant opening and closing of his jaws, then she turned and marched into the road, where Matt was patting the roof of the cab as it pulled away.

'Matt?'

He looked up, seemingly perplexed by the speed at which she was tottering towards him.

'What were you going to say? Before the dinner – about your boss?'

'Oh.' Matt nodded apologetically, holding out his hand as another cab pulled up. 'After you.'

Alexa stumbled inside, falling back against the seat. 'Tell me,' she said, feeling her eyes drop shut.

Matt slipped an arm around her shoulder and drew her towards him so that her head was on his lap. 'I was just going to say that he's not one for respecting women.'

Alexa managed a laugh. 'Really?'

'Sorry.' Matt started stroking her hair. 'I would've swapped places if there'd been time.'

Alexa let out a quiet sigh. She was exhausted and very drunk, but she recognised the feeling inside her. It felt like fire. She had made up her mind about something.

'Matt?' she said again.

He stopped stroking her hair for a second and looked down at her face.

'I'm going to take the job at *Banter*.'

4

Alexa stepped into the lift, trying to align her thoughts. Her hands were clammy and her legs felt weak. She wanted to swallow, but her throat was devoid of anything to swallow.

The doors started to slide shut, then juddered to a halt as the other woman in the lift thrust a limb between its jaws, calling out to a colleague in the atrium. Alexa leaned back on the reflective wall and exhaled, grateful to the woman for adding an extra few seconds to her journey.

The women's small talk washed over her as the lift lurched upwards. Alexa stared straight ahead, struggling to focus. The adrenaline was having a strange effect on her mind – muddling up the important things, like how she would hit the revenue targets laid down by Peterson, with the small, insignificant details that ought not to be taking up space in her head, like whether her shoes made her look too tall and whether she ought to have pinned back her fringe. It was only when the two women stepped out on the fourth floor that she realised she wasn't going anywhere.

Alexa snapped to, pressing '5' and checking her makeup in the mirrored wall. The shoes definitely made her look too tall, she decided, and her light brown fringe was hanging limply over her eyes like an unkempt mane. Why hadn't she noticed that before? She turned away from her reflection in disgust.

Stepping onto the fifth floor, Alexa turned left, suddenly very aware of the fact that she was stooping. She pulled back her shoulders and forced her legs forward, one after the other, fighting the urge to turn and flee.

She had caught glimpses of the *Banter* office in the past, but she had never taken much in. The life-size pin-ups on the door had rather put her off. This was her first proper sight of the place she would inhabit for the next nine months.

The office was a colourful, dirty mess. It looked like a teenage boy's bedroom. There were piles of magazines, DVDs and clothes all over the floor and copies of *Banter* strewn across every surface. Lodged in the gaps between piles were random objects that included, at first glance: a water pistol, a set of elf costumes, a pyramid of baked bean cans, a giant beer mug in the shape of a naked woman and a lawnmower.

Alexa drew to a halt in the gangway that ran along the middle of the office. There was nobody there. She looked at the clock. It was only ten past eight. Her nerves had woken her at six and she hadn't been able to get back to sleep.

She felt a vibration and felt around for her phone, suddenly hoping for an email from Peterson saying he'd changed his mind and urgently needed her back on *Hers*. It wasn't an email though; it was a text message from Matt.

Thinking of U. Mx

Alexa smiled, feeling a little more confident as she looked up at the fifty-inch plasma TV at the end of the office. It showed two semi-naked teenage girls, writhing around on a bed together, looking very unsure about what they were supposed to be doing. Alexa grimaced. Something had to be done about Banter TV. It was essentially a ten-minute roll of filmed photo shoots on loop, interspersed with amateur ads for cheap phone-ins that looked as though they'd been filmed in somebody's garage. It was little wonder that Banter TV had no viewers.

Alexa scanned the five banks of desks, trying to identify her seat. *It was only pin-ups,* she told herself, wandering to the next bank of desks and coming face to face with a pair of giant breasts hanging from a filing cabinet door. She shuddered as the image of her mother flitted across her mind.

Alexa continued to scan the desks, wondering where Derek Piggott sat in relation to her. At Peterson's request, she had had no contact with the deputy editor since the press release had gone out about her appointment. That was typical of how things were done at Senate: behind closed doors, with no collaboration, creating maximum potential for resentment. She didn't even know how the deputy editor had taken the news of his effective demotion.

She jumped. Someone was clearing his throat behind her.

'Sorry, didn't mean to scare you.'

Alexa felt her heart rate triple. She turned to find herself staring at someone who looked exactly like Amir Khan. His hair was jet black, short and spiky, his angular jaw coated in a few days' worth of stubble and his eyes were dark, like pools of ink.

'Um, hi.' She collected herself together and managed some kind of smile.

He was tall, she noticed. Alexa rarely found herself looking up to meet someone's eye.

'Alexa?' he said, at exactly the moment Alexa chose to say her name.

They laughed awkwardly.

'I'm Riz,' he said, shaking her hand with the grip of a champion boxer. 'Sports editor.'

'Right.' Alexa straightened up. It was refreshing, not having to stoop. 'Great to meet you. I'm . . . well, you already know. I'm going to be managing director for the next few months. Launching new initiatives, that sort of thing.' She glanced around. 'That's the plan, anyway.'

Alexa inwardly screamed at herself for adding the unnecessary final sentence. This had always been a problem. It wasn't just first-day nerves; it was her pathetic inability to talk in a normal way to attractive men. It maddened her. She could devise a ten-million-pound business plan and execute it within a year, she could build websites and draw up cross-platform strategies, but she couldn't have a normal conversation with a good-looking guy.

'Yeah, we got the email.' Riz moved a little closer, lowering his voice. 'That caused a few ripples.'

Alexa tried to laugh, but nothing came out. *The email.* What had Peterson told them? How much did they know about the ultimate purpose of her secondment to *Banter*? The fact that the title's future was in jeopardy would have been kept from the team, surely, in which case, why the 'ripples'? She couldn't think of a subtle way to ask.

Riz looked around the office. 'You're looking for a desk, I presume?'

Alexa nodded, still thinking about the email. 'A desk would be good.'

He was wearing low-slung, casual jeans and a T-shirt, she noted, clocking his muscular shoulders as he headed off along the gangway. The trouser suit had been a mistake, she thought, cursing her lack of foresight. This was media; she knew how people dressed here. Why had she gone for the formal look?

Riz walked quickly to the far corner of the office and then stopped.

'Hmm.'

Alexa followed, as speedily as her inappropriate high heels would allow.

Riz was squinting at one of the monitors on the last bank of desks, gently stroking the stubble on his chin.

'I think . . .' He grimaced. 'I think the news desk might have got here first.'

Alexa drew level with Riz and then froze. On the desk in front of her, gleaming in the weak morning sunlight, was a black rubber dildo about four times the size of any she had seen in any shops. It rose up above her monitor like an obelisk.

'Delightful.' She managed a smile, but inside, she felt anxious. She could imagine it now, half a dozen grown men crowding round her desk like little school boys, smirking as they tried to agree on the optimal position.

Riz stepped forward and made as if to remove the offending article. 'Shall I?'

Alexa nodded. 'If you don't mind.'

He lifted it off the desk and then looked around, surveying the mounds of paper and toys around them.

Alexa was about to suggest the nearest waste paper bin when she had a better idea.

'Put it there,' she instructed, clearing a space on the window sill next to her desk.

Riz looked at her. 'You sure?'

Alexa nodded. 'Yeah. It's a lovely gesture, don't you think?'

He smiled, slowly. 'I see. Yes. *Lovely.*'

Alexa pulled out her chair and was only half surprised to find an A3 poster of a glamour model, spread-eagled, staring up at her with a wanton expression.

'Am I to expect . . . quite a few of these little treats?' she asked, unsticking the poster from her seat and folding it inside-out, only to find another image on the reverse, this one of a blonde on all fours.

He looked at her, one eyebrow raised. 'You're not at *Hers* any more.'

Alexa watched out of the corner of her eye as Riz returned to his desk, allowing herself a quick moment to wonder what might be going on two floors below. It was nearly half-past eight. Annabel would be sifting through the post in her slow, dreamy way, waiting for the kettle to boil for her herbal tea. Deirdre would be moaning about over-crowding on the Central line and

Lily would be printing off knitting patterns. Riz was right; she wasn't at *Hers* any more.

Logging on was a predictably slow, painful process that involved a multitude of error messages and three phone calls to the IT help desk. It was while she was on one of these calls that she realised she was being watched. The office had been slowly filling up with boisterous young men and until now, Alexa had kept her head down, waiting for a full house before she started to make her introductions. But it was becoming increasingly hard to ignore the man in his early thirties who was bearing down on her from across the desk. He had shoulder-length, oily brown hair and a small tuft of stubble at the base of his chin.

'Oi oi!' he cried, as she put down the phone.

'Hi,' she said, smiling up at the man. She couldn't help thinking that he might be reasonably good-looking, if it weren't for the hair or the goatee.

'I'm Derek,' he bellowed, despite the fact that Alexa's ear was no more than a metre from his mouth. 'And you must be our new managing director.'

He said the last two words slowly, with emphasis, as though expecting some kind of applause. Alexa looked over his shoulder and realised that, in fact, the deputy editor did have something of an audience. Half a dozen young men from the nearest bank of desks were looking over, smirking. Derek Piggott clearly had a following.

Alexa rose to her feet with what she hoped was a mixture of grace and poise, offering out her hand. It was only as she did so that she realised how incredibly short the man was. He couldn't have been more than five foot six.

'Alexa,' she declared, as boldly as she dared. She had a feeling that Derek was not the type of man who liked to be talked down to, but there was little she could do about the practicalities of the situation.

'Well,' he replied loudly, having offered a surprisingly weak handshake. 'I look forward to seeing your *managing* and your *directing*.'

She held his fake smile. This was bad. Already there was hostility between them and she had barely taken off her coat. Alexa wondered again about the contents of that email. Perhaps Derek felt that she was partly to blame for his demotion. He obviously saw her as some kind of threat.

'I'm looking forward to working together to monetise all the great content you produce,' she said calmly.

Alexa instantly regretted her choice of words. They were too condescending. She could see that in the way Derek turned his back on her, clearly pulling a face to the other members of the team and sitting back down at his desk, which, she realised with dismay, was the one diagonally opposite hers.

'Oh,' he said, in the same oratory tone. 'Alexa, the kitchen's down the corridor, on the left.'

There were sniggers from the nearby band of desks. Alexa could hear the laughter travel through the office like a wave. Her cheeks burned, her whole body starting to shake with a mixture of rage and embarrassment.

What was the appropriate response? The longer she stood there, the more she felt like a freak: tall and conspicuous, the butt of the joke. Sitting down now would be to concede defeat. She had to say something. But what? She didn't understand the office dynamics yet. It seemed very much as though everyone looked up to the deputy editor. In her head, she could hear the voice of Miss Calder, her old English teacher: *Do you find something funny? Hmm? Would you care to share the joke with the rest of the class?* The last thing she wanted was to come across like Miss Calder.

Eventually, after what felt like hours of standing in mute panic, Alexa was saved. She didn't need to say anything, because, she realised, nobody was looking at her any more. All heads had swivelled towards the peroxide blonde who was sashaying across the office in a pair of gold hotpants, stilettos and a push-up bra.

'Hi,' the girl purred, winking flirtatiously at the rather un-attractive redhead on the near bank of desks and sliding into the seat next to Derek's. Alexa could just make out the sight of her round, tanned buttocks, slowly escaping from the shiny hotpants as she logged onto her computer.

It took a while for Alexa to realise that she was the only one left staring at this spectacle. The men, of which there were now seven or eight, had reverted to throwing parcels around, playing with gadgets and flipping through newspapers. Occasionally, eyes would return to the girl's backside, but there was no sense that the sight of it was anything unusual. Slowly, Alexa sat back down, wondering whether she had had all the conversations she was going to have for the day. Only two men had bothered to make eye contact so far – and in Derek's case, it was only so that he could set her up for public humiliation.

She opened up her email and pretended to scan her empty inbox, glancing sideways at Sienna Pageant. This, she thought, was her PA. Or at least, this was the 'Editor's PA/Editorial Assistant', according to the credits in the magazine, which was all she had to go on. Once she had agreed to the role, Peterson had become distinctly vague about how exactly the power share would work between Derek and herself.

'PADDY.'

A loud, robotic voice fired out across the office. A scruffy-looking lad in shorts was talking through some kind of voice-distorting megaphone.

'GET THE COFFEES IN.'

A lanky young man with wild, curly hair and braces sprung to his feet in the middle of the office.

Alexa watched as, to her surprise, the young man bounded towards her.

'Nice t'meetcha,' he said. He was Irish. 'I'm Paddy.'

'Nice to meet you too.' Alexa smiled, grateful for the non-confrontational human contact. 'What do you do here?'

'Anything they tell me.' He jerked a thumb in the direction of the man with the megaphone. 'I'm the office gopher. D'you want a tea or coffee?'

'I'm fine, but thanks for the offer.'

'Not a problem.'

'PADDY! COFFEES!'

Alexa risked a smile as she watched the lad spring off towards the kitchen. Again, her thoughts were drawn to what was probably happening two floors down. At *Hers*, they took turns to make the coffee. Nobody bellowed when they wanted a drink and the juniors were treated like valued members of the team. Still, Paddy didn't seem to mind. He didn't even look put-out when someone from the sports desk tried to garrotte him with an elf hat as he passed.

Alexa jumped as her phone buzzed on the desk.

Go get em, Lex!
Good luck with Day 1. Kx

She looked back at her empty inbox, trying not to let the situation get to her. She wondered how Kate would react, in her shoes. Alexa was pretending not to notice, but it was clear that the redheaded man on the next bank of desks was talking about her to one of his colleagues. They kept looking up at her and then nudging one another, muttering quietly and sniggering.

Would Kate put up with this? Would she have remained silent in response to Derek's joke? It was unlikely. In fact, by now, Kate would probably have reprimanded the deputy editor and the redheaded man like a parent with a child, alienating them and anyone else who dared cross her path. That was the difference between Alexa and Kate. Kate didn't care what people thought of her. Alexa cared too much.

The office continued to fill up. Alexa opened a browser, trying to decide the best way to get to know everyone. At *Hers*, she had held a company meeting and played ice-breaker games before holding a brainstorm to generate ideas for reviving the title. Somehow, that didn't seem like a viable tactic here. She needed to meet the section teams individually. She needed some introductions.

Alexa leaned across the desk, catching the attention of the busty blonde.

'Hi. Is it Sienna?'

The girl's plump, red lips melted into a false-looking smile. 'That's right.'

Alexa swallowed. It was like talking to a lap dancer.

'I'm Alexa. It's nice to meet you.'

It was difficult to know whether a handshake was appropriate, given not only the volume of clutter between them but also the potential for a wardrobe malfunction on the part of Sienna's low-cut top. Alexa opted for a cheery wave.

'Can I ask a favour?'

'Sure,' she said, batting her eyelashes for the benefit of Derek, who was making no secret of the fact that his foot had worked its way over to Sienna's side of the desk and was foraging for a playmate.

'I . . .' Alexa tried to focus. The deputy editor was playing footsie with his PA. 'Can you tell me whether any meetings have been set up for this week?'

'Meetings?' She jerked sideways, trying not to smile.

'Yes. You know, introductory . . .'

'Oh. Right. Um . . .' Sienna glared playfully at her male boss. 'Not that I know, no. Ow!'

Alexa thought for a second. She didn't want to start throwing her weight around but she really did need some help setting up meetings for all the departments. It would take hours to trawl through the names and send out blind invitations to all the people she had never met.

36

'Could you . . . might you be able to help set some up for me? Introductions with each of the teams?'

For a moment it looked as though Sienna was too preoccupied with her under-the-desk tousle to hear the question. Then she looked up. Suddenly, she was no longer smiling.

'With all due respect, Alexa, that's not my job.'

'Oh.' Alexa recoiled, suddenly wondering whether she'd misread the credits. Perhaps Sienna wasn't a PA after all. 'I'm so sorry. I must have made a mistake. What . . . What *is* your role?'

Sienna glanced salaciously at Derek, who grinned back at her.

'Editorial assistant.'

'Oh.' Alexa frowned. She wanted to grab a nearby copy of *Banter* to check. 'I thought you were also the editor's PA. Perhaps I—'

'I *was*, but we agreed to drop the PA bit, didn't we, Derek?'

Derek was no longer looking at Sienna, no longer grinning. His eyes were resolutely fixed on Alexa. 'That's right.'

'But . . .' Alexa was struggling to understand. 'Who does the administrative work?'

Sienna shrugged slowly. 'I guess we don't really have much, do we, Derek? We all just *muck in*.'

Alexa was about to reply and then stopped herself. The situation was impossible to navigate. Derek had accepted Sienna's effective promotion because, presumably, he was getting sexual favours in return. It was not in his interest to restore her official title and Alexa already knew that sexual favours or no sexual favours, Derek would not be siding with her in an argument. But she needed a PA.

The question was, should she go in heavy-handed and demand that Sienna do what she was paid to do, or should she accept the situation and just *muck in*?

'Look,' she began, preparing to lay down some terms. Behind Sienna, she noticed, the redhead and colleagues were passing around pieces of paper, looking in her direction and collapsing in fits of hysterics. Alexa tried to concentrate. She opened her mouth to address the PA and as she did so, she thought of an alternative. 'I'll ask Peterson for the headcount to recruit a PA. Someone who can do the administrative work.'

For a fleeting moment, Sienna lost it. 'Wait!' she spluttered, before quickly recovering her composure. 'There's no need. I'll do it. I'll set up your meetings, no problem. I just meant, *generally*, we don't have much admin.'

Alexa smiled. 'Great. Thanks.'

She was about to set off on an introductory tour of the office when something occurred to her.

'Sienna?'

The girl looked up with a fake, breezy smile. 'Mmm?'

'Can you please thank whoever gave me my gift?' She nodded to the giant dildo on the window sill.

Sienna glanced sideways at Derek, then back at the pasty-faced redhead, both of whom were pretending not to be listening.

'Sure,' she said, with another false smile. 'I'll pass it on.'

5

'Just remember, don't mention my job.'

Matt rolled his eyes, glancing sideways through a wisp of blond hair as they waited for the lights.

'Sorry.' Alexa waited for him to look round again, so she could show him how grateful she was for putting up with her neuroticism today, but the lights were about to change and Matt was clearly intent on making a quick getaway. Not that any getaway was ever slow in the Aston Martin DB9.

The lights went green and Alexa's head jerked back against the seat. She wondered what her parents would think when they saw the car. Her mother would instantly want to know one thing: was it paid for with earnings or family money? She would probably spend the whole afternoon trying to work it out. Her father would probably pretend not to care, while secretly yearning for a ride. Maybe Alexa would engineer some sort of outing for Matt and her father, if the opportunity arose. That might give her a chance to break the news to her mother about the job, too.

'Why are you so stressed, anyway?'

'I'm not stressed.'

Matt gave a half-smile and put his foot down, propelling them onto the motorway.

Alexa closed her eyes, feeling slightly sick. Annoyingly, Matt was right. She felt stressed. It was partly the new job, but mainly, she knew, it was the prospect of telling her parents about the new job.

'You're jiggling,' he pointed out.

Alexa looked down at her bare knees and clamped them together, forcing the involuntary movement to stop.

'Why is it such an issue, telling your folks?'

Alexa shrugged. 'It's just . . .' She tried to think of a way of putting it. 'They're quite old-fashioned.'

'So? Shock them. No big deal.'

She said nothing. Matt hadn't met her parents. He hadn't met her mother, or witnessed the power that she still exerted over her daughter. To be fair, it was Alexa's fault that Matt didn't understand. She was the one who had put off the introduction for so long. It wasn't that she was ashamed of her boyfriend. Nor was she ashamed of her parents – despite her mother's overbearing manner and embarrassingly loud voice. No, she was ashamed of *herself* and the crushing sense of impending failure she felt every time she saw her mother. She knew how absurd it would seem to a handsome, confident city lawyer that a twenty-nine year old woman still lived by her mother's rule book and *that* was why it had taken seven months for her to summon the courage.

'Would it be better if I wasn't here?' asked Matt.

'Of course not!' Alexa recoiled at the thought. 'That's the whole point of the barbecue. Mum and Dad want to meet you. Anyway, *I* want them to meet you. I think Mum's worried I might be gay.'

Matt whipped round, his blue eyes squinting at her in the sunlight. 'Why would she think that?'

Alexa forced a shrug, wishing she hadn't said anything. 'I dunno.'

She did know, but she wasn't going to tell him.

Matt accelerated up the slip road and onto the dual carriageway that led to her parents' village. He still looked perplexed.

For a moment, Alexa considered explaining the truth – that he was the first boyfriend to meet her parents, the first to make it past the two-month mark. But she couldn't bring herself to do it. Again, it was something she couldn't explain – not just because she didn't want to ruin her chances with Matt but because she didn't *know*. She was as keen as her mother was to work out why her relationships had never lasted more than a few weeks in the past.

It wasn't that Alexa chose to break up; she didn't get through men in the same way that Kate did. This was something that happened *to* her. It was like a recurring nightmare, always ending the same way: a note or a text message or a painful conversation to say, 'it's not working out.' Never a full explanation, never an opportunity to patch things up.

Alexa reached out and touched the sun-bleached hairs on Matt's forearm, stroking it as he changed down a gear to turn into Elm Rise. This time, there would be no note or text message or painful conversation. This time, it was going to last.

The satnav was lost, she noted, smiling. There was no reception of any kind in the village. Usually, that annoyed her, but today it seemed like a blessing. Her mother thought Alexa's BlackBerry addiction was bad, but she hadn't seen Matt's.

They drew up outside the pebbledash exterior of number twelve.

'So.' Matt turned to her. 'If in doubt, talk Girl Guides or band camp, right?'

Alexa smiled. He had obviously been listening. Her mother was involved in just about every community activity within a twenty-mile radius of the village: Averley Youth Club, the Green Streets project, North Surrey YMCA, Kids' Canoe Club and the local nature reserve. And those were just the ones that Alexa could remember. She secretly wondered whether her mother was attempting to fulfil her own ambitions through the members of her various groups in the same way she had done with Alexa.

'I don't think there's a band camp, but I may be wrong.'

'Can't hurt to ask.' Matt pulled on the handbrake, smiling.

41

Then he placed a hand on her thigh, pinned her back against the seat and gave her a quick, hard kiss. 'You should wear dresses more often,' he said, glancing down at her legs before swinging himself out of the car.

The front door opened before they'd even reached the garden gate. Alexa's mother had clearly been waiting.

'Hi!' she cried, at a volume that might, thought Alexa, feeling anxious and paranoid, have been more for the benefit of alerting the neighbours to the expensive car than for greeting them. Averley was a reasonably affluent village, but nobody here drove an Aston Martin.

Alexa raised her right hand, feeling grateful for Matt's hot, strong grip around her left. Her mother had had her hair done for the occasion, she noted, taking in the flash of auburn between the wands of wisteria around the door.

'How are you, darling?' cooed her mother, before they had even made contact. 'And you must be Matthew? Lovely to meet you! Did you have a good journey?' There was the briefest of pauses for air-kissing. 'Goodness! Is that your car out there? Super! Is it new? Are you hungry? Shall we go through to the garden? Let's go through to the garden.'

Alexa squeezed Matt's hand as her mother led the way through to the small patio at the back of the house, which appeared to be filling with a bluish smoke. She tightened her grip on Matt's hand and felt her way over to where her dad was haphazardly fanning flames on the barbecue.

'Hi, Dad.' She put her spare arm round his shoulders and squeezed. She was taller than him now, she noted. Either he was shrinking or – God forbid – she was still growing. 'This is Matt. Need a hand?'

'Darling! Come and meet Matthew!' cried Alexa's mother, unnecessarily, adding, in a noisy hiss, '*I think you've used too much charcoal!*'

Alexa grimaced, wondering why her mother had been so intent

42

on holding a barbecue in the first place. A pub lunch would have been perfectly adequate and they all knew that Dad wasn't famous for his culinary skills. In fact, thought Alexa, he wasn't famous for much at all, now that he was retired – except perhaps being the most hen-pecked man in Averley.

Poor Dad. She didn't remember things being like this before, when she was growing up. Although, thinking about it, Alexa realised that this was probably because he'd spent most of his time at the office, preferring company accounts to the company of his wife. Alexa felt bad for thinking such things, but it was true. Her mother was a control freak. She had never been able to trust other people to get things done. Alexa had learned this at an early age. One of her earliest memories was of her mother dropping her off at a gym lesson and then reappearing in the doorway, giving pointers to her daughter from the back of the room. Eventually, the instructor had asked her to leave, but that hadn't seemed to deter her. Music, swimming, art and virtually every other extra-curricular activity that had featured in Alexa's privileged upbringing – as well as most academic ones – had involved input from her mother. She meant well, Alexa knew that, but she had trouble letting go.

Matt had moved over to the barbecue and was talking quietly to her dad.

'. . . the air vents . . .'

'. . . wasn't sure . . .'

'. . . slide that along?'

Alexa smiled as the air began to clear.

'Well! Marvellous!' Alexa's mum clasped her hands together in jubilation. 'I'll go and get the drinks! What would people like?'

Drinks were served, with only a small mishap involving the wobbly garden table, and after a couple of glasses of Pimm's, Alexa felt herself starting to unwind. Her dad also looked more relaxed, she noted. In unspoken agreement, Matt had taken the seat nearest to the barbecue and was discreetly tending to the smouldering coals as he sipped his drink.

'So, Matthew! That's a very nice car out the front. Is that a family heirloom?'

Alexa felt like screaming. She wanted to launch herself at her mother and tell her to stop being so *obvious*. How could a DB9 be a family heirloom? How, mathematically, given the model of car, would that be possible?

'No,' replied Matt, unable to resist a little smile. 'I bought it with my bonus last year.'

'Oh!' Alexa's mother gave a nervous laugh, clearly impressed and a little overwhelmed. '*Gosh.*'

'I was lucky,' he explained modestly. 'We had a bumper year for deals last year.'

'Yes. Right.' Alexa's mother nodded, raising her eyebrows at her husband, who was trying to look through two sets of windows to catch a glimpse of the car.

More questions followed. Where had Matt grown up? What had he studied? Did he have brothers or sisters? Which area of law was his focus? Matt passed with flying colours. He kept up with the questions, laughed at Alexa's mother's jokes and masterfully down-played his lifetime achievements, even managing to weave in a reference to his time doing pro-bono work for a local children's charity. The only slight hiccup came when Matt had pulled out his phone to check the name of his old scout group and noticed the lack of message alerts.

'Oh. Don't you have any reception around here?'

'No,' replied Alexa's mother, suddenly caustic.

'Amazing.' Matt shook his head, clearly not picking up on the vibe. 'I didn't think there were places like that left . . .'

'I hope you're not addicted, as well?'

Alexa took it upon herself to step in. She hadn't warned Matt about this. 'It's not an addiction, Mum; it's communication. It's the way things work these days. '

Her mother leaned over to Matt, speaking directly to him.

'She's addicted,' she said softly. 'Don't you think? She can't stop looking at that thing.'

Matt smiled tactfully.

Alexa said nothing. She knew that she ought to move on, to think of a neutral topic of conversation, but she couldn't. She was so angry with her mother.

It wasn't simply that she was imposing her old-fashioned views on people who didn't want to hear, or that she was insulting her guest for doing something as innocent as checking his phone. It was that she was so damned *contradictory*.

If there was one personality trait that Alexa attributed to her mother, it was her drive to succeed. Where else had it come from, if not the woman who had allowed her only educational toys as a child – the woman who had withheld her evening meal until her homework was done? Alexa could still remember the time her mother had denied her a place on the Year 11 post-exam holiday to Barcelona – could still feel the wrench of disappointment in her gut as she took in her mother's words. It was all because of the B she had attained in her Geography coursework – and it hadn't even been her fault. The teacher had slipped up and set an unsuitable piece of work. *Nobody* in her class had got anything higher than a B grade. It was no wonder Alexa had found herself working her way into a top university, desperately seeking out a top graduate job and flinging herself into every piece of work in a desperate attempt to succeed. It was no wonder that now, ten years later, she was still feeling the same compulsion to achieve, achieve, achieve – yet her mother *did* wonder. She wondered why Alexa was continually checking her email. It seemed so hypocritical that Alexa wondered whether she might have missed something along the way – whether she had misinterpreted her mother's words of 'encouragement' over the years.

She reached out and topped up her father's empty glass. Her hands were shaking.

Matt stoked the coals on the barbecue. He had picked up on it now.

'Nearly time to put the meat on,' he said, cautiously. 'Five minutes, I'd say.'

Nobody moved.

Eventually, Alexa could bear it no longer. The pressure inside her was too great. She got up and stormed inside, locking herself into the downstairs bathroom. Flipping down the lid of the toilet, she sat, head in hands, waiting for the rage to pass.

Her mother didn't say those things to annoy her, she knew that. That was the ironic thing. She said them because she *cared*. She was worried about her daughter turning into a workaholic and failing to keep hold of Mr Right – risking a life of lonely, work-fuelled celibacy. Like most mothers, she just wanted her daughter to have it all. She couldn't see, of course, that it was *she* who had created the workaholic. Alexa *was* addicted to her BlackBerry. She *was* wedded to her career. She *did* have trouble holding down a boyfriend and, frankly, it was unlikely that she would succeed in 'having it all'. Did anyone, these days? What did that mean, anyway?

She thought about her friend, Kate – the only person she knew who stood a chance of having it all. In a year's time, barring disasters, she would be a partner at TDS. She would continue to churn through men, keeping an eye out for husband material and then once she decided on 'the one', she would engineer a proposal and a year later, they'd be married with their first kid on the way. Knowing Kate, she probably had it all mapped out in an Excel spreadsheet.

It wasn't so simple for Alexa. At least, it didn't feel simple. Matt was the only man she had been with for more than a couple of months and every day, she felt privileged to still be with him. She couldn't pick and choose like Kate. Ironically, from her mother's perspective, Alexa had become so afraid of failure that she found it almost impossible to focus on anything other than upcoming challenges in the workplace. She *tried* to loosen up when it came to relationships, but it wasn't something that came naturally.

Alexa breathed deeply and exhaled, slowly. She felt calmer now; the shaking had subsided. Rising to her feet, she studied her face in the mirror. The sun had brought out the freckles on her cheeks and her eyes looked paler in comparison. She watched as her reflection started to smile back at her. She was ready to face the world again.

The scene to which she returned was unexpected. It was as though she had turned up at somebody else's party. Matt and her father were chatting happily by the barbecue, her father threading kebab meat onto skewers while Matt turned the slabs of steak, and her mother was flitting from kitchen to garden, humming as she arranged the salads.

'Can I help?' Alexa asked lamely.

The men were lost in conversation and didn't reply. Her mother stood for a moment, appraising her handiwork on the table. Then she turned, as if suddenly remembering something.

'Yes – yes, you can. Come and fetch a couple of things from the kitchen, will you?'

Alexa was familiar enough with her mother's tricks to know that there was no urgent barbecue-related mission awaiting her in the kitchen. She trampled inside, wondering which of her mother's lectures she was about to hear. On the plus side, she thought, at least by being alone together in the kitchen, there might be an opportunity to tell her mother about the job.

'So!' Alexa's mother pressed the kitchen door shut behind them 'Oh, Alexa, you're stooping.'

Alexa straightened up, pushing a wisp of fringe out of her eyes. It was a criticism she had heard so many times, over the years. She tried so hard to be proud of her looks – all five foot ten of them – but too often, it just felt more comfortable to be at eye level with others. Not that that was an argument worth having with her mother.

'I just wanted to say,' her mother began, in a whisper that equated to anyone else's normal speaking volume, 'I think Matthew is wonderful. So does your father. He gave me the nod, just now.'

'Good. I'm glad you think so.' Alexa smiled hesitantly. *The nod.* It was as though Matt had come under scrutiny by virtue of his association with her. 'I think he is, too.'

She waited with trepidation as her mother continued to wring her hands.

'And . . . well, I just want to say . . . try to make time for him, won't you? I know what you're like, always rushing around, working all hours . . .'

Alexa frowned. She couldn't quite believe these words were coming out of her mother's mouth. Make time? *Time?* Coming from the person who believed that productivity was the ultimate goal, that life was all about using time efficiently?

Alexa found herself nodding, too stunned to object.

'He seems like a perfect match,' her mother went on. 'Obviously very ambitious.'

Alexa nodded again. The hypocrisy was astounding. What did they *want* from her? Was ambition seen as a good thing or not? Throughout all of her life so far, Alexa had been working on the assumption that ambition was good – that it was an essential ingredient of a fulfilling life. Matt's ambition was being lauded and yet, here was her mother, effectively telling Alexa to take her foot off the gas and to 'make time'. Making time meant borrowing it from other activities, of course. There was only a finite number of hours in the day and Alexa's waking ones were already filled – her mother had made sure of that. So what exactly was her mother trying to say?

'You're coming to the end of your contract at the magazine now, aren't you? Perhaps you can take it a bit easier for a few months?'

Through the blur of confusion, Alexa spotted an opportunity.

'Actually, my contract has—'

'Have we got any more peppers?' Her father appeared in the doorway. 'Just need a half or so for the last kebab.'

'Try the bottom of the fridge.' Alexa's mum moved over to the sink and started scrubbing a burnt pan – a good use of six seconds, thought Alexa, watching in annoyance.

'Alexa, don't leave your guest out there on his own. Go on – you go and entertain Matthew. We'll sort out the food.'

Alexa toyed with the idea of telling them now, both at once, but it didn't feel right. Her mother would overreact, she would get angry again and her dad wouldn't know how to respond, and all the while Matt would be outside on his own.

'Oh, Alexa?' Her mother called out as she made her escape. 'I meant to ask. You remember Lara Fielding, don't you? The little girl you used to babysit, from the village?'

'You mean the spoilt brat who would only eat food that was pink?'

'Well, yes. I'm sure she's grown out of that now. I was talking to Janice the other day and she mentioned that Lara has just finished a Media Studies degree and is looking for work! So, naturally, I said that you might be able to put in a good word with the ladies at *Hers*.'

Alexa sighed. She wouldn't inflict Lara Fielding on anyone – especially not her friends on the third floor.

'I'll see what I can do.'

Matt raised an eyebrow as she re-emerged.

She shook her head. 'Got interrupted.'

He looked unimpressed.

'I *will* tell them,' she said, 'just—'

'Tell who what?' her mother asked breezily, reappearing with a bowl of chopped peppers.

'Oh.' Alexa panicked. 'Just . . .' She couldn't say it. Not yet.

49

'Alexa has some news,' Matt said, unhelpfully.

'I . . .' Alexa said the line in her head, but she kept getting stuck on the word *Banter*. 'I have a new job,' she managed.

'Do you?' cooed her mother.

'Do you?' her dad echoed.

'Yes.' She pressed on. 'It's a managing director role, a bit like my last one, but for a men's title.'

'Oh! Congratulations!'

'Which title, darling?'

'Um . . . it's . . . well,' Alexa looked at the patio. Matt was looking at her, eyebrows raised. 'It's . . .' She tried again to push the word out, but she just couldn't do it. 'A niche magazine,' she said, eventually. 'You won't have heard of it.'

'Well!' cried her mother, clearly perplexed that the news wasn't more significant, given the build-up. 'That's . . . fabulous!'

She didn't look as disappointed as she might have done, thought Alexa – presumably because she saw the role as offering more potential for her daughter to make time for Matt. Within seconds, she was popping the cork on a bottle of champagne.

'Well done, Alexa!' she cried, filling the glasses.

'Hear hear!' said her dad. 'Well done.'

'Yes,' Matt added woodenly. 'Well done.'

Alexa held up her glass as the toast was made, feeling shaky and slightly sick.

6

'Pig Out?'

'Hogwarts?'

'Pig Headed?' Derek sniggered and scratched his goatee, clearly finding the whole thing hilarious. 'No, hang on, how about Pigs Might Fly? Ha!'

Alexa sighed. They were nearly two hours into the weekly editorial meeting and they'd barely scratched the surface of features. For the last ten minutes, conversation had revolved around possible funny headlines for Paddy's first editorial assignment – a trip to a Suffolk pig farm. Alexa suspected that the location had been carefully chosen by the other members of the team to ensure maximum ridicule for the junior writer.

'How about Pig Tales!' roared Derek, looking around the table for a response.

Marcus, the ginger-haired news editor, guffawed appropriately and Sienna let out a girly squeal, rearranging her blouse to display a little more cleavage.

Alexa cleared her throat. 'Shall we move on? I'm sure the features team will come up with something suitably funny.' She looked at the balding, energetic features editor who nodded back at her. 'Neil? What else?'

Before Neil could speak, Derek leaned forward, his head cocked aggressively to one side.

'How about,' he said, in a slow, condescending tone, 'we carry

51

on going round the table, like we've been doing, shall we? That's tends to be how we do it, see.' He smiled patronisingly at her.

Alexa managed to nod, despite the burning rage inside her. There were so many things she wanted to say. They *weren't* going round the table; they were going through the magazine, section by section, as was customary in such meetings. She had looked to Neil because, as features editor, he was best placed to summarise the next topic of discussion. And to use that disdainful tone in front of the entire staff was not just unprofessional; it was *pathetic*. Alexa remained silent.

'Er . . . same as,' said the scruffy young man next to Paddy, who, for reasons unknown to Alexa, was known as Biscuit. She remembered him from her first day; he'd been the one brandishing the voice-distorting megaphone. He was responsible for the jokes pages of Banter.

'Any news on the Guy Thomas thing?' asked someone.

Biscuit screwed up his face. 'He's threatening to sue.'

'Bastard.'

'Fucker.'

Alexa looked around, perturbed. 'Sorry . . . could someone explain the *Guy Thomas thing*?'

Derek sighed, loudly. 'Could someone please explain the Guy Thomas thing, for the benefit of our *managing director*,' he said, in a tired monotone.

'We, um, printed a "fun fact" about him in the Celebrity Banter section,' said Biscuit, not meeting Alexa's eye. 'Said he had a phobia of peas. He's claiming it's not a phobia, it's an *aversion*.'

'He's going to court over an aversion to peas?' Alexa frowned.

'He always threatens.'

Derek leaned forward again. He had the same look on his face as before.

'Round here, you see, lawsuits come with the territory. Not a lot you can do about them.'

Alexa disagreed, but said nothing.

'Anyway! Good news,' said Neil, tactfully changing the subject. 'We've had Ricky Lewis confirmed as our lead feature next week. Got the green light for a "Love Rat Tells All" piece.'

'Fan-fuckin'-tastic,' said Derek, shaking his fist in what Alexa could only interpret as a display of jubilation. There were nods of respect from all round the room. A couple of men punched the air.

Alexa said nothing. She didn't share their enthusiasm. Ricky Lewis was a premiership footballer whose exploits, as far as she knew, included: drink-driving, speeding, cheating on his girlfriend with a teenage prostitute and then walking out on said girlfriend, who had taken him back and was five months pregnant with his child. Was it right, she wondered, to splash heroic images of such a man across the pages of a magazine aimed at impressionable young lads?

'Love the angle, too,' added Derek. 'Really get him to talk – you might get some juicy tit-bits.'

'Some sordid truths about the wife, maybe?' someone else suggested.

Neil nodded and jotted it down. Alexa nearly spoke out, but stopped herself. She was new to this market. There was clearly a lot for her to learn about what worked and what didn't. If this was a feature that pulled in the readers, she could hardly speak out against it.

'Other stuff . . .' Neil was taking the lead as Alexa had suggested, she noted, his shiny pate bobbing from side to side as he skimmed down his list. 'Ah, yes. This week's Ten Sexiest is nurses, which is always a winner. I think there was only one that didn't get her baps out, so that brings the nipple count to eighteen, from just the one feature.'

Alexa joined in with the general noises of appreciation, finding herself inadvertently glancing down, checking that her own nipples were hidden away under the dark, shapeless top – one of five almost identical garments that had become her own unofficial uniform since the day one *faux pas* with the suit. She felt uneasy. Did they seriously use nipple count as a metric to gauge an edition's prospects?

'Then we're just deciding on whether to do a men's summer diet feature – "The Mankini Diet", we were thinking – or just a how-to on barbecuing. Or maybe some sort of how-much-sex-do-you-need-to-burn-off-the-calories type thing.'

Alexa tuned out as various suggestions were bandied about. It amazed her, how differently things happened here compared to two floors down. At *Hers*, features writing was seen as an art form. It was hard enough just to think of a theme that was topical – not just appropriate for the time of year, but based on real-life global trends. On discovering that, say, a wave of fifty-somethings were taking up extreme sports, or that refugees were crossing the channel and moving in with local pensioners, the challenge would be to find a hapless features writer willing to find a fifty-something mountain-biker or a Dover landlady harbouring immigrants. At *Banter*, it seemed, features were plucked from thin air. Funny surnames, whacky hair-dos, tasty breakfast cereals – anything would do.

The discussion eventually ran its course and Alexa looked around hopefully. She wasn't going to bring the meeting to a close – not with Derek sitting three seats down.

'One more thing,' said Neil, just as Derek started noisily bashing his papers against the desk in a conclusive manner.

'Mmm?'

'As usual, we've had a shockingly bad set of Banter Confessions in this week.' He pulled a face. 'I was hoping Sienna might have time to write a few?'

All eyes turned to the peroxide blonde next to Derek.

'I reckon I could fit it in,' she replied, with extra emphasis on her last three words.

Alexa frowned, ignoring the ripple of smutty laughter that

was travelling across the room. 'Sorry,' she said. 'But shouldn't we be getting real girls to send in their confessions?'

Derek rolled his eyes. 'That's the *idea*, yeah,' he said. 'But like Neil said, we don't always get enough and most of them are too crap to print. Sienna does a much better job, don't you, darling?' He turned to his PA and winked.

'Apparently I do a very good "compliant",' explained Sienna, smiling demurely at Alexa as the dirty laughter flared up again.

'I just wonder . . .' Alexa feared that she might already be testing Derek's patience, but she wanted to get something straight. 'I was just wondering *why* we don't get more confessions in. We offer a fifty pound incentive for the best one, right?'

Derek nodded reluctantly. Marcus rolled his eyes. The pallid redheaded news editor always seemed to side with Derek. It was as though they had some secret allegiance. Alexa persevered, nonetheless.

'We have nearly fifty thousand female readers . . . But we have trouble eliciting *three* decent confessions from them each week?'

'Yeah. Look, this isn't exactly a new problem.' Derek rolled his eyes impatiently and exchanged a look with Marcus. 'It's just the way it is.'

Alexa disagreed, again, but this time she was willing to speak out. Something was ringing bells.

'Last year,' she said, 'when I was working at *Hers*, we noticed a massive drop-off in letters coming through to our agony aunt.' She looked around. Sienna was inspecting her nails. Derek was spinning a pen around his thumb. Marcus was trying to do the same only failing and most of the others looked half-asleep. Only Neil and Riz seemed to be listening.

'We realised that the drop-off coincided with the new editor mugshots. Our agony aunt's new photo made her look about twenty years younger and a lot more attractive. It was putting the readers off. They wanted to see someone they could relate to. What mugshot are you using for the confessions?'

Neil looked up immediately. 'It's a picture of a random lad, looking kind of curious. I've always thought it's a bit seedy, actually. My wife thinks it looks like a paedophile. Maybe we should change it? We could pitch it as "send your confessions to our secretary, Sienna".'

'Hey,' Sienna pouted, pushing her breasts a little further onto the desk. 'Not if it means an ugly mugshot.'

'It doesn't have to be ugly.'

'Medium-ugly,' said Marcus, raising a ginger eyebrow.

'Oi!'

'Tell you what.' Neil was obviously adept at spotting potential deviations. 'We'll make someone up. Give her a medium-ugly mugshot and create a fake email address for her, then we'll see what she brings in.'

'Hallelujah!' cried Derek, rolling his eyes. 'Thank *God* that's sorted. Real girls confessing to a fake secretary, saving Sienna about . . . what, half an hour a week? Fucking marvellous.'

There was silence for a moment. Alexa managed to maintain some semblance of a smile and then, since Derek was pre-occupied with throwing his arms about and pulling stupid expressions, she checked for any other business and dismissed the team.

The deputy editor was one of the last to leave the room.

'Derek?' She caught his attention as he passed. 'Can I have a word?'

Derek stopped in his tracks, holding his position in the doorway as though deliberating over whether to heed or ignore the request. Eventually, when everyone else had returned to their desks, he turned to face Alexa.

'I'd *love* to have a word with you,' he sneered.

Alexa could feel herself tense up as she watched him return to his seat at the head of the table. They were now separated by four chairs, which seemed odd, but she didn't comment.

'I just wanted to say . . .' Alexa took a breath and pushed out the words. 'Well, I thought it would be sensible to talk about our roles and responsibilities.'

'Our *roles and responsibilities*,' he echoed mockingly. 'Yes, let's.'

Alexa thought for a second. She had known that this wouldn't be easy, but she hadn't quite anticipated the extent of Derek's resentment towards her.

'So, to clarify,' she persevered. 'In my mind, you are still the acting editor of this magazine.'

Derek snorted. 'I don't know what the fuck is going on in your mind. All I know is that a few weeks ago, I was demoted to *deputy editor* for no apparent reason and then you come along with a fancy title and start talking about *rejuvenation* and *engagement*.'

Alexa sighed. So this was what it was all about. Derek blamed Alexa for his demotion. It wasn't exactly a revelation, but at least there was no longer any room for doubt. Alexa wished she had spoken out when Peterson had told her of his plans. She ought to have foreseen this problem; she should have realised from Peterson's cryptic mumblings that Derek Piggott would prove to be a problem. She should have advised the chief executive not to demote him. Inflated egos were far easier to deal with than crushed ones.

'Look,' she said, picking up on Derek's last few words. 'We *need* to get this magazine back on its feet. That's why I'm here, and as soon as I've done my job, I'll be out of your hair.'

'Back on its feet?' Derek stared at her, nostrils flaring. 'Who said it wasn't on its feet?'

Alexa was about to reply and then stopped.

He had no idea.

For the last few weeks, she had been working on the assumption that Terry Peterson had told Derek about the Americans' plans to dispose of the title if it didn't improve its profitability. She had assumed that he was being discreet by not mentioning it around the office. She should have thought. Derek wasn't capable of discretion. Peterson had clearly kept him in the dark on purpose.

'Sorry,' she said, watching Derek tug irritably at his goatee. 'That was melodramatic. I just mean, I'm here to try and help *Banter* hit its April targets. I'm not here to run the editorial side of the magazine.'

Derek just stared at her, shaking his head.

'Primarily,' she said when it became apparent that nothing more was forthcoming from the man, 'I see this involving new channels for the existing content – *your* content. But it's inevitable that at times, there may be a need to look at the content itself, maybe make a few changes.'

Derek continued to stare hatefully at Alexa, slowly shaking his head.

'For that, I need your support.' She could hear the desperation in her voice. 'I need to feel that you trust me to get involved. I need to . . .' Alexa faltered. This was the real reason she had called him in. She could barely bring herself to say the words. 'I need to know that you won't undermine me in front of the team.'

Initially, there was no reaction from Derek. Then he sat back, slowly, still looking at her through the dark slits that his eyes had become. All of a sudden, he launched himself forwards. Alexa jumped.

'*Banter*,' he spat, pressing his face right up to hers, 'is a fucking good magazine.'

Alexa nodded mutely. He was so close she couldn't breathe.

'I *know* that,' he said, through gritted teeth, 'because I've worked here for *six years*. So when some *bint* in a suit comes in here on some crazy salary and starts telling me how to run my magazine and how to talk to my team . . .' He sniffed loudly, angrily, only millimetres from her face, 'then it's hardly surprising when I don't take too *kindly* to her. *Is it?*'

Alexa shook her head, saying nothing.

Eventually, Derek threw himself back into his chair, shaking

58

his head and looking into the main office with a cold, hard stare.

Alexa slowly exhaled. She was about to say, tentatively, that she wasn't trying to dictate how he ran his magazine or talked to his team, but as she opened her mouth to speak, Derek threw back his chair and stood up, marching out of the meeting room and slamming the door on his way out.

Alexa sank down in her chair and pressed her fingers against her closed eyes. She was so close to crying, but something inside her was blocking the tears. She *couldn't* cry. She wouldn't allow it. This was just part of the challenge, she told herself. This was the lion's den Matt had warned her against. This was the all-male environment Leonie had been so worried about. She had to stay strong. She thought about Kate's reaction to the girl in her boyfriend's office who had let her tears show. She wasn't going to be like that.

Alexa grabbed her notepad and stood up. She was going to go back into the office and continue to do what she was being paid to do. She was going back into the lions' den.

7

The photographer squinted critically at his digital display.

'Okay, that last one again, if you don't mind. Yeah, move your hands about, that's it, like you're really enjoying yourself.'

The girl grabbed her breasts with fresh gusto, flicking her long, dark hair to one side and pouting at the camera. Alexa swallowed nervously, wondering whether the girl actually was enjoying herself. Going by the shaky knees and the look of forced ecstasy on her face, Alexa suspected not.

Kayleigh Williams was nineteen years old. This was her first modelling shoot – a fact that Alexa could probably have deduced by the girl's demeanour, had it not been written on the call sheet in front of her. She couldn't help thinking that it might also be the girl's last.

It wasn't that Kayleigh didn't have the looks: she was tall and curvy with dark eyes and glossy, chestnut-coloured hair that cascaded in waves down her back. Her breasts, as noted on the call sheet, were a sizeable 32DD. The problem was the way she held herself. It was her confidence – or lack thereof. The girl looked petrified.

'Can you move a bit more slowly, Kayleigh?' Jamie, the pictures editor, obviously felt compelled to intervene. 'That's it. Much more sexual, yeah.'

The videographer gave a nod of approval as he changed angle. This was why amateur photographs never looked anything like those in the magazine. Aside from the photographer there was a photographer's assistant, a lighting guy, a junior lighting guy, makeup and a young lad whose job it was to run around the set looking busy and repeatedly offering drinks. For this shoot there was also a videographer. *Banter* now filmed, as well as shot, all of its most popular features, for the website and Banter TV.

The 'Brainy Banter' feature was up there among the readers' favourites. The concept was simple: get a female university student to take off her clothes and then ask her some trivia questions that she would inevitably get wrong under pressure, then print the airbrushed pictures beside her incorrect answers, thus offering the readers a dumb, compliant bimbo with a perfect body. It wasn't exactly a fair representation of the female student population, but then, nothing was ever a fair representation. *Banter* was no different from other publications when it came to manipulating the truth.

'We call that the hand-bra,' whispered Jamie, leaning over.

'Right.' Alexa nodded awkwardly as the girl leaned forward, lightly clutching her heavy breasts.

'Got to get plenty of nipple-free shots, for the website and so on,' he explained softly.

She nodded again, feeling distinctly uncomfortable. It wasn't just that she was sitting, watching another woman grope her own breasts; it was something else. She couldn't quite put a finger on it, but Alexa didn't feel right.

'Makeup?' Jamie was talking at full volume again, which wasn't particularly loud. Unlike most of the staff at *Banter*, Jamie had a quietly authoritative manner. He was boyishly good-looking, with high cheekbones, plump lips and piercing blue eyes that shone out from beneath long, blond lashes.

The makeup artist emerged from a far corner of the room, munching on a sandwich.

'Can you try and do something about the mark on her thigh?'

The makeup artist brushed the crumbs from her hands and bent down, grimacing at the sight of the girl's leg. 'Hmm.' She looked up. 'Is that a birthmark?'

Kayleigh nodded apologetically.

The woman screwed up her face. 'I'll see what I can do.'

The makeup artist retreated and started rummaging through her enormous kit bag, leaving Kayleigh standing self-consciously under the lights wearing a G-string and a pair of stilettos.

That was it, thought Alexa. That was what made her feel so uncomfortable: it was the fact that *Kayleigh* looked so uncomfortable. The girl didn't *want* to be exposing her every pimple and blemish to the nation, to be scrutinised by two hundred thousand strangers. True, she had volunteered for the shoot – probably encouraged to do so by a boyfriend who saw it as some kind of trophy to show his mates – but it was clear from the way she was hugging her chest that now that she was here, she felt over-exposed.

Alexa felt a surge of pity for the girl. *She* wouldn't stand up there, half naked, in front of a bunch of strangers. Even though she understood the rationale for appearing in *Banter* – that it was flattering to know that men saw you as a source of sexual stimulation – she still couldn't imagine herself doing it. Alexa wondered what it was that was stopping her. What made her different from Kayleigh?

A thick layer of foundation was applied to the offending birthmark, rendering it invisible to the camera – although from where Alexa and Jamie sat, it looked like a bad cement job. Close-up, the girl wasn't as gorgeous as she initially appeared. Beneath the streaky tan, her skin was pitted and her front teeth were stained brown with nicotine. Alexa couldn't help wondering whether this modelling shoot was some kind of ironic attempt to boost the girl's self-esteem.

Alexa thought about this for a moment, wondering whether she had hit on something. Was it self-esteem that made her different from the nineteen-year-old standing in front of her? Or self-respect? Alexa squirmed uncomfortably as the makeup artist surveyed her handiwork. She was trying to work out who had more self-respect: the woman who took her clothes off for a lads' mag, or the woman who refused to do so. She couldn't help thinking that the last six weeks had done something to dent her confidence.

'Have you got enough clean stills?' asked Jamie, jolting Alexa out of her thoughts. 'I was thinking, we could do a couple of hair-bra shots – you've got lovely hair, Kayleigh.'

Kayleigh giggled nervously. 'Thanks.'

The photographer nodded. 'Good idea. Let's give it a go.'

'Maybe using the props?' Jamie suggested, nodding at the desk by the window, which supported a selection of pens, papers and books that were presumably there to remind the reader that Kayleigh was a student.

The props helped, Alexa noticed. Kayleigh looked almost sassy, crawling along the desk on all fours, her buttocks raised in the air and her breasts hanging low, obscured by a thin veil of hair. On the photographer's advice, she played with the various items of stationery provided, sucking pencils, slapping rulers against her backside and pretending to read while donning a pair of fake glasses.

'That's great!' cried the videographer. 'More please!'

'Awesome.' The photographer nodded at Jamie. 'We've got something here.'

Alexa felt a vibration in her pocket and pulled out her phone. She had two text messages.

Of course I remember
Loopy Lara. Didn't she
only eat pink food or
sthing? Horrible little
brat. Wouldn't wish her
on my worst enemy. xL

Alexa smiled and opened the message from Matt.

Is she hot? Would
U be tempted . . .?

She stifled a laugh. Matt had seemed genuinely concerned about the risk of Alexa being 'converted', having latched on to some bizarre idea that girl-on-girl action was something that happened quite frequently, out of the blue. He had obviously been reading too much *Banter*, she thought wryly.

She's young. Currently
posing for a 'knee bra'
shot. Extremely turned
on. Ax

Alexa tucked her phone away and refocused on the action. Jamie seemed to be pleased with how things were going.

'Well done, Kayleigh. That's really great. Are you okay to do a few topless shots now?'

Kayleigh nodded, slowly reaching round and gathering the dark locks of hair to reveal her full, heavy breasts.

'That's good,' said Jamie, under his breath. 'They're real. The readers prefer real ones.'

Alexa nodded, watching as the photographer directed Kayleigh to sit on the chair, open her legs and straighten her back. She didn't feel right. Perhaps it was the muted references to various parts of the girl's body that bothered her. Jamie seemed respectful enough, but Alexa couldn't help noticing the way his brief exchanges with the photographer centred around Kayleigh's hair, thigh or breasts as though they were parts of a mannequin in a window display.

'Okay!' The photographer eventually ran out of poses and started checking through his shots. 'I think we're done.' He beckoned for Kayleigh to take a look. 'Loads of great stuff here.'

Kayleigh grabbed her bra from the floor and pulled it on, her inhibitions visibly returning.

'Oh my God!' Kayleigh gasped as she caught sight of herself on the screen. 'I look like a real model!'

The photographer smiled modestly, flicking through a selection for the girl to see. Alexa wondered what it must be like to see topless photographs of yourself, knowing that in a couple of weeks' time, they would be plastered across the back pages of a national magazine. She couldn't help feeling a shudder of panic on Kayleigh's behalf.

The videographer caught Jamie's eye. 'Can we do a few words to the camera?'

'Oh yes, of course.' Jamie wandered over to the tripod and gently interrupted. He was very genteel, noted Alexa. They all were. She didn't know what she'd been expecting, but perhaps she had foreseen an element of seediness in today's shoot – a lewd remark or possibly some inappropriate gestures. There had been nothing like that. The only crudeness at *Banter*, as far as she could tell, went on behind women's backs – in the office upstairs.

The videographer checked the settings on his camera and looked at Kayleigh, who was subtly plumping her breasts inside her bra.

'I want you to say "Hi, I'm Kayleigh and you're watching Banter TV." Okay?'

Kayleigh nodded, looking down to check on her cleavage. She suddenly looked nervous again.

'Ready when you are.'

'Hi, I'm Banter TV and . . . oh, sorry.'

'That's okay.' The videographer smiled. 'Try again.'

'Hi, I'm Kayleigh and – sorry. What was it again?'

'Don't panic. Just take it slowly. It's "Hi, I'm Kayleigh and you're watching Banter TV."'

'Okay.' Kayleigh took a deep breath and looked down the barrel of the video camera. Then she turned away, flushed and exasperated. 'Oh God. I can't do it!'

Jamie wandered over, offering a glass of water.

'Hey, Kayleigh, there's no rush. We can take all afternoon if you like.'

Alexa admired his tact. She knew how much work Jamie had on his plate upstairs; he was always the last to leave the office at night. He certainly wouldn't want to take all afternoon.

With a shaky hand, Kayleigh returned the empty glass to the pictures editor and flashed him an apologetic look.

'Tell you what,' said Jamie. 'Just do a dry-run. No pressure; we'll leave the camera off and you can just practise what you're going to say.'

'Okay.' She nodded. 'Right.' Kayleigh looked darkly into the camera and in a slow, sexy voice, growled: 'Hi, I'm Kayleigh and you're watching Banter TV.'

The videographer smiled. 'Got it.'

Kayleigh frowned. 'What d'you mean? That was a practice.'

'Oh, I must have left the camera running by mistake.' The videographer glanced at Jamie. 'That's lucky, isn't it?'

Alexa had to stop herself from laughing. Kayleigh was an ideal candidate for 'Brainy Banter'.

She looked at her watch. Strictly speaking, they were ten minutes into Kayleigh's 'exam', but the junior editor who was supposed to be asking the questions had wandered off in search of a pen and hadn't been seen since. She was about to suggest popping upstairs to find the young man when the door flew open to reveal a windswept-looking Paddy, towering in the doorway, panting.

'Hey!' He made a half-hearted attempt at taming his wild, curly hair as he looked around the room, his eyes settling on the lingerie-clad student. 'Sorry I'm late. I'm stepping in as exam master. Had to track down some questions.'

Kayleigh smiled timidly. Alexa breathed a sigh of relief. Paddy, she was beginning to realise, was one of the gems shining out from a mixed team at *Banter*. She raised a hand to the lad in a gesture of appreciation.

'I'm Paddy,' he said, bounding over. 'Pleasure to meet you.'

'Kayleigh,' she replied, shaking his hand.

'You can put your clothes on if you like,' suggested Jamie, quietly.

Quickly, Kayleigh slipped on a translucent white blouse and a leather skirt, perching nervously at the desk, opposite Paddy.

Alexa wondered whether it was fair for her to stick around while the questions were asked. The photographer and videographer were already packing away. She doubted that exam conditions were necessary, but it didn't seem fair for her to listen in. Her phone buzzed.

I knew it. I will have
to remind U tonight of
what U would miss if
you turned . . . Mmm,
looking forward to it.

Alexa hid her smile as she tucked away her phone. Paddy had already started the exam.

'You're at Leeds Uni, right?' he asked. 'Studying Sociology and hoping to get . . . a third?'

Kayleigh nodded.

'And most importantly . . . you're a 32DD, right?'

Alexa watched as the junior editor glanced approvingly at the girl's flimsy top. There it was again: the blatant reference to parts of Kayleigh's body as though they were joints of ham.

'Okay . . . let's begin. What is the main ingredient of the German dish, sauerkraut?'

'Um . . .' Kayleigh's face crumpled. 'Sausage?'

Paddy smiled. 'That'll go down well with the readers.'

Alexa followed Jamie out, trying not to cringe as Kayleigh struggled to decide whether a baby fox was called a cub or a puppy.

'Jamie?' she said, as the lift started to propel them up to the fifth floor. 'D'you think, generally, we'd do better to get some higher-calibre models in for our features?'

He looked at her, raising an eyebrow. 'You mean models with a higher IQ?'

Alexa shook her head. She knew that intelligence, sadly, was not a desirable trait for the girls. 'No, I mean . . . more professional models. Ones that know how to love the camera.'

Jamie started to smile. 'You don't have any brothers, do you?'

She frowned. 'No.'

'I only ask because if you did, then you'd know that the thing about *Banter* and all the other lads' mags – the thing that makes them sell – is *not* using chic glamour models who love the camera.'

'What?'

'They want photos of the girl-next-door. Or rather, they want photos of *their fantasy of* the girl-next-door. Chicks like Kayleigh . . . perfect.'

'But . . .' Alexa was struggling to understand what he meant. 'All the airbrushing and touching up that you do . . . surely that's because the readers want pictures of the perfect woman?'

Jamie motioned for Alexa to exit the lift before him. He was shaking his head and smiling.

'Nope. They want her to look sexy, but approachable. They want to believe that they can get their hands on tits like Kayleigh's – that girls like Kayleigh will let them into their pants.' He leaned forward and yanked open the door. 'Sexy, but rough. That's what we do best.'

Alexa headed back into the office, lost in thought.

'And the best bit?' he said, eyes twinkling.

She looked at him.

Jamie smiled. 'We don't have to pay them a penny.'

8

Alexa laid out the cuttings on the desk in front of her, re-reading the headlines that were splashed strategically across backdrops of nipples and flesh.

The 'Win Your Girlfriend a Boob Job' competition had been the most popular one of the year. That was closely followed by the search for the nation's horniest girlfriend, and at number three was Chick Strip, an appeal for readers to send in videos of their other halves undressing – a contest that probably could have performed even better, had it not been curtailed by some women's rights group declaring it 'insulting to women'.

Alexa pushed the cuttings aside, thinking about the campaigners' argument for a moment. Was it insulting? She was a woman and she didn't feel insulted. But then, she wasn't one of the subjects of the video footage. She tried to imagine how she would feel to be one of the girls in the winning clips, having her body subjected to scrutiny by hundreds of thousands of hormonal young men. It was difficult. She wasn't likely to find herself in such a position. Alexa turned back to the blank document on her screen. 'Competitions', she typed. Carriage-return. She drummed her fingers against the keyboard.

It wasn't that she didn't know what to say. She knew, conceptually, what she needed to recommend to Peterson in the way of features and competitions. She knew that they needed greater reader engagement: more blogging, more uploads, more general banter. They needed to run more contests with compelling incentives – although Alexa was not convinced that cosmetic surgery for girlfriends was necessarily the right way to go on this. No, the problem was not a lack of inspiration. The problem was that she was completely demoralised.

More than a month had passed since Alexa had first set foot in the *Banter* offices. For weeks, she had read, watched, assessed and observed, pulling together recommendations and starting to make small changes where possible. She had no doubt that she could make an impact, perhaps even meet the ambitious April targets, given the chance – but that was the problem. She wasn't being given the chance. The weight of resentment felt by certain members of the team was such that she *couldn't* make an impact, however hard she tried. Changes couldn't be made by Alexa alone; they had to be instigated by the senior editors. Of the five senior editors at *Banter* – Derek, Marcus, Neil, Jamie and Riz – the most critical two were ardently opposed to Alexa's very existence. It simply wasn't possible to turn things around with only half of the team on board.

Alexa sighed. It was a quarter to seven. Her brain had given up for the night. She closed the document, emailed it to herself, realising that yet again, she would be opening up her laptop after dinner. Matt would be disappointed. Already, Alexa had down-graded his suggested 'drinks and dinner' to a takeaway at her place and now she was effectively writing off any chance of a relaxing evening by committing herself to more work. Her thoughts flitted back to the advice her mother had given her: *Make time for him.* Where was this time supposed to come from?

'Not watching the game?'

Alexa jumped. She had assumed she was the only one left in the office. Riz was standing halfway between her desk and his, a sports bag slung over one shoulder and his hair spiky and wet. He must have been to the gym.

'Um . . . no.' Alexa blinked. She had heard the guys talk about some match tonight, but nobody had mentioned it to her directly. 'I'm . . . working late.'

Riz nodded casually. 'Well, we'll be in the Eagle if you manage to get away. See ya.'

Alexa lifted a hand. 'Goodnight, Riz.'

She waited for the door to slam before she exhaled, feeling embarrassed and ashamed on top of everything else. Riz was being charitable. She probably should have felt grateful to him for trying to include her in the team's plans, but all she could think about was the fact that she'd been left out in the first place.

Alexa started to shut down, her eyes glazing over as she waited for the programmes to close. She looked across the office, wondering vaguely why her outlook seemed more restricted than usual. There was a remote-control helicopter, obscuring a large part of the features desk, but that wasn't it. Then she realised. On Sienna's desk was a stack of old copies of *Banter*. They were piled up, she realised, in a way that completely obscured Alexa's view of Sienna and of the news desk beyond that. Sienna had erected a barrier between them.

Alexa reached down for her bag, wondering whether there was anything she could have done differently with regards to the surly assistant. It was never going to be easy, walking into a situation like this. Sienna had spent two years carving herself a cosy little niche, being the only female amid a bunch of alpha males who enjoyed her presence on their desks, in their laps and anywhere else they fancied. Here was Alexa, diluting her minority, ignoring her female wiles and restoring her role to the administrative one she was being paid to do. It was probably fair to say that no amount of lenience or kindness would persuade Sienna to switch her allegiance from the lads to the new, female MD.

Alexa trod forlornly towards the lift. Derek was her biggest problem. Derek had been knocked off his perch, just as Sienna had, but he had further to fall. Not only that, but he had more influence within the team. Whereas Sienna was seen as the office totty, Derek had respect. He was the deputy editor and people listened to him. His attitude towards Alexa had infected the minds of others.

Alexa could see it happening around her. She knew that most of the news desk saw her as some kind of joke – thanks to Marcus, the news editor who worshipped Derek's every movement. Louis Carrillo was just one example. Loud, sexist and one of the team's most senior writers, he laughed openly at Derek's laddish remarks that were clearly designed to offend Alexa. Then there were others, in the middle ranks, who clearly didn't know what to think.

Raising a limp hand in the direction of the security guard, Alexa pushed through the glass doors and took in a lungful of warm, polluted air. Her phone was ringing.

'Hey, it's me.'

A smile formed on Alexa's lips, despite her mood.

'Still on for a takeaway?' Matt's voice sounded tired, but warm.

'Yeah.' Alexa stopped just outside Senate House, staring at the words on the mock Tudor building opposite. *The Eagle*, read the gold lettering. Below the name hung a banner, announcing that Premier League games would be shown on Wednesdays and Saturdays throughout the season.

'I'm just finishing up now,' said Matt. 'Shall I come straight over?'

Alexa continued to stare at the gold lettering, thinking about what might be going on inside.

'Um . . .'

That was the problem. If she was going to make an impact at *Banter*, she had to get the team on her side – and to do that, she had to *know* them. She had to bond with them. Turning a business around wasn't just about changing business models or distribution channels; it was about changing *minds*. She had to face up to the likes of Derek and Marcus and persuade them that she was a force for good. She had to go across the road and watch the football with them.

'I . . .' Alexa pictured her boyfriend's face. His blue eyes would be narrowed questioningly, his tanned brow furrowed. 'The thing is, I'm going to have to work this evening.'

Matt sighed quietly. Alexa wasn't sure what to do. Her heart was telling her to salvage the date, to reverse the disappointment she had already caused and leave the *Banter* boys to watch the game. But her mind was telling her to cancel on Matt and cross the road. She loved Matt. She wished she could offer him something more than the distracted, exhausted wreck that was all that remained of her at the end of each working day. But that was the point. The only way she could ensure proper quality time with Matt was to get these things off her plate and then, once the teething problems were over and life at *Banter* developed more of a predictable rhythm, she would be able to devote herself fully to Matt.

She faltered for a moment and then made her decision.

'How about we do a proper date, this weekend?' she asked, as enthusiastically as she could with the guilt and shame weighing her down. 'There's no point in you coming round and falling asleep while I work.'

'I guess.' Matt sounded disappointed.

'Hey, we could go to that place in Mayfair – the one that all your colleagues were raving about.'

'Maybe, yeah.' He seemed to brighten a little at this suggestion.

Alexa smiled. She knew how important it was for Matt to keep up with all the ridiculously expensive new restaurants in town. It wasn't so much that he enjoyed the experience; it was more, as far as she could tell, that he liked to have something to talk about with his firm's wealthy client base.

'I'll make a booking,' said Alexa. 'See you on Saturday. Mine at six?'

'See you then.'

Alexa slipped her phone into her bag and stepped up to the road, waiting for a gap in the traffic. She was determined not to think about Matt, not to feel bad about letting him down. She had to leave that part of her behind, for now. It was time to mix with the lads.

The Eagle was a traditional pub with small wooden tables and benches that were nowhere near sufficient for the hordes of beer-fuelled revellers that filled the place. A giant screen had been erected on the end wall, directly above one of the tables, around which sat a group of girls who were clearly oblivious to the focus of attention above their heads.

It wasn't hard to identify the *Banter* team. They were by far the largest group in the bar, and the noisiest. Alexa watched from the doorway as Derek pushed a pint into Marcus' face, whereupon, to the sound of a slow hand-clap, the news editor gripped the glass in his teeth and downed it in about four seconds, hands-free. The clapping was drowned in a roar of jeering as the editor received another pint as his prize. Alexa hung back, wondering whether this venture was wise after all. Sienna wasn't here, she noted.

The noise level swelled as a line of players in red kit filled the giant screen. She pushed herself further into the pub, one foot after the other.

Derek was the first to spot her, his expression morphing quickly from one of surprise to one of smug anticipation.

'Ahha!' he cried, pausing for a moment in the distribution of beers around the team. 'Our esteemed leader has arrived!'

All faces turned towards Alexa, who continued to venture towards them, ignoring the sarcasm. She couldn't meet anyone's eye.

'You getting the beers in?' she asked. Her approach, she had decided, was to be bold – not laddish; she didn't want to try and emulate the deputy editor – she just wanted to make it known

74

that she too could drink beer and enjoy a game of football like the rest of them.

'What're you drinking?' asked Derek, reluctantly. There was a spot of beer froth on the tip of his goatee.

'Pint of Grolsch, please.'

Derek raised his eyebrows at the nearest team members, who responded with looks of amusement.

Alexa grabbed her lager and tried to retreat to the edge of the group, but Derek reached out and nudged her elbow with just enough force to spill her beer.

'Have to say,' he announced, competing with the TV for volume, 'I didn't think I'd see you here, Ms Long!'

Alexa turned to him, frowning. 'Ms—'

'Oi, Derek!' Marcus yelled from the group nearest the screen. 'You ain't got Lewis!'

'Don't need 'im to beat a bunch a poofters like you!'

Alexa pretended to find the exchange amusing. In fact, she felt mildly repulsed by the way men turned into inarticulate, fist-waving tribesmen the moment a competitive game came on. She wondered whether Matt was the same when he got with his rugby mates.

'Won't 'ave 'im for a while, most likely,' muttered Derek, wiping a bare arm across his mouth and removing the beer foam. 'Be partying too bloody hard, after the boost we gave 'im.' He laughed.

Alexa realised that in the din, she was probably the only person who could hear him. She wondered whether he might be making conversation.

'Ricky Lewis?' she clarified.

Derek looked at her. In an instant, Alexa realised that she had been mistaken. Derek's face was a picture of contempt.

'Yeah,' he sneered. 'You know? As in, the subject of a four-page spread in our magazine this week?' He rolled his eyes and strutted off towards the front of the group, where Marcus and other disciples were standing, bellowing at the screen.

Alexa fought back the tears of humiliation. She knew that Derek felt threatened – that they all did. They thought she was after their jobs. The irony was that she was here to *save* their jobs, not to steal them, but she had no way of telling them this. They had no idea how close they had already come to losing their livelihoods. Alexa could see why Peterson had kept the Americans' threats from the team; he knew as well as she did that fragile egos did not cope well under stress and that *Banter* would quickly collapse if news of the plans to fold leaked out. She couldn't, therefore, expect everyone to understand why she was there. But still . . . couldn't they see she was *trying*?

Having fought her way into the thick of the group, Alexa suddenly found herself standing by the bar, alone. One by one, her colleagues had pushed forward towards the screen, turning their backs on her. At first, Alexa had surged forward with them, but she couldn't help feeling that the further she pushed, the further *they* pushed, so that she was always left at the back.

She pretended to watch the game, forcing her face into various expressions as a player on either team made a run for the goal, occasionally joining in with the cries of exasperation as the shot went wide or the keeper made a save. She gulped down her beer, taking refuge in its cold, bitter taste and its mildly numbing effect. It was only her sense of self-preservation that was stopping the tears from flowing.

Alexa stood, her eyes blindly following the movements on the pitch, too scared to blink in case a tear leaked out. What had she expected? That she could win them over by turning up to a football match and drinking pints? That Derek's followers would suddenly start listening to a young female management consultant who had worked in magazines for all of two years? Alexa tipped back another slug of lager, slowly coming to the conclusion that there was no point in her being here. Expecting to command respect by coming over all laddish was no better than turning up in a low-cut top, Sienna-style, and joining in with the banter. Sienna wasn't a respected member of the team and nor was she. As a woman, was it even possible to command respect in an environment like *Banter*'s? She drained her glass and took a step back, planning her exit. If she waited for half-time, Derek would almost certainly draw attention to her disappearance, but if she sloped off now then he'd do so behind her back, which was probably worse. Alexa stared at the referee, willing him to blow the whistle for half-time and wishing she were back at her flat, with Matt.

'Who d'you support?'

She looked round, still wearing her vague, open-mouthed expression from some player's attempt at goal. She shut her mouth and returned Riz's smile. Then she opened it again, realising that in the whole time she had been staring at the screen, she hadn't once thought to figure out who was playing.

'Well . . .' Alexa remembered her pledge to be bold and decided she had nothing to lose. 'Do I look like a reds supporter?'

He smiled. 'I'm glad you said that. I'm with Spurs, too. Way too many Arsenal fans in our office, if you ask me.'

Alexa laughed. She could have deduced one of the teams, she realised, from her conversation with Derek; Ricky Lewis played for Arsenal. She felt glad, somehow, that she and Derek were on different sides.

'Get it all done?'

It took a couple of seconds for Alexa to understand the question.

'Oh. Most of it,' she said quickly. 'I decided a game of football would help me think.' She laughed unnecessarily, wishing she could learn to stop filling gaps in conversation with noise.

He nodded. 'And the pint.'

Alexa smiled. They turned their attention back to the game – or rather, Riz did. Alexa's eyes were focused on the screen, but her mind was still on her sports editor. She couldn't work him out. Of all the young men in the office, Riz was the only one who spoke openly to her, like this. Neil, Jamie, Paddy and the rest – they spoke to her, but only in a professional capacity. Riz would just come up to her and ask how things were, seemingly oblivious to the sideways looks from the others. In fact, that was the strange thing: Riz's reputation didn't appear to be damaged by his conversations with the estranged MD. He wasn't best buddies with Derek, but they got on well enough. Riz seemed to have a way of getting on with everybody. Alexa wished he could impart his secret to her.

'Oh, shit.'

Alexa came to and followed Riz's gaze. Beneath the big screen, the group of girls were finishing their drinks, putting on jackets and hugging one another. They were in blissful ignorance of the obstruction caused by their heads and limbs as they said their farewells.

Alexa watched, amused, as the expressions on the men's faces around the bar became more and more irate. Then suddenly, a man lunged forward from the crowd.

'Get the fuck out of the way!' yelled the redhead, pointing at the screen with one hand and trying to force them aside with the other.

Riz groaned. Alexa closed her eyes, embarrassed and ashamed. The aggressive man was Marcus.

'Jesus.' Riz shook his head as someone from the news desk stepped forward and hauled his boss out of the way.

Alexa turned to see whether the commotion had alerted the bar staff. Remarkably, they seemed oblivious, too busy serving customers.

'Is that normal?' she asked.

Riz shrugged. 'I guess he has more respect for the game than for women.'

Alexa didn't reply. She couldn't tell whether Riz was joking, but she had a feeling he might be right.

The whistle blew for half-time and Alexa found herself lifted off her feet, buckling under the force of a hundred thirsty men, surging towards the bar.

'Drink?' she found herself saying, as Riz, swept up in the same surge, appeared at her side. The idea of disappearing back to her flat seemed both strategically unwise and physically impossible, all of a sudden.

'Go on then.'

Several minutes later, Alexa emerged with two pints of beer and two dripping, sticky wrists.

'Thanks.' Riz lifted his glass against hers, laughing as a drunk football fan stumbled between them. 'The downside to watching the game in a shit-hole, eh?'

Alexa frowned. 'What's the upside?'

'Well, er . . .' Riz looked slightly embarrassed. 'It means not going home. I'm living with my folks for a bit – between houses.'

Alexa nodded understandingly. She too had moved back with her parents the previous year, in an effort to save money to buy her flat. It had lasted six days.

They sipped their drinks, glancing instinctively at the ads on the screen.

'You're pretty young, to be a managing director.'

Alexa looked at him. For once, the words didn't sound like an accusation.

'You're young,' she returned, 'for a sports editor.'

'Thirty-two.'

'Twenty-nine.'

'See?' He nodded. 'Young.'

'I'm only an interim.' Alexa shrugged, making out that it was no big deal while secretly feeling flattered that Riz was taking such an interest in her career. 'Fixed contract, fixed targets. Then I'm out of here.'

'Like a Premiership football manager.'

'Do they have targets?'

He thought for a moment. 'Good point.'

Alexa smiled. This was incredible. She hadn't reverted to babbling.

'Maybe they should,' she suggested.

Riz nodded. 'I'll put it to our readers.'

The second half passed much more quickly and seemed significantly more enjoyable. As a newfound Spurs supporter, Alexa no longer made expectant noises as Arsenal players took shots at goal. She noticed things, too. Like, for example, the way the Arsenal players spat more and tended to writhe around, feigning injury after every tackle. From what she could tell, Spurs had the upper hand. They just needed to score.

With one minute to go, there were still no goals from either side. Alexa found herself willing the players on, muttering words of encouragement, desperate to see them win. She was about to ask Riz what would happen if the score was nil–all at the end when she felt a vibration in her pocket. She pulled out her phone. *Mum – home,* said the display. After a moment's deliberation, she took the call.

'Hi!' she cried, above the din. 'Hold on a second.'

With hindsight, thought Alexa as she fought her way through the crowds, taking a call in the final minute of a local derby in a crowded pub was not the best idea. She spilled onto the pavement and looked at the phone, taking a couple of seconds to regain her breath.

'Sorry about that,' she said. 'Watching the football.'

'Oh.'

Alexa smiled. Bewilderment, disdain, disappointment . . . it was incredible how much could be conveyed in a single syllable.

'Is it urgent, or shall I call you back at the weekend?'

'Oh, well . . . it's nothing much.' There it was again. Watching a game of football was clearly not deemed a sensible use of time.

'Go on,' Alexa prompted.

'Well, I just wanted to find out whether you'd managed to

talk to your colleagues yet. About Lara. Only I was talking to Janice at youth group and she said that Lara hadn't heard.'

'Sorry.' Alexa grimaced at the thought of her unmet promise. 'I'll do it this week.'

'Only if it's not too much trouble.'

A deafening roar emanated from inside the pub.

'No trouble.'

'Lovely. Thank you, darling. Um . . . how is Matthew?'

Alexa was already in the doorway, waiting to return to the game. 'He's fine.'

'Good. That's good. Do send him our love.'

'I will. Bye, Mum.'

'Right, yes. Bye, darling!'

Alexa took a moment before returning to the pub. She was beginning to realise that she didn't actually need to tell her mother about the job. It was only a nine-month contract, of which she had already served one. Her mother didn't need to know. She would be better off not knowing. Alexa could just imagine the pained expression on her mother's face whenever somebody from youth group or scouts asked what her daughter was up to. This way, her mother wouldn't have to lie. Alexa felt the relief engulf her as she came to terms with her decision. It was better for everyone this way.

Even before she got close enough to see the TV, Alexa knew that she'd missed a goal. The pub was alive with activity: men standing on chairs, fists clenched in exasperation, eyes fixed on the screen. The question was: which team?

Riz's expression told her the answer.

'You should disappear more often!'

Alexa laughed. The score was one–nil to Spurs and there were only seconds of injury time left to go. As she watched, though, an Arsenal midfielder lobbed the ball half the length of the pitch and Alexa watched, dismayed, as a waiting team-mate crossed it perfectly into the goal.

'Offside!' Alexa found herself yelling. She knew the rules.

'Fuck off!' shouted a man, very close to her ear.

Alexa reeled sideways and realised with dismay that the man was Derek.

'No way was that offside!' he bellowed aggressively, both hands flying into the air above his stumpy little body. He seemed to be shouting at both the referee and Alexa at once.

Alexa became aware of a movement in the crowd around her. Bodies were shifting, making a clearing around her and Derek.

'He was offside,' she stated, calmly.

Alexa knew that she had the upper hand, not only in that she had drunk fewer pints than the deputy editor, but in that she was right. On the TV, a slow-motion replay was indicating, quite clearly, that the Arsenal player had been hanging around by the goal, a long way from the nearest defender.

Derek seemed unperturbed. 'You're a woman!' he yelled. 'You don't even *understand* the offside rule!'

Alexa caught Riz's eye, incredulous. He nodded at the TV, where the referee was signalling for the goal to be disallowed.

'*That's bollocks,*' Derek spat in Alexa's direction as he turned, barging through the ring of onlookers and heading for the bar.

Alexa stood for a moment, waiting for her reflexes to catch up with what had just happened. Adrenaline flooded her veins and she realised that her pint glass was shaking.

'Wow,' said Riz, softly. 'You okay?'

'Nice one!' cried somebody behind her, more loudly.

Alexa turned to see a pasty white face framed with ginger hair.

'Good call,' said Marcus. He was a Spurs fan, of course. 'Very good call, Ms Long.'

'What?' Alexa frowned. That was the second time tonight she had heard that name.

Riz leaned over, smiling apologetically. 'It's your nickname.'

Alexa said it a few times in her head, rolling the words together. Ms Long. Alexa Long. *AlexaLong*.

'Oh. Right.'

The shaking began to subside. Alexa let out a shallow breath. For a nickname, she considered, it could have been worse – and besides, it wasn't the nickname that mattered. What mattered was the fact that one of Derek's disciples was standing in front of her, grinning from ear to ear and offering her another drink.

9

'I thought Sienna and Derek were sleeping together,' said Alexa, topping up Matt's wine. 'But then I heard a rumour that Sienna and *Riz* were an item, which just seems wrong. Riz is too straight-forward. He's . . . well, I just can't see him getting involved with such a—'

'Such a what?' challenged Matt, as she faltered. 'Go on, say it. Insult the poor girl.'

Alexa shook her head. 'Sorry. Slut, I was going to say.'

She felt bad. Sienna hadn't actually done anything to deserve such a name. It was just a combination of things. The way she dressed. The voice she used with the men. Her permanently puckered lips.

'Anyway,' she said, 'I heard another rumour on Friday, that Sienna was sleeping with *Marcus*.'

'Who's Marcus?'

'News editor. You know, the one I told you about. Piggy-eyed, ginger guy. I'd be surprised if anyone wanted to sleep with him, to be honest.'

Matt raised an eyebrow, pushing the remains of his prawn cocktail away. 'I hope nobody says that about me.'

Alexa rolled her eyes. She hadn't asked, but she was willing to bet that Matt had never been turned down by anyone. Even first thing in the morning, he was irresistible – as she had discovered on New Year's Day, nearly eight months ago. Alexa had

84

woken in Kate's spare bed with a crick in her neck as a result of Matt's arm around her. She still remembered the look of surprise in his sleepy blue eyes, mirroring her own as they woke up and started to recall what had happened – still felt a rush of excitement when she pictured the scene.

'Have you told your parents yet?'

Alexa emerged from her daydream. 'I've decided . . . I'm not going to.'

'What?'

'Well, it's only a short-term contract. They wouldn't approve; they'd never see things from my point of view. There's no need to tell them.'

'Well . . .' Matt looked at her, slowly shaking his head in bewilderment. 'It's up to you, I suppose.'

They sipped their wine in silence. Alexa felt angry, all of a sudden. She resented the way Matt judged her relationship with her parents. He couldn't possibly know how it felt to be constantly striving to live up to her mother's standards. He didn't understand how appalled they would be to discover that their daughter was working for *Banter*. He just didn't get it.

'It is up to me,' she declared, 'and I've made up my mind. I just have to hit the fifty-four million, then I'm out of there.'

Matt nodded, leaning back to allow the waiter to remove his debris.

Alexa sat, staring into her expensive glass of wine, waiting for some kind of reaction to the mention of her ambitious target and realising, as the seconds passed, that she wasn't going to get one. Deep down, she wanted Matt to be impressed by the scale of the task she had undertaken. He knew that *Banter*'s current revenues were only thirty-two million. The next eight months weren't going to be easy. But Matt didn't seem to care.

She took a large sip of wine and watched as the main courses were slid onto the table. It was becoming evident that the boutique Mayfair hotel specialised in exotic cuisine of miniature proportions. Alexa's plate, despite being one of the largest she had ever eaten off, was almost entirely empty. In the centre sat a twisted, glazed noodle and three slim, perfectly formed slivers of duck.

'Bon appétit,' said Matt, eyeing his steak with glee. He seemed to have ordered the only dish on the menu that came in a standard size.

Alexa busied herself dissecting the duck, trying not to let her frustration show. What she wanted, desperately, was to find out what Matt really thought of her job at *Banter*. She had noticed that whenever conversation turned to her work then something changed in him. He became curt, indifferent. He would feign interest, but Alexa often got the impression he was thinking about something else.

She moved on to her second sliver of duck, her frustration finally winning over her composure.

'You're not interested, are you?' Alexa looked at him. 'You think my job's a waste of time.'

Matt stopped chewing, recoiling in surprise. 'Why d'you say that?'

'It just seems as though you don't really care.' Alexa waited for him to meet her eye. 'I guess it's just loose change, for you . . . child's play.'

'No.' Matt seemed genuinely surprised. 'No. That's not true. Fifty-two million is fifty-two million. That's not child's play.'

'It's fifty-four million.'

'Sorry.' Matt flinched. 'That's what I meant.'

Alexa took a deep breath. She didn't want to come across as a psychopathic workaholic but she really, really wanted to know why Matt seemed so disinterested in the things that occupied her mind for half of her waking hours. It was looking less and less likely that his reservations were borne out of concerns for her wellbeing in the 'lions' den'. Tales of her battles with Derek or the stalemate she seemed to have reached with Sienna were greeted with the same vague nods as the mention of financial targets.

'I am impressed.' Matt was looking at her intensely. 'I'm impressed with everything you do. You're . . . you're amazing. I don't know how you do it – how you keep going the whole time, always . . .'

Alexa watched as he struggled to finish his sentence. She felt instantly guilty. Matt's blue eyes were looking intently into hers, pleadingly. He clearly meant every word.

'Always living up to your own high standards.'

Alexa reached out and locked fingers with him across the table. 'Sorry for being paranoid.'

Matt started to smile. 'So go on, tell me.' He was poised for a forkful of steak, but his eyes were still fixed on Alexa's.

She frowned. 'Tell you what?'

'How the hell will you make the fifty-two million?'

Alexa smiled. 'Fifty-four million.'

Matt winced. 'Sorry.'

'Well, if you really want to know . . .'

Alexa gave him one last chance to back out, but he didn't take it. So she told him. She told him about the proposed tablet app, her plans for rejuvenating Banter TV, the new feature ideas that she and Neil had devised and the ways in which she was going to 'up the nipple count'.

'Ah,' said Matt, nodding wisely as he polished off his steak. 'I like that idea. Reckon that'll net you at least ten million.'

Alexa smiled. It wasn't quite fair to say that Matt had shown no interest in her work in recent weeks. He had, she recalled, sat through at least an hour of Banter TV and scanned the 'Girls' section of every issue she brought home. He therefore considered himself an expert in such things as submissive positions and nipple counts.

'Oh,' she said, remembering something else. 'And we'll have no more sending our junior editors on mad expeditions for the hell of it. From now on, we're going to try and get locations to *pay us* for being featured.'

Matt looked at her quizzically. 'Didn't you send the last one to a pig farm?'

'Well, yes, but—'

'I'm not sure how much money a pig farm would be willing to spend on being featured in *Banter*.'

'Okay,' Alexa conceded, impressed that he remembered Paddy's feature. 'But that was a one-off. Usually, it's track days and adventure weekends. That kind of thing.'

'Ah.' Matt nodded.

'There's one other thing that I want to do,' said Alexa, thinking back to her list for Peterson.

'What's that?'

'A mobile app.'

Matt pushed his plate away and sat back, looking contemplative.

The mobile app was the only outstanding initiative that Alexa had yet to figure out. It had to be good – so good that every lad in the country felt compelled to download it. So good that lads who downloaded all their music and films for free would actually *pay* for it.

'Naked girls straight to your mobile phone, you mean? That sort of thing?'

'I don't know.' Alexa shook her head pensively. Her initial thoughts had been along those lines, but she knew that the idea wasn't imaginative enough. Men had been accessing porn on their phones for years, for free.

Matt leaned forward, his eyes fixed intently on hers.

'Here's an idea,' he said. 'How about you stop trying to fix everything yourself and get the guys on your team to help?'

Alexa smiled, straightening her back and squaring up to Matt. 'You know, I might actually have to resort to that.'

10

'So, let's have a think about the things that have really worked for *Banter* over the last few years.'

Alexa stood, one arm hooked over the top of the flipchart, the other poised to write. A silence descended on the room. A few people started scanning their notes and adopting pensive expressions.

'Come on, guys.' Alexa reached over and opened a window. It was a warm afternoon, but for some reason the heating was on full-blast throughout the building.

'Chimp on a pogo-stick?' suggested Biscuit, eventually. 'That got, like, a zillion hits on the website.'

'Chimp riding a cow?' added Greg, one of the junior writers next to him. 'Didn't we do something like that?'

'It was a monkey,' corrected Marcus.

'Juggling monkeys?' Paddy called out.

Marcus frowned. 'I don't remember that.'

'Monkey tennis!' cried Greg, receiving a swift blow to the head from Biscuit with a giant, inflatable mallet that had somehow made its way into the meeting.

'It was just a suggestion,' explained Paddy. The mallet swung round and another blow was administered.

Alexa nodded, surveying the list of words on the flipchart and wondering how such insight might eventually contribute to a business case for a ground-breaking mobile app. *Primates. Sports.*

Animals riding other animals. It didn't seem promising, but then, this was a brainstorm; there was no such thing as a bad idea.

'Topless tennis?' suggested Jamie. 'We often get sent topless pics by the female readers.'

'Topless gardening,' added someone, having evidently forgotten the overall purpose and just randomly word-associating.

'Topless hairdressers? Or topless occupations in general. We could definitely make something of that. There must be a topless librarian out there.'

'If there isn't, we'll invent one!' cried Derek, clearly too amused by the idea to keep his mouth shut any longer.

'Good . . .' Alexa continued to write, trying not to lose faith. This, she thought, was why magazine editors should not be put in charge of strategic initiatives. They were all talking in terms of one-off features. What *Banter* needed was a concept; an idea that could be run over and over again, that provided lads all over the world with a perpetual source of entertainment.

'Topless dancing?' muttered Louis, from behind his wall of greasy black hair.

'Like it.' Derek winked at him from across the table.

Reluctantly, Alexa wrote it down. She knew that both Derek and the lascivious senior news writer, Louis, along with Marcus, were no strangers to topless dancing. The three longest-standing members of the *Banter* team regularly rolled in at around midday, sweating alcohol and revelling in misguided fantasies about love-struck strippers in gentlemen's clubs.

'Dancing-gone-wrong?' suggested Neil. 'Our readers love a bit of that.'

'Anything gone wrong,' said Riz, speaking for the first time. 'The most popular feature we ever ran was on footballers getting kicked in the nads.'

There were reminiscent mumblings, followed by a long conversation about whether actually, the feature on geriatric sumo wrestling had drawn in more readers.

'How about: "Look Out, I Just Ate a House"?'

Alexa looked at Biscuit for a moment, along with everybody else, and sighed. She had to try to steer them onto a more constructive train of thought.

'That's great,' she said, with as much energy as she could muster. 'So . . . what have we learned from all this? What drives our reader engagement? What types of thing could we do that would really boost their loyalty to the brand?'

The room fell silent.

Alexa started flipping through the pages of notes, hoping that something would catch someone's eye. Unfortunately, the only person willing to speak was Derek.

'*Boost their loyalty to the brand,*' he echoed, in a squeaky voice. '*Drive reader engagement* . . . what does that even *mean*?'

Alexa stood for a moment, hating her deputy editor more than ever and realising with dismay that the brief display of solidarity she had witnessed from Marcus had been driven solely by their supposed football allegiance. Marcus' appreciation for Derek's words was spreading throughout the news team.

The only way to proceed, Alexa decided, ripping the pages off the pad and sticking them around the room, was to ignore the deputy editor. She knew that his childish behaviour was affecting people's perceptions of her, but she also knew that certain members of the team were mature enough to see through it and respect her for what she was trying to do. It was just a clique, she told herself. Old boys' clubs were to be expected in all-male environments.

'What I'm talking about is getting the readers really *involved* with our stuff. Offering them an experience that they can't get anywhere else. Making them *love* our app – and everything else – for our amazing sporting disasters or animal games or topless girls or whatever it is we decide to do.'

There was some tentative nodding. Alexa scanned the notes

again, feeling more fired up than defeatist after Derek's outburst. She couldn't help noticing how many times the word 'topless' cropped up.

'What about the girls?' she asked. 'Is there anything more we could offer, to get the lads really hooked?'

Alexa had thought a lot about what Jamie had told her after the Brainy Banter photo shoot. It was clear to her now why girls like Kayleigh were such a hit with the readers. She understood the girl-next-door thing, she saw why it worked so much better than hiring real glamour models. In fact, she had been slowly coming to the conclusion that they ought to be doing *more* to exploit the girls – she just wasn't sure what.

'We already film the photo shoots,' said Louis. 'Short of offering live performances, I'm not sure what else we could do.'

'We could film the interviews?' suggested someone. 'Get them to answer all sexily, into the camera?'

Neil reached for the inflatable mallet and walloped the lad on the head.

'Sorry, but have you attended a photo shoot recently? Have you witnessed the moment when the stunning blonde 34DD opens her mouth to speak?'

Jamie nodded. 'A real turn-off. I agree. Keep it to visuals only.'

Alexa nodded too, but she wasn't convinced they could write off the idea entirely. The appeal of these girls, as she now knew, was that they were *real*. They had flaws. The readers wanted to see their imperfections – or at least, some of their imperfections. At the same time, Alexa knew that men were willing to throw away good money to hear a girl – any girl – talk dirty on the phone. There had to be a way of putting the ideas together.

'Okay,' she said, putting the thought aside and going for one last push on the app front. 'Topless hairdressers . . . topless tennis . . . Jamie, did you say we got lots of topless pictures sent in?'

He nodded.

'By our female readers?'

'From blokes, mainly.' Neil leaned in. 'That's how we get most of our models. Their boyfriends send in a photo, then they get flattered into doing the shoot.'

Alexa looked around the room, wondering whether anyone else was thinking along the same lines as her. There were smiles creeping up some of their faces but nobody seemed to want to voice their thoughts. Alexa seized the opportunity.

'How about the *My Girlfriend* app? A video upload service where men can watch clips of other people's girlfriends?'

Biscuit looked up immediately. 'I'd pay for that!'

'Fuck, yeah.' Louis rubbed his hands together, letting out a dirty growl.

'What?' The only person not voicing his approval was Neil. He frowned at his colleagues. 'Isn't this going a bit *too* far? I mean, you can't just let any old body upload videos of girls.'

'Yes you can!' Louis quickly drowned out Neil's protest. Alexa was surprised to hear the strength of support for her idea, but then remembered how things worked around here. Louis wasn't in favour of the idea because it was hers; he was backing it because it was bold and laddish and out there. Just as Marcus had appeared to stand by her side at the football match a couple of weeks ago and then reverted to his old ways when back in the office, Louis's apparent cooperation was transient.

'Shut the fuck up,' roared Marcus. 'Don't be such a homo!'

'You're too old for this game, mate. We're not talking about *married men*.' Louis spat out the term like an insult. 'We're talking about young blokes with girlfriends. It's a bloody brilliant idea.'

'Okay . . .' Neil wasn't the type to back down without a fight. 'How about we ask someone with a girlfriend.' He looked around. 'Um . . .'

It quickly transpired that nobody in the room had a girlfriend.

'Riz!' cried Marcus, with sudden vindictiveness in his voice. 'How about you?'

'Ha ha.' Riz dipped his head and looked at the table. Alexa wondered what was going on. Did Riz have a girlfriend? Clearly there was some in-joke between the men from which Alexa had been excluded.

'Look, I just think this thing would have to be carefully implemented,' said Neil, although nobody was listening any more.

A discussion broke out about exactly how the app might work: whether it would require users to upload footage in order to view other people's videos, who would censor the clips and how the breast-rating system would work. Alexa started pulling flip-chart pages off the wall, deep in her own thoughts and suddenly feeling excited. Neil was right about the careful implementation, but on the face of it, this app was a no-brainer. They already knew that two of their top-performing competitions last year had involved sending in pictures of readers' semi-naked girl-friends. Unsolicited topless photos were pouring in via the *Banter* text line and video was surely the next step. This app made perfect sense.

My Girlfriend, mused Alexa, as the rabble poured out of the meeting room and returned to work. It had a nice ring to it. Simple, memorable, descriptive. She folded the pages of notes and stuffed them under her desk, not intending to ever look at them again. There was a small, niggling feeling at the back of her mind about the ethics of such blatant female objectification, but the feeling was dwarfed by the anticipation of what could be achieved with such an initiative.

The proofs for this week's edition of *Banter* lay neatly arranged on the desk in front of her. Strictly speaking, they were a priority, but Alexa could do little more than turn the pages as her brain raced from mobile app developers to content censorship and onto legislation and, finally, how to pitch such a radical idea to the technophobic chief executive.

She smiled, focusing briefly on the proofs as she noted the high volume of Banter Confessions this week. The mugshot Jamie had chosen for 'Joanne', their secretary, was the perfect mix of sassy and approachable. Alexa flipped the page, wondering what Sienna thought of her reduction in workload this week. Then she stopped. A surge of bile rose up inside her as she looked at the image staring up at her from the desk.

The image on the page was porn. Not just the tanned flesh and nipples to which she had become accustomed; this was serious, hardcore porn involving penetration and bodily fluids and carefully sculpted pubic hair – and *her own face*, amateurishly Photoshopped onto the woman's prostrate figure.

Alexa forced herself to turn the page. She sat stock still for a moment, waiting for the nausea to pass. It felt as though she might vomit, right there at her desk.

Questions quickly filled her mind as she sat, shaking and panicking. How had the image been created? Who was responsible? How had it found its way into the proofs? What was she supposed to do about it? Alexa tried to push the questions away, to allow her body to recover from the shock, but they kept coming. Who knew about this? How did they expect her to react?

Eventually, the nausea subsided a little, enabling Alexa to look up and scan the office. Derek, Marcus and Louis went straight onto her shortlist of culprits. In fact, she couldn't think of anyone else with the same combination of arrogance and vindictiveness to attempt to pull off a stunt like this.

She shuddered inwardly at the thought of one – or, more likely, more than one – of them overlaying the image of her face onto the hideous picture. There were office pranks, like leaving a giant dildo on somebody's desk or changing the screensaver message to a mild obscenity, both of which had happened to Alexa during her first fortnight – both of which she had accepted with good humour, as part of the 'office banter' – but this was something else. This was grotesque and offensive and apart from anything else, it was a sackable offence.

Alexa feigned interest in the remaining pages, turning them

slowly to give herself time to think. Derek was at his desk. It seemed to Alexa as though he was making less noise than usual. In fact, he seemed to be glancing up from his screen more often, too. He was definitely involved, she decided. Alexa kept turning the pages, desperately hoping that the initial shock hadn't registered on her face. She still didn't feel right, even now, but she couldn't bear to let him think he had won. Eventually, she reached the last page and calmly slid the whole pack away, face down.

Her email to Leonie and Kate was brief, mainly because she knew that Sienna had access to her inbox and the last thing she wanted was to alert the PA's suspicion. Sienna, thankfully, was some distance away, perched on the edge of Louis' desk and giggling as he encouraged her to bend over and suck on the controls of the Nintendo Wii.

Alexa was fairly sure that Sienna hadn't been involved; it had all the hallmarks of a male sense of humour and given the severity of an incident like this in the eyes of Senate HR, she could only assume that the guilty parties would want to keep the details of their endeavour to themselves. This, thought Alexa as she waited for a response from her friends, was what perplexed her. The perpetrators were effectively bound to secrecy; they couldn't share the joke with the rest of the team. So what was the point? She pressed Refresh, staring desperately at her inbox. She realised, unhappily, that she already knew the answer.

The point of the stunt was to hurt her.

She pounced on an incoming message.

Lex,
    This is horrible. I can't believe they'd do that. Are you OK?
    I really think you should go to HR about this. You have to get it dealt with the proper way. These men have to learn, Lex – they can't get away with this sort of thing. You have to make an example of them.

Call me if you want to chat – am on hols until Mon.
Leonie xx

Alexa squinted at the screen, thinking hard about her friend's advice. Leonie was right. Going to HR was the only way. It wasn't a prospect she relished, having the case opened up to the political correctness brigade on the second floor and anyone else who might be involved, but she had to draw the crime to people's attention in order for the perpetrators to be brought to justice. If she allowed them to get away with it this time, then there would be other incidents down the line – either directed at her or at someone else. It wasn't fair on future victims to keep quiet.

The problem was, of course, that there would be no way for HR to prove who was responsible. Alexa had a good idea of who the culprit or culprits might be, but there was no *proof*. These men were smart enough to have covered their tracks and even after hours of painful questioning by HR investigators, there would be little chance of a verdict. The likes of Derek would just laugh it off; nobody would take the blame.

Alexa shuddered at the thought of what the investigation might entail. No doubt, there would be weeks of interviews resulting in little more than a vague set of eliminations and a whole host of rumours and accusations. They would all be forced by HR to sit through hours of pointless videos about corporate policies and sexual equality, which would serve no purpose except to strengthen the 'them and us' sentiment and provide a good laugh for Derek's clan. Worst of all, every employee of Senate Media would at some point see a leaked copy of the offending material, making Alexa the laughing stock of the firm. Any credibility she had managed to build up in her first two months at *Banter* would be wiped out in an instant. It would be the end of her job – possibly the end of her career.

It would be easier to keep quiet, thought Alexa, wondering whether she could exact her revenge in some other way – bringing

Derek and his close-knit crew down in some other way. She sighed. That was the cop-out option. It was the selfish, safe option.

This was exactly why so many women opted not to go to court after being wronged in the workplace: it wasn't pleasant, having your personal and professional life scrutinised and judged in public, while the perpetrators sat smugly in the dock, waiting for their rap on the knuckles. No, she thought. To brush it under the carpet was to let the whole side down. Every woman who kept quiet about an incident like this was inadvertently perpetuating the problem.

Alexa started clicking randomly on old emails, thinking about the email she would send to HR. Her breathing was still quick and shallow and her eyes kept wandering to the pile of upturned pages on her desk. She needed to extract the porn from the main deck, ready for the pre-press meeting in the morning, then somehow she needed to slip the porn into her bag and dispose of it, somewhere a long way from the office. She stopped clicking. Kate had replied.

Jesus, Lex!

Leonie is right – this is bloody awful. What a bunch of t*ssers.

I have to say, in my experience, HR does more harm than good. They'd hang out your dirty washing for all to see and you still wouldn't know who to blame. Unless you have a way of pinning it on someone then the risk is that you're left looking pathetic and the tw*ts get away with it.

Sorry, not sure that helps.

Good luck – and don't let the b*stards get you down.

Kx

PS See you next Sun for an update? Hyde Park café at 12?

Alexa re-read her friends' emails, both of them, and let out a quiet sigh. Their responses were as predictable and contradictory as ever. She could have guessed that Leonie would opt for the official line, while Kate went for the course of action that minimised the risk of career disruption. The question was, which was the right option for her?

She looked at her friends' emails one last time before deleting them both. Sienna was returning to her desk, via Marcus', where she bent over obligingly as he made to slap her backside. Alexa stared venomously at the upturned pack of proofs, willing her brain to make the decision.

The office was starting to empty out for lunch. Derek, who was usually the first to lead the mass exodus, seemed unusually reluctant to vacate his seat. It was particularly odd, thought Alexa, considering that it was a Friday – fish and chips day at The Eagle. She watched out of the corner of her eye as Marcus rallied the news desk and cast a questioning eye at the deputy editor. It was impossible to tell whether Marcus' expression was suggestive of anything more than an invitation to lunch. Derek shook his head and turned back to his monitor.

Before long, Derek and Alexa were alone in their part of the office. In the far corner, Jamie was one-handedly airbrushing a cleavage while biting into a baguette. Dark thoughts occupied Alexa's mind as her suspicions converged into theories: the exchange between Marcus and Derek had not been about lunch, but about whether she had seen the porn yet. The quick shake of Derek's head had referred to *her*.

Derek checked his watch and rose to his feet, heading briskly for the door. Alexa exhaled, trying to relieve some of the tension inside her. Perhaps he hadn't been monitoring her after all. Slowly, she flicked through the corners of the upturned pages, looking out for rogue obscenity. Even though the office was virtually deserted, she couldn't risk exposing the image.

It was harder than she had imagined, telling the pages apart, so she found herself peeling each page up, slowly, from the corner, to establish which one to extract. Eventually, she identified the page and slid it free of the main pack. Slowly, keeping the page face down, she started to fold it into two, so that the porn was turned in on itself for her to hide in her bag.

'Alexa?'

She froze. Her hands were trembling in front of her, clutching either side of the half-folded page. If she let go with either one, the exposed side would drop down and swing into view. Jamie was standing right behind her.

In one swift movement, Alexa pressed the two halves together and dropped the folded sheet on the desk. 'Yes?'

'I just wanted to check something on this Back to School feature.' He tentatively offered a print-out of the page in question. Perhaps he sensed her unease. 'In the absence of Derek, can you confirm that we're including all the girls? It's just that this one, on the left, looks a bit . . . young.'

Alexa took the print-out, dropping the page on the desk so that Jamie wouldn't have time to register her shaking hands. Her heart was beating so hard in her chest it felt as though something might burst.

She peered at the image – four busty blondes wearing mini-skirts, stockings and skin-tight shirts tied in knots under their pneumatic breasts – trying to breathe normally and to concentrate. Jamie was right. The girl on the left looked prepubescent.

'Crop her off,' she said, handing back the page and trying to smile. 'Just in case.'

Jamie nodded. He made to leave and then hesitated, looking at Alexa.

'Are you alright?'

'Mmm?' She tried to smile. 'Yeah, fine.'

'It's just, you look a bit . . . pale.'

'Do I?'

'Yeah.'

'Oh.' Alexa shrugged. 'Probably tired.'

He nodded unconvincingly.

Alexa watched as he slowly turned and walked back down the office. He was almost back in his seat by the time she looked down and realised that the page had gone. She froze for a second, unable to breathe. A wave of hot, sticky sickness rose up inside her. Then, hearing the crash of her own chair against the filing cabinet, she launched herself across the office.

'Jamie?' she called out, breathlessly. 'Jamie . . . um . . .'

It was too late. Jamie was unfolding the page, his face distorted by a mixture of horror and disbelief.

11

'He saw it?' Leonie looked at her, aghast. '*Shit*, Lex. What did he say?'

Alexa grimaced as she recalled the hideous moment when Jamie had finally met her eye.

'He didn't say anything, for a while. Then he told me he knew who'd done it.'

'What?' Leonie leaned across the picnic bench. 'Who?'

Alexa looked around, in case Kate was on her way. It would be bad enough recalling the situation once, but twice would be torturous.

'*Who?*' repeated Leonie, insistently.

Hyde Park was buzzing with noisy tourists and Londoners catching the last of the summer sun, but Kate didn't appear to be among them.

'It was Marcus, apparently. Jamie said he recognised the handiwork. "A unique way of using Photoshop," he said.'

'But . . .' Leonie looked up as a pigeon fluttered clumsily onto their table and headed towards the half-eaten muffin between them. 'How d'you know you can trust this Jamie guy? What if *he* was in on it?'

Alexa shook her head, shooing the pigeon away. 'I trust him. Besides, if he'd been in on it, the graphics would've been better.' She managed a half-smile.

'But . . .' Leonie clearly wasn't convinced. 'It's such a disgusting thing, Lex . . . what if—'

'Honestly,' Alexa assured her. 'Jamie's one of the good guys.'

'One of the *good guys*?' She pulled back her head, scathingly.

Alexa gave a defensive nod. It was hard to explain, but she was beginning to understand the men who worked on *Banter*. There were, broadly speaking, two types. There were those who wrote sexist, condescending, bigoted words for the magazine and then left the office each night to become regular guys with wives and families and a conscience. Then there were men like Derek and Marcus and Louis who really *believed* in those words. Alexa had observed Jamie's calm, sensitive manner with Kaylcigh at the photo shoot. She had worked with him a few times now, she'd seen the way he treated his colleagues. He was definitely one of the good guys.

'So, you know it was Marcus who did it? Can you prove it?'

Alexa swilled the remains of her coffee around the paper cup, then tipped it back and swallowed, avoiding Leonie's eye as she slowly crumpled the cup in her hand. This was the tricky part.

'The thing is . . . I'm sure Jamie's right about Marcus, but I don't think he was the only one involved.'

'Why d'you say that?'

'Because . . .' Alexa faltered, trying to articulate her thoughts. She had never suspected Marcus as the sole perpetrator of the crime, even when Jamie had identified him as the culprit. It was something to do with Marcus' manner. His attitude. He wasn't an ardent chauvinist and he wasn't ardently against Alexa's presence at *Banter*; in fact, he wasn't ardently anything. He was a sheep. He followed the person with the largest following – which, in most cases, was Derek. Marcus believed whatever Derek believed. He laughed at whatever Derek was laughing at, he drank whatever Derek was drinking and he did whatever Derek told him to do. The only instance Alexa could think of where Marcus had deviated from this pattern was when he had admitted to supporting a different football team – but then, perhaps Tottenham Hotspurs had a larger following than Arsenal.

'Marcus isn't capable of thinking for himself,' she explained. 'I'm fairly sure Derek set him up.'

'*The deputy editor?*'

Alexa nodded, cringing as she envisioned the moment Derek had goaded Marcus into accepting the challenge. It *had* to be Derek, she thought. Nobody else would instil such audacity in the pallid news editor. It was just like Derek, too, to palm off his dirty work to an underling. This way, Marcus got to feel big in front of the man he idolised and Derek got to hurt Alexa without the risk of taking any blame.

'That's a big accusation, Lex. Can you prove it?'

Alexa looked away. Pedalos puttered slowly across the surface of the Serpentine. A pair of swans squawked over a lump of bread.

'I'm not going to prove it,' she said, eventually.

Leonie frowned. 'What, you mean you'll leave HR to try and—'

'No, I mean I'm not going to HR.'

'*What?*'

Alexa sighed, looking around again for Kate. She had a feeling her ex-colleague would understand better than Leonie what she was about to say. There was still no sign.

'I was going to,' she explained, 'but Jamie told me not to.'

'So what—'

'No, Leonie,' Alexa silenced her friend. 'He's right. He's worked at *Banter* for years – he knows how things work. If I went to HR, waving a piece of porn with my face on it, my placement would be over tomorrow and I'd never lead a team at Senate again.'

'But . . .' Leonie was shaking her head, lost for words. 'Surely there's a way? I mean, *you're* not to blame – you shouldn't be persecuted for something *they've* done?'

Alexa lifted her shoulders. She'd been through this exact

thought process herself. 'That's the problem. There's no way of avoiding persecution if I expose what they've done. That's exactly why they did what they did.'

Leonie wiped a hand across her furrowed brow. 'I just think . . . well, if something like this had happened to me at school, there'd be no question about what to do.'

'This isn't school,' said Alexa, suddenly realising the irony of the statement. Her office environment was worse than that of a school playground.

'But . . .' Leonie trailed off again, clearly coming to the same conclusion that Alexa had eventually drawn in front of Jamie. 'So, that's it, then? You're just going to forget it ever happened? Let them get away with it?'

Alexa shook her head. 'Not exactly.'

Leonie looked at her suspiciously. 'What does that mean?'

'It means I'll get them back, just not through official channels.'

'*Not through official channels.* What's that supposed to mean?'

Alexa smiled weakly. 'Don't worry. I won't be taking Jamie's advice. He gave me a memory stick full of gay porn and offered to mock something up for me.'

'*What?*' Leonie stared at her, horrified. 'So what *are* you going to do?'

Alexa shook her head. 'I don't know yet. I'll think of something else.'

Leonie sighed, shaking her head. 'Honestly, Lex . . . that place.'

Alexa said nothing. She felt an unexpected sense of loyalty to her workplace, all of a sudden. *That place.* She knew what Leonie was thinking. Leonie saw *Banter* as nothing more than an amoral, soulless pit of inequity that was harming society. She hadn't said it in so many words, but Alexa could tell. She wanted to explain to her friend that, in context, Jamie's plan wasn't altogether inappropriate. For a man who got called 'Cuntface' and 'Fuckwit' on a daily basis, retaliation in the form of Photoshopped gay porn was a viable, possibly even sensible, option.

'Why did he have gay porn on his computer anyway?' asked Leonie, derisively.

'I guess it goes with the job,' she said, thinking about the massive library of fleshy images that resided on Jamie's Mac. It was a fair question. She had been so overwhelmed with relief at finding an ally that she hadn't actually stopped to ask about the origin of Jamie's stash.

The picnic table vibrated as their phones buzzed simultaneously.

'She's not coming,' they both guessed, in unison.

Sure enough, the message was from Kate, apologising for the fact that she was still in the office and would probably be there all afternoon.

'That's shit,' declared Leonie, staring furiously at her phone. 'It's a Sunday; she has to have *some* kind of break.'

Alexa nodded, remembering that sinking feeling she used to get on a Sunday afternoon when she started to realise that Friday's workload was going to wipe out her entire weekend.

'Unless she's seeing that guy?' Alexa raised an eyebrow.

'Who, Damo?' Leonie frowned. 'Didn't you hear? She's not with him any more – she's seeing some friend of her dad's accountant.'

'*What?*'

Leonie lifted her shoulders. 'I know. Let's see if this one breaks the three-week record.'

Alexa divided the remaining chunk of muffin into two, feeling relieved that conversation had moved off the subject of Marcus' and Derek's prank.

'Well,' she said, popping one half into her mouth. 'More for us, I guess. Shall we wander?'

Leonie nodded, smiling brightly as they set off on the tarmac path that circled the lake.

'How's it going outside work, anyway?' she asked. 'How's Matt?'

Alexa smiled, feeling about fourteen years old again. 'He's fine.'

Leonie raised an eyebrow. 'Why do you always go like that when we talk about Matt?'

'Like what?' she asked, despite knowing exactly what. The mere mention of her boyfriend's name induced a feeling of hopeful excitement, mingled with fear that it would all end tomorrow. She didn't know why – it just felt too brilliant to last. She didn't deserve it. It was hard to describe.

Leonie was shaking her head, still looking at Alexa.

'Honestly,' she said, smiling as though bemused. 'You can single-handedly take on a forty million-pound business, but you can't work out what's going on with the man in your life.'

Alexa looked up, apologetically. Leonie had hit the nail on the head. That was exactly the problem – always had been. She was supremely confident when it came to figures and forecasts and strategies but when it came to relationships, she was a wreck.

'Hey, I gave Loopy Lara's CV to the cretins on *Ciao!*,' she said, changing the subject.

Leonie raised an eyebrow. 'Not *Hers*, then?'

'I thought about it, but decided it wouldn't be fair on them. *Ciao!*'s probably more up her street, anyway. It's basically adding two-word captions to trashy photos bought from the paps. She might even get to meet some F-listers.'

'Spoilt little brat. I wonder whether she eats multi-coloured food now?'

Alexa laughed. 'Speaking of brats, what's your new class like?'

Leonie's head danced from side to side. 'Mixed. I've got a couple of really smart ones, but most of them are just apathetic kids who use up all their brain power on mobile games and Facebook. Then there's Roger, who's on his third attempt at repeating the year. He's nearly nineteen.' She cringed.

'Any classroom assistants this time?'

Leonie puffed out her cheeks and exhaled. 'One, but she spends most of her time with the Romanian boy who doesn't speak a word of English.'

'At fifteen?'

'Yup.'

Alexa felt suddenly guilty for having spent the last twenty minutes discussing who had planted porn in her proofs. Leonie had real issues to think about.

They walked on in silence for a while, looking out at the lake and taking occasional sidesteps to avoid oncoming joggers. The sun was still high overhead, heating the back of Alexa's head through her hair.

'You're thinking about work,' Leonie guessed, accusingly.

Alexa replied with a guilty nod. She did spend too much time thinking about her work. It wasn't deliberate; she just found her thoughts drifting that way by default.

'The porn thing?'

Alexa shook her head. 'A new mobile app we're hoping to launch.'

Leonie raised an eyebrow. 'What does it do?'

Alexa hesitated. She wasn't sure whether Leonie would approve of the *My Girlfriend* idea. To Leonie, even the magazine was distasteful. This would be one step further over the line.

'It's . . .' Alexa considered changing the subject, but something inside her was telling her not to. Deep down, she wanted Leonie to know. She wanted Leonie to approve of the app – to condone it. She wanted to convince her friend that the idea was acceptable. After all, if she couldn't convince her friend, then how would she convince millions of strangers across the nation?

'It's a simple principle,' she said, finally. 'Basically, lads upload videos of their girlfriends and other lads view the videos, tag their favourites, rate and rank them, that sort of thing.'

'What sort of videos?'

'Well . . .' Alexa shrugged. 'Dirty ones. But not *too* dirty.'

Leonie squinted thoughtfully into the distance. The smile had gone from her face.

'You're serious, right?' she asked, eventually.

'Yeah.' Alexa swallowed, feeling uncomfortable all of a sudden. 'It sounds a bit crass, I know, but with the branding and interface and . . .'

She lost the thread of her argument, glancing sideways at Leonie's stricken face. *Lads upload videos of their girlfriends.* Alexa replayed her explanatory sentence in her head, hearing the words as though for the first time. Not only did it sound crass, but also exceedingly basic and not even very original. She couldn't help wondering whether this app really was the brainwave it had appeared to be, three days ago, or whether she was simply looking at it through the eyes of a profit-hungry media consultant with targets to meet.

'What about the girls in the videos?' asked Leonie, stopping abruptly and looking Alexa in the eye. 'Do they get a say in what gets uploaded?'

'Oh, they have to give consent,' Alexa said quickly. The words came out before she'd had a chance to think about what had actually been discussed. Consent was on the list of 'risks to address', but as yet, nothing had been decided about how exactly the subject of the video would offer her approval.

'Right.' Leonie nodded, not looking entirely convinced. 'I've seen some horrible things at school, Lex. Bullying, revenge acts . . . you'd *have* to make sure the girls give consent.'

Alexa nodded guiltily. She would make it her first priority the next day to address the issue of consent.

'And the guys,' Leonie went on, frowning earnestly. 'Are they allowed to upload whatever they want?'

Alexa shook her head. 'There's a moderator. Only moderated content goes up.'

'So . . .' Leonie bit her lip, her eyes flitting down to the gravel path and roaming around randomly. 'I'm just thinking of some of the boys in my class.' Her gaze flickered up to meet Alexa's. 'There'd have to be a strict age limit on the girls.'

'Absolutely,' Alexa found herself saying. 'Over-eighteens only.'

The issue of age restrictions had also come up in the planning meeting, but everybody knew that appearances could be deceptive. There was no foolproof way of saying that the subject of a mobile video was eighteen years of age.

Slowly, Leonie started to walk on. Alexa followed, finding herself clenching and unclenching her fists. It wasn't just that Leonie's response was a good representation of how ordinary people, removed from the debauched environment on the fifth floor of Senate House, would see their app, if the release were to go ahead. It was that her response *mattered*. Alexa hadn't realised until now how much she wanted Leonie's approval.

'I'm a mentor for the Year 10s,' said Leonie, quietly. Her face was turned away, looking in the direction of a bunch of teenagers playing frisbee. 'I have a surgery hour every week, where kids can come and talk to me about their problems. Drugs, violence at home, that kind of thing.'

Alexa nodded anxiously. She didn't like the tone of Leonie's voice.

'I had a girl come to me this week,' said Leonie, finally wrenching her gaze from the teenagers and turning to Alexa. 'A really bubbly, self-confident fourteen-year-old. Well, that's what I thought. She's won prizes in English literature and she always plays the leading lady in our school productions. But it turns out, her boyfriend's pressuring her into having sex. She doesn't know what to do. She's fourteen, Lex. The boyfriend expects her to sleep with him, because he thinks that's what all the kids are doing.'

It was Alexa's turn to look away. Leonie's point was coming across loud and clear.

'Look,' Leonie stopped again, reaching out and laying a hand on Alexa's arm. 'I can see what you're trying to do. But just . . .

be careful, Lex.' She sighed. 'Think about the kids, as well as the lads. Everyone has a mobile phone, these days.'

Alexa nodded solemnly. She couldn't think of anything adequate to say, so she said nothing.

Leonie gave her arm a little squeeze and let go, with a smile that didn't quite reach her eyes. 'Don't underestimate the power of a tool like this.'

12

Alexa clicked the mouse button and, with a sense of relief, saw the final slide appear on the projector screen.

'So, in summary, this is how we intend to hit our targets.'

She stood to one side, counting the seconds as she waited for heads to start nodding. The finance director was squinting sceptically at the figures on the right-hand side, which showed the investment required and estimated the pay-back period. Peterson's executive assistant, Vincent Chang, was peering sideways, trying to decipher his boss' notes, an impossible task due to Peterson's handwriting. Andrew Lake, head of men's titles, was typing a message on his phone and the COO was propped up on one elbow, asleep.

'Okay!' cried Alexa, forcing a breezy smile. 'Any questions?'

Inevitably, there were questions. The FD required further convincing that the tablet app would break even within two years. Lake wanted to know how the editorial improvements would drive ten thousand additional readers, even with the renewed focus on flesh. Chang asked a brown-nosing question about the proposed rejuvenation of Banter TV and its effects on other Senate channels, which was clearly designed to impress Peterson – who, sadly for Chang, was engaged in a battle with his BlackBerry to turn off the alarm, which was inexplicably going off at five-minute intervals.

'Anything else?' Alexa held the smile, desperate not to let her frayed nerves show.

'Yes,' said Peterson, pushing his BlackBerry aside. 'I have a question.'

Alexa nodded, praying that the chief executive's query wouldn't topple the carefully constructed set of arguments that seemed to have just about satisfied everybody else in the room. She was so close; she just needed this one person's approval.

'This *app*,' Peterson went on, as though reading from a foreign dictionary. 'Is it something that will work on any phone?'

'Any smart phone, yes.'

Peterson frowned. '*Smart* phone?'

'As in, um . . .' Alexa was careful not to look at anybody's face as she explained. 'Any phone that allows you to browse the web, check emails, that sort of thing.'

The chief executive looked dubious. 'And how popular are these *smart* phones? They're not just a fad, are they?'

Alexa looked at him. 'The number of smart phone handsets in the UK is doubling every three years and most of the people buying them are teens and young adults. They're not a fad, no.'

She thought about adding that Peterson's own device – the one lying face-down on the desk in front of him – was a breed of smart phone, but decided that what with the rogue alarm issue, this might weaken her case.

Peterson took in the information, nodding thoughtfully for several seconds. He was smiling, Alexa noted – but then, Terry Peterson always smiled.

It was absurd, thought Alexa, standing rigidly beside the projector screen, that of all the research and preliminary work she had undertaken to make sure this initiative stacked up – the meetings, the calculations, the costing and planning – it was this ridiculous question that determined whether the app went to market. *How popular are smart phones?* In another context, she might have laughed.

Alexa waited, keeping her eyes on Peterson's, too afraid to look at anyone else in case it prompted more questions.

113

After what seemed like a very long time, he began to nod. Then, breaking through the stony silence, came the familiar sound of his BlackBerry.

Peterson stabbed at the keys with his sausage-like fingers, making no impact on the ascending alarm call.

Alexa stepped forward. 'D'you want me to . . .'

Peterson sent the beeping device sliding along the table to Alexa, who silenced the noise in an instant by pressing Stop.

'Thanks,' muttered Peterson, taking the device back and stuffing it disdainfully into his pocket. Then he looked up and smiled. 'I think, where mobile phones are concerned, we should probably bow to your superior judgement.' He turned to Chang, who nodded keenly. Peterson glanced at the other faces around the table in turn. 'Are we happy for Alexa to proceed with her six-month plan?'

The question was answered, slowly, with a succession of sleepy nods. Alexa let out a long sigh of relief. She hadn't realised how heavily the burden of today's decision had been weighing on her mind. There were no guarantees when it came to hitting the targets, but at least she had cleared the first hurdle.

She stooped to retrieve the memory stick from the back of the computer and returned to the table to gather her notes. Around her, the room was emptying out.

Peterson stopped on his way through the door and looked back.

'I meant to ask,' he said, with his customary smile. 'How's it all going on the fifth floor?'

'Great!' Alexa replied, enthusiastically.

Peterson tilted his head to one side. 'Truthfully?'

Alexa was about to back up her first response, but then she stopped herself. Terry Peterson knew nothing about new technology, but there were two things he understood better than anyone: magazines and people. There was no point in lying.

'To be honest,' she said quietly, 'I'm seeing more opposition than I'd expected from certain members of the team.'

He nodded. There was a twinkle in his eye.

'I'm finding it . . . well . . .' Alexa broke away. She didn't want Peterson thinking she was incompetent. 'It's not easy.'

The chief executive laughed softly to himself, shaking his head as he slipped through the door.

'I never for a moment thought it would be, Alexa.'

13

Neil leafed through his papers, pulling out two photocopies of an elaborate sketch – one for Alexa, one for Derek.

'Well,' he said, with a sigh. 'You said you wanted something to hook into the girlfriend theme, for the app . . .'

Alexa nodded. She was aware of the fact that Neil still had reservations about the app, but after a few weeks of meetings and debate where they had spoken at length, the features editor had come round to Alexa's way of thinking.

'So, this is it,' he said. 'It's called, "How Much Do You Pay For Sex?"'

Alexa nodded, studying the photocopy. It looked like a child's sketch of a coffee filter. Beside her, Derek sat, shaking his head. It wasn't Neil's idea he objected to; it was the whole concept of the app.

'Right.' Neil scratched his bald head, glancing at Alexa's copy as though unsure about where to begin. 'It's a reader participation feature, okay? I've tested it on the lads – it seems to work.'

Alexa looked sideways at Derek, who was stroking his goatee, his eyes revealing a complete lack of confidence.

'Along the top, that's all the different ways they pay for sex every month: dinner dates, drinks, chocolates and so on. That all gets added up in the box underneath.' He pointed to the box marked 'COST'. 'And in this box here,' he motioned to the box marked 'SHAGS', 'they enter the number of times they've had sex this month.'

Derek squinted at his copy and slowly began to nod.

'So then,' Neil explained, 'dividing one by the other, you get a cost per shag, and down at the bottom here, we've got what that equates to – so the reader can tell whether they're getting their money's worth, so to speak.'

'Genius,' muttered Derek. 'Romanian whore, Dutch hooker, Essex slag . . . that's fuckin' fantastic, mate. Love it.'

Alexa nodded too. She had to admit, the feature was entertaining. It would go down brilliantly with the readers. She waited for Derek to finish applauding the idea, wondering whether two months ago, she might have found these suggestions offensive. It was mildly disturbing to think that men viewed their other halves purely as a means of having sex; it devalued the whole principle of a relationship. Alexa couldn't imagine how she would feel if she discovered that sex was Matt's only motivation for going out with her. But then, this wasn't real. Everybody knew that *Banter* wasn't real. How else would they get away with the vast expanses of airbrushed flesh, the fake breasts or the 'up for it' girls? The whole thing was tongue-in-cheek, set in a fantasy world that didn't exist, and the readers knew it.

'I think it's great,' she said, enthusiastically. 'And we can put the *My Girlfriend* mini-feature somewhere alongside it?'

'Inset,' Neil nodded, stabbing the page with a finger.

'Perfect.' She smiled. The developers had almost finished testing the app and it would be ready for launch next week, barring any last-minute disasters.

Neil rubbed his forehead. 'Other stuff . . . ah, yes. This one's just a standard boobs feature. Freshers' Week Fitties. Always goes down well with the students.' He quickly leafed through the unedited proofs.

Alexa nodded as breast after breast was revealed, each of them heavy yet pert, almost all of them surgically enhanced. Images like these no longer shocked her. In her first few weeks, the unedited proofs had seemed particularly fascinating. Pre-airbrushing, there were all sorts of details that never made it into print: scars, moles, lopsidedness, discolouration, stretch-marks, hairy nipples . . . . Now, Alexa barely noticed such things. She had seen how Jamie's team transformed raw material like this into a caramel-skinned, dewy-eyed work of art that made up the centrefold of the magazine. She was used to looking at breasts. They were everywhere: on the walls, as screensavers, lying around on the desks . . . . She had become desensitised.

'Anything else?' asked Derek, planting an elbow on the table and cutting Alexa out of his field of vision.

Neil hesitated, slowly gathering his papers and picking up a memory stick from among them.

'There is . . . something.' He tapped the little storage device on the table and looked at Alexa. 'The interviews trial for Banter TV.'

'Oh?' Alexa tried to maintain a calm exterior. She couldn't bear for Derek to sense her unease. A week ago, she had asked Neil to arrange for the 'Bi-Banter' interview – so-called because it featured two girls and their supposed bisexual tendencies – to be *filmed* during the photo shoot. The idea was that viewers would get to see more than just writhing around on a bed; they would actually get to hear the girls speak.

'Maybe . . . maybe you should see them for yourself.'

Alexa squirmed. Beside her, Derek caught on immediately.

'Oh, let's take a look!' He made a grab for the memory stick. 'Shall we put it on?'

He looked around the meeting room, seeking out a device on which he could play the files and then poking his head out of the meeting room and yelling for Marcus to join them.

Alexa glanced anxiously at Neil, who just lifted his shoulders apologetically.

'Derek, can we just . . .' Alexa started to protest, but too late.

Various members of the news team were already following Marcus into the room. Derek waved them over, ramming the memory stick into the projector and rubbing his hands together with glee as the machine warmed up.

'Gentlemen,' he cried, looking up expectantly at the projector screen. 'Prepare for some titillating pillow-talk!'

Alexa felt herself crumple inside. She could tell from Neil's demeanour that he regretted his decision to mention the trial in front of the deputy editor, but there was nothing that either of them could do about it now.

Before long, a faint image started to appear on the end wall: two girls on a cream, shag-pile rug, wearing matching black string underwear and pouting a lot. One was petite and blonde; the other was a tall, striking brunette with enormous, plum-coloured lips.

'Looks okay so far!' cried Marcus, swinging his feet up onto the table in what looked like an attempt to emulate Derek's position.

The two girls leaned towards the camera, kneeling so that their breasts were pressing up against one another. Derek nodded approvingly, but there was a look in his eye that implied the best was yet to come.

All of a sudden, a loud crackling sound came out of the speakers, followed by a deafening squeal.

Alexa covered her ears.

'Oh my God,' said Derek as the wailing continued, varying slightly in pitch.

'Is that them, talking?' yelled Louis, above the din.

Alexa slowly removed her hands from her ears and realised that Louis was right; this was the start of the interview.

Neil pulled a face. 'Can you turn it down a bit, mate?'

Reluctantly, Derek reached for the remote control and lowered the volume to an audible level. It still hurt Alexa's ears to listen.

'. . . and this is Sam, and you're watchin' Banter TV!' they shrieked in unison.

Alexa forced herself to stare at the screen, where the two girls were looking blankly at one another as though they didn't know what to do next.

'They warm up,' said Neil, awkwardly. 'Sort of.'

A muffled conversation could be heard in which someone behind the camera, possibly Neil, instructed one of the girls to start playing with the straps on the other girl's bra. There were a few seconds of awkward foreplay that might just have passed the screen test for a very bad porn movie, then the brunette spoke again.

'We're gonna tell you abat the worst fing we ever done.' She paused to stroke her friend's shoulder in a manner that might conceivably have been considered sexy, had she not proceeded to let out a peal of cackling laughter.

Alexa couldn't bring herself to look at Derek, who was practically pissing himself. She knew what he was doing. His laughter was a prompt – a way of getting everyone else laughing. In a few minutes, he would find a way of establishing in no uncertain terms that this was Alexa's fault. He would make sure the whole team knew that the joke was on her.

Alexa stared straight ahead, trying not to listen to either the audio or the hysterics. They had warned her about this. Neil and Jamie had told her exactly what happened when amateur glamour models opened their mouths to the camera. She ought to have listened. But she hadn't been able to let go of this feeling that somehow they had to show *more* of their girls. Photo shoot footage was sexy, but it was repetitive. One shoot looked much like another, just with a different girl under the lights. There had to be something else they could do to keep the lads coming back for more. Clearly, though, a filmed interview was not the answer.

'Once,' yowled the blonde, tugging at the brunette's bra strap and slowly pulling it down her shoulder, allowing one enormous, weighty breast to spill out. 'We was at a party, and—'

'Okay!' cried Alexa, reaching for the controls. 'That's enough.' She pressed Stop and slammed the remote down on the table.

For a moment, she thought she might get away with dismissing the lads, as Derek seemed unable to speak for laughing. But as the noise died down and people started drifting back to the office, Derek suddenly pulled himself together.

'If anyone has any more brainwaves for improving "reader engagement",' he said, loudly, 'Ms Long would love to hear them!'

Alexa fixed a weary smile on her face and sat, waiting for the room to empty. Eventually, the cavalcade dispersed and she turned to face Neil, who had sat, head in hands, throughout.

'Sorry,' he said, stretching the skin around his eyes and shaking his head despairingly. 'I should've waited.'

Alexa shrugged. 'It wasn't your fault. I should've listened to you in the first place.'

Neil let out a sigh, looking up at the frozen image on the screen.

'I presume . . .' Alexa decided to have one last go at exploiting her terrible idea. 'I presume we can't use any of it, can we?'

Neil grimaced, sucking air through his teeth. 'My wife works in post-production. She's an editor. I showed it to her and she reckoned we might be able to salvage about twenty seconds' worth.'

Alexa pulled a face.

'There is . . . one thing I thought of, though,' offered Neil.

She looked up hopefully.

'Well, we've got the footage of them playing on the rug . . . and we've got the words that we want them to say . . .' He looked meaningfully at Alexa.

Clearly there was some sort of obvious implication, but she couldn't ascertain what it was.

'We could get someone *else* to say the words,' Neil suggested.

'A professional. Not entirely fair on the girls, but there's no law against it. That way, the viewer gets his naughty interview and he only sees the sexy part of the visuals.'

Alexa nodded, contemplatively. She was thinking about the cost of hiring someone to talk dirty on the girls' behalf, trying to calculate whether the benefits justified the means. How did the other channels do it? Could she really hope to entice more viewers with scripted 'chats' to the camera? She needed to do *something*, that was for sure. If she couldn't generate more ad revenue for Banter TV then the only option was to shut it down.

'Maybe,' she said, eventually. She smiled at Neil. 'Thanks for trying, anyway.'

They rose to their feet and returned to the office, where Derek appeared to be rousing the troops yet again, but this time towards the exit. Alexa checked the time. It was only four o'clock. She stepped up to Sienna's desk and peered over the barricade of magazines.

'Sienna?'

Reluctantly, the blonde looked up from her typing.

Alexa faltered. It pained her to ask, but she had to know. 'Where's everyone going?'

'Oh.' Sienna's surly pout slowly spread into a smile and her voice rose a notch in volume. 'Didn't you get your invitation?'

Several heads turned. Lads halfway to the door stopped, looking back at Sienna and then at Alexa, as though they sensed something kicking off.

'It's the Senate advertising do,' Sienna explained loudly, rising from her seat and slinging a miniature gold jacket around her bare shoulders. '*Everybody* goes.'

Everybody, thought Alexa, feeling the humiliation burn her cheeks, *except her*.

'Of course,' she muttered. 'Have fun.'

Alexa willed her assistant to leave, but Sienna was clearly having too much fun.

'I'm sure we could get you in,' she said, glancing playfully at Marcus as he hovered nearby, enjoying the spectacle. She clearly wanted the whole team to hear. 'We could just explain to the bouncer that you don't have an invitation.'

Alexa held her gaze. 'That's very kind,' she said, calmly. 'But I have way too much work.'

Eventually, Sienna slung an arm around Marcus' sizeable waist and indicated for the rest of the team to follow them out.

Waiting for the door to slam, Alexa stared straight ahead, the image of the news editor's hand on the girl's backside emblazoned on her mind. Sienna was worse than all the lads put together. She didn't say much, but what she did say was masterfully devised to cause maximum pain without actually crossing any lines. Derek and Marcus were crude, but Sienna was devious.

Alexa slumped down in her chair, too exhausted and demoralised to even think about what this mysterious 'advertising do' might be. No doubt it would be another opportunity for Derek's boys to spread the word about her latest display of incompetence – another chance for Sienna to ingratiate herself further with the team and to alienate the new MD. Alexa closed her eyes. She felt like crying.

A gentle tapping noise prompted her to open her eyes. In the far corner of the office, Jamie was still working. Alexa looked over at his screen, which was filled with a detailed close-up of a girl's armpit. One by one, the little dots of stubble were disappearing as he worked his way from left to right, leaving a smooth, flawless finish in his wake. Alexa fell forwards, onto her elbows, staring blankly at her screensaver.

Until now, things had seemed manageable. She had a plan, she had the backing of the chief executive and she had the confidence to see it through. But all of a sudden, that confidence had gone. The barriers seemed higher, the targets further away. It seemed inconceivable that seven months from now, she would be proving to the New York board that they should keep the *Banter* brand alive. She had no plan. There were no reasons.

She was every bit as incompetent as Derek was busy telling people she was.

Alexa's phone vibrated against the desk. Through tear-filled eyes, she looked down. It was Matt. She rejected the call. She couldn't let him hear her like this. At no point in the last nine months had Matt seen this side of her and Alexa was determined that he never should. Her strength and energy were the things he loved about her; he'd run a mile if he was suddenly confronted with this meek, over-sensitive cry-baby. Besides, she didn't need to burden him with her troubles. Her mother had always taught her to tackle problems – not wallow in self-pity when they got too much. Her phone bleeped again with a text message.

> Hey gorgeous. Will
> U B my date for the
> Annual Law Society
> Dinner next Fri? Mx

A warm, salty tear trickled down her nose and onto her trembling lip. Alone and exhausted, the sound of Derek's vindictive laughter still fresh in her mind and the sight of Matt's words, blurring on the screen in front of her, Alexa couldn't think of what else to do but cry.

A phone was ringing, somewhere nearby. Alexa blinked, waiting for Jamie to pick it up, but he seemed engrossed in one of the last remaining hair follicles. It continued to ring. After a few more seconds, she drew a shaky breath and picked up the call.

'*Banter* magazine,' she offered, the tears choking her voice.

'Afternoon!' The good-humoured, Cockney twang jarred with Alexa's mood. 'Frankie here. How ya doing, sweet-cheeks? Dezza not around?'

'No,' stammered Alexa, assuming the man was referring to Derek. It occurred to her that he had mistaken her for Sienna – Sienna being, until now, the only female in the office.

'Take a message for me, yeah? Tell 'im the stripper's all booked for tomorra, name of Crystal. Tall, like he said, but blonde. I couldn't get an Asian for love nor money – they're all fuckin' booked. Tell 'im we're all meetin' at mine, eightish, then we'll hit the town. The bird's booked for 'alf eleven, my place.'

Alexa couldn't speak.

'Cheers, sweet-cheeks. Don't forget, will ya?'

Alexa's breathing quickened as she found her misery turning to rage. 'No,' she said. 'I won't forget.'

Crystal. Alexa looked at the Post-it note in front of her, on which she had inadvertently scribbled the name. *Couldn't get an Asian . . .* Alexa stared, dumbfounded, at the little yellow note. She hated Derek even more than she had done five minutes ago. *The bird's booked for half eleven.* Like a taxi or a pizza delivery. That was how they thought. He really did *believe* all that misogynistic crap he wrote about each week. It was incredible. Or rather, it would have been incredible, had somebody told her about this two months ago. Sadly, Alexa now knew that that was exactly how Derek's mind worked.

She laid down the Post-it on her desk, her pen hovering over its surface as she thought about whether to pass on the message. She quite liked the idea of Derek missing out on a night with the lads – but then, she reasoned, it was more likely that if she failed to give him the message, he'd simply call his mates, catch up with them in time for the stripper and work out that it had been Alexa taking the call. She didn't want to have to explain herself to Derek. Reluctantly, she appended the note with instructions on where and when to meet and reached over to Derek's desk. Then she stopped.

A wry smile began to form through the tears as an idea crept into her mind. She retracted the note, added two of Sienna's customary kisses to the end and then stuck it on the corner of Derek's monitor. This, she realised, was the start of her revenge.

14

'Two hundred and eighty-three views,' Sienna announced proudly.

'That's bollocks,' accused Marcus, wheeling himself backwards and colliding with Derek's chair. 'Let's see.'

With a flash of scarlet fingernails, Sienna handed Marcus her mobile phone.

Derek gave the news editor a playful thump. 'You're only asking so you can see my videos again.'

Marcus squared up to him. 'If I wanted to see your videos, I'd just do this.' He reached for his own mobile phone, pressed a button and waited as the familiar, tinny beat started to emanate from the device.

'Am I on your favourites?' squeaked Sienna.

'You might be.' Marcus raised a ginger eyebrow.

Alexa looked away. Usually, she would have found the whole conversation mildly abhorrent, but today, it was also a sign of encouragement.

The *My Girlfriend* app had gone live at eight o'clock in the morning. Alexa had spent most of the day in a state of nervous agitation, petrified that the app would go unnoticed, or prove too expensive for their readers, or attract bad press. She had almost convinced herself in the run-up to the launch that this would prove to be an expensive, high-profile flop for Senate, but early results suggested that the initiative promised to be anything but.

By midday, the app had been downloaded eight hundred times. By three o'clock, it had achieved twelve hundred downloads, of which a hundred and fifty users had uploaded a video. The total video viewing figure was just under four thousand – of which several hundred had taken place on the fifth floor of Senate House. As far as Alexa could tell, nobody had done any work since noon, when Sienna had uploaded her first clip.

'Fuck me,' gasped Marcus, passing Sienna's phone around the news team. 'She's not lying. Look – two hundred and eighty-nine . . . ninety! Popular girl.'

'What's your average rating, though?' yelled Louis, grabbing the handset. 'I gave you a zero, for not getting your kit off at the end.'

Sienna replied with a sulky pout, snatching her phone out of Louis' hand.

Quite why Sienna possessed a video of herself, stripping down to her underwear in what looked like somebody's kitchen, or why she would upload such a thing to the app for the whole world to see – not least, the whole *Banter* workforce – was an interesting question. Alexa wondered how much thought had gone into those videos on Sienna's part. Almost certainly, she had prepared for today – cherry-picking her raunchiest videos, possibly even recording them afresh in the last few weeks, for this purpose alone.

The whole point of the mobile app was that *men* uploaded footage of their wives and girlfriends, for other men to appreciate. But Sienna didn't have a boyfriend. At least, Alexa didn't think she did. She might have been sleeping with one or more members of the *Banter* team, but the videos hadn't been posted by them. *She had uploaded the videos herself.*

Alexa picked up the phone and dialled the number for the stats analyst.

'Hi, Jason. It's Alexa.'

'Thought it might be.' There was a smile in his voice. 'You want an update, do you?'

127

'No, actually – I have a question. Um . . . do we know the split of male to female, for our uploaders?'

'For our *up*loaders?'

'Yes – you know, the ones posting videos.'

'Er, no. We don't ask for gender when they download the app. Only email address.'

Alexa sighed. There was no way of verifying her theory.

'Oh!' Jason yelped down the phone. 'But if the user subscribes to our newsletter, which most of them do, then we can cross-reference it and get the split from that.'

'Can we?' Alexa brightened. 'I mean . . . can you?'

Jason laughed. 'I'll get back to you.'

Alexa thanked him and put down the phone. She looked up, suddenly aware that several heads around the office were turning in her direction.

'It's in widescreen!' yelled Derek.

Alexa followed his stare and realised that the centre of attention was in fact the plasma TV on the wall above her head. One of the junior writers had hooked up his phone to the monitor and was fiddling with the remote control.

'That's it!' Derek leaned back in his chair, arms crossed, a childish grin spreading across his face. Around the room, others adopted similar positions. On Biscuit's instruction, Paddy started pulling down the blinds, while someone else switched off the lights. The dance music pumping out of the news desk stereo was turned up a notch, providing an instant nightclub feel.

Alexa wheeled sideways, craning her neck to see what all the fuss was about. On the screen, she could just make out the image of a buxom girl in a bra and white mini-skirt, flicking her blonde hair about and moving seductively on what looked like some kind of stage. Alexa looked around the office, taking in the gormless, mesmerised faces of her staff. Sienna had uploaded another video.

The footage was jerky, pixelated and poorly lit; it was hard to make out what was going on. Occasionally, the writhing silhouette would light up in the flash of a camera, revealing every contour of Sienna's curvaceous body, then the details would be lost again.

It was ironic, thought Alexa. Banter TV was played on this screen all day, every day. Leggy, busty blondes in dental-floss bikinis, wearing half a kilogram of makeup were shown non-stop and yet the lads barely batted an eyelid. But this poorly-shot footage of a drunken PA in her underwear – *their* drunken PA in her underwear – was turning them into salivating wrecks.

'Oi, Jamie!' Louis rose from his chair, picking up an inflatable armchair and lobbing it into the corner of the office, where Jamie sat, his face lit up by the blue glow of his Mac. 'Not interested in this?'

Jamie turned round, removing a pair of headphones from his ears. 'What's that?'

Louis was clearly on a high after his earlier brush with Sienna. 'Don't you wanna see a piece of ass?'

'Oh.' Jamie shrugged. 'No offence, Sienna, but I see enough pieces of ass as it is, in this job.'

Sienna and Louis exchanged a look, before settling back to watch the show.

Alexa wondered what was going through the girl's mind. Her colleague had just referred to her as a 'piece of ass'. Was that a compliment? Perhaps in *Banter* terms, it was – in the sense that it represented eye candy for the readers. For a colleague to be judged in that way, it implied that the same set of criteria were being applied. Alexa knew that there was a hint of misogyny around the office, but she liked to think that *she* was being judged on something other than her looks. Then again, *she* wasn't the one uploading smutty videos of herself to the mobile app.

Alexa sat, staring into the darkness while the video played, contemplating her own hypocrisy. She didn't want to be judged by her looks, and yet she had just launched an app that was making money from men who did exactly that. What did that say about her? And was it really accurate to say that she didn't want to be judged by her looks? If that was the case, then why did she bother with makeup? Why did she wear trousers that fitted snugly around her backside? If she really wanted to be judged on merit alone, she wouldn't bother checking her disastrous hair in the mirrored walls of the lift each morning; she'd wear a sack to work.

The video finished abruptly and was replaced by the app menu bar.

'Replay!' yelled Marcus, pointing at the option on the screen. 'Replay!'

Alexa leaned over to the nearest window and yanked on the cord of the blind. All of a sudden she felt angry. Sienna's videos had uncovered an uncomfortable contradiction inside her.

'Sorry, guys!' She pulled the next blind amid cries of protest. 'We've got a magazine to produce.'

Someone turned down the music and slowly, men swivelled back to their desks, blinking resentfully in the weak September sunshine.

Alexa sighed. As well as feeling angry, she felt stupid. Yet again, she was coming across as the bad cop, while Derek was hanging out with the lads. She had an idea.

'Okay, here's the deal!' she yelled. 'Next Friday, we finish at four o'clock and we head to the pub.'

There were a few tentative roars of approval. Alexa had never suggested a social activity before.

'Free drinks all night,' she went on, 'to celebrate the successful launch of our first app.'

There was more roaring. Derek raised his voice above it. 'What's the catch?'

Alexa forced a smile, looking around at the attentive faces. It was amazing what effect the promise of free alcohol had on young men. 'The catch is that we have to achieve ten thousand downloads by the time we leave for the pub. Otherwise, no drinks.'

'Ten thousand?' echoed Louis, peevishly.

'That's impossible,' declared Marcus.

Alexa shrugged. 'We're nearly at two thousand already.'

'We can't control how many people download it.'

Alexa looked at him, not sure where to begin.

'Feature it in the magazine,' she said. 'Do a "best and worst" for the website. Put your favourites in the newsletter. Tell your mates about it. Jesus, Marcus. If you can't control it, who can?'

Marcus quietly admitted defeat, but clearly the conversation wasn't over yet – not for Derek, at least.

'Tell you what!' he yelled, drawing attention to himself as usual. 'If we reach ten thousand, we go out on the lash and Ms Long pays for drinks. If we don't, we go out anyway and *I* pay for drinks!'

Alexa sighed, shrinking down behind her monitor. She was trying to incentivise the team to hit a target. Meanwhile, her deputy editor was offering the same incentive for *not* hitting the target, while simultaneously establishing himself as the popular boss.

The office went unusually quiet, either because people were busy working towards their incentive or – more likely, Alexa suspected – because they were watching videos on their mobile phones. The only noise she could hear was coming from Derek, across the desk.

'Yeah!' he yelled into his phone. 'I know! Fat chance. Hey, listen, mate. You've got an iPhone, haven't you? You gotta get this app. It's called *My Girlfriend*. No, *girl*-friend. Check it out. Yeah, *Banter*. Well, me really. Yeah, well, I've been thinking about it for a while . . . Yeah, I know. Really popular, yeah . . . I'm a genius. Ha! Yeah, cool beans. Laters. Ciao!'

Alexa hid her smile. She didn't mind that Derek was taking credit for the app's success. Nor did she mind that he seemed determined that she should pay for drinks next Friday. At least this way, they were working towards the same goal.

Next Friday. Alexa leaned forward and opened her calendar. She clicked on the following week and saw, with dismay, why the phrase rang a bell. Next Friday was Matt's annual law dinner. She had promised to be his date. She closed her eyes and pressed her fingers into the sockets.

She was doing it again. She was so wrapped up in the moment, so excited by the prospect of the new, lucrative revenue stream and so keen to get the boys on her side that she had forgotten everything else in her life. Work, yet again, had floated to the top of her agenda.

Hi Matt,

I'm so sorry – bad news. I just promised the team I'd take them out for drinks next Fri to celebrate the launch of this app. Completely forgot about your law dinner. I guess I could come along afterwards? How formal is it? I am an idiot – sorry.

Lex xx

PS app going really well – have you downloaded it?

Alexa pressed Send and sat, trying to focus on the launch summary for Peterson. She couldn't concentrate. All she could think about was her own thoughtlessness. She had known about Matt's dinner for nearly a week. It was in her diary. Why hadn't she checked before standing up and making the promise to the team?

'Download it!' Derek shouted into the phone. 'Loads of fit birds getting naked, basically. I tell you . . . always knew it'd be a winner.'

Alexa stuffed her headphones into her ears, trying to block out the noise. The summary document remained blank on her screen. She wondered vaguely how the chief executive would react to the launch figures. He could only think in terms of circulation figures and revenue; he didn't understand uploads and downloads. An email alert appeared at the bottom of her screen.

Don't worry – I'll take Dickie.

Alexa frowned, scrolling down in case there was more to the message. There wasn't. There was no mention of the possibility that she might join him after the dinner, no mention of the app, no mention of how her big day was going.

Alexa tried not to read too much into it. Matt was a busy lawyer. He didn't have time for long-winded emails. Clearly, he was saving his words for when they could talk, face to face. She would apologise properly when they next met and he would congratulate her on the launch of the app. They would work out a way for her to go to the law dinner, even if it was just for the last hour. Alexa had almost convinced herself of this when she realised her phone was ringing.

'Hey, it's Jason.'

'Oh, hi. Did you manage to find out—'

'Yes!' he interrupted. 'Yes, and you know what? There's something funny going on. Of the two hundred uploaders we know about, a hundred and seventy are female! Eighty-five percent. Weird, eh?'

'Yes,' she said, feeling something leap inside her. 'That is weird. Thanks, Jason.'

She replaced the receiver, looking across at Sienna, who was busy texting friends about her newfound fame. Accidentally, they had discovered a new market: a new and potentially very lucrative market.

15

'So, drinks are on you, then?' Riz appeared at the bar, eyeing the square of red card in Alexa's hand that represented her credit card behind the bar.

She smiled. 'What can I get you?'

'Becks, please.'

Alexa didn't even need to summon the barman; the young Australian was already looking at her, awaiting instructions. It was barely six o'clock and already she had spent over two hundred pounds; the Aussie was at her service.

Riz tapped his glass against hers. 'Money well spent?' He jerked his head in the direction of the reserved sofas and armchairs in the corner, where members of the *Banter* team were sprawled in various states of consciousness.

Alexa nodded. 'Definitely.'

She thought back to when she had offered her incentive to the team. It seemed almost laughable that eight days ago, the prospect of ten thousand downloads had seemed over ambitious. The target had been met within two days. At last count, the app had been downloaded eighty-two thousand times, exceeding Alexa's estimates by a factor of ten. She would probably end up spending a grand tonight, but it would be worth every penny.

'Come on,' said Riz. 'You can't hang out here all night. Let them get their own drinks – you can trust them with the tab.'

Alexa cocked her head to one side, eyeing him sceptically.

'Some of them,' he corrected himself.

As they approached the group, Derek rose from his seat, arms raised above his stubby frame as though rousing the crowd before a comedy show.

'A drinking game!' he announced.

Alexa groaned quietly. Derek was like a child; he had to make everything into a game. She smiled gratefully as Riz steered her to a spot behind the sofas, just outside Derek's field of view.

'Easy one to begin with . . . let's start with Fuzzy Duck!'

Alexa leaned against the back of one of the armchairs.

'How's it going, living with your folks?' she asked.

'Oh.' Riz grimaced. 'I escaped.'

'Yeah? You got your own place?'

He nodded. 'Eventually – we moved in on Saturday. Not a minute too soon. I must've put on about ten kilos with my mum's cooking.'

Alexa wanted to ask what he meant by 'we', but couldn't think of a tactful way. She couldn't help glancing down at the reference to his weight. Riz's T-shirt was just tight enough to show a lean, muscular stomach – not a hint of a belly.

A commotion broke out as Paddy fell for the trap in the drinking game.

'You said, "does he fuck",' cried Louis, pointing accusingly at the young Irishman. 'Drink!'

'Drink! Drink!' chanted the team around him.

Alexa wondered whether she ought to intervene. The junior editor was looking rather pale.

'Guys . . .' She stopped, realising that Paddy had already downed his pint of Guinness.

Promptly removing the upturned glass from his head, Paddy stumbled to his feet and wandered off, muttering something about a road trip.

Alexa tapped Biscuit on the shoulder. 'Can you go and check he's okay?'

Biscuit nodded, grabbing the red card as he went. 'I'll get a round of shots in on my way back!'

Alexa exchanged a look with Riz.

'Anyway,' she said, motioning for them to take the corner sofa that Biscuit had just vacated. 'Where's the place?'

Riz quickly commandeered the seat and opened his mouth to reply, but Alexa never got to hear it.

'Drink!' roared Derek.

'Drink!' echoed Marcus.

'Drink!' chorused various members of the news team.

'You're supposed to say, "Yes, Harry",' explained Neil, somewhat apologetically.

Alexa frowned. 'But your name's not Harry.' It wasn't clear which of them had fouled, but she didn't mind taking it on herself. The beer had given her an injection of courage.

'It's a game!' yelled Derek, casting a despairing look at Marcus.

Before Alexa could reply, Riz gave her a gentle nudge, lifted his pint glass and poured the entire contents down his throat.

'My mistake,' he said, placing the empty glass on the table.

For a moment, the players were speechless. Then slowly, heads began to turn. Alexa glanced at the faces, beginning to understand what was expected of her. She looked down at her glass, which still contained three-quarters of a pint. She hadn't downed beer in a long time.

'Drink, drink,' muttered Louis, quietly but persistently.

'Drink, drink,' echoed other voices in the group.

She had two options: crumble under the pressure as they expected her to do, or surprise them by rising to the challenge. Alexa straightened up, held her pint glass aloft and opened her throat. The bubbles filled her mouth and nose, hitting the back of her throat and making her gag. She ignored it and kept on swallowing. Beer sloshed over the edges of the glass and ran in two lines down her chin. She ignored that too, tilting the glass so that the last few droplets joined the lake in her mouth.

136

Eventually, the liquid slipped down her throat and Alexa lunged forward, slamming the glass on the table and wiping the beer from her chin. It wasn't the quickest execution, or the most elegant, but at least she had tried. Nobody could say she wasn't joining in.

Slowly, Alexa looked up, expecting to see shaking heads and derisive expressions. The sight that greeted her came as something of a surprise. Derek and Marcus were looking at one another, eyebrows raised – perhaps sarcastically, but Alexa didn't care. Some of the other lads were nodding, slowly. Specs, the new writer on the news desk, was raising his glass to her. Alexa smiled. For the first time in months, it felt as though she had earned a little respect.

'Sorry,' Riz said quietly. 'Waste of good beer. I'll get the next lot.'

'Tequila!' cried Biscuit, setting down a giant tray full of shots on the table.

'Did you check on Paddy?' asked Alexa, grabbing two glasses and passing one to Riz. 'Is he okay?'

Biscuit nodded. 'He's fine.'

'Where is he?' asked Riz.

'Couldn't find him.' Biscuit shrugged.

'So . . .'

Alexa looked around in search of someone more sober than Biscuit who might have another go at finding the junior writer. She felt slightly ill after the quick consumption of beer and thought about using this as an excuse to get some fresh air and avoid drinking her shot. As she thought about this, though, she caught sight of Paddy, stumbling through the crowds towards them. Her relief was offset only by the realisation that Paddy was carrying a large Give Way sign under his arm.

Paddy's haul was greeted with a round of applause, the new owner being treated to not one but two shots of tequila and the road sign itself enjoying pride of place on the back of Derek's chair.

Alexa threw back her shot along with everyone else, feeling her stomach rebel as the fiery liquid burned down her insides. She slammed her empty glass against the table and found herself staring at the scene unfolding on the sofa opposite.

Sienna, who had until this point remained relatively inconspicuous on the lap of the new pictures assistant, was now perched on the edge of the sofa, propped up on the cushions with her back arched, her breasts making a break for freedom from inside a lacy black corset. Meanwhile, Specs was hovering over her, licking rivulets of tequila from her chest.

'You're not still surprised, are you?' asked Riz, barely batting an eyelid.

Alexa continued to stare as Sienna suddenly pushed herself up, brushing Specs aside and looking around at the incredulous faces, ensuring she had everyone's attention.

'Mmm,' murmured the PA, in a loud, rasping voice. 'That was good. Let's do some more shots!'

There was a stampede towards the bar as multiple editors offered to buy the next round.

'She's not stupid,' Alexa observed.

Riz shook his head. 'God, no. She knows exactly what she's doing.'

Alexa continued to drink her beer, feeling it mix with the tequila inside her and thinking about Riz's words. He was right. There wasn't a single move that the PA made that didn't have a motive. She kept Derek sweet because she wanted to work her way into an editorial post. She played the dumb blonde because she wanted the team to see her as compliant and sexy – the perfect *Banter* girl. An outsider might say that she was the victim of sexual harassment at work, but in fact, it was the other way round. It was her male colleagues who were being played.

'She's just biding her time,' Riz said quietly.

'What d'you mean?'

'She wants to do more editorial – not just the shitty problem letters she does for Neil. She's looking around, I bet.'

Alexa looked at him. 'Do you think?'

He nodded.

Alexa considered this. It occurred to her that despite Sienna's flaws – the distracting outfits, the surly attitude towards administrative work, the mind-numbingly irritating purr that she put on for men – she was a good writer. Her 'Dear Joanne' letters were far more interesting and well written than the hundreds they now received from readers, thanks to Alexa's suggestion to introduce the fake secretary. Alexa felt guilty, all of a sudden. She had taken away a part of Sienna's job that she enjoyed and did well. If the girl was looking around, then Alexa was partly to blame.

Alexa swilled the remains of her beer around in her glass, drunkenly resolving to have a word with Derek and find out whether there were any other editorial opportunities for Sienna. As she did so, something dawned on her. There *was* an opportunity for Sienna. A perfect opportunity. The latest proposal for Banter TV was to show the original footage and overlay the girls' interview responses on top. Only, of course, they couldn't use the actual responses because they weren't sexy. *Sienna could do the voiceover.* Sienna could write the responses *and* purr convincingly for the camera.

It might have been partly the drink, but Alexa felt overwhelmingly excited by this new idea. This way, Sienna became a valuable part of the editorial team and Banter TV got a facelift, at no extra cost. Alexa would also request a pay rise and promotion for Sienna, as an extra incentive.

Derek's voice interrupted her thoughts. He was nominally talking to Marcus, but the volume was such that he clearly intended for the whole group to hear – perhaps the whole of Soho.

'She's six foot tall, blonde, 32FF, and she takes her fucking clothes off for a living. Guess who's just had a text message from her, asking if we can meet up . . .?'

'No way.' Marcus looked gobsmacked. Colleagues glanced sceptically at one another, but nobody dared confront the editor.

'That guy is so full of shit,' said Riz, quietly.

Alexa smiled. 'Maybe he really is going out with her.'

Riz looked at her strangely.

For a moment, Alexa considered telling Riz about the ongoing practical joke she was playing on the deputy editor, but quickly decided against it. She was about to change the subject when Riz suddenly drew closer and put his mouth right up to her ear.

'You do realise that most people think he's a prick, don't you?'

She looked at him, unsure as to what exactly he meant.

'Just saying,' he shrugged. 'In case you think he's got fans in the office. He hasn't. Not really.'

Alexa's smile broadened. She felt happier than she had done in weeks.

'So.' He rose to his feet. 'Same again?'

16

Alexa looked up as the sound of high heels echoed off the polished stone walls of the atrium.

'Sorry!' called Kate, tugging on her suit jacket as she clip-clopped her way to the visitors' area, arms outstretched. 'My PowerPoint crashed.' They hugged tightly, then Kate turned to the security guard behind the desk. 'I'll be back,' she said, unhappily.

'D'you have time for a drink, or would you prefer to cancel?'

Kate was already heading for the revolving door. 'I've *always* got time for a drink,' she said, smiling. 'But d'you mind if it's coffee? I don't think I'll stay awake otherwise.'

Alexa smiled sympathetically. 'Suits me. I'm not the one going back to the office to redo an hour's work.'

'Two hours,' corrected Kate, pulling a face. 'It's a nightmare. D'you think I'd have a case to sue Microsoft?'

Alexa laughed. 'I'll ask Matt.'

They squeezed into the same pod of the door and shuffled through.

'Bloody hell,' muttered Kate, pulling her thin suit jacket around her. 'It's freezing.'

'It is October,' Alexa pointed out.

'Mmm. You tend to forget, up there.'

Alexa couldn't help glancing back at the imposing building, just to remind herself. Sure enough, the white glow of strip-lights illuminated the air around the three floors occupied by TDS. Kate was right. Day or night, summer or winter, it was all the same up there.

'So, your app's causing a bit of a stir, you say?'

Alexa's mood instantly plummeted. 'A bit.'

They crossed the road and headed down a side street towards Piccadilly. An Arctic wind ripped through their clothes, prompting Kate to huff ineffectively on her hands. 'So, what sort of a – phh – stir?'

Alexa hesitated, slowly realising something. *Kate didn't know.* She slowed her pace, wondering which of them was more wrapped up in her work: her or Kate. 'Have you read any newspapers in the last day or so?'

Kate squinted into the night sky. 'Only the financial pages.'

It was Kate, Alexa decided. News of *Banter*'s 'despicable mobile app' was all over the front pages of most of the national newspapers.

They emerged on Piccadilly, where Alexa guided her friend into the nearest store, directing her to the news racks.

'Look,' she said, picking up a copy of the tabloid that Derek had gleefully dropped on her desk that morning. She flipped to page four, where the headline took up most of the left-hand page: PORNO MOBILE APP SHOCKS NATION.

She picked up another. BANTER LAUNCHES OFFENSIVE MOBILE APP. Kate drew a sharp breath. She was clearly reading the headlines for the first time. SEXIST APP DRAWS MAX NUMBER OF COMPLAINTS. Alexa worked her way along, leaving the newspapers open on the racks for Kate to see. It was only when somebody coughed, just behind her, that she realised they were being watched.

'You gonna buy dem papers?' growled the shopkeeper.

'Sorry.' Alexa nodded apologetically and started restoring the newspapers to their rightful positions on the shelf.

'It's not a library, you know.'

'No. Right.' Alexa continued to whip shut the pages. Meanwhile, Kate just stood, staring at the display, shaking her head.

'I see what you mean,' she said, as they beat a hasty retreat from the shop.

Alexa nodded, looking for a suitable café. Starbucks was open, a few doors down. She looked enquiringly at Kate, who gave a distracted nod.

'They're just jealous,' declared Kate, as they queued for their drinks. 'Everyone knows the tabloids hate lads' mags for stealing their page three readers.'

'It's not just the tabloids,' Alexa pointed out. 'It's the broadsheets too. And half the women's rights groups in the UK.' She turned to the barista. 'Skinny latte, please.'

'Cappuccino with an extra shot – actually, can you make it a triple shot?'

Alexa looked at her friend. 'Don't you want to sleep at some point?'

Kate shrugged. 'Probably not.' She moved to the end of the counter and extracted two sachets of sugar.

Alexa sighed, leaning against the wooden surface as they waited for their coffees. Perhaps there was a hint of bitterness in the media's reaction to the app. After all, they were all competing for the same share of the reader's attention. Time spent ogling half-naked girls on a mobile app was time *not* spent reading the news headlines, but . . . no. That wasn't it. The reason for the coverage was one of genuine outrage.

'*Women's rights groups,*' said Kate, scathingly. 'Haven't they got better things to be doing? I mean, whose rights are at risk here? The women who appear in the videos? They *want* to appear in the videos! Didn't you say most of the videos were uploaded by women?'

Alexa nodded. She reached for her coffee as it appeared on the surface between them.

Kate furiously stirred the sugars into her cappuccino while

Alexa scanned the place for somewhere to sit. The only option seemed to be a small, round table by the door that was covered in wrappers and paper cups.

'It's ridiculous,' declared Kate, sweeping the debris to one side and slamming her mug down on the table. 'I mean, hasn't feminism moved on a bit? I thought feminism was supposed to be all about choice – about *choosing* what we do with our bodies. If girls choose to share footage of themselves in their underwear, then let them! It's flattering that people want to watch. It's *liberating.*'

'Is it?' asked Alexa, sipping her latte. She didn't feel sure about anything anymore.

Kate looked at her as though she were mad. 'Jesus, Lex! You launched the thing!'

'Yeah, but . . .' She sighed, picturing the headlines again. 'There seem to be a lot of people against it.'

Kate shook her head despairingly. 'Lex, you care *way* too much about what people think.'

Alexa said nothing. Kate was right about that. She did care too much about what other people thought. She always had done. That was the reason she hadn't told her parents where she worked. It was the reason she hadn't confronted Derek or Marcus about their behaviour. It was the reason she felt so bad about this media backlash today. She sometimes wondered whether it was the underlying reason for her unending drive to achieve. Was it simply because she wanted others to think better of her? If that was the case, then ironically she had succeeded in doing exactly the opposite.

'What do other people think, within Senate?' asked Kate. 'Do they think you've overstepped the mark with this thing?'

Alexa shrugged helplessly. That was the ridiculous thing. While she was having heart palpitations at the sight of these headlines, envisioning feminist crusaders smashing windows and appealing to have the brand shut down, for the rest of the team it seemed to be business as usual. Derek and the other editorial staff had seemed rather amused by the whole debacle, proclaiming their app to be 'one in the eye for Global Media' – Global Media being the owner of not only two of the nation's biggest-selling tabloids but also the owner of *Banter*'s main rival, *Diss*. Meanwhile, Peterson had simply looked baffled at her suggestion that the app's survival might be at risk.

'The chief executive wants to showcase the app at the October board meeting. He sees it as a roaring success.'

'And it is!' Kate lowered her cup firmly onto the table. 'It *is* a success. Not only have you created a whole new revenue stream for the business, you've generated a whole lot of PR to go with it!'

Alexa nodded, uncertainly.

'You know what they say . . . all publicity's good publicity.'

'Except when it's bad publicity.'

Kate made a guttural noise. 'Lex,' she growled. 'Think of all the lads that will've seen those headlines and thought, "awesome – I'd better check that out". Seriously, have a little confidence.' Kate gulped down some syrupy coffee. 'This is a brilliant innovation. Be proud of it. Don't let the fuckers get you down.'

Reluctantly, Alexa smiled back at her friend.

'Nobody scorned Ben & Jerry when they launched their first ice cream parlour, did they?'

'But they weren't cashing in on women's insecurities or objectifying the female form, were they?'

'Neither are you! For God's sake, nobody's making these girls get their kit off, are they? They want to do it – it's *empowering*.'

Alexa buried herself in her coffee cup. She agreed with Kate's argument, but she was also beginning to see flaws in it. There was an element of empowerment for the girls in the videos – but at the same time, it did seem a bit like exploitation.

'Bloody feminists,' Kate muttered angrily. 'They are *so*

misguided, they give women a bad name. If they stopped waving their bras about for one second, then they might realise that the best route to equality is for women to start *thinking* like men. Being bullish. Embracing initiatives like this. Having the balls to take a risk on a project and to see it through. *That's* what they ought to be doing. Not standing in the way of progress.'

The young Starbucks employee who had been hovering nearby took the opportunity to dart over and clear the table of debris.

Alexa thought about Kate's words. She wasn't sure whether she could speak for the entire female race, but for her, to some extent, it was true. She needed to think more like a man. Sure, she was assertive on the outside; she talked a good game and could hold her own. But deep down, there was always this nagging doubt. She could never feel entirely sure that what she was doing was right. It didn't take much to uncover this deep-rooted lack of confidence, either. A negative comment or a doubtful look did the trick. So when the entire British press and half of the nation's feminist organisations seemed to be ganging up against her, it was hardly surprising that she was having second thoughts.

'You should hear some of my male colleagues,' said Kate, smiling. 'Hey. D'you remember Jeremy Cartwright, from our intake?'

'How could I forget?' Alexa grimaced at the thought. Jeremy Cartwright had been the obnoxious MBA graduate in their year group at TDS. Having been to business school, he considered himself several cuts above the rest and liked to exert his authority by making loud phone calls about important projects that nobody else knew anything about.

'He managed to convince the board of Lexicom to invest all their earnings in that crappy website—'

'My-pet.com!' Alexa finished, remembering it vividly.

'They paid fifty million pounds for it!' Kate cackled.

Alexa laughed too.

'Now *he* knew how to think like a man.' Kate gasped for air.

'He was still convinced it was a winner, a year later when it went belly-up!' She shook her head. There were tears of laughter in her eyes.

Alexa was so wrapped up in the memory of the square-headed, arrogant MBA that she almost didn't notice her phone vibrating on the table between them.

'Oh.' She looked at the screen. 'It's Leonie. Hi!'

'You sound chipper.'

Alexa tried to banish the thoughts of Jeremy's overly-gelled hair and black-rimmed glasses from her mind. 'I'm with Kate,' she said, sobering up. 'We're near Green Park. Are you around?'

'Dulwich,' she said, apologetically. 'I'm on supper duty – Piers has rugby. I just called to check you were okay.'

'What . . . d'you mean?' Alexa already knew what she meant, but she had to ask.

'The *My Girlfriend* app. It's all over the papers. That's your thing, isn't it?'

Alexa sighed. She could feel herself sinking back into her earlier mood. Kate had just spent the last ten minutes persuading her not to care what people thought, but in an instant, she cared again. 'Yes,' she said, solemnly.

'So, is this it, then? Are you going to have to shut it down?'

Alexa couldn't help noticing a hint of optimism in her friend's voice.

'No,' she said firmly. She was reminded of the indignation with which Peterson had greeted her suggestion that they might have to pull the app. He wasn't going to shut off a revenue stream like this – and neither was she. Kate's stern words were still ringing in her ears. 'Of course not. It's just a storm in a teacup.'

'Oh. Well, that's good then,' Leonie replied uncertainly.

'Yeah – I think it'll be fine.' Alexa looked at Kate, who was clearly trying to decipher the other end of the conversation. 'We'll see how things pan out, but I imagine it'll all blow over within the week.'

'Great,' said Leonie, with false jollity.

They lapsed into an awkward silence. Alexa felt guilty for coming across so cockily. Had Leonie caught her half an hour earlier, she would have been greeted with a very different response, but for some reason Alexa didn't want to let on to her friend how badly the negative press was affecting her.

'How are things with you, anyway?' she asked, brightly. 'How's the class?'

'Oh, not bad. Andrei can now swear in English and Roger looks to be on track to repeat the year again.'

Alexa forced a laugh. The guilt was still weighing heavily upon her – guilt for her earlier flippancy and guilt for going down a career path that so appalled her friend.

'One of my boys nearly got suspended this week for opening a newspaper in class.'

'What?' Alexa tuned in to what Leonie was saying. 'That seems a bit melodramatic. Just for opening a newspaper?'

There was a pause. 'It was page three of the *Star*.'

'Oh.' Alexa didn't know how to respond. She knew what her friend was implying: that the material on page three of a tabloid was no different to the material inside her magazine and that both were freely available to any adult or child in a newsagent. Leonie was making a point. 'Probably the same newspaper that was slating our app,' she said, in a half-hearted attempt at a joke.

'Mmm.' There was another pause, then a clattering noise in the background. 'Oh, I'd better go. Piers has just come in and he's covered in mud. He needs to be undressed at the door, otherwise he'll trample it everywhere. Catch up soon, yeah?'

'Yeah,' Alexa said rigidly. 'See ya.'

Kate had given up on the eavesdropping and gone to the ladies'. Alexa sat at the table, Leonie's words ringing in her ears. There was friction between them that she hadn't been aware of before. It wasn't the words that gave it away, so much as the tone. Alexa couldn't help wondering whether the primary reason for Leonie's call hadn't been to check on her wellbeing after all, but to make her feel guilty for the incident that had happened in class.

Her phone buzzed on the table. Alexa grabbed it, grateful for the distraction from her thoughts. It was a text message from an unknown number.

> Hey Alexa, THANX 4 putting
> me in touch w Ciao! U R a star
> – I got Jnr Asst Editorial position!
> And hey- I didn't know u were at
> BANTER?!?! That is SO cool. Can I
> pop up & C U?! LARA XXX

Alexa let her head roll back, leaving her eyes closed in despair. When she opened them, Kate was standing over her, frowning.

'Problem?'

Alexa nodded. 'Potentially. Remember I told you about that little cow that Leonie and I used to babysit?'

'The one that—'

'Only ate pink food, yeah. Well, thanks to me, she just got a job at *Ciao!*.'

'Cool. Why is that a problem?'

Alexa screwed up her face. 'It becomes a problem when she tells her mummy that I work at *Banter*.'

Kate looked down at her, slowly shaking her head. 'You're scared of what your parents will think,' she surmised. Then she leaned down and pressed her face right up to Alexa's. '*You have to stop caring about what other people think.*'

Alexa nodded. Kate was right. She had to stop caring. She had to have confidence. She had to get rid of that deep, niggling doubt that kept rising up inside her and causing her to question her beliefs. She took a deep breath.

She had to start thinking like a man.

17

A tuneless, trombone-like noise blasted through the hubbub, prompting Alexa to look up from the pile of paperwork on her desk.

Biscuit was balanced on a swivel chair at the far end of the office, blowing through a traffic cone. Alexa recognised the instrument. It had made its first appearance shortly after the team night out – alongside Paddy's Give Way sign, a section of water mains pipe and flashing orange lamp, which, sadly, had given up flashing on arrival. Having succeeded in attracting the team's attention, Biscuit handed over to Greg, one of the junior writers, who was clambering onto the adjacent chair.

Greg cleared his throat. 'Ladies and gentlemen!' he cried. 'I bring to you great news. News of a lucrative advertorial feature deal. News – Josh, turn the music down, will you? News . . . of Paddy's next assignment!'

Amid jeers and drum rolls, Paddy leaned back on the photocopier and groaned. Already this month, he had been sent on a 'his and hers' horse-riding holiday (on his own), an advanced driving course and a Territorial Army boot camp that had nearly killed him.

'And the location is . . .' Greg slowly unfolded the piece of paper in his hands. Silence reigned. 'The Kingsley Health and Beauty Spa, Cheshire!'

The office erupted in laddish laughter. Paddy held his head in his hands.

Alexa smiled. She knew that the junior writer wasn't really disappointed. Paddy lapped up whatever was thrown his way; he relished these challenges. He wrote good articles on the back of them, too. If he carried on like this, thought Alexa, he would rise quickly from the sticky floor of the junior writer pool.

The hilarity continued. Someone remarked that Paddy should take a member of the team as his 'date' for the spa weekend. Someone else suggested Jamie, on account of the tight-fitting polo neck he was wearing.

'What's with the shoes, too?' asked Louis. 'They're hurting my eyes, they're so shiny. Ooh – don't move! Flash of light!' He shielded his eyes and leapt from foot to foot.

Derek swooped up to Jamie's desk, clearly spotting an opportunity for public ridicule. 'Suits you, sir!' he cried, with a camp flick of the wrist. Marcus was quick to catch on, wheeling himself along the gangway and giving a tuneless rendition of 'Beautiful Boy'. Jamie ignored it all, keeping his headphones firmly clamped over his ears and scrolling through images.

It was just harmless banter, Alexa told herself. Besides, there was nothing she could do about it. This was what happened when you put twenty-five young, sexually-charged males in an over-heated room together for eight hours every day. The testosterone was bound to come out somehow.

She turned the pages of the print-out in front of her. In two weeks' time, Peterson would be taking the Americans through these slides in an attempt to reassure them that *Banter* was on track to meet its April targets. Alexa couldn't concentrate. In the far corner of the office, Marcus and Louis were serenading the pictures editor with some kind of duet that sounded rather like a tribal burial chant. She didn't like the way in which certain members of the team took such a disproportionate share of abuse from the ringleaders. Too often, it felt less like banter and more like . . . well, bullying.

Alexa decided to intervene, but too late. The deputy editor

was already grabbing his coat from the back of his chair, encouraging Marcus and Louis to do the same.

'Pub's calling,' muttered Derek, by way of explanation. 'Oh, yeah.' He reached into his coat pocket and pulled out a crumpled page that looked to have been torn from a magazine. He tossed it across the desk for Alexa to retrieve. 'Our app's even causing trouble across the pond.'

He raised an eyebrow and then, with a dismissive wave, swaggered out with Marcus and Louis in tow.

Alexa looked down at the cutting. It was from the weekend supplement of the *New York Times*. The headline read, BRITISH PORN HITS US CELL PHONES. It was only a quarter-page article, but it wasn't the size that mattered. The *New York Times* had a readership of nearly a million – and then there were online readers on top of that. The article was a recycled argument against modern 'overtness', written from the same outraged standpoint as its UK equivalents. Alexa wondered whether it had been picked up on by the board of Senate Inc. She cringed at the thought. Peterson was planning to promote the app at the October board meeting as one of the key success stories of the quarter.

'Ignore it,' came the suggestion from across the desk.

Alexa looked up. Her body language must have given away her concerns. Sienna was looking at her with an expression that bordered on sympathetic.

'Ignore it,' she said again, more gently.

Alexa managed a weak smile in return. Sienna was talking to her. It was progress. Ever since she'd been assigned to write and act out the voiceover for Banter TV, she had seemed significantly more acquiescent towards Alexa. With a pay rise and promotion pending on the basis of a successful two-month trial, the editorial assistant-cum-PA had clearly had a change of heart.

'Some people take themselves too seriously,' said Sienna. 'They're just a bunch of backward-thinking prunes.'

Alexa frowned, unable to resist a little laugh. 'Do you mean prudes?'

'Whatever.' Sienna shrugged.

Alexa found herself smiling, despite herself. Sienna was right. It didn't matter what the editor of the *New York Times* supplement thought of their mobile app. It was clearly successful enough to have attracted a sufficient number of US downloaders to catch his or her eye, and would no doubt attract more, with the additional press. Alexa screwed up the article and lobbed it into the bin. She picked up the stack of pages in front of her and laid them back down on the desk, starting again on page one.

The office began to empty out. Alexa lost herself in the PowerPoint, scribbling notes in margins, imagining Peterson's voice, authoritatively reading her words to a roomful of impatient Americans who clearly had no more time for this brand. She had to change the tone. ~~Profitable~~ Highly profitable mobile app. Legal bill ~~reduced~~ vastly reduced. ~~Improvement~~ Significant improvement in brand engagement.

'Night.' Sienna rose a well-manicured hand in her direction as she tottered towards the door in her stiletto heels.

Alexa raised a hand in acknowledgement and watched as the girl sashayed past each row of desks, checking out her reflection in the darkened windows. It was only when she had reached the door when Alexa thought to call out. 'Sienna?'

Sienna executed a perfect catwalk turn. 'Mmm?'

'Nice work, on the Cowgirl interview. I watched it this morning.'

Sienna gave a coy smile, lifting her shoulders so that her entire ensemble rose to the level of her stocking-clad buttocks. 'Thanks.'

Alexa let out a sigh of relief. The ice was finally melting. Administrative tasks were now greeted with only a hint of resentment and although Alexa couldn't be certain, she wondered whether the barrier of magazines between them might have come down by a copy or two in the last few days.

Alexa checked the time on her monitor and prepared to go

through the pack one last time. It was half-past seven. She had said she'd be at Matt's in Pimlico by eight. She stared at the page on her screen. Her vision blurred. She was too exhausted to focus. Alexa tried one more time, but gave up. She'd done enough. If there were any more changes to be made then Peterson would just have to make them himself. She logged off, piling up the various pieces of paper and gathering the week-old coffee cups around one finger.

She lingered on her way to the kitchen. Jamie was staring at his screen, diligently ironing out the cellulite from a girl's backside. His headphones were lying on the desk, Alexa noted. She wondered whether he actually played music through them during the day, or whether they were simply a defence mechanism to protect against the playground banter.

'Jesus!' he cried, clutching his chest as he turned. 'You made me jump.'

'Sorry.' Alexa smiled. 'Just taking empties back to the kitchen. Have you got . . .' She looked on Jamie's desk, but there was no debris to collect. There was nothing, in fact. The area around his Mac was entirely devoid of clutter.

He shook his head, but didn't return to his work.

'Are you . . .' Alexa started the sentence, just for something to say. An awkward silence fell. 'Are you going to be staying late?'

'Not too late,' he replied, smiling. 'I hope.'

Alexa nodded. Jamie was nearly always the last to leave at night. She felt bad about that. He was nowhere near the highest paid member of staff.

'Does your wife mind you spending your nights here, doing . . . that,' she said, nodding at the butt-cheek on his screen.

'Oh. Um . . .' Jamie's eyes darted towards the image and then roamed the floor by Alexa's feet. 'I don't have a wife.'

'Sorry,' Alexa shook her head apologetically. 'Girlfriend, I mean.' He had definitely mentioned another half at some point. She looked again at the editor's ring finger. There was a thin

154

gold band around it. Alexa suddenly realised what she had done, and panicked. *He was a widower. At thirty-something.* It was so tragic – and Alexa had stirred everything up by mentioning . . .

'I don't have a girlfriend,' he said, calmly.

Alexa was about to issue a profound apology and retreat to the kitchen, when she noticed the emphasis placed on Jamie's penultimate syllable.

'Oh. Um, right.' She nodded, feeling relieved and embarrassed. She tried to think of something to say. Jamie was gay. *Of course Jamie was gay.* How had she missed this before? There were so many clues. The fashionable clothes. The lack of raucous girl-talk. The easy manner with semi-naked girls. The *gay porn on his computer,* for God's sake. 'Your . . . partner,' she stammered, finally.

Jamie shrugged. 'He doesn't mind. He's a nurse, so he works shifts, anyway.'

'Oh, right!' Alexa gushed.

She wasn't shocked about Jamie being gay; she was just shocked by her own lack of observational skills. Had she been operating in a vacuum, these past twelve weeks? Were there other blatantly obvious things that she had failed to spot?

Alexa thought back to the homophobic bullying earlier and wondered how much people knew. She mentally replayed some of the conversations she had overheard. It was impossible to glean anything from them. Derek and his cronies were as cruel to Jamie as they were to everyone else. The term 'gay' was bandied about but usually as an insult, not meant literally.

'So,' Jamie looked at her, his head cocked to one side. 'You never asked me to do your revenge airbrushing. Didn't lose your nerve, did you?'

'Ah,' Alexa nodded, relieved to be back on home turf. She glanced again at Jamie's screen, thinking back to the images on the memory stick he had provided. She still couldn't believe she hadn't twigged, at that point. Perhaps it was the atmosphere within *Banter* that distorted her thinking. There was so much machismo and aggression – it was just *assumed* that everyone working on the title was heterosexual. 'I . . . I thought of another way.'

'Oh yeah?'

Alexa just smiled, visualising Derek Piggott's face as he regaled the team with tales of his latest electronic exploits with the pneumatic blonde. She hadn't yet worked out how she would use the situation to her advantage, but she felt confident that the situation would arise at some point.

'I'm afraid I can't tell you how,' she said. 'Not yet.'

Jamie's eyes twinkled. 'Saving the punchline for when you need it most?'

She nodded. 'Something like that.'

Alexa raised her collection of mugs in a gesture of solidarity and hurried off to the kitchen. It was a quarter to eight; she was late. She rushed back to her desk, swung her coat over her shoulders and stopped. Her phone was ringing. She hesitated. It was an external call. She considered leaving it unanswered, but then remembered that Peterson was in New York for pre-board meetings. It could be urgent.

'Alexa Harris.'

'Hi there, Alexa.' It was a high-pitched female voice. She sounded young and highly assertive. 'My name's Wendy and I'm calling from *BBC Breakfast*. We're hoping to do a feature on the *My Girlfriend* mobile app tomorrow morning and we were wondering whether you'd represent Banter's views on the programme?'

'Um, right.' Alexa's heart started pounding. She felt sick. The thought of going on live TV turned her stomach. She started trying to think of alternatives. She couldn't trust Derek or anyone else from the editorial team. Peterson was too senior and besides, he wouldn't know enough about the app. But *somebody* had to speak; they had to have representation.

'Sure,' she heard herself say. 'I'd be happy to.'

'Great!' cooed Wendy. 'It'll be around six thirty, so you'll need to be here for five forty-five. I presume you'll want a car – whereabouts d'you live?'

'I'll be . . .' Alexa was about to give the producer Matt's address, but then realised that staying at Matt's would involve turning up in the crumpled set of clothes in her bag, or the ones she was wearing now. She desperately wanted to see Matt tonight, but this was national television. She was being asked to defend the brand in front of millions of viewers. 'Hammersmith,' she said, spelling out her full address.

Maybe Matt would come to hers, she thought, feeling increasingly queasy as the young woman talked her through the details.

'Oh, and I forgot to mention,' said Wendy in a sing-song voice, just as Alexa was about to sign off. 'We've also got the head of campaigns for a charity called REACT – you know it, I presume?'

'Er, no.' The knot in Alexa's stomach tightened a little. 'Not really.'

'It's an award-winning human rights organisation that challenges the sexual objectification of women,' explained Wendy. 'You'll probably want to check them out.'

'Yes. Of course.'

Alexa thanked the producer and replaced the receiver. Her hands were trembling uncontrollably. She stared at the note on the desk, trying to imagine herself on TV. It was too frightening to contemplate. She wasn't made for public speaking. Small groups were fine; one on one was preferable. This, though . . . they were talking millions of viewers. What if she said the wrong thing? What if she froze with the nerves? What if someone she knew was watching?

Alexa closed her eyes for a moment, feeling the dread fill her body as she realised what it was that really scared her. It wasn't the risk of someone she knew watching; it was the risk of *her parents* watching.

For three months, she had kept her dirty secret from them. It would be worse if they found out now than if she had just come clean, right at the beginning. She pictured her mother, staring in horror at the kitchen TV as the image of her daughter came on, the sound of her voice, defending the brand . . . Alexa stopped herself. It wasn't going to happen. Her parents didn't watch morning television – especially not at six thirty a.m. She gathered her belongings and stood up, slowly becoming aware of a vibration inside her bag.

It was Matt.

'Hey.' Alexa let out a weary sigh. She could already feel the weight of the guilt from what she was about to do.

'Just checking you hadn't forgotten.'

'Um, no.' Alexa grimaced, picturing his blue eyes as they looked searchingly around his bachelor pad, waiting. 'I'm so sorry, Matt. Something's come up. I've said I'll go on TV tomorrow, talking about the app.'

'Oh.' Matt's reply was almost inaudible.

'The thing is,' Alexa went on, feeling the need to fill the silence. 'I need to go home to get fresh clothes and by the time I'm back in Pimlico after that . . .'

'Right.'

'Sorry,' she said again. 'You could come to mine? Or maybe tomorrow, instead?'

'I'm meeting Dickie for drinks tomorrow. Look, it's late. Don't worry about it. Good luck on TV, eh?'

Alexa was about to suggest another alternative – she didn't know what, but it didn't matter anyway. The line was already dead. She sighed, shoving the note into a side pocket of her bag and leaving the office for what she knew would be another sleepless night.

18

'Try to relax.'

The makeup woman clipped back a stray wisp of fringe and looked appraisingly at Alexa's face. Alexa sat rigidly in the chair, staring at her tense reflection and trying to do as she was told.

'Have you been airbrushed before?'

Alexa faltered. Jamie had airbrushed her mugshot for the 'About Us' section of the website, but she couldn't see why that was relevant for a television appearance.

The woman responded to her silence by holding up a small gun-like instrument and telling Alexa to shut her eyes. Alexa opened them again to find that her face had been spray-painted. Like an adept graffiti artist, the woman had re-coloured her skin in various shades: tan for the forehead, darker brown for the cheeks, charcoal grey around the eyes and plum for her lips. She looked like a pristine china doll.

Feeling slightly perturbed by her inconceivably flawless complexion but too nervous to voice her concerns, Alexa glanced sideways at the girl in the next chair along. She was short, with a button nose and big, round eyes. Her hair was light brown – not dissimilar in colour to Alexa's, but wavier and pulled back in a bushy ponytail. Alexa recognised her from the YouTube clips. She was head of campaigns for REACT and her name was Georgie Caraway.

Alexa continued to watch through the gap in her fringe, which was being tugged and straightened using some kind of miniature steam-roller device, as the girl raised her voice to the adjacent makeup artist.

'It's fine,' she said firmly. 'I don't need any more.'

The woman tried to dab something on Georgie's cheek. The intense, round eyes stared up at the woman. 'I said, I don't *need* any more.'

Alexa's attention returned to her own reflection as she sensed that the sculpting was finally complete. If this was the treatment Georgie Caraway doled out to the makeup artist, she didn't like to think about how she reacted to her opposition in a live debate.

The woman bent down and gave Alexa's face a quick once-over. 'All set.'

Alexa thanked her, vaguely. She was too distracted and nervous to have a fully formed opinion of the woman's handiwork, but she sensed that the result was something significantly more striking than the effect she usually achieved each morning. Too striking, probably, but appropriate for the cameras, she hoped. Alexa breathed deeply and smiled as Wendy reappeared in the doorway.

'Follow me!' Wendy looked cheerily from Alexa to Georgie and then strode off down the corridor. She led them to an area of seating that formed part of the studio. Alexa's stomach flipped. The news desk was only a few metres away; if she screamed now, it would be heard on national television. She began to feel short of breath, as though the air in the studio was low on oxygen.

'Wait here and someone will call you when it's time to go on.' Wendy flashed an effusive smile and strutted off down the corridor.

Georgie took the seat furthest from Alexa, clearly making her stance known. For a moment, Alexa considered attempting to alleviate her nerves and test her vocal chords by engaging the campaigner in conversation, but then thought better of it. She had studied Georgie Caraway's form on YouTube. The girl was clearly very bright. She was also highly opposed to the likes of *Banter* and was therefore unlikely to have much to say to Alexa. Or rather, she might have a good deal to say, but it wouldn't be an ideal way to warm up for a live debate.

Alexa felt sick. She looked over at the brightly lit news desk, feeling her knees shake against one another. The female presenter was laughing over newspaper headlines with the waxy-haired man who had been in the makeup room before her. They looked so relaxed. How did they do that? Were they *really* relaxed, or were they just experts at masking their nerves?

There were magazines splayed out on the coffee table in front of them, but Alexa couldn't bring herself to look at them. Her nerves were draining her energy, stealing her focus. She wanted to reach into her bag and glance at the notes she had scribbled in the car on the way in, but she didn't want Georgie to catch her revising. There was nothing she could do but sit and wait. She couldn't even text Matt because mobile phones weren't allowed in the studio.

'Alexa and Georgie?' A handsome young man with a headset hovered over them, hands clasped and features set in a broad grin. It was the same grin that Wendy had worn. Alexa rose shakily to her feet, feeling the nausea surge up again inside her. Two million people were tuned into the show at this very moment. Two million people were about to hear her speak.

Alexa and Georgie were taken to their seats on the news desk. The presenter switched on a brilliant smile and introduced herself as Christine – as though they didn't already know who she was. Alexa tested her own smile. She could feel the nerves dragging down the corners of her mouth, distorting her face. The bright lights were melting her makeup and she could feel a lock of her fringe, rigid with hairspray, falling down over her eyes.

'We'll be on after the jingle,' Christine said calmly.

All too soon, a countdown could be heard from behind one of the cameras. Alexa looked around, suddenly realising how many cameras there were. There was one facing Christine, one hovering above them and at least three gliding about the studio on booms. Which one were they supposed to look at?

'. . . also with us today is Alexa Harris, from the lads' mag behind the mobile app, *Banter*. Alexa, why don't you start by telling us what prompted you to launch the app?'

Alexa gave what she hoped was a professional-looking nod, opting to focus on the presenter and not the cameras.

'Well,' she said, hearing her voice as a high-pitched squeak. She cleared her throat. 'It was an opportunity for us to extend the *Banter* brand and offer our readers and viewers something more. Our male readers take pleasure from watching the female form and our female readers are keen to provide them with something to watch. It's a perfect match.'

'A perfect match. Georgie Caraway, from REACT, how do you see this new offering?'

Georgie looked straight into the presenter's eyes. She didn't even appear to be nervous.

'Unfortunately, we see it as yet another example of objectifying women – something we're working very hard to oppose. This application is perpetuating a vicious cycle of degradation and sexual abuse that harms not just women but our whole society.'

Alexa tried to swallow but her throat was dry. The presenter was looking at her.

'Alexa Harris, from *Banter*,' she prompted. 'Perhaps you could just clarify: are you denying that your application objectifies women, or are you simply claiming that the objectification isn't an issue?'

'The app does not objectify women,' stated Alexa. 'If it did, why would women use it to upload their videos?'

'Because,' replied Georgie, without waiting for a cue, 'there are women who see it as acceptable to be treated like objects. This in itself is a result of the chauvinist culture created by magazines such as *Banter*. Lads' mags have *caused* this problem and now they're pointing at the effects as some kind of argument for going even further and causing even more harm.'

Alexa took a breath, grappling for a quick response. The girl was good. She was upping the game. Alexa had to think of a compelling argument that said lads' mags were not the problem.

'Women find it liberating, having their videos viewed on the app,' she said, suddenly remembering Kate's claim. 'It's quite the opposite of objectification; it's *empowering* for women.'

Christine turned to Georgie, her mouth open for another question, but Georgie was already on the offensive.

'One of the most dangerous myths of this century,' she said, shaking her head, 'is the whole "empowerment" charade. Women who say they feel "empowered" by uploading footage of their sexual exploits for the benefit of strangers are either lying or they're so downtrodden by the pressure to conform to the beauty ideal set upon them by today's media and advertising industries that they'll do anything to attract so-called admirers.'

'So, you're saying that our female readers don't *know* what they really want?' asked Alexa, quickly. 'That they're confused?'

Georgie looked at her, bug-eyed and attentive. 'I'm saying that there's nothing empowering about being looked at like a piece of meat. And I'd also like to point out that it's not just adults, looking at this meat. Children as young as eight now have mobile phones.'

The presenter leaned in between them. 'Alexa? Is there an issue with young children getting hold of these images?'

Alexa shook her head. 'We have very strict controls over what gets uploaded and who downloads it. There's an age limit of sixteen for all users and our moderators keep a very close eye on the subjects of the videos.'

'I'm sorry,' Georgie responded quickly, 'but those controls really don't go far enough. There's no law against looking over an adult's shoulder and watching what's on the screen, is there?'

'There's no law against looking over an adult's shoulder and seeing page three of a tabloid,' Alexa pointed out.

'Exactly!' Georgie's eyes widened. 'That's precisely the problem. Our children are growing up in an ever more sexualised society, and it's magazines and mobile apps like yours that are driving it forward. Sex is everywhere: on TV, on advertising hoardings, on our computer screens . . . we've become so used to it that we don't see a problem any more when a yoghurt company decides to use a glamour model in its ad campaign or an airline sells seats on the basis of its air hostess' cup size.'

'You're right,' said Alexa, simply. 'Sex *is* everywhere, but I'm afraid that's not the fault of our magazine. I think you'll find a lot more of it on the hard drives of teenage boys' computers than on our pages.'

The presenter's head swivelled, ready for the inevitable come-back.

'That's porn,' argued Georgie, calmly. 'And porn is fine. Although it's degrading to women, at least when we look at it, we *know* it's porn. We go out of our way to find it. We know it's not real. What magazines like yours have done is brought sex into the *mainstream*. That's far more dangerous than hardcore porn on obscure websites.'

'I don't—'

'Inch by inch,' Georgie went on, ignoring the interjection, 'you bring sexual images and language into our everyday lives. Most of us hardly notice it happening – we just accept it as "the way things are".' She drew quotation marks in the air. 'But look back ten years and think about what was considered mainstream then. Did *you* see videos of half-naked women on a regular basis, when you were growing up?'

Alexa let out a quiet sigh. 'Things have changed,' she said. 'You can't put the genie back in the bottle.'

'But you can—'

'And unfortunately, we're going to have to leave it there,' said Christine, producing another Colgate smile. 'Next up, we ask whether a new breed of pony can transform the Scottish tourism industry and we take a look at the fashionable side of UK politics. You're watching *BBC Breakfast.*'

The man with the headset reappeared, giving Alexa and Georgie the thumbs-up. It had all happened so quickly. They had barely got started on the debate and suddenly they were being wheeled off again. Alexa's heart was still hammering inside her chest, the adrenaline racing around her veins.

'That was great, ladies!' sung Christine as they were led away to the percussion jingle. 'Thanks for coming in!'

Wendy reappeared, still bearing the same fixed smile, and escorted them through the rabbit warren of corridors that led, eventually, to the main exit.

Alexa was so overwhelmed with a mixture of latent anxiety and relief that she barely noticed when Georgie started talking. She glanced down at the campaigner, who was scuttling along beside her, taking twice as many steps to keep up.

'I said, your arguments weren't too bad,' she said, waiting for Alexa to catch her eye again. 'Considering you didn't have a leg to stand on.'

They were in the atrium now. Wendy flashed them another smile. 'I'll leave you to see yourselves out, okay? Take a car to wherever you need to get to. Just tell them you were on *Breakfast.* Thanks again!'

Alexa returned Wendy's expression, muttered her thanks and then turned back to Georgie.

'*I* don't have a . . .'

She stopped. Georgie was already halfway through the revolving doors, heading for the cab rank. Alexa waited a moment to put a suitable distance between them, then followed her into the car park.

Sinking into the folds of soft, warm leather of the BBC car, Alexa allowed herself a moment to reflect. It hadn't gone as badly as it might have done. In fact, no, she was being hard on herself. It had gone reasonably well. Georgie had won in the articulacy stakes, but at least Alexa hadn't embarrassed herself. By a stroke of luck, the debate had been curtailed at a good point in her argument; viewers would be left with her genie comment ringing in their ears and the sight of Georgie not quite forming a response in time.

It felt good to have defended the app to the nation, but at the same time, it felt as though . . . well, it felt as though this might be only the start. The app had been out for less than a month and, so far, *Banter* had avoided the regulators. Alexa wasn't naïve enough to think that the battle had been won; she knew that the likes of Georgie would be back for another round. She just couldn't tell when it would be or how it might happen.

She reached into her bag and switched on her phone. Matt had promised to record her appearance, although currently, the idea of reliving the last ten minutes of her life was not an appealing one.

Her phone vibrated with a text message. Several text messages. And several emails, Alexa noted with alarm. The phone was buzzing continuously as a flood of alerts popped up on the screen. Alexa opened the text messages first.

U were great. Mxx

OMG! Saw U on TV –
coooool. Lara X

Hey Lex, U used my
words! Next time, tell
me when ur on TV?!
Kxx

Alexa smiled, still feeling anxious from all the adrenaline in her system. She opened the emails.

Hi Alexa,
Wow. Saw you on TV. Did they give you a facelift or something?
Sienna

Hey Lex,
Saw you on BBC Breakfast just now – very good! We miss you at Hers. Come back! Hope all is well at Banter.
Annabel xx

Nice one, boss.
Good to see someone talking sense.
Riz

Alexa let the phone drop into her lap and let out a long, shaky breath. She hadn't anticipated such a reaction. It was barely seven o'clock; most people were in bed at this time, surely? Alexa lifted the phone to her ear to play the voicemail, feeling suddenly panicked. It felt as though an iron jaw had been clamped around her chest. She knew, even before she heard a word, who had left her the message.

'Alexa, it's your mother.' There was a pause, then a rasping sound, as though she was struggling for breath. 'I can't believe—' There was a muffled whimper. She was crying, Alexa realised. 'You said it was a *specialist* title!' The jaws closed around Alexa's chest. She had never heard her mother cry. 'Janice says the whole village has known for weeks!' There was more muffled sniffing, then an uncharacteristically weak groan, and then silence.

Alexa fell back in the seat and closed her eyes, feeling the pressure build up behind them. This was the worst possible way for her mother to find out. Not only was she discovering her daughter's sordid profession by watching national television; she was also – it now transpired – the last to know. Alexa cursed her foolish decision to give Lara Fielding a leg-up in her career. Of

167

course she would have told her mother that Alexa worked at *Banter*. It was juicy gossip. Both Lara and her mother, Janice, were known for their love of gossip. With hindsight, thought Alexa, it was a wonder that the news hadn't travelled back to her mother before now.

She opened her eyes and stared, unseeing, as the streets of Soho crawled past, her vision starting to blur. Lara Fielding wasn't really to blame. She had made things worse, but ultimately, the blame lay squarely at Alexa's feet. She was the one who had opted to stand for *Banter* in a live television debate. She was the one who had put off telling her parents for three months. Why? Because she was a coward. That was why. She could have simply broken the news, gently, at the beginning of her contract, but she had convinced herself that it would be simpler and kinder just to keep quiet – to keep her parents in the dark. Now she had hurt them so badly that her mother was in tears. How could she possibly have thought this was kinder than telling the truth?

It was starting to rain. Through the tears, she watched the droplets hit the cab window and trickle down, feeling her mood sink further as they fell.

'Here y'go,' announced the driver.

Slowly, Alexa climbed out and headed up the steps of Senate House. The night security guard called out a cheery greeting but Alexa didn't turn round. She waited for the lift, tears streaming down her cheeks, seeing nothing but the image of her mother's face: red, angry and hurt.

Her mobile phone rang again as she entered the office. Wiping a sleeve across her eyes, she looked down. It was Matt.

'Hi,' she said, sniffing away the tears.

'Hey! Are you pleased?'

'Well, yeah.' Alexa exhaled, shakily. 'But my mum was watching.'

There was a change in sound quality, as though Matt

was stepping into a building from a noisy street. '*Any post? No?* Sorry, Lex. What did you say?'

'I said, *my mum was watching.*'

'Oh.' There was a muted hissing noise in the background. 'That's not good, is it? Still, at least she knows now, eh? *No milk!*'

Alexa felt a surge of anger rise up inside her. 'Matt, did you hear what I said?'

'Of course I did. You said your mum was watching. What's up with you? You sound tetchy.'

'What's up with me?' Alexa stood in the middle of the office, tears running down her airbrushed face. She wanted to punch something. Matt *knew* what her parents were like. He knew how hard it was for her to live up to her mother's standards – how much pressure she felt to comply. He knew that she had been living a lie for the last three months because she was too scared to tell her parents – and here he was, asking *what was up with her.*

'Are you okay?' asked Matt, sounding more perplexed than concerned.

Alexa let out a despairing sigh. He had no idea. He didn't understand and he didn't care. 'Yeah,' she said, choking back a fresh wave of sobs. 'Yeah, I'm absolutely fine.'

'Right. Good. Well, I'll see you soon.'

Alexa tried to speak, but something was blocking her throat. She nodded helplessly into the handset, hearing the click as Matt ended the call. Slowly, the realisation dawned on her that this wasn't something that Matt or anyone else could help with. She switched off her phone and headed slowly towards her desk. This was her problem. They were her parents. It was up to her to make amends.

19

Like a droid, Alexa paid for her coffee and headed up Charing Cross Road, waiting at the lights before turning left and taking the same route she had done every weekday for the last two years. Her legs felt heavy. Each step was an effort, as though there was some kind of resistance pulling back against her shins.

The resistance, she knew, was in her head. She couldn't continue with this routine – couldn't keep going into work each morning as though nothing had happened. Her mother had made her feelings clear in the voicemail, so now every day that Alexa worked was another day spent with this black cloud looming over her. Of course, she had always known that her mother wouldn't approve of her job at *Banter*. But until three days ago, her mother had lived in blissful ignorance. It was a form of deception, but it was one that made everybody happy. Now, she was officially acting against her mother's will and she couldn't bear it any longer. She had to summon the courage to call her mother back.

Alexa found herself slowing down as Senate House loomed into view, casting a long shadow across the street in the early morning sun. Then she stopped altogether. Something was happening on the steps outside the building. There was a large group of people, huddled around the entrance to the building, stamping their feet and . . . Alexa felt suddenly cold. They were *chanting*.

Cautiously, she headed towards the protesters, squinting at their gaudy signs. WOMEN NOT OBJECTS, read one. SEXISM SELLS, read another. Draped across the brickwork above the main entrance hung a banner that said LADS' MAGS PROMOTE VIOLENCE AGAINST WOMEN. Alexa felt the last remaining energy reserves drain from her body. They were here to object about *Banter*. More specifically, she suspected, they were here to object about *Banter*'s latest initiative – *her* latest initiative, the mobile app.

Alexa forced herself forwards, every muscle in her body rebelling. As she got closer to the building, she managed to pick out the words of the chant. *'LADS' MAGS ARE PORNOGRAPHIC, PORN PROMOTES HUMAN TRAFFIC. LADS' MAGS ARE PORNOGRAPHIC, PORN PROMOTES HUMAN TRAFFIC . . .'* Those who weren't chanting were blowing whistles, banging drums and rattling tambourines.

There must have been nearly a hundred protesters, Alexa estimated. Most were wearing matching black and white T-shirts bearing feminist slogans and she was surprised to see that a good number of the protesters were men. On the fringes of the group, Alexa noted, were half a dozen spectators with cameras and notebooks. Journalists.

She jumped. A woman in a fluorescent yellow vest stepped into her path.

'D'you work for Senate?' she asked, wearily. It was Dee, the facilities manager.

Alexa nodded, too stressed and preoccupied to point out that their paths crossed nearly every day in the fifth-floor kitchen.

'There's a protest goin' on,' Dee said, unnecessarily.

Alexa nodded again, realising that she might be able to make use of her anonymity. 'What's it about?'

Dee rolled her eyes. 'Something to do with *Banter*, as usual. Feminist clap-trap.'

Alexa gave a weak smile. At least Dee was on her side, even

if a hundred angry protesters were lined up outside her place of work.

'No point in tryin' to get in. They're not lettin' anyone through. The advice is to work from home today.'

'But . . .' Alexa looked at Dee. She couldn't believe there was no contingency plan. Senate was a twenty-four-hour business. The radio producers and DJs must have been let in somehow. She looked again at the hordes of chanting protesters. They were standing shoulder to shoulder, ten deep around the steps. 'Can't we use a back entrance or something?'

Dee shook her head. 'Too many people. It's a fire hazard. Only essential staff are allowed in.'

Alexa was about to point out that as managing director of *Banter* she probably fell into this category, but then quickly reconsidered. The idea of working from home was significantly more appealing than spending the day with those other members of staff who deemed themselves 'essential staff'. She wondered whether today might be the day she found a way to make amends with her mother. Maybe she would muster the courage to pick up the phone.

Dee stormed off to accost another Senate employee, leaving Alexa alone on the pavement, unexpectedly transfixed by the raging protesters. They had so much energy. Their rhythmic chanting and rattling seemed to strengthen with every syllable, their placards jerking up and down in perfect unison.

'Do you believe that women are objects?' said a voice, close by.

Alexa turned. Her heart was pounding. She recognised the voice.

'Do you?' it asked again.

Georgie Caraway was grinning up at her, holding out a leaflet. 'Hello, Alexa.'

Instinctively, Alexa took the leaflet, giving it a cursory glance before stuffing it dismissively into her pocket. *ABUSE STARTS*

WITH LADS' MAGS, read the heading, below which was a disturbing image of a young woman's face, bruised and bloodied beyond recognition.

'Georgie,' she said curtly, her pulse still racing. 'How can I help you?'

'How can *you* help *me?*' Georgie smiled sweetly. 'With respect, Alexa, I don't think I'm the one who needs help.' She nodded towards the group of protesters surrounding the Senate entrance.

'Well, maybe that's where you're wrong.' Alexa maintained her focus on the girl. Her heart was hammering inside her ribcage but she was determined not to lose her nerve. Georgie may have won in the articulacy stakes on their TV debate, but she didn't have the right to stop Alexa from doing her job. 'I've never been better, see. We're enjoying one of our best week's trading, thanks to this nifty new app we launched recently. You may have heard of it – it's called *My Girlfriend?*'

Georgie flipped her eyes heavenward. 'Yes, thanks Alexa. That's actually why we're here. You might remember, we were on television together, discussing the issue?'

Alexa was about to point out, sarcastically, that the campaigners might have done better to choose a more sympathetic audience for their protest, when she realised that she would be wasting her time. She didn't want to engage Georgie in conversation. She was here to make the brand stronger – not to discuss its morality with a feminist campaigner.

'I'm sorry,' she said. 'I've got work to do. Good luck with your protest.' Alexa cast a disparaging look in the direction of the crowds and then turned on her heel and marched off.

She maintained her purposeful stride all the way to the lights, where she stopped. She looked left and right and then, eventually, over her shoulder to see whether she was being watched – or worse, followed. Senate House was several blocks away and not in the line of sight. The streets were heaving with commuters, but neither Georgie nor any of her feminist friends seemed to be among them. Alexa breathed a long, shaky sigh of relief and crossed the road. She took her first sip of her coffee as she went underground at Leicester Square and nearly spat it back into the cup. It was lukewarm and bitter – like her thoughts.

Sinking into her seat on the train, Alexa closed her eyes, waiting for the jerky, rocking motion to shake off some of the tension inside her. It didn't work. Her core remained rigid, her breathing shallow and fast. The campaigners had affected her more than she liked to admit. She couldn't seem to push away the thought of those people in their black and white T-shirts with their giant, home-made placards – couldn't block out the echo of their robotic chant.

Kate was right, of course. These people were ardent feminists with an axe to grind. It just happened to be *Banter* on the receiving end of the axe – not because *Banter* was doing anything worse than the other magazines out there but because *Banter*, thanks to her, was making more money than its competitors. She should have felt proud that the campaigners had chosen to protest outside her offices. It was a compliment; she had made such an impact in her first four months that they were seeing a backlash to the brand's success.

She thought about what Kate would say, if she were here with her. She would probably tell Alexa to laugh it off and think like a man, which was exactly what she knew she should be doing. Derek would be laughing, for sure. In fact, he had probably found a way into the building, simply so that he could parade up and down the fifth floor, crowing to the empty desks and blasting out emails describing the reaction to his fantastic idea.

Alexa leaned forward, resting her elbows on her knees and pressing her palms into her closed eyes. She *wanted* to be proud, but it was hard in the face of so much opposition. Those protesters resented her and everything she stood for. Alexa had put on a show for Georgie, feigning bravado, but deep down she hadn't gone unscathed by their display. It was something to do with her parents' disapproval, Alexa suspected. The protesters held the same beliefs and the same set of values as her prudish parents. Every stamp of the campaigners' feet was a reminder of what her mother thought about her career. *Lads' mags are pornographic* – their chant was ringing in her ears.

If only Leonie were here, she thought. Leonie knew what her mother was like. She understood Alexa's perpetual conflict between pleasing her mother and going her own way. Except . . . Alexa looked up as the automated voice announced her stop. She couldn't call Leonie, because she couldn't bear to hear the disappointment in her voice as she learned what the outcry was all about. Leonie wouldn't ever say so directly, but Alexa suspected she disapproved of the initiatives at *Banter* as much as her parents did. They hadn't spoken in weeks.

Taking a deep breath, she pushed herself to her feet and moved towards the exit. She needed to speak to her parents, to clear the air, but she wasn't ready yet. It felt as though somehow she couldn't make contact with them until she had proved herself right – or at least, proved that *Banter* wasn't wrong. Soon, when her changes were starting to make a difference and she had something to show for herself, she would make amends and explain. The app was starting to make serious money and, for the first time since she'd taken the job, Alexa felt that the targets might actually be within reach.

She mounted the steps to her flat and dragged herself to the door, feeling heavier than ever. There was something different about the hallway, she noticed as she dropped her bag and wandered into the lounge. She collapsed sideways on the sofa, lifting her legs as she fell and lying completely still. She knew there were things she needed to be doing, like checking the app stats and circulating updates to the team and reading the messages from Peterson, who was in New York, presenting the app to the Americans as – ironically – the 'success story of the quarter', but all that could wait.

Alexa's eyes sprang open. She stared at the ceiling, then slowly turned her head. *Matt's rugby bag.* That was what made the hallway seem different. It was missing. Matt kept it at hers so that he could go straight to his matches on a Saturday morning, but the shoe rack had been bare when she'd passed it.

She jumped up and ran back to the hall, her heart in her mouth. The panic mounted inside her as she stood, looking at the space where the bag had been, thinking about what it meant. Matt wouldn't have a rugby match on a Wednesday.

She ran back into the lounge, looking around, kidding herself that she didn't know what she might find. She knew exactly what she was looking for. She ran into the kitchen and, with a sinking feeling that left her gasping for air, she saw it. The despair ripped through her, sucking what little energy remained from her limbs and filling her throat with tears. The note was taped to the door of the oven at eye level, fluttering slightly in the breeze.

Alexa pulled it off and collapsed on the counter, her vision blurring with the tears. She wiped a shaky hand across her face and tried to focus on Matt's handwriting, knowing already what it meant.

Dear Lex,
    You are the most lively, intelligent, beautiful girl I have ever met. Your ambition puts me to shame and I'm in awe of how far you go to meet your goals. But that's the thing. I'm tired of playing second fiddle to your career. I know you don't see it, but you work *too hard*. Maybe you think others don't work hard enough – I know you think I earn way too much for the hours I put in – but that's just it. I'll never be like you and I don't think I can be *with* you either. There's more to life than work, Lex.
    I'm sorry that things have changed. We were good together. I'll miss you.
    Matt

Alexa slowly screwed up the note in her hand, feeling the salty tears stream down her face. She clenched her fist into a ball, squeezing the words together until her nails dug into her palm. She wanted to feel physical pain, as much pain as her body could handle – anything, to distract from the pain inside.

Matt was gone.

He had walked out of her life. *She* had driven him out of her life. Alexa clutched at the kitchen counter, feeling herself slipping away. They had lasted ten months. Ten glorious months. They were good together – he said so himself. What went wrong? Alexa scrunched shut her eyes, pushing out more tears. *She* had gone wrong. That was the problem. Just like the last time, and the time before that.

She banged on the edge of the worktop, hurting her fists in an attempt to distract from the misery inside her. Matt was gone. She couldn't move. Couldn't think. Couldn't function.

It took several seconds for Alexa to register the sound of the doorbell. Her anguish had blotted out the real world. She straightened up and looked into the hallway. A glimmer of hope shone through the wretchedness, followed by a wave of self-loathing for thinking such ludicrous thoughts. Of course Matt wasn't returning to tell her he'd made an enormous mistake.

The bell rang again. Alexa tried to think rationally. *Could* it be Matt? She looked at the ball of paper in her hand. Definitely not. He had moved on . . . and besides, he'd be at work by now.

Cautiously, she moved towards the front door, wiping a sleeve across her eyes and checking her face in the hall mirror. It was blotchy and red, with traces of mascara running down from the corners of her eyes. She made a half-hearted attempt at cleaning herself up and then opened the door.

'Hi.'

Alexa's disappointment quickly turned to despair as she took stock of her visitor. She tried to slam the door shut, but Georgie was too quick.

'Hey!' The girl's elfin face looked up at Alexa with a mixture of pain and indignation.

Alexa opened the door a little, just enough to encourage the foot to move. It didn't.

'Hear me out!' Georgie looked pleadingly through her thick, dark lashes. 'I don't normally follow people across London, I swear.'

Alexa sighed. Thankfully, the stairwell was dark enough to cast shadows on her face, hiding the streaks, but that wasn't her main concern. All she really wanted was for Georgie to leave her alone.

'I just thought we could talk,' explained the campaigner, with a look that almost qualified as apologetic.

'Look, Georgie,' Alexa could hear the weakness in her voice, 'I've got a lot on.'

'This won't take long,' Georgie replied, clearly not clocking Alexa's tone. 'I just wanted to give you this.' She thrust a booklet through the half-open door and waited for Alexa to take it.

Alexa looked down at what she was holding, ignoring the girl's blinking eyes. She didn't have the energy for this, or the head space. There were too many thoughts crashing around inside her head, too many painful memories.

LADS' MAGS PROMOTE VIOLENCE AGAINST WOMEN, she read, mechanically. She recognised the slogan from the banner that had been strung up above the entrance to Senate House. It was different from the leaflet that the girl had thrust into her hand at the rally – more substantial, but printed on the same, cheap paper. 'Fine. Thanks. I'll take a read.' She started to push the door shut but Georgie's foot remained in position.

'Just in case you don't get a chance,' she said brightly, 'I'll just quickly tell you what's inside.'

'Look, Georg—'

'It tells the story of a young woman called Lisa. She's twenty-eight and she came to us through a women's outreach charity because her boyfriend beat her so badly she ended up in intensive care with head wounds and when she came out she had nowhere to go.'

'Please, Georgie,' Alexa begged. 'I'll read the booklet.'

She knew it was wrong to object, but she didn't want to hear about this Lisa character or anyone else in the feminist propaganda booklet. She had enough to deal with.

'For four years,' Georgie went on, 'Lisa stayed with this man, while he hit her, strangled her and raped her. She took to wearing scarves to hide her injuries and after a while, she avoided going out in public altogether. But she stayed with him.' Georgie waited to catch her eye. 'You know why?'

Eventually, Alexa gave in and looked at the girl.

'Because she thought she deserved it. She thought it was this man's God-given right to abuse her, because that was what *he* believed.'

Alexa looked at the floor, unable to bear the pleading eyes any longer. She wanted Georgie to leave, but clearly that wasn't going to happen until the girl had brought it all back to lads' mags.

'He thought it was okay to strangle his girlfriend because that's what he'd seen in the magazines,' Georgie explained, predictably. 'He was wrapped up in this world of hyper-masculinity, where men are alpha-males and women are inferior, weak, pathetic . . . where women comply with men's fantasies – fantasies that are derived from images in *your* magazine. The whole principle of the lads' mag is to ridicule and degrade women. They perpetuate a culture of contempt against women.'

Alexa waited for a moment, in case there was more to come. After a couple of seconds, she lifted the booklet into view and promised, quietly, that she'd read it sometime. She knew it was selfish, but she just wanted to see the back of Georgie. She was thinking about the note that had been taped to the oven door and she could feel the tears building up behind her eyes. It was only a matter of time before they spilled out again.

'Can I put you on the REACT mailing list?' asked Georgie. 'That way, you'll get stuff like this straight through your door.'

'Great.'

'And email, too?' she pressed, missing Alexa's morbid sarcasm. 'I'll need your email address. In fact, can I grab a card?'

At the back of her mind, Alexa knew that it was a bad idea to give Georgie her business card. But images of Matt kept flashing through her mind and the tears were about to start flowing and this seemed like the quickest way of getting rid of the girl.

'Thanks.' Georgie took the card and handed one over in return. 'I'll see you around.'

Finally, the girl was gone. Alexa pressed the door shut and stood with her back against it, looking at the empty shoe rack where Matt's bag had been. She felt her lower lip quiver and a fresh surge of pressure against her eyes as the image of his smile flashed through her mind. The tears spilled out as she felt herself sliding down against the door, falling into a crumpled heap on the floor. She knew there were people far worse off than her, like Lisa and probably hundreds of other women that Georgie could tell her about, but right now, it felt as though her life was just about as bad as it could get.

20

'How can he say you work *too hard*?' Kate screwed up her face and looked out at the flailing skaters.

Alexa buried her face in the folds of her coat sleeves, wrapping her hands around the cold, metal barrier. Leonie's expression said it all. Kate was talking rubbish to try and make her feel better.

'If he thought you were working too hard then why didn't he say so at the time?'

Alexa's head remained nestled in the woollen fabric, her eyes scrunched shut. She couldn't be bothered to explain to Kate that he *had* said, although not in so many words. She ought to have realised that Matt's lack of response to her preoccupied business babble was a sign; his silence ought to have been enough.

'Watch out.' Leonie struck out a protective arm as a young teenage boy came sliding towards them at high speed. In an instant, Alexa was forced out of her cocoon of self-pity.

The boy slammed into the barrier at the exact spot where Alexa's head had been and rebounded onto the ice, backside first. Alexa watched expressionlessly as a young woman attempted to skirt round the boy's writhing body, wobbled for a moment and then lurched forwards, shrieking as her knees smacked against the ice.

Somerset House had been Kate's idea. She had obviously hoped to tempt her friend out of her misery by providing a source of fresh air and exercise, but frankly, Alexa would have preferred the stale air and warmth of her flat and she had told Kate as much. After a period of unsuccessful cajoling on Kate's part, they had settled for watching the other skaters from inside the grounds, which were apparently spectacular, although Alexa wasn't in the mood to take anything in.

'Honestly, though, it's not as if *he* never worked late, is it?' Kate clearly wasn't going to let up until she had drawn out every one of Matt's supposed faults. 'Think of all those fancy dinners he made you go to. That was effectively work, wasn't it?'

Alexa shrugged, reverting to her slumped position on the barrier as the commotion on the rink died down. Her thoughts flitted back to the last formal dinner she had attended with Matt. At the time, it had seemed a little like a chore, but . . . . She pictured him, standing at the top of the steps in his perfectly fitting suit. He had looked so adorable. It hadn't been a chore at all. And even if it had been, at least it was a chore of finite commitment. Her involvement with *Banter* must have seemed to Matt like a never-ending, all-consuming cloud hanging between them. How often had she found herself thinking about branding or app regulations in the middle of dinner?

'I'm just sorry I got you together in the first place,' Kate went on, shaking her head. 'I thought he was a decent guy, but clearly . . .' Alexa was barely listening. She was thinking about all the times she had forced Matt to sit through her selfish ramblings when they could have been talking about, well, anything. Anything would have been better than another conversation about her wretched work.

She wondered what Matt was doing right now. Probably watching the game, she thought, possibly with Dickie or more likely with his uni mates, in town. Alexa tortured herself by imagining him sitting at a table in the pub, beer in one hand, a pretty blonde girl on his knee. The girls would flock to him now that he was single again. Maybe he had a new girlfriend already. Maybe they were – no. Alexa forced herself to stop. She had deleted his number and email address from her phone and removed him from her list of Facebook friends, just in case she was tempted to check. Matt had made his feelings clear; it was over.

'I guess I should've known better,' sighed Kate, 'him being a lawyer. Law is so outdated. He obviously didn't get the fact that these days, women have careers too.'

Eventually, Alexa lifted her head.

'Look,' she said. 'I appreciate what you're trying to do, but please don't bother.'

Kate drew her head back, frowning. She looked genuinely perplexed.

'It's very sweet of you to try and pin the blame on Matt,' Alexa explained, 'but we all know this wasn't his fault.'

'What?' Kate looked agitated. 'That's not—'

'*Kate . . .*' Leonie looked at her meaningfully. 'Leave it.'

Alexa flashed her a look of appreciation, but Leonie was staring out at the ice rink. Alexa tried to do the same, but her eyes wouldn't focus. They were filling with tears again. It wasn't just Matt, this time; it was Leonie.

She hadn't expected to see her here today. They hadn't spoken since their brief phone call nearly a month ago, when Alexa had ignored Leonie's offer of support during the first wave of bad press. Alexa wondered how much persuasion it had taken on Kate's part to get her along today. She seemed amicable, if a little quiet, but there was a distance between them that she had never sensed before.

Alexa stepped back from the barrier, feeling suddenly cold. She crossed her arms, tucking her fists up behind them and looking around aimlessly. There was too much going on in her head for her to be able to think straight.

Leonie glanced sideways, not meeting her eye.

'Shall we get a hot drink?' She waved a gloved hand in the direction of the house.

Mutely, Alexa followed her friends into the warm, steamy fug of the café. The bright colours and polka-dots on the walls did nothing to improve her mood. She sank into a plastic moulded chair and stared blankly at the tablecloth while Kate and Leonie queued for the drinks. Her hand went instinctively to her pocket and she found herself extracting her mobile phone and navigating to the text message that had arrived that morning.

Hey Lex. Just
checking U R
OK. M

'M'. That was all. Every text message she had received from Matt until now had been signed 'Mx'. It was as though he was officially making the distinction. 'Mx' was for a time when kisses had been a part of their relationship – albeit brief, hurried kisses towards the end, due to Alexa's wretched work – and now kisses were officially not required.

She looked up to see how the others were doing and, noting that there were still four people ahead of the girls in the queue, pressed Reply.

There was only really one way of responding to such a text. *Fine thanks. A.* Or words to that effect. There was no warmth in the question, so there was no point in adding any to the response. But the problem was, Alexa didn't *want* to be all curt and formal. She didn't *want* to be no longer going out with Matt. If she'd had things her way, then there would still be kisses at the end of every message – there would be proper, long kisses at the start and end of every encounter. But that was just it. *She* had been responsible for the dwindling affection between them. She had taken him for granted, prioritising her work over their relationship, knowing he'd always be there tomorrow.

Fine thanks. Missing U.
Lx

It was too sentimental, she knew that, but Alexa felt as though she had nothing to lose. It wasn't that she expected a sentimental response in return – although that was what she secretly wanted. It just seemed as though nothing really mattered, so there was no harm in letting Matt know how she really felt. Besides, it would serve as a test. If there was a tiny hint of a chance that he might regret walking out on her, then here was his chance to say so. She didn't hold out much hope.

'We got marshmallows!' announced Kate, reappearing with two giant mugs overflowing with frothy toppings.

Alexa quickly tucked her phone away, lifting the giant cup and taking a sip. At least it was sugar; she'd barely eaten in days.

'You'll find someone else in no time,' Kate declared, with a firm smile.

Alexa noticed Leonie's head quickly disappear into her cup. Leonie understood. However much she disapproved of the other parts of Alexa's life, she understood the problem. Alexa didn't want to find someone else; she wanted Matt. Unlike Kate, Alexa didn't have an issue with being single. She didn't see relationships in terms of conquests or projects. She just wanted to feel loved again, the way she had felt with Matt. That was the worst part: she hadn't even seen it coming. If only she'd realised the damage she was doing to the relationship – if she had only *noticed* the lack of hugging and kissing – she might have been able to reverse the change.

'There must be hundreds of eligible men at your work?' Kate pushed her face into Alexa's field of vision.

Alexa sighed. Even if there had been hundreds of eligible men, she couldn't think of anything more likely to end her career than starting a relationship with one of them. Mixing business with sex was career suicide – especially at a place like *Banter*.

'I don't want to think about my work,' she said, shuddering as the weight of all her problems came down on her again. Matt, Leonie, Georgie and her feminist campaigners, her parents . . . . It suddenly felt as though everybody was against her. There were probably people in this café who would turn their backs in disgust if they knew what she was doing for a living. She had alienated herself. And for what? A set of revenue targets. A nine-month contract. It was pathetic.

'Oh, shit. Sorry.' Kate grimaced. 'I forgot.'

Alexa closed her eyes and sank down in the uncomfortable plastic chair. Kate was presumably referring to the protests, which, thankfully, had received minimal coverage in the press – just a couple of posts on some feminist blogs and a small article in a north London paper. The app was continuing to do well and Peterson saw the opposition campaigns as nothing to worry about. But despite the lack of support for the protesters' cause, she couldn't help feeling anxious. Alongside the painful ache inside her was a seed of anxiety that grew every time someone mentioned *Banter*. Perhaps Georgie had caught her at a vulnerable time, or perhaps it was to do with her parents, but the protests had had more of an impact on her than she had anticipated.

The booklet lay on the hall floor, next to the door, the image of the ravaged, bleeding face staring up at her every time she entered or left the flat. Every time she passed a woman in a headscarf, she thought of Lisa. Every couple she saw, kissing or cuddling on the tube, made her wonder whether the man was a violent alpha-male in the bedroom, forcing his partner to comply against her will. She looked at advertisements differently, noticing sexual innuendos where before she might have seen frivolous slogans. The mere sight of a child made her feel guilty.

She opened her eyes and looked at Leonie.

'How's that girl?'

'What girl?'

'The one who came to see you about the . . . her boyfriend. You know.'

Leonie took a second to work out what Alexa meant.

'Well, she hasn't been back, so I guess that's good news.'

Alexa nodded uncertainly. She knew it seemed odd to Leonie that she cared about a girl she didn't know and was unlikely to ever meet, but for some reason she felt protective towards the fourteen-year-old. She wanted to know that the girl had stood up to her boyfriend and explained that she wasn't ready to have sex. Maybe it was guilt, Alexa conceded unhappily. What she really wanted was for Leonie to tell her that everything was fine, that the incident had been a one-off, that it was nothing to do with the sexualisation of media or the content of her magazine.

Alexa tilted her mug, stirring the remains of the marshmallows into the milky drink. Out of the corner of her eye, she could see Kate's frown, boring into the side of Leonie's head, clearly trying to work out what they were talking about, but Leonie maintained her silence.

Eventually, Alexa swallowed the last of the frothy dregs and set the mug down on the table. She looked sideways at Leonie and waited for her friend to turn round.

'Leonie?'

There was a hint of warmth in Leonie's expression as she looked up.

'Do you hate what I'm doing at *Banter*?'

Leonie looked at her for a moment, then gave a sad smile, shaking her head.

'What I think,' she said, softly, 'is that you should slow down a bit. Decide what you really believe in, then aim for that. Remember that project we did for Mr Dibben when we were twelve?'

Alexa nodded, perplexed by the reference to their Year 8 design project. She remembered it well; the task had been to build a vehicle that would transport all four members of the team around the school playing field in the quickest time possible. Their entry had been the first to make it to the start line, but it had fallen apart on the first bend, thanks to a fault with one of the wheels.

'D'you remember how we were given eight weeks to finish it, but you went ahead and built it in a fortnight? Then we spent the next six weeks trying to fix all the problems that we wouldn't have had if we'd planned it properly?'

Alexa cringed. She hadn't remembered it like that, but it was true. She had been so intent on getting the thing built, she hadn't stopped to think about what they really wanted to make. The wheel had fallen off because they hadn't had time to design proper bearings. That was exactly the mistake she had made with *Banter*.

'Slow down, Lex.' Leonie smiled tentatively. 'Take a bit of time to think about the consequences.'

21

'Check me out!'

It was nearly half-past ten. Derek swaggered nonchalantly to his desk, belched loudly and turned on the spot, clearly expecting some kind of reaction.

Reluctantly, Alexa looked up. She rarely enjoyed the deputy editor's attempts at humour and she suspected that this morning would be no different, but her curiosity was getting the better of her.

She saw all she needed to see and then looked away quickly, before Derek had time to make eye contact. The sight was not an attractive one. In addition to the usual hairy tuft on the editor's chin, this morning there were disfiguring patches of ginger stubble coating the entire bottom half of Derek's face.

'You like it?' he asked, leaning over in Alexa's direction. She pretended not to notice. 'Wanna touch it?' he asked, loudly. 'It's grow-a-tash month. For charity. Come on – have a feel.'

Alexa sighed. Usually, she would have made some kind of derogatory remark, perhaps advising him that the ginger tufts on his face did not constitute a moustache, but today she had other things on her mind.

Obligingly, Sienna leapt up from her desk and pressed her palm against Derek's patchy stubble.

'Is your girlfriend into facial hair?' She raised an eyebrow.

'My *girlfriend* . . .' Derek looked around to check that people were listening. 'Is gonna *love it!* I'm meeting her tonight, as it happens.'

Alexa stayed vaguely tuned in, on the off chance that Derek gave away any useful information that might impact her revenge act, but her thoughts were elsewhere. Specifically, they were five floors down, where the remnants of the latest protest were still smeared all over the glass-walled atrium.

Nobody else seemed to care. There had been a brief flurry of excitement among those who had made it into the office in time to see the half-scraped remains, but in the absence of their leader, who, thankfully, had arrived too late to see anything more than a team of window cleaners at work, it had soon blown over. To them, it was just another pathetic campaign by a bunch of bra-burning feminists. Alexa wondered whether she'd feel equally blasé had the campaign carried a different slogan or been fronted by a different image. She couldn't tell. All she could think about was that picture on all the posters and that bright green caption: *DO YOU FEEL LIBERATED NOW?*

Yet again, her mugshot had been used against her. This time, though, the product was not meant for her eyes only. It was meant for the whole world to see. Her face, superimposed onto the body of a naked, squatting glamour model, had been pasted all over the walls and windows of Senate House.

The posters had appeared in the dead of night, when the night porter was doing his rounds of the building. The full extent of the vandalism had only been realised at eight o'clock, when the morning receptionists had arrived for work. A maintenance team had been called in, but it transpired that the campaigners had used some sort of wallpaper glue that didn't easily come off. When Alexa had arrived, there were still half-stripped remains of posters and streaks of paint all over the windows.

It was illegal, of course. 'Criminal damage' was the term the police had used, but presumably the protesters didn't care. They had taken care to cover their tracks so that nobody could know who was to blame. Alexa knew who was to blame. She had sat face-to-face with the ringleader, under the hot, bright lights of the BBC studio. She had slammed a door against the girl's shoe and begged her to leave her flat. Clearly trespassing wasn't any more of a crime in Georgie Caraway's eyes than vandalism.

Alexa's screensaver kicked in. She jiggled the mouse and continued to stare at the desktop background. The worst was yet to come. The protesters would have taken photos – hundreds of them, probably, at dawn this morning, while the night porter snoozed – and soon enough, those photos would find their way into the pages of newspapers and magazines across the country. The press hadn't shown much interest in the previous campaign, but that was because there was nothing original about it. This, though . . . Alexa shuddered. She had to hand it to Georgie Caraway's crusaders; using the face of *Banter*'s MD to front a campaign against the magazine was original. It was eye-catching and probably funny, too – if you weren't the subject of the joke. Alexa grimaced. The press would lap it up.

Eventually, Sienna finished stroking the deputy editor's face and tottered over to the printer in her patent, thigh-high boots. She was perpetually chirpy these days – not just because of the excessive attention lavished upon her by the all-male editorial team but because now, thanks to Alexa's intervention, she was the voice of Banter TV, as well as writing a good proportion of the content for the magazine.

'Who are we sending for the fitness challenge against *Monsieur*?' she asked, shimmying up to the nearest desk, which happened to be Louis'.

Louis raised an eyebrow as though there was something going on between them, which Alexa supposed there might have been. She was too preoccupied to care either way. *Monsieur* was another one of Senate's men's titles. It considered itself a cut above *Banter*, due to its supposedly up-market readership, but for some time now, Peterson had been encouraging the two magazines to cross-promote.

'Fitness?' Louis leaned forward in his seat and looked the assistant up and down. 'Is that anything to do with birds being fit?'

'It's to do with *you* being fit,' she replied, flirtatiously.

Biscuit wandered up and took a look at the print-out in Sienna's hand. 'Ah.' He started to chuckle, then took the page and wandered over to the features desk, where Paddy was handing out coffees. 'Listen up,' he said loudly. 'I think we have a project for you.'

Before long, the office was filled with the familiar sound of Paddy-baiting. Alexa continued to stare at her screen, vaguely relieved by the knowledge that the posters downstairs were now officially considered old news and that attention had drifted to the next victim. She didn't like the way Paddy got treated in the office, but then, it didn't seem to bother him. He got his fill of semi-naked models each week, so presumably that was enough of an upside to compensate for the perpetual bullying. Besides, right now it felt to Alexa as though she had too many problems of her own to start thinking about other people's.

Alexa jumped. She could hear breathing very close to her ear. She whipped round to find Sienna standing next to her, quietly observing her inactivity.

'Don't worry,' she said, bending down so that her mouth was against Alexa's ear. 'At least they chose a bird with a hot body, eh?'

Alexa's heart was pounding, but she managed a half-smile. She was grateful for Sienna's perceptiveness, but also mildly perturbed. She had witnessed the *Banter* gossip machine in action and the last thing she wanted was for the whole team to know how badly the posters were affecting her.

'Just harmless fun, I guess.' Alexa forced a breezy smile. 'What can I do for you?'

Sienna held out a print-out that looked similar to the one she'd relinquished to Biscuit. 'It's for the fitness challenge. We thought, well, they thought . . .' She trailed off, looking embarrassed and stifling a phoney laugh.

Alexa was beginning to wonder what was going on when Derek leaned over, grinning.

'How 'bout it, eh?' He stroked the prickles on his face. 'You and Paddy, to make up Team Banter? It's only a 10K run and a bit of swimming and cycling. We thought you might look good in a bit of Lycra.'

Alexa handed the sheet back to Sienna, her eyes focused intently on Derek. This was yet another attempt to erode her self-esteem. She thought about accepting the challenge, just to spite him, but then thought about what it would entail and realised that the joke would be on her.

'How about,' she said, slowly and deliberately, 'you send someone who enjoys running and swimming and cycling, whose job it is to *write* about it in the magazine that you're supposed to be editing?'

They stared at one another for a couple of seconds and then Alexa swivelled back to her screen and swiftly opened a document – any document. She just picked one at random in an attempt to look busy.

She was still staring at the same document ten minutes later, pretending to work and thinking about the assistant editor. Sienna wasn't a cruel person. She was irritating and conniving and she knew how to get her own way with the boys, but she wasn't one of them. Alexa could tell from the look of shame that had crossed her face as she had chickened out of the joke. It was the same look that Alexa had seen the previous week, when she'd admitted to Paddy that Marcus was trying to trick him into going to the strip club. Sienna wasn't afraid to use people, but she didn't like to hurt them either – at least, that was how it seemed to Alexa. She looked down and realised that her phone was ringing.

'Alexa Harris.'

'Hey,' sang a bright, female voice. 'I heard there was a bit of a commotion over at your building this morning?'

Alexa felt a flutter of nerves inside her. It was Georgie.

'That was a cool strapline, don't you think? I guess it would feel pretty liberating, seeing your naked body splashed all over the place like that.'

Alexa was starting to tremble with a mixture of rage and fear. She could picture the girl's face, her irritating smile shining out from the dark mass of curls. She couldn't believe Georgie had the audacity to call and discuss her crime while the police were still following up leads. It was practically an admission of guilt. And *why*? Alexa wondered. Why was Georgie calling her like this?

'I'm busy,' Alexa said quietly. She didn't want anyone else to hear – didn't want anyone recognising the vulnerability in her voice. In her mind, she wanted to pull the phone from her ear and end the call, but at the same time, she couldn't help feeling a little intrigued by what the girl had to say.

'Busy brainstorming ideas for how you might make even *more* money from turning women into objects?'

Alexa tried again to put the phone down, but Georgie's voice streamed down the line, strong and fluent. It had been a big mistake to give the girl her card.

'. . . the one I read in last week's issue. Apparently, most women fantasise about rape. Is that true, Alexa? Because over a hundred thousand women are raped in this country every year – that's one for every three of your readers. Do you think they fantasise about rape? Do you?'

Alexa could hear the blood in her ears. She wanted to scream at the girl, but she couldn't. It was like one of those hideous nightmares in which nobody could hear your cries of distress. She couldn't let her colleagues know what Georgie was doing to her, just as she couldn't let Georgie know what her colleagues were doing to her. That was the worst part. What would Georgie say, Alexa wondered, if she realised that only weeks earlier, members of her own team had defaced the very same image that she had used for the posters, but for an even more offensive and harmful purpose? How would *she* feel, thought Alexa angrily, if she became the victim of bullying from both outside *and* inside her own team? Because that was what it was. It was bullying.

Suddenly, the rage boiled over inside her.

'Listen,' she growled down the phone. 'Do you want me to call the police? Because I will. Even if you get away with the posters, you're breaking the law by harassing me like this.'

'No, please—'

Alexa wrenched the phone from her ear and slammed it into the cradle, the echo of Georgie's protest still haunting her, the image of her guileless expression still imprinted on her brain from that morning at the BBC. She tried to focus on her work, but flashbacks from the last few weeks started racing through her mind: the on-air discussion with Georgie, her mother's phone call, the series of one-way conversations with Matt, Leonie's warning, the hideous posters downstairs. The campaigner's call seemed to have stirred it all up in her head.

Realising just in time that the tears were about to spill out, Alexa swiped her bag from under the desk and rushed out, her jaw trembling and her vision starting to blur. She made it to the ladies' just as the tears began to gush down her cheeks, but as she opened the door, she heard a toilet flush and saw that the cubicles were all occupied. The idea of some unknown female employee offering to help – or worse, Sienna – was just too awful to contemplate. Alexa retreated quickly, heading for the stairwell and plunging blindly down five flights of stairs.

She stumbled across the atrium, head down, avoiding the raft of ladders and cleaning equipment being used to remove the last few posters. She pushed on the heavy glass door and threw herself across the road, into a café she'd never even noticed before.

Scanning quickly for colleagues, she ordered a coffee and hid herself away at the table behind the counter, feeling the tears choke her throat as her chest went into spasms. She pulled a tissue out of her bag and pressed it against her face, waiting for the shuddering and crying to stop.

It was ridiculous, this feeling of insecurity. Alexa knew that, but it didn't stop the tears from flowing. Perhaps it was just the shock of seeing her face on the walls like that – or the fear of not knowing what was to come. She couldn't pretend that she wasn't bothered about the attention that this latest protest was likely to attract. There was no telling what impact it would have – on the brand, on the industry or on Alexa.

She couldn't help thinking, again, about what her mother would say if she caught sight of those posters. No mother would enjoy seeing her daughter in that position, strung up from a building like that. But *Alexa's* mother, of all people . . . she cringed, feeling helpless and ashamed and filled with regret. She wished she could turn back the clock and undo some of the things she had done, but she knew, from years of aggressive schooling, that this was no way to look at the problem. The way forward, according to her mother, was to tackle the problem head-on. But that involved confrontation. At this point in time, Alexa couldn't even contemplate such a thing, let alone act. She pulled out her phone, suddenly desperate for reassurance.

'Kate? It's me.'

'*Hey,*' Kate replied in a whisper. There was a rustling noise at the other end, then a clip-clop of shoes. Alexa pictured her friend strutting purposefully through the glass-walled offices of TDS towards the lobby and wondered whether Kate ever lost her nerve like this.

'Is that you, Lex?' Kate said, reverting to normal volume. 'You sound weird.'

'Sorry for calling you at work.' Alexa sniffed, making a fresh effort to compose herself.

'No, no worries.' Kate's voice softened a little. 'You know what it's like . . . millions of urgent projects, but nothing really urgent. What's up?'

Alexa sighed. 'Everything.'

'Well, maybe you can filter it down a bit.' Kate laughed softly.

Alexa felt suddenly overcome with relief at the thought of sharing her problems.

'The protesters came back.'

'Oh yeah? What did they do this time? Set fire to copies of *Banter* along with their bras?'

'If only,' replied Alexa, appreciating her friend's dismissive tone. She told Kate about the posters and the slogan and the call from Georgie and the inevitable press that would follow. 'The nationals are gonna have a field day.'

Kate groaned. 'Bloody feminists. You're right – I'm sure the press will love it. Still, it might be a good form of subliminal marketing for *Banter*, eh?'

Alexa felt something lift inside her. Even though Kate was confirming her worst fear – that the poster campaign would soon make national headlines – at least she was making light of the situation, putting it in perspective. There were worse things that could have happened than a bunch of feminist crusaders vandalising the Senate HQ.

'You know what this is about,' said Kate, suddenly sounding angry. 'It's about you being a woman. It makes me so cross, all this *equality* crap that they rave about. If the campaigners had just thought for a second about what they were doing to you today, then they'd realise that *they* were the ones being sexist – not you.'

'Sorry?' Alexa liked her friend's conclusion, but she had no idea how it had come about.

'If you'd been a male MD, they wouldn't have had such a problem, I bet. They *definitely* wouldn't have used your face on their stupid campaign. It's because you're a woman that they're so bloody aggrieved – a woman who's bold enough to do a man's job. They want equality, but when it happens, they kick up a stink because you've abandoned the sisterhood. It's so ironic it's untrue!'

Alexa was beginning to see Kate's point. Perhaps it was true that she wouldn't have suffered such persecution, had she been born a man.

'It was the same with Margaret Thatcher,' Kate went on in the same, steely tone. 'If she'd been *Mr* Thatcher, she would have been deemed a strong, masterful leader. A decisive visionary. But as a woman, she was seen as bossy and conniving and mean.'

Kate continued to make points to back up her theory, but Alexa was only half-listening. Her friend's words had triggered a new train of thought. *Equality*. Up until now, she hadn't really considered inequality an issue. Feminism had done its job in the seventies and eighties; women had equal rights, equal status and equal pay – at least, in theory they did. In practice, they earned twenty percent less than their male counterparts, but in Alexa's mind, that was largely because women weren't actively exerting their rights. Any woman who complained about the status quo was just giving women a bad name. That was one of the reasons she had gone for the job at *Banter*. She had wanted to prove to the old-fashioned types like David Winterbottom that men and women could now be equal. They had equality.

Alexa pushed away her untouched coffee, tuning into Kate's words, then out again. But they *didn't* have equality. She knew that because she saw it, every day in the office. The laws may have dictated that she had equal rights, status and pay, but none of those things were happening. And besides, nobody ever talked about equal respect. She knew for sure that the attitude of certain colleagues towards her would be different, had one of her X chromosomes been a Y chromosome.

'Just because you're daring to reverse the pattern,' Kate's tirade went on, 'putting a woman at the top . . .'

The pattern. Alexa thought for a second. Kate was right. In the workplace and in her industry in particular, there was a pattern. Men sat at the top of the food chain – male directors, male editors, male photographers, male writers – and women sat (or lay) at the bottom – taking their clothes off for little or no money. Alexa stopped her thoughts in their tracks, not liking where they were going.

'. . . so you have *no* reason to feel guilty,' Kate declared. 'They asked for equality and that's what they got. You can tell Georgie that from me, next time she calls.'

Alexa wiped her free hand across one cheek, then the other. The tears had dried, leaving her skin feeling salty and tight. She thanked Kate for her words of reassurance and promised to call again soon for a proper catch-up. She wasn't entirely sure whether Kate's words had reassured her or not, but she no longer felt shaken or tense. The poster campaign seemed like less of a big deal, but now there were other issues, issues that had been lurking at the back of her mind for a while, beginning to surface.

Alexa leaned sideways and checked her reflection in the shiny brass counter. Her eyes looked a little sore, but her complexion was restored to its usual colour and she was surprised to note that the fringe was behaving itself on her forehead for once. She gave her reflection a tentative smile and rose from the seat, bracing herself for a return to the fifth floor. Kate was right about one thing: she had no reason to feel guilty. She was just doing her job. It may have been a job usually reserved for men, but she had secured it and she was going to see it through – posters or no posters.

She was still grappling with the multitude of arguments spawned by Kate's words when she exited the lift on the fifth floor. She was so deep in thought as she hurried into the kitchen that she nearly slammed straight into the jeans-clad backside that was blocking the doorway. Riz was bent over with his back to her, dropping teabags into the miniscule pedal bin.

'Oh! Sorry.' Alexa withdrew, watching as he picked the stray teabag off the floor and straightened up to his full height.

He smiled and nodded at the tray of mugs. 'Want a tea?'

Alexa was about to accept the offer when she caught sight of something in the corner, behind the bin. It was crumpled, but she recognised it immediately from the fleshy tones and the bright green font. It was one of the posters from the atrium. She could feel her confidence crumble as she stood there, eyeing its lurid tones. Why was it here, in the kitchen? How had it travelled up five floors? Had one of the lads saved it to show Derek? Or had one of the campaigners somehow got into the building?

Riz followed her gaze and in one swift movement, reached down, scrunched the poster into a ball, deposited it in the bin and turned to face her. 'I was thinking we could use it as next week's front cover,' he said, taking one of the mugs from the tray and offering it out for her to take.

'Thanks,' she said, referring more to the joke than the tea. It felt good to know that someone was laughing with her – not just laughing at her.

Riz shrugged, leaning down to pick up the tray of mugs. 'Don't let it get to you. You shouldn't feel responsible. It's like you said on TV. *Banter* reflects what society wants; it doesn't drive it.'

Alexa nodded, watching him carry the tray back to his desk. He was right. Kate was right. She was only doing her job and that job was a perfectly harmless one. Taking a deep breath, Alexa pushed herself off from the counter and walked purposefully back to the office. She had targets to meet and she wasn't going to let a bunch of feminists stand in her way.

22

Alexa rubbed her eyes and blinked at the images, taking another sip of lukewarm coffee. It was no good. The iPad wireframes were blurring into one on the screen and the annotations had lost their meaning. She knew, deep down, that she ought to go home and come in early the next day to finish the job, but it wasn't in her nature to give up and besides, it was her own fault she was still here; if she'd just focused properly during working hours, she would have been away by six.

She had tried all day to focus, but it had proved impossible with that stack of newspapers on the desk beside her – each bearing gleeful headlines and garish photos of the latest anti-*Banter* campaign. Alexa could still taste bile in her throat from the moment she'd opened the papers that morning and again, whenever her gaze had drifted sideways or Derek had made one of his needling 'jokes'. In the end, she had shoved the newspapers into a bag and stashed them under the desk, but that hadn't stopped her thoughts drifting. Nor had it prevented her imagination from conjuring up scenes: her mother opening the newspaper, her father reeling backwards in horror, old acquaintances laughing and showing their friends, strangers seeing only one side of the story and taking offence at her magazine.

She loathed Georgie Caraway. The initial protest had riled her, as had the TV debate, but this was *personal*. Alexa would rather have gone through a hundred live television appearances than have her friends and family see her like this, spread naked across the pages of every tabloid. It was below the belt. Of course, Georgie would claim that Alexa was being treated in exactly the way that her magazine treated its models. That would be her argument. But that wasn't true. Those models *wanted* to have their bodies revered by the nation. Alexa didn't. It was about choice. Surely, the members of REACT understood the concept of consent?

Alexa's gaze slipped away from the screen. She found herself wondering whether Matt had seen the press and if so, what he thought. She had had no reply to her text message, leading Alexa to the reluctant conclusion that is really was over, for good. Matt wasn't the type to keep in touch with ex-girlfriends. His message to her had obviously been a form of courtesy call to check that the note on the oven door had done its job. Alexa closed her tired eyes, picturing his reaction to the hideous pictures all over the newspapers. Would he feel angry on her behalf? Or would he feel in some way vindicated by the know-ledge that her corrosive career was starting to eat away at itself?

She opened her eyes. Her phone was ringing in her bag. She reached down and drew it out, her eyes almost too tired to read the display. She squinted, feeling a lurch of apprehension. Leonie could only be calling about one thing – the same thing that everybody else had called about and the same thing that had occupied her mind for most of the day. Alexa considered leaving the call to ring out, as she had done for the others, but something inside her wouldn't allow it. Leonie was her best friend. She didn't approve of what Alexa was doing, but she hadn't turned her back on her either – which was more than could be said for her mother.

'Hey.'

'Hi, Lex. How's things?' Leonie's voice sounded stilted, Alexa thought, but it might have been the line. There was a lot of background noise. 'I saw the thing . . . in the paper . . .' There was a high-pitched bleeping sound as though Leonie was passing through store security. 'You okay?'

'I'm fine,' Alexa lied. 'It's not as bad as it could have been.'

Leonie hesitated. 'Are you . . . still at work?'

'Unfortunately.'

'I'm in town,' said Leonie. There was definitely something different about her tone, Alexa decided. It was as though she didn't know how to talk to her. Alexa wondered whether the press had anything to do with it. 'Wanna come shopping?'

Alexa checked the time and frowned. 'Now?'

'Late-night shopping,' Leonie explained. 'Most of them are open 'til ten. I'm trying to find my goddaughter a birthday present – think I might have to resort to Oxford Street.'

Alexa shuddered at the thought of the over-crowded children's stores nearby. She looked at the wireframes on the screen, thinking again of the stash of bad press in the bag next to her feet and feeling a fresh wave of resentment towards the protesters. Now, more than ever, she had to try and hit those April targets. She couldn't let Georgie's lot win after such public humiliation. But at the same time, she couldn't turn Leonie down. As it was, she felt bad enough for not being a better friend.

'Sounds great,' she said, with a smile. 'Mothercare at eight?'

Alexa shut down her computer and shrugged on her coat, taking the bag of newspapers with her as she left. She wasn't exactly sure what she intended to do with the stash, but she knew that concentration would be impossible for all the time it sat there, under the desk. Upon reaching the fifth-floor lobby, Alexa stopped. She lifted the lid of the recycling bin and ceremoniously tipped the contents of the bag inside.

As she stepped out of the lift downstairs, Alexa felt unusually light, as though a huge load had been lifted from her shoulders. She waved to the security guard and skipped down the steps, pushing away the morose thoughts that had plagued her all day. Maybe Kate was right. Perhaps all publicity was good publicity and perhaps the bad press would actually benefit the magazine.

Alexa jumped as someone leapt out of the darkness onto the pavement in front of her.

Her heart fluttered with a surge of adrenaline. She stepped sideways, out of the stranger's way, feeling her grip tighten on her handbag. Then she realised who it was.

'You're working late.'

Alexa's panic quickly turned to rage as she took in the dark, curly hair. She pushed past, quickening her pace and looking straight ahead. What was wrong with this girl? First she followed Alexa across London to her home, then she plastered her office in offensive material and *phoned to talk about it* and now she was lurking in the darkness, jumping out from behind trees.

'Got lots on, have you?' Georgie called, trotting to keep up with Alexa.

Alexa could taste it again in her mouth: the bitter, salty taste of bile. This was harassment. It was a form of stalking. She was within her rights to call the police.

'Go away,' she said, upping her pace another notch so that Georgie was running to keep up.

'Hold on,' Georgie cried breathlessly. 'I can explain . . .'

'Save it for the police,' said Alexa, pulling out her mobile phone.

'No!' Georgie was panting now as she trotted along beside her. 'No – listen. I know it seems weird, me following you around like this.'

Alexa crossed a side street, looking right but not left, so she didn't have to meet Georgie's eye. A motorcyclist honked his horn as she strode out in front of him, missing his handlebars by only millimetres.

'It's just . . . well, look.' She caught up with Alexa and looked her in the eye. Alexa kept walking. 'I've been with REACT since the beginning. For seven years, we've been . . .' She was panting

204

with the exertion of walking and talking. 'We've been doing the same things: leaflets, sit-ins, lobbying MPs, petitions . . . every single form of protest you're allowed to do in this country. But nobody takes any notice. They just think we'll eventually go away.'

Alexa wished *Georgie* would go away. They were nearly at Mothercare. She had to think of a way to shake off her tail before Leonie arrived.

'But that's just it,' said Georgie, scuttling along beside her. 'We've had enough of playing by the rules. It doesn't work. That's why we're hounding you. We want—'

'*Hounding?*' Alexa rounded on her. She wanted to hurl something. She wanted to pin the girl against a wall and tell her how she had felt, opening those newspapers this morning. 'So you admit that you're *hounding* me, do you?'

'Look, we want to . . .'

Georgie trailed off, distracted by something over Alexa's left shoulder. Alexa followed her gaze and realised that Leonie was waving at her from inside the store. She closed her eyes for a second, wondering whether she had time to lose her stalker in the late-night shoppers, but Leonie was already shouting her name. It was too late.

'Hey,' Alexa reached out and hugged her friend, prolonging the embrace while she tried to think of a way to explain. '*Listen*,' she hissed, as they drew apart. '*This*—'

'I'm Georgie,' said the girl, swiftly inserting her hand between them.

Leonie glanced sideways at Alexa as though she sensed there was something peculiar going on. Being Leonie, though, she shook hands politely and returned Georgie's eager smile.

'Georgie's one of the campaigners that illegally put the posters all over our building,' Alexa said quickly. 'You probably read about it in the paper this morning.'

Leonie opened her mouth and then shut it again, looking

confused. Alexa felt a sudden lurch in her gut. The idea crossed her mind that Leonie might actually *like* the campaigner. It was quite possible that they would get on well, on the basis that Leonie saw things from the school children's perspective – it was possible that she disapproved of the app and the magazine almost as much as Georgie did.

'I wasn't involved in the posters,' said Georgie, rolling her eyes as though Alexa was mistaken.

'Then how do you—'

'The posters were there, so we drew attention to the matter in the press,' Georgie explained.

Alexa was about to retaliate but then suddenly turned her back on the girl, surveying the store. 'So! What shall we buy your goddaughter?'

Leonie faltered for a moment and then followed Alexa inside, clearly bewildered but too tactful to ask what was going on. Georgie stayed with them, but thankfully she remained quiet. Alexa turned to the nearest rack of clothes, fingering the fabric of a miniature duffle coat while pressing her shoulder up against Leonie's, sealing them off from Georgie.

'How old is she?'

'She'll be turning three,' Leonie replied, awkwardly.

Alexa nodded, moving on to the next rack. They had to lose the girl. *She* had to lose the girl.

'Are we thinking dresses, or something a bit more practical?' She held up a long-sleeved pullover covered in pink butterflies and bearing the slogan, *MUMMY'S LITTLE ANGEL*. 'It's all a bit pink, isn't it?'

'I guess . . .' Leonie looked at the top and quickly moved on. 'Practical, probably.'

'You won't find that in the girls' section,' said a voice from behind them.

Alexa stared straight ahead but Leonie's head instinctively whipped round.

'That's the problem,' declared Georgie, clearly pleased to have caught Leonie's eye. 'We're conditioned as soon as we're born, according to gender stereotypes. Look around you. This half of the shop is all about being a beautiful princess, while that half's all about being a big, strong adventurer.'

Alexa tried to turn Leonie's attention back to the matter in hand by holding up a white cotton T-shirt, but Georgie was clearly on a roll and Leonie was either too polite or too rapt in what she was saying to look away.

'There's no difference between boys and girls in terms of what they're good at or how they behave,' said Georgie. 'Not when they're born, anyway. It's just how we condition them that's different.' She picked up a fuschia party dress and slammed it dramatically back on the rail. Alexa looked away, pretending not to be listening. 'Girls are praised for looking pretty, while boys are praised for achieving and winning.'

Out of the corner of her eye, Alexa saw Leonie's head swivel from the cotton T-shirt back to the party dress, then back to the T-shirt. Alexa felt a plummeting sensation. It was irrational, she knew, but she was scared that Leonie would bond with the feminist campaigner.

As it happened, Alexa agreed with some of what Georgie was saying. The difference between the frilly clothes on one side of the shop and the hard-wearing outfits across the aisle was stark; it was no wonder girls grew up wanting to be glamour models and the boardrooms were filled with men. But being preached to by the person who had humiliated her in front of the nation was not why Alexa had come here tonight. She also took umbrage at the fact that Georgie seemed to be directing her points at *her*, as though somehow the whole childhood conditioning thing was her fault.

'What about this?' she asked, picking out the one neutral-coloured set of tops on display. Next to the tops were some bog-standard children's jeans.

Leonie seemed taken by the choice – or possibly just grateful to have something to distract from the feminist tirade in their wake. They picked out the appropriate sizes and took the outfit to the checkout.

While paying, using a combination of sign language and whispers, Alexa and Leonie agreed to go for a drink, on the understanding that they could first shrug off their shadow.

Alexa turned to Georgie as they left the shop. The venom rose up inside her as she registered the girl's breezy smile.

'Can you leave us alone now?' she asked, brusquely.

Georgie grinned back. Perhaps she was used to rejection, thought Alexa. The campaigners had been thrown out of nearly every supermarket in London in a failed attempt to get retailers to stop selling lads' mags.

'Sure,' she said, brightly. 'I didn't plan on hanging around. I just wanted to have a quick chat.'

Alexa sighed. The last thing she wanted was a 'chat', but if it meant Georgie would leave them alone, she would humour the girl.

They hovered in the shop doorway. It looked ominously as though Georgie was about to begin another speech.

'This is what I've been trying to tell you,' she said, looking at Alexa. 'We're not stupid. We know it's not going to be easy, trying to put the genie back in the bottle. Lads' mags are out there now and society is littered with images of sex. It'll take something bigger than a poster campaign to reverse the change.'

Alexa met her gaze, reluctantly finding herself drawn in by the girl's words.

'We also realise that if we bring down one magazine, then another will spring up in its place, or some other form of media – like your obscene app, for example.'

Alexa said nothing.

'Like I said, we've tried all the legal protest options, but they haven't worked. So what we need is an insider. Someone who will bring them all down as an industry. Someone who knows how it all works, who—'

'Someone who isn't me,' Alexa cut in. She was beginning to understand what Georgie was getting at and she didn't like where it was going. She had a career to think about. She wasn't about to risk everything for a bunch of feminists with an axe to grind.

'Just think about it.'

Alexa sighed, glancing up at the unlit Christmas lights above them. Then she looked back at Georgie. 'I thought about it. And I still say no. Goodnight, Georgie.'

Quickly, before the girl could come up with another argument, Alexa caught Leonie's eye and led them across Oxford Street ahead of an oncoming bus, putting a wall of traffic between them and the campaigner. They weaved through the Christmas shoppers and disappeared down a narrow Soho street.

'Jesus!' Alexa gasped as they hurried into the first pub they came to. 'Sorry about that.'

Leonie glanced over her shoulder, catching her breath. On seeing that they were finally alone, she smiled. 'It was quite interesting, actually. I've never met anyone quite so determined. It's uncanny. She gives *you* a run for your money.'

Alexa shot her a warning look as they weaved their way to the bar. Inside, the relief was washing over her. Leonie hadn't bonded with Georgie. She must have been feeling paranoid.

They took their drinks and retreated to a table in the corner of the pub. Neither said anything, but Alexa suspected they had subconsciously opted for the darkest spot in case Georgie came looking for them.

'You're shaking,' Leonie pointed out.

Alexa looked down as she took her first sip of wine. Her glass was trembling in her hand.

'I'm stressed. She followed me from my office, for God's sake. She's a maniac.'

Alexa took some deep breaths and sank back in the worn,

high-backed leather seat. 'I just . . .' She wanted to explain the problem, but it was hard to articulate. 'I know what they're saying and it makes sense . . . some of it. But I don't see why they think stamping out lads' mags is going to solve the world's problems. Lads' mags aren't the evil thing everyone thinks they are. They just *reflect* what people want. If there weren't lads' mags, there'd be something else – she said so herself.' Alexa took another gulp of wine, feeling panicky again. 'And I don't see why they think it helps to victimise *me* in their campaigns. If they want to slate the brand, fine. They can complain all they like about *Banter* but why do they think they have the right to humiliate *me*, personally, in public like that?'

Leonie moved closer on the seat and laid a hand gently on her upper arm.

'They're doing it for attention, Lex. They tried slating the brand but nobody noticed. They went on TV and nobody noticed. You heard what she said just then. It's going to be a long battle and they want an insider on their team. That's why they're targeting you.'

Alexa shook her head helplessly. It was nice to be able to talk about it to someone, but she was beginning to realise that the more she talked, the more there was, bottled up inside her.

'They're not going to get me on their team by splashing me across the national press, looking like a porn star,' she said, baulking at the thought of the papers in the recycling bin.

Leonie looked as though she was about to reply, then sat back, taking a sip of her drink.

They sat quietly for a while. Alexa was running through the events of the last few hours, few days, trying to untangle all the arguments and straighten out her opinions. She thought back to the advice Leonie had given her the previous weekend. *Decide what you really believe in, then aim for that.* A few months ago, she had done exactly that. She believed in the value of *Banter* as an entertainment brand and she had set off with the aim of boosting it further. The question was, did she still believe? Or had Georgie and the likes of Derek changed her mind about what the magazine really stood for? *It's just an entertainment brand*, she told herself, testing the strength of her conviction.

'What?'

Alexa looked up. She realised she'd muttered it out loud.

'*Banter*,' she said, sheepishly. 'It's just an entertainment brand that offers young men what they want.'

'Is it?' Leonie asked the question openly, without sarcasm.

Alexa thought for a second, then replied.

'Yes,' she said firmly. While a lot had changed in the last few months, her fundamental opinion hadn't. *Banter* was an entertainment brand that did a good job of catering for today's generation of young men. She wasn't ashamed to represent it. 'It does contain nudity, but that's not its primary function. We cover sport and jokes and news and . . .' Alexa stopped, realising that semi-naked women did make up a large proportion of the coverage. But then, a lot of that content was interviews and commentary – like Sienna's editorial, for example. It was by no means the soft porn people made it out to be.

'What?' asked Alexa, seeing the look of scepticism on Leonie's face. 'You don't believe me, do you?'

She lifted her shoulders tentatively. 'I can't say, either way. I don't read it.'

'It's more than just tits and ass. It really is.' Alexa could hear the pleading in her voice, but she didn't care. She wanted Leonie to believe her.

'So show them that.'

Alexa frowned. 'Show who?'

'The campaigners. Show Georgie's clan that your magazine's not responsible for our society's ills. If you really believe it's not.'

There it was again. Leonie's last sentence was unnecessary. Alexa wanted to prove it, desperately – to the campaigners and now to Leonie, too, but she wasn't sure how.

'What d'you mean?'

'Do a nipple-free edition,' said Leonie, shrugging again. 'That way, if lads still buy it then you've proved that it's more than just tits and ass; it's an entertainment brand.'

Alexa swallowed a large slug of wine. *A nipple-free edition.* She could imagine how the editorial team would take that. Nipples were the talking point of most internal meetings. Could she really risk taking away what some saw as the lifeblood of the magazine?

She thought for a moment. It would be a bold statement. If it backfired, it could be an expensive one, too. But if it worked . . .

She started to smile. 'That sounds like a challenge, Leonie.'

23

Alexa spread out the pages across the meeting room table, eyeing each one critically as she went. The first few didn't look all that different from usual. The *Banter–Monsieur* fitness challenge was the leading feature, with a photo of Paddy and Riz squaring up to an equally unmatched pair from their sister title and a selection of bicep and six-pack shots – mostly of Riz – interspersed throughout the text. There was a one-pager on the cast of a new TV comedy show and a double page on a man who had made a full-scale model of an Aston Martin out of Edam cheese. It was only by page eight or nine that the content started to look a little different.

She continued to lay out the print-outs, comparing the features to those of the previous week, from memory. Some of the regulars had been adapted for the purpose, like Popping Out, the weekly collection of photos revealing female celebrities' nipples, which had been renamed Staying In and this week featuring the fully-clothed equivalents. In Bed With, which usually involved full nudity with strategically placed bedroom toys, this week revealed only the girl's face, sticking out from a thick double duvet and bearing a cheeky smile. Other features had been developed especially, with more emphasis on gaming, gadgets, sport and TV. Alexa felt they had a good mix.

She set down the final sheet, gave it a once-over and returned to the cover page, trying to visualise it on the shelf alongside

Diss and the other lads' mags. The headline image was of Jemima Wolf, the actress who had quit Hollywood to set up an Alzheimer's charity in the UK. She was wearing a long, white dress and brown winter boots that gave her a faraway, gypsy look. She was beautiful, and there wasn't a hint of cleavage. The surrounding images were breast-free, too: a teaser shot from the fitness challenge, a gaming screen-grab and some quotes from various interviews. Alexa smiled. It was tasteful. The colours and fonts still screamed *lads' mag* and of course, it still said 'Banter' in bold across the top, but the content was clean. It was making a point. And in fact, thought Alexa, picturing the cover next to the fleshy vulgarity of *Diss*, it had the potential to do quite well.

There was a knock on the door. Alexa looked round to find Riz leaning into the meeting room, looking at her with a hint of awkwardness.

He nodded towards the collage of papers on the table. 'Can I have a look?'

Alexa stepped aside as Riz surveyed the display. He looked pensive, bending over and studying the cover page carefully before scanning the others and then returning to the cover page. Alexa felt her chest tighten. There was something about Riz's expression that made her feel distinctly uneasy.

'I think . . .' He continued to stare at the cover page, then eventually looked at Alexa. 'I think maybe we should knock up a second cover option. You know, like when we have a blonde and a brunette version, to cater for all tastes.'

Alexa frowned. 'Who would we use for the blonde?'

'No, I mean . . .' Riz reached for the cover page, holding it up in the light. 'One clean version and one, well, *normal*.'

Alexa suddenly realised what he meant. He was worried about going to market with such a prudish front cover.

'Oh,' she said, feeling suddenly anxious. Riz had worked on the magazine for years. He knew the market. If he was voicing concerns about this edition, then it probably meant they had a problem. But on the other hand, if they didn't make their point about being more than just soft porn, then they might have an even more serious problem. Alexa knew better than anyone how important it was not to underestimate the power of the press. If the public took the feminists' side then they could well see the lads' mag market disappearing altogether.

'No,' she said, eventually. 'No, we have to keep it totally clean. That's the point. We have to make a statement – to prove that there's more to *Banter* than just tits and ass.'

Riz studied the page in his hand for a second, then placed it back on the table. He nodded thoughtfully and took a step back.

'Well,' he said, turning to Alexa. 'It's your call.' He gave a mock salute. 'G'night, Boss. Fingers crossed.'

Alexa raised a hand in return, watching as he headed out towards the lobby, scooping up his gym kit as he went. She pulled out a chair at the head of the meeting room table and sat, head in hands, thinking about what she was about to do.

The announcement to the team at the start of the week had gone just about as badly as it could have done. Derek had found the whole 'clean' concept so amusing that he kept breaking into hysterics as she talked them through it, asking her to repeat whole swathes of her carefully prepared speech, leaving her stammering like a junior candidate at an interview. Marcus and the news team had quickly followed suit, spending most of the session thinking up hilarious headlines for the edition by replacing the words 'nipple' and 'boobs' with other, less erotic bodily parts such as 'elbow' and 'ear'. Had it not been for the mental image of those newspaper clippings or Georgie's smug grin, Alexa might have walked out and given up. But she had remained strong. She knew that if it came to choosing between victory against Georgie and victory against her chauvinist deputy editor, then Georgie was the bigger target. Derek had the potential to bring down her reputation, but Georgie could bring down the magazine – possibly even the whole industry.

Nonetheless, Riz's words had unsettled her. If the words had come from anyone else on the team, she might not have cared so much. Everyone was doubtful about the prospects of the nipple-free edition, so it wasn't as though Riz's opinion was unique. Alexa's concern was that Riz understood the point she was trying to make – he believed that *Banter* was an entertainment brand – yet still he seemed unsure. Despite being sports editor, Riz clearly saw the topless girls as the main selling point for the magazine.

Alexa looked again at the picture of Jemima Wolf in her long white dress and sighed. She knew the risks, had weighed up the consequences. There was no way she'd back down now. There was no time, anyway. The clean edition of *Banter* would appear on news stands across the country on Thursday morning and short of pulping three hundred thousand copies, there was nothing she could do to stop it. Alexa gathered up the pages in front of her and headed back into the office.

It was half-past six. The only sounds were the gentle hum of machines and the occasional click of Jamie's mouse as he worked his way along an arm, erasing hairs. Alexa returned to her desk, feeling quietly confident and looking forward to seeing Georgie's expression when she saw the sales figures for this week's *Banter* and realised that the assumptions on which she based her whole feminist mantra were totally wrong.

She saved her work and shut down the computer, relishing the prospect of spending an evening in front of the TV with a glass of wine. It was the first time in weeks that she had left the office at a reasonable hour – the first time, she realised with an unexpected tug of sadness, since she had split up with Matt. She hadn't thought so much about Matt recently. There was too much else going on. She wondered again whether he had seen the tabloid press last week and what he thought, seeing her face on that body . . .

She looked up. There was a noise coming from across

the desk. It sounded like short, sharp bursts of breath, or sniffing.

Alexa rose from her seat, peering across the magazine barricade between her desk and Sienna's. A mass of blonde hair was splayed out across the desk, almost completely eclipsing her keyboard. In short, sharp spasms, the girl's slender shoulders heaved against the black lace of her halterneck, straining with each sob.

'Sienna?' Alexa pushed back her chair and stood, watching the convulsions from above. She wasn't sure what to say. She hadn't even realised Sienna was there.

The sobs continued. Alexa couldn't tell whether the girl was ignoring her or hadn't heard her, so she called out again, a little louder but not so loud that Jamie could hear.

The blonde hair fell away quickly. Sienna's eyes were bloodshot and her cheeks mottled with makeup, like a watercolour left out in the rain.

'What's wrong?' Alexa could hear the uncertainty in her voice. She had never been good at showing affection to strangers – let alone strangers who had actively maintained that status despite working less than two metres apart for five months.

Sienna blinked a few times, running a talon-like fingernail under each eye. Her hand was dripping with tears and mascara. She gave one final sob, then inhaled and let it out in one long, shaky breath.

'Nothing,' she said, pulling her lips into a smile through the tears.

Alexa felt a stab of sympathy, recognising the false bravado and wondering whether her own had been any less transparent. She waited, in case Sienna wanted to say more. Quietly, Alexa walked round the bank of desks and crouched down beside the girl's desk. She looked so young and vulnerable without the sultry pout, her skin blotchy and raw.

Alexa reached round and placed an arm tentatively around

the girl's shoulders. Clearly, she thought, considering the emphasis Sienna usually put on her appearance and the state of her now, something serious had happened. She had let go of her self-respect.

Sienna tried again to wipe her cheeks free of makeup, but she succeeded only in smearing it further. Alexa reached across to her side of the desk and grabbed a handful of tissues.

'Thanks,' Sienna breathed, peering into a small mirror that had been tacked to the side of her monitor. She recoiled at the sight of her face, then discarded the tissues on the floor as if giving up on the clear-up operation. Alexa looked at the mirror, wondering whether its purpose was purely cosmetic or whether it served an additional function, alerting Sienna of oncoming males and general action behind her. It was while she was thinking about this that she noticed the image on the screen.

It was a photograph of Sienna. She was sporting her usual, come-get-me pout and the border was a familiar blue, indicating a profile picture for a Facebook group. It wasn't this that worried Alexa; she already knew that the assistant spent large parts of her day on the social networking site. It was the name of the group. Alexa baulked as she read the words. *WIN A RIDE WITH SIENNA.*

She scanned the page, feeling increasingly uncomfortable. The group had three hundred and forty members, all male as far as she could see, and most of the comments in the central column looked to relate to sexual positions involving Sienna.

Does she ride any style?
Reverse Cowgirl?
Deckchair, anyone?
HOW DO WE WIN? I'M IN!

Alexa looked away, trying to think rationally about the situation. She felt anxious and sick, not sure what to do. It was the same feeling of panic that had consumed her when she had found the porn in the proofs, back in the summer.

'Is this . . .' Alexa twisted so that she could see the girl's face. 'Is this what you're crying about?'

It was a stupid question, but she had to check. Sienna's mind worked in a different way to hers and there was a possibility that, despite its grotesqueness, the Facebook group wasn't actually the source of the girl's discontent. In this instance, however, their thoughts were aligned. Sienna nodded miserably.

Alexa looked back at the screen. 'Who set it up?'

Sienna shrugged. 'Someone at *Monsieur*.' She looked close to tears again.

'Someone . . .' Alexa was about to ask whether it was somebody Sienna knew, but then she remembered. When Sienna had liaised with the *Monsieur* editorial team to organise the fitness challenge, there had been rumours of a relationship between Sienna and one particular senior writer at *Monsieur*. Alexa didn't usually find herself privy to rumours – she was shut out from most of the cliques – but this one had been impossible to miss.

'Were you . . . seeing one of the writers on *Monsieur*?'

Sienna hesitated again. 'Sort of.' She looked away. 'Two of them,' she said quietly.

Alexa closed her eyes. This didn't surprise her. It was just like Sienna to take on not one, but two men from the same magazine. She was probably trying to wheedle her way onto the editorial team – maybe hoping to play one off against another, using her power to get the job that she wanted. Whatever her motives, the plan had backfired. The only surprise to Alexa was that something like this hadn't happened before – or that Sienna hadn't seen it coming.

Alexa tried to think of something comforting or helpful to say. She wanted to reassure Sienna that this would blow over once the Facebook group got shut down, but the girl wasn't stupid. She would know it was a lie. This would live on, making a dent in Sienna's reputation throughout Senate – possibly beyond. Alexa became very aware of her arm, resting across the girl's shoulders, and felt a sudden compulsion to rub the girl's back, like a mother winding her baby. For the first time since she'd been introduced to the surly PA, Alexa found herself feeling a tug of fondness for the girl.

Without warning, Sienna shifted in her seat, turning and burying herself in Alexa's shoulder. Alexa held her, feeling the warm moisture from Sienna's face seep through her blouse, her long fingernails lightly scratching her sleeve. She almost couldn't believe this was happening. It was like a dream – a nightmare – after which, tomorrow morning, Sienna would come in bearing her usual sultry pout, apply some more lipstick and hold a brusque exchange with Alexa before getting on with her TV script. Alexa shifted her hand from the girl's back and reached out, switching off the monitor so that the Facebook page was no longer bearing down on them.

Slowly, Sienna emerged and let out a shaky breath. Her face was so streaky and dark, she was almost unrecognisable.

'I shouldn't have tried it on with them,' she said, choking on her words.

Alexa said nothing. Then, when Sienna eventually met her eye, she said what she'd been meaning to say for a long time.

'Sienna, you don't have to try it on with anyone.'

A defensive look flashed across Sienna's face and, for a moment, it looked as though she was going to turn away. But she held Alexa's gaze, saying nothing.

'You're smart,' Alexa went on. 'People will respect you for that, if you let them.'

Still Sienna said nothing.

'I know you find it easy to charm them and to some extent, that's what they've come to expect. But . . . you could use your brain, instead of your body.'

Alexa hesitated, listening to her last sentence again in her head. She had wanted to talk to Sienna about this for so long, never quite finding the opportunity, and now it had finally come and she had the girl in her arms, listening, waiting . . . her advice sounded flaky and hollow. Sienna knew as well as she did that their monthly pay packet came from a magazine that promoted women's bodies over and above their brains.

Eventually, Sienna took a deep breath and straightened up, looking gratefully at the blank screen. She gave an exhausted sigh and attempted a smile.

'Thanks,' she said, rising from her seat. 'I don't believe you, but thanks.'

24

Terry Peterson sighed and removed his glasses, massaging the bridge of his nose.

'I don't know what to say.'

Alexa didn't reply. She couldn't think of a response that wouldn't sound facetious, and that was the last thing she wanted, given his state of mind.

Peterson closed his eyes for a moment and then slowly replaced the glasses. Alexa was vaguely aware that she had never seen him in glasses before; presumably he wore contact lenses. She wondered whether it had been the stress of today's circulation figures that had driven him to abandon his pride – whether it was her fault that, for once, he looked every one of his fifty-seven years. He hadn't shown a glimmer of his trademark smile since she had walked into the room.

The nipple-free edition of *Banter* had been a disaster. Usually selling between two and three hundred thousand copies, this week's circulation stood at seventy-eight thousand – an all-time low. Most of those had been subscription sales, too. Meanwhile, *Diss* was enjoying one of its best ever weeks, outstripping *Banter* by a factor of four.

'What were you *thinking*?' he asked angrily.

Alexa wasn't sure whether the question was supposed to be rhetorical, but chose to presume that it wasn't.

'I wanted to make a point,' she replied. 'We've had so much

bad press recently, with the success of the mobile app . . . ' She paused for the briefest of moments, to ensure the reminder of her previous conquest had sunk in. 'I was worried our readers would turn against us.'

Peterson looked at her, eyebrows raised. 'And you had evidence to suggest that this was a risk?'

'There are more and more protests,' she explained. 'They're starting to attract attention and it's turning the public against us. In a worst-case scenario, we could see our whole market wiped out by top-shelf or brown-bag legislation. I wanted to protect the brand by proving that *Banter* has more to offer than cheap smut.'

Peterson winced as Alexa delivered her last two words. He didn't speak for a moment. When he did, it was in a tone more severe than she had ever heard.

'Alexa,' he said, looking angrily at her over the top of his glasses. 'I am concerned that you're losing your focus. I understand that some of the recent campaigns have been directed against you personally, and I can imagine that might be unpleasant. But please don't try to protect your own reputation at the expense of the magazine's.'

Alexa stared at him, horrified. She *hadn't* been trying to protect her own reputation. She had been trying to protect the brand. This was about *Banter*, not her. The clean edition was all about making a point about what the magazine stood for – trying to ensure it had longevity in the face of a growing body of opinion against it. The accusation hit her so hard that she felt winded, unable to think of a response that adequately refuted the charge.

'When I heard about what you were planning, I was dubious,' said Peterson, oblivious to her mute outrage. 'But I let it pass because I thought you knew what you were doing.'

It took a couple of seconds for Alexa to unravel Peterson's words but when she did, she felt something sink inside her. Derek must have gone to see Peterson when she had first announced the idea. He had obviously opted to creep to the chief executive in favour of simply talking to her, face to face. He had gone for the brownie points. Alexa felt like a victim of a playground prank. She'd been stitched up in front of the headmaster.

Peterson continued to voice his concerns, but Alexa was only partially tuned in. The vision of Derek sitting in this very chair, making snide comments about her to the chief executive, made her feel sick. She could picture him now, leaning forward in that conspiratorial, boysy way. She could hear his voice. '*To be honest, mate, I'm not sure she knows what she's doing.*' It was pathetic. Alexa would have been perfectly amenable to a discussion. She might even have changed her mind about the whole idea, had he presented his arguments coherently instead of parading around the office, inventing comedy headlines for when the whole thing backfired – which it had now, and no doubt the headlines would follow once the press got hold of the figures. In fact, it wasn't inconceivable that Derek would leak them himself, given his determination to muddy her name. The appalling results seemed to have really brightened up his day.

Alexa listened to the man's tirade, not even trying to interject. She felt low, not just because the disastrous results had left her looking inept but because they had also proved to her and everybody else that *Banter* wasn't the all-round entertainment brand that she had made it out to be. In the face of such strong opposition – not only from Georgie's brigade but also from close friends and family – Alexa had managed to convince herself that the magazine was not soft porn. This stunt was conclusive proof that she'd got it wrong.

This depressing revelation brought on a wave of sadness. Alexa was only now beginning to realise the extent of her own delusion. Riz had tried to warn her that she was on the wrong track by suggesting the alternative cover design. Neil had talked often enough about the nipple count and Jamie was always going on about the optimal cleavage-to-words ratio and what made a good double spread. She hadn't taken it in. Stubbornly, she had stuck with her own unfounded belief that there was more to the magazine than tits and ass. Alexa couldn't help wondering whether a small part of her had wanted to issue the clean edition to appease the doubters in her own close circle – namely, her mother.

Alexa thought about this as Peterson continued to list reasons for his concern. The more she thought about it, the more it seemed to make sense. It was an unpleasant realisation, but Alexa felt increasingly certain that subconsciously, her mother's approval had been a factor in her decision. It made sense. She had spent her whole life trying to satisfy her mother's demands and having failed so spectacularly in recent months, this was an obvious way to try and regain respect. Alexa couldn't help thinking back to the time she had accompanied her mother, as a five year-old, to the supermarket and refused to recite her multiplication tables on the way round. Such was the power of her mother's wrath that Alexa had taken a bar of chocolate from the racks at check-out and offered the peace offering to her mother on the way home. Of course, Alexa's plan had backfired when her mother realised that the bar of chocolate had not been paid for and it wasn't an altogether dissimilar situation now, twenty-four years later. The penalty for trying to earn back her mother's approval was just as harsh as the original punishment.

'. . . massive exposure for the *Diss* mobile app?'

Alexa looked up, the feeling of failure compounding itself inside her. *Diss* had taken the opportunity to launch its own equivalent of the *My Girlfriend* app, *Voyeur*, in the same week as *Banter*'s clean edition, giving it heavy in-mag promotion and a radio campaign across all Global Media stations.

'It's not ideal, no,' Alexa agreed meekly, cursing her deputy editor again. It was no secret that he was on good terms with the editor of *Diss*. He must have tipped Peterson off about that, too. There was no way Peterson had found this information for himself; he couldn't even work his BlackBerry.

After a pause that seemed unbearably long, Peterson leaned across the desk and looked at Alexa.

'Look,' he said, gravely, 'I brought you in because I thought you understood the market. I thought you had a good grasp of what our readers want. That's why I pay you such vast sums of money.' He raised his eyebrows and gave her a meaningful look.

Alexa swallowed nervously. Somewhere deep inside her, she felt a stab of indignation. She knew that both Derek and Marcus earned higher equivalent day rates than her and they were responsible for a perpetual drop in circulation over a period of years – not just a week. Now was clearly not the time to point this out, however. Alexa remained silent, watching as Peterson clasped his hands together as though preparing to conclude his speech.

'I'm disappointed, Alexa. You clearly don't understand the readership as well as I had thought and for that reason, I'm making a change to the governance structure. As of today, I want Derek Piggott to have the final say on all editorial decisions. Your primary remit remains to be to launch new revenue streams and boost existing ones. Please, Alexa, don't let me down again.'

Alexa nodded, taking her cue to leave. She slipped through the door and walked quickly through the management offices, across the lobby and into the ladies' toilets. She only stopped when she reached the privacy of the cubicle, where she leaned back on the door and scrunched her fists into balls, banging them hard against the door, making the lock rattle.

The frustration burned through Alexa's insides as she realised the extent of her mistake. To single-handedly lose the business a hundred thousand pounds was disastrous enough, but this wasn't just about the lost revenues from the previous week. As Peterson had pointed out, this was about her complete lack of understanding of the market. She had failed to grasp the whole basis of the magazine – of the lads' mag industry. Despite all the warnings and all the advice to the contrary, she had gone ahead, like a maverick, pursuing some crazy theory about its entertainment qualities that had been dreamed up in a pub.

Alexa banged her fists against the door again. This was the worst mistake of her career. And now, as a result, she had to report in to Derek. She closed her eyes, trying to imagine her life under this new regime. The thought of it made her want to retch.

25

Alexa padded into the kitchen and pulled open the fridge, squinting at its brightly lit contents. She didn't really care what she found inside – as long as it was edible.

There was a bag of limp lettuce, a bottle of juice with a September sell-by date and a small lump of cheese that would whittle down to almost nothing once the mould had been scraped off. In the door was a lone carton of milk whose contents were slowly solidifying and at the back, a bulky, foil-wrapped slab oozing brown liquid onto the shelf below. Alexa started to unwrap it and then stopped. It was the remains of her mother's cake from the barbecue back in July.

She let the fridge door fall shut and settled for a mug of water, as there were no clean glasses. It was ironic. For weeks, she had lived off takeaway pizza and microwave meals, forgetting to eat at times, all for the sake of a magazine that made its money from promoting the female physique.

Alexa wandered over to the sofa, sinking into it and closing her eyes, wondering what might happen if she simply stayed here for the rest of the weekend, the rest of the week – as long as it took for someone to find her. Would anyone come looking? The only people expecting to see her would be her colleagues and they wouldn't give a damn if she didn't turn up.

Alexa propped herself up, just enough to take a sip of water, then fell back onto the cushions. The office was beginning to depress her. The new working arrangement with Derek was proving every bit as unbearable as she had feared. What made things worse was that his attitude seemed to be permeating the rest of the team. He had taken to explaining things to her, slowly and loudly, in front of the others, as though she took a while to catch on – a habit that Marcus seemed to have adopted, although with less conviction. There was also a noticeable difference in the attitude of the junior writers towards her. It was like going back to her first day, when lewd jokes had been avoided within her earshot, punchlines delivered in a hushed snigger and conversations conducted in cryptic, laddish code. She had worked so hard to be accepted by the team, slowly building relationships, showing them that she wasn't that different to them after all. And now, thanks to her own obstinate thinking and Derek's insecurity, she was back to square one.

For the first time since she had started at *Banter*, Alexa was seriously beginning to wonder whether it was worth her while sticking around. The combination of this newfound internal resistance and the public sentiment against the magazine was making the targets seem more distant than ever. She knew, even if Derek didn't have the full picture, that if the targets couldn't be met then that would be it. The Americans would cut off their lifeline in April and the brand would die.

Alexa opened one eye and rolled sideways as her phone buzzed on the coffee table beside her. It was an email. She considered leaving it unread, but her curiosity got the better of her and she found herself reaching for the device. A surge of frustration ran through her as she caught sight of the name of the sender.

Hi Alexa,
    Just wanted to congratulate you on the first half-decent edition of Banter. I have a framed copy of it on my bedroom wall. Does this mean you have a conscience after all? I hear the sales figures weren't too rosy, though, so

maybe it's time to start thinking about joining the
opposition . . .?
    Yours patiently,
    Georgie

Alexa sat up, staring at the words with a mixture of hatred
and shame. No matter how many times she heard from the girl,
no matter how predictable her appearances became, Alexa still
got a shock every time she made contact. It was like a curse. She
popped up when Alexa was least expecting it, rubbing salt into
the wounds, taking pleasure in Alexa's misfortune. Yes, Alexa had
a conscience. But no, she wasn't thinking about joining the
opposition. She never would. Not after what the opposition had
done to her.

Alexa sighed, draining the mug of water. Her head was throb-
bing. It had been another sleepless night. She had tossed and
turned until the early hours, then found herself drifting in and out
of a stressful dream in which she and a faceless child were being
hunted down by a masked gunman. Maybe her conscience was
playing tricks on her, she thought. Maybe deep down, she
was considering the option of switching allegiances and joining
REACT as their insider. She dismissed the thought instantly. There
was no way she'd do such a thing. The very thought of joining
an organisation that scaled buildings in the dead of night,
plastering office blocks with offensive material, was laughable –
even if she approved of their cause. But she didn't, anyway.

REACT may have won their fight to prove that *Banter* made
its money from the portrayal of half-naked women in sexual
positions, but that didn't mean it could be held responsible for
everything wrong with today's society. The whole point of *Banter*
was that it was exactly that – banter. It did contain some crass
remarks but they were meant in jest. 'The most important thing:
she's a 34DD!' 'How to get in this girl's knickers!' 'Escape the
nagging with this' – they were deliberately contentious headlines

that nobody, least of all the readers, took seriously. Apart from Derek, perhaps. She looked down as her phone buzzed again in her hand.

Hey Lex,
How did the clean issue sell? I bought a copy! Very proud that you made a stand. Hope it's all going well. Goddaughter loved the outfit! Fancy coming to our school nativity play on 10th Dec? It's a bit alternative – I'm one of the lorry drivers. Kate's invited too . . . Let me know.
Leonie x

Alexa sighed, trying to distract herself by picturing Leonie as a lorry driver and working out where such a character might fit in the nativity play. It didn't make her laugh. Right now, it felt as though nothing would ever make her laugh again. She thought about calling Leonie, then quickly shied away from the idea. Alexa didn't feel ready to admit to her friend that their idea had failed.

She considered calling Kate, but rejected that too. It was too easy to be brainwashed by Kate's exuberant, post-feminism rants and right now, Alexa didn't want to be brainwashed. She wanted to decide for herself whether her goals were worth pursuing – whether she had it in her to turn *Banter* around, despite everything that had happened.

Alexa scrolled through the favourites on her phone and then stopped, her thumb hovering above the screen. She had considered doing this so many times, but never got as far as making the call. There was too much to explain, too much to apologise for. But now, for some reason, the explanations and apologies didn't seem so daunting. Perhaps it was because she had opened her mind to the possibility of quitting. Or perhaps all the other problems put things into perspective. Alexa took a breath and pressed the button.

'Averley nine-two-eight?'

Alexa smiled, despite her apprehension. No matter how many times she explained to her mother that the system had changed and that 'Averley nine-two-eight' didn't actually mean anything anymore, her mother's telephone greeting remained the same.

'Mum, it's me.'

There was a pause.

'Hello, dear.' Her voice sounded stilted all of a sudden – quite different to the jolly, sing-song tone that had greeted Alexa. 'How are you?'

'I'm fine, thanks,' Alexa lied. 'You?'

'I'm fine too.' There was a pause. 'Your father's helping out at the canoe club regatta. I'm just going down there now.'

'Oh, right. Good.' Alexa wondered whether this was an attempt to curtail the conversation. 'Shall I call back another time?'

'No,' her mother replied, quickly. 'Now's good.'

Now's good, thought Alexa. *Good for what?* She hadn't planned what she was going to say. She just knew that she had to break the deadlock between them – soon, before the weeks turned into months. She tried to think of a neutral topic. It was absurd; this was her mother, not some stranger at a cocktail party. They had so much to say to one another, yet here she was, searching for idle chit-chat as though they were barely acquainted.

'How's canoe club going?' she asked, lamely.

'Not bad. We had our end-of-season party a few weeks back. I'm trying to get some of the youth club members to join, but you know how they are . . .' She trailed off.

Alexa was about to follow on with a question about the youth club, but suddenly she could bear it no longer. She bent forward and stood up, her tired eyes wandering the apartment as she forced herself to say the words.

'Mum, I'm sorry,' she said.

There was no reply. Alexa hadn't really expected one.

'I wanted to tell you about the job – I tried to, but it just

232

never seemed like the right time. I'm so sorry you found out by seeing me on TV.'

Alexa could hear her mother's breathing down the line: one long, inhalation and then a shaky sigh. She remained silent, waiting for some kind of reply.

After a painful pause, it came.

'It was rather a shock,' said Alexa's mother, quietly.

'I'm sorry,' Alexa said again. She felt mildly relieved to have elicited a response from her mother, but she wasn't naïve enough to think that the response qualified as forgiveness.

'I should've thought,' she went on, struggling to articulate her feelings. 'I should've . . . well, I should have told you, back in July.'

There was another pause. Alexa was conscious of repeating herself, but her thoughts were so muddled up in her head, she couldn't come up with a coherent apology. The problem was that there were so many parts to her wrongdoing, she didn't know where to start. Her mother wasn't making it any easier, by staying silent while she stuttered on.

'I just thought . . . well, I thought it would be easier for you if you didn't know . . .'

'It was a good debate,' her mother said quietly. 'I thought you did well, given the circumstances.'

Alexa stopped talking. She was too stunned to reply. Her mother was saying something positive – almost *praising* her performance. Of course, she disapproved of her daughter's stance in the debate, but still, this was just about as close to a compliment as Alexa's mother had come in years.

'You're still there, I presume?'

Alexa hesitated. 'Sort of,' she heard herself saying.

'What does that mean? How can you be *sort of* there?' Her voice had reverted to its usual, scalding tone, Alexa noted.

'Well . . .' Alexa wished she had just replied honestly. She was considering leaving her job at *Banter*, but that was all.

233

'I'm still there, but it's not turning out quite how I thought it would.'

Alexa's mother gave a brief snort of amusement. 'And how did you think it would turn out, working in the pornographic industry?'

'It's not . . .' Alexa started to argue, then stopped herself. Her mother wasn't entirely wrong. 'I thought . . . I wanted to . . .' She grappled for the words to explain what she had envisaged when Peterson had offered her the job. 'I think I convinced myself that I could turn it into something better,' she said.

Alexa waited for the derisory snort, but it never came. Instead, there was more stony silence.

'I was only thinking about the business,' she explained. 'I thought it would be a challenge. I wanted to take it on – to show them what I could do.'

A heavy sigh came down the line. 'You always do.'

Alexa opened her mouth to reply, but nothing came out. That was *rich*, she thought, coming from the person who had instilled the sense of determination in her in the first place. She said nothing. She didn't want to antagonise her mother any more – and besides, Alexa thought she detected a hint of fondness in her mother's tone, mixed in with the despair.

'I'll be working somewhere else, soon,' she assured her mother. 'I'll do something more worthy. Something you can tell your friends about. Something you can be proud of.'

There was another pause. Alexa looked out of the window, trying to think of a change of subject. She knew that there was more to say on the matter but it felt as though she had said the important things.

'Darling?' Her mother's voice remained stilted, but there was a slight softness in its tone. 'We *are* proud.'

Alexa felt something swell inside her. She had never heard her mother say anything like that before. Of course, she knew that the words weren't unconditional; her mother wasn't proud of certain, specific achievements and she wasn't proud of anything Alexa had done regarding *Banter*, but she was proud. *They were proud.*

'Anyway . . .' Her mother quickly reverted to her scout-leader tone. 'How's Matt?'

Alexa's heart lurched. Her parents didn't know. She hadn't spoken to them in such a long time that they thought she was still with Matt.

'He's . . .' Alexa hesitated. 'He's fine,' she heard herself saying. It was something to do with wanting to make her mother proud, she thought. She couldn't disappoint her on too many fronts at once. One thing at a time, she decided. She would tell them about Matt next time they spoke.

'Good. And you'll be home for Christmas? Both of you?'

Alexa cringed. 'We, um . . . we haven't worked out what we're doing yet. But I'll be there, for sure.' *On my own,* she thought, *as I have been for the last thirty years.* If she had still been with Matt, this would have been the first Christmas she had ever spent with a boyfriend. She tried not to dwell on this thought. It would be fine. She would get through it, as she always did, sitting among all the coupled-up cousins and divorced aunts.

'Oh – I haven't told you!' Alexa's mother was almost back to her old, exuberant self. 'I've been nominated for an award.'

'An award?' Alexa tried not to sound too surprised. She couldn't imagine what her mother might have done to qualify for such a thing.

'It's called the Unsung Hero award and it's open to the whole of Surrey. The helpers at the youth group nominated me!'

Alexa felt a rush of joy for her mother. 'That's brilliant!' she cried, meaning it. Her mother deserved some recognition for all the hours of voluntary work she put in every week at her various charities.

'I'm sure I won't win it,' her mother said modestly. 'But it's nice to be nominated, anyway.'

'It's great!' Alexa agreed. 'And don't put yourself down – you might win.'

She recognised the hope in her mother's voice and felt a sudden surge of affection for the woman who, throughout her whole life, had witnessed the achievements of others, pushing and goading and propelling them to success. Now, for the first time, she had the potential to experience it first-hand. The modesty was a veneer, thought Alexa; winning this award would mean everything to her mother.

'I'm keeping my fingers crossed for you.'

'Thanks, darling. Likewise.'

Alexa tried to smile, but she couldn't. Unexpectedly, her lower lip stiffened and she could feel tears welling up in her eyes – tears of joy or relief or sheer exhaustion, she didn't know which. *Likewise.* Her mother was keeping her fingers crossed for her.

26

'Footballers' wives?' suggested Greg, the junior writer.

Riz shook his head. 'Done to death.'

'Footballers' cars?' Greg tried.

'Maybe.'

'Stupid purchases made by footballers' wives?' Sienna raised an eyebrow provocatively.

'*That* might work.' Riz nodded and jotted something on his pad.

'Hey.' Derek leaned forward, grinning from behind the tufts of ginger hair that continued to sprout from his upper lip, despite the fact that his month of charity was officially over. 'How about stupid purchases made by *footballers*? That way we can include all the minging prossies they slept with!'

Riz and Greg chuckled politely, but the suggestion wasn't noted.

Alexa sighed. She wanted to help mould the sports section of the tablet app for its launch in the new year and she knew that Riz was relying on her support, but she couldn't bear to hear the inevitable condescending reaction of the deputy editor to her suggestions. Besides, Alexa was all too aware now that *Banter*'s sports coverage was not its main asset. To be honest, she couldn't understand why Riz remained so enthusiastic about his section, given its lowly positioning each week between the TV guide and the 'Dirty MILF Slags That Want to Jerk Your Dick Till You Shoot Your Load' classified ads.

'Let's try and come up with some *interactive* ideas, shall we?' asked Riz, looking around brightly. 'It's for a tablet, remember.'

'What about . . .' Greg narrowed his eyes in thought. 'Bad haircuts?'

Riz nodded tactfully. Alexa wondered whether Greg might have spent too much time with Biscuit on the jokes pages in recent weeks.

The suggestions reeled forth, their quality gradually improving under the masterful guidance of Riz. Other sports made brief appearances in conversation, but there was a tendency to gravitate towards the national sport.

'What about women footballers?' Alexa suggested, unable to stop herself. She had read a short feature in *Diss* on a female professional soccer player in the US who now had her own clothing line.

Sienna looked up. 'Footie Fitties, you could call it!'

Riz nodded approvingly. 'I like it.'

'What?' cried Derek, screwing up his face in Alexa's direction. 'Footie Fitties? As in, the players? That's a contradiction in terms.' He grimaced. 'Load of ugly dykes.'

Alexa said nothing. She glanced at Sienna, expecting to see a crumpled expression in response to the put-down, but she was just looking blankly at Derek, not even offering her usual simpering smile. Alexa watched her out of the corner of her eye. She couldn't be sure, but she thought she had detected a slight difference in Sienna's behaviour of late. She was still flirtatious around the office, but only in a general sense – pouting and flicking her hair as she always did. Alexa hadn't seen her wrap herself around Derek or Marcus in the last few days.

Little more had been said on the matter of the *Monsieur* Facebook group. Sienna had requested that the incident go unreported to Senate HR and Alexa hadn't tried to convince her otherwise. She had had the group marked as offensive and the page had been taken down immediately. Aside from the slight change that Alexa detected in the girl's attitude, it was as though the whole thing had never happened.

A discussion broke out about whether the Footie Fitties feature was a viable option, given the apparent lack – according to Derek – of attractive female footballers. Alexa remained silent, trying not to let the insulting generalisations get to her but aware that her blood pressure was rising.

'Even if there were enough,' declared Derek, 'they'd have to be prepared to get their kit off.' He laughed at his own incidental pun. 'Ha – get it?'

'Yeah,' said Alexa, suddenly unable to stop herself. 'They'd have to get their kit off. We couldn't just feature a woman in the magazine because she was *good* at something, could we? Those rights are reserved for *men*. No, women are only good if they've got nice legs and big tits!'

Derek stared, eyes wide, letting out a slow, soft cat-call. Everyone around the table was looking at her.

Alexa sat back in her chair, feeling suddenly flushed and wondering what on earth had possessed her to come out with such a remark. It was like something Georgie Caraway would have said in one of her feminist rants.

Derek began to nod, clearly enjoying himself. 'Oh, of course,' he said, patronisingly. 'I forgot. *Banter* should be about fully-clothed women and clean jokes, right?' He glanced sideways, trying to catch someone's eye. No one looked up. 'Because that's what sells copies, isn't it? That's what really boosts our numbers.'

Alexa managed to hold his gaze. She stared hatefully into the man's beady eyes, trying to temper the response that was on her lips. *At least I tried something*, she wanted to say. For seven years, Derek had sat around, watching *Banter*'s circulation slide and doing nothing about it. She opened her mouth to speak, but someone else got there first.

'It was a stunt, Derek. The idea was to make a point, not to boost our numbers.'

Alexa clamped her mouth shut, gobsmacked. She had never heard Sienna answer anyone back, let alone the deputy editor – and let alone in defence of Alexa. She wasn't even pouting, either. She was just staring pointedly at Derek.

For a moment, nobody spoke. Derek glared back at his PA with a mixture of bewilderment and outrage, then quickly pulled himself together.

'Jesus Christ,' he muttered, with a brisk shake of the head. 'Thank God it's me making the decisions around here and not you women. We'd never get anything right.'

Alexa resisted the urge to lean over and punch the deputy editor in the face. She could feel herself shaking with anger, the heat passing up through her body in a wave. He really meant it. That was what got to her the most. He really believed that she and Sienna were inferior to their male counterparts and that sportswomen deserved no coverage if they didn't look good topless.

'I guess we could do grassroots WAGs?' Riz suggested, tentatively.

Greg gave a vigorous nod, even though Riz hadn't explained what he meant.

'Like, Saturday league players send in a video of their girlfriend – ooh, we could feature them on the mobile app, too. Then we could do a photo shoot, if they're up for it, and maybe a footie-related interview . . .'

Riz continued to brainstorm with himself, with occasional noises of encouragement from Greg. Derek, Alexa and Sienna remained silent. Alexa was having her own private brainstorm. She was thinking about her battle with Derek.

'Okay, so each week we'll have one video interview with a sports personality, one footballer's car slash house slash yacht slash WAG's stupid purchase feature, one caption spread and one Footie Fittie of some sort – either a player or a grassroots WAG.' He looked up from his notes with a valiant smile. 'That's great! Thanks, guys. I think that'll really work on the app.'

Riz and Greg left the room in a hurry, followed shortly by Sienna, who mumbled something about organising the Christmas do and scurried off, head down. Alexa stayed put. She had just remembered something.

'Well!' Derek stood up and rubbed his belly, looking pleased with himself. 'That went well, didn't it? Or are you still sulking about the dyke thing?'

Alexa knew he was deliberately riling her. It was working. Suddenly, the full force of his arrogance hit her afresh and she rose from her seat, feeling furious but at the same time strangely excited about what she was about to do.

'Derek?' she called, as he turned to leave the room. 'Have you got a minute?'

He whipped round, one eyebrow raised in anticipation.

Alexa picked up her phone from the meeting room table and scrolled through the messages. She had been holding onto this for a while now – two months, at least. She hadn't thought about exactly how she would use it, but she had known it would be useful at some point. It was clear to her now that this was the perfect opportunity.

She located the string of messages, lowered the phone and fixed her gaze on Derek. 'I've asked you before, but you don't seem to have taken it on board. So I'll ask you again. Please show some respect towards me in front of our colleagues.'

One side of Derek's mouth curled up in a slow, gloating smile. 'I'm sorry,' he said, 'but that's all the respect you're gonna get from me.'

Alexa closed her eyes for a moment, the fire burning inside her. The urge to tell Derek the truth about *Banter*'s precarious status within Senate was stronger than ever, but she managed to rein it in. She knew that to let slip about the Americans' stance would effectively set the magazine on a path of self-destruction. She raised the handset to eye level. There was only one way to keep Derek in check, she decided, and this was it.

241

'In which case,' she said, 'I might have to think about forwarding this to the rest of the team.'

She tilted the screen towards him to reveal a long string of dirty text messages from Derek to the double-F stripper named Crystal – or rather, from Derek to Alexa's spare mobile phone. It had taken weeks to achieve the desired result, not that Alexa had had a precise view of what the desired result looked like at the start. She had initially embarked on the plan in a fit of rage against Derek's sexist, unpleasant behaviour. It was a direct result of the phone call from his Cockney friend who had addressed her as 'sweet-cheeks' and explained that the Asian strippers were all booked up. Over time, Alexa had begun to realise that there was mileage in the late-night text conversations that her deputy editor thought he was conducting with the beautiful blonde. The messages, of which there were literally hundreds, some of which made Alexa feel physically sick, each required a carefully crafted, provocative response, sent at a suitable time of night – and then, of course, there was the date.

'She never showed up for that date, did she?' Alexa smiled, quickly navigating to the photos on her phone: photo after photo of Derek, sitting alone at a candlelit table for two in an expensive restaurant in Soho, looking increasingly anxious and pathetic.

That had been Alexa's favourite part of the ruse. He had waited for nearly an hour at that table. It was enough time for Alexa to take her photos, grab a pizza from around the corner and return to take a few final shots that really captured the look of dejection. It was a childish prank and this was a childish threat she was making, but Alexa was beginning to realise that childish was the only level on which Derek operated.

Slowly, Derek looked up. The cocky smirk had vanished from his face.

'You wouldn't dare,' he said, quietly.

Alexa gave a beatific smile. 'Wouldn't I?'

242

27

'Mary, you are gonna have a baby,' proclaimed the leather-clad teenager, bringing his cardboard Harley Davidson to a halt in the middle of the stage.

'What . . . me?' The pretty young blonde feigned surprise. 'But . . . but . . .' She glanced behind her.

'I'm a virgin!' came the hissed prompt from the wings.

'I'm a virgin,' she declared. A ripple of smutty laughter travelled across the school hall.

Alexa watched as the Hell's Angel drove off on his makeshift machine. She wasn't laughing. She was thinking about the significance of the line in the girl's real life. She didn't know for sure that the pretty young blonde was the girl that Leonie had mentioned, back in summer, but she had all but convinced herself that it was. There were too many coincidences for it not to be. The girl looked about fourteen or fifteen, she was pretty, she was playing the leading lady and she had a look of vulnerability about her that made it easy to picture her coming to Leonie in distress.

Following a noisy scene change, the girl reappeared, dressed in striped pyjamas and accompanied by a new character, an acne-ridden teenager whom Alexa took to be Joseph.

'Joe, I gotta tell you something,' said the girl, perching on the high-jump mattress that was presumably meant to be their bed. 'I'm pregnant.'

'What!' yelled the boy, with surprising vigour. 'How? How're you pregnant when we never—'

A silence fell. Alexa guessed that Mary was supposed to interject at this point, but she didn't – not until after another hissed prompt from behind the scenes. Alexa glanced at the empty seat next to her as the lines continued to be mechanically recited on stage. Kate had texted to say she'd be late, but that could mean anything. Alexa was half-expecting another text any minute to say that she wouldn't make it after all. She hoped, for Leonie's sake, that Kate would arrive in time for the curtain-call.

An unconvincing row ensued between Mary and Joe about the supposedly immaculate conception, which concluded with Joe sleeping on the gym bench at the side of the stage and the Hell's Angel returning, in his dreams, to explain that Mary was in fact telling the truth and that he should call a halt to the divorce proceedings.

Kate arrived just as Mary and Joe completed their arduous journey to Bethlehem, only to discover that there were no rooms at the Holiday Inn.

'Hey!' Kate slipped into her seat, grinning guiltily at Alexa. 'Have I missed the lorry driver?'

Alexa smiled and shook her head. 'No sign as yet.'

'I can't give birth at a motorway service station!' cried Mary, looking up at the painted hoarding along the top of the stage that read HAPPY CHEF SERVICES.

Kate exchanged a bewildered look with Alexa, who said nothing.

Inevitably, baby Jesus was born in the motorway service station, with roadside recovery blankets and Burger King napkins used as swaddling.

The stage lights dimmed and then brightened again, focusing on three large, tattooed men in the middle of the stage, smoking fake cigarettes and swigging from cans. Alexa's thoughts were still with the actress playing Mary. She wanted to know for sure that the girl had held firm with her boyfriend, that she hadn't consented to sex. Seeing her in the flesh, so gawky and anxious and naïve, brought back all the guilt that Alexa had felt when Leonie had first told her. She shifted uncomfortably in her seat, wondering whether Leonie had heard any more from the girl. It was only when Kate nudged her in the ribs that she realised that one of the fat men on stage was in fact Leonie. Her face was hidden beneath a baseball cap, her chin was adorned with a fake beard and her petite frame enlarged with some sort of padding beneath her clothes.

'. . . been driving all night,' boomed one of the men, presumably another teacher.

'Too right,' said the next, taking a swig of Coke. 'Need something to keep us going.'

Just as Leonie looked up to speak, the stage was invaded with not one, but six Hell's Angels, all wearing ill-fitting leather and riding matching cardboard motorbikes.

'Word up!' cried one of the lads, as the sound effects from the bikes died down.

'A woman called Mary's up the duff, right?' said another.

'The kid is gonna be a superstar!'

'You need to get to Bethlehem.'

'Follow our tail lights!'

The Hell's Angels thundered off stage with the three lorry drivers in tow. Alexa became aware that Kate was sniggering hysterically in the seat beside her, but she didn't look round. Even the sight of Leonie steering her way around the stage in an invisible HGV cab didn't make Alexa laugh. It was as though the sight of the young girl playing Mary had cast a spell of sadness upon her; she couldn't find the play amusing when such serious issues were going on behind the scenes.

Eventually, the truck drivers tracked down baby Jesus in the service station car park and knelt to worship him in a variety of religious rituals.

'That was great,' said Kate, when the actors eventually lined the stage to take their bows.

'Yeah,' Alexa replied, not sure whether her friend was being sarcastic. 'I have to say, I had no idea the Hell's Angels played such a crucial role in the nativity story.'

Kate threw her a warning look. 'Come on, now. At least it was original. Shall we extract our friend from her articulated vehicle and go for a drink?'

Alexa nodded. Apart from anything else, she wanted an update on the girl's situation.

The night air was refreshingly cold on her skin after the stuffy, over-heated school hall. They stood by the gates, waiting for Leonie to emerge and watching the stream of teenagers pour out. They formed clusters: threes and fours, mainly, with occasional larger gaggles made up of sixth-formers. Most of the girls were wearing high heels and were clearly very aware of the young men around them. The teenage boys kept their heads down, pretending not to notice.

Alexa spotted the acne-ridden face of the young man who had played Joe, standing still in the flowing crowd and glancing back as though waiting for someone to catch up. Alexa felt a lurch of apprehension as she saw the blonde head bobbing towards him. Mary and Joe were an item in real life. Which meant . . . Alexa watched as the pair of them skulked off, hand in hand. That was the boyfriend. *He* was the boy who had tried to pressure her into having sex. He looked so young. He was a child. They both were. It seemed wrong that they were making such big decisions – taking such risks – so young.

'It's freezing,' moaned Kate, squinting up at the ugly concrete building. 'What's she doing in there?'

Alexa shivered, suddenly feeling the cold herself. She shoved her hands deep into her coat pockets and scrunched them into balls for warmth. Something grazed the knuckle of her right hand. A piece of paper. She drew it out and felt all her worries

246

intensify. It was the leaflet that Georgie had thrust at her during the protest. *ABUSE STARTS WITH LADS' MAGS*, she read, before stuffing it back into her pocket and trying not to register the image of the woman's bloodied face on the front.

It was too late, of course. Alexa was already thinking about the woman that Georgie had told her about in the doorway – the one whose boyfriend had battered her nearly to death. Her thoughts flitted between the woman and the girl she had just seen disappearing with the young teenager and she knew that the problems were inextricably linked. Alexa didn't feel responsible, exactly; she knew that lads' mags weren't to blame for the way people behaved, but she felt troubled by the very existence of the problem.

'Sorry about that!' Leonie came hurrying down the path. 'Took a while to get out of my fat suit.'

Kate laughed. 'You were great.'

Leonie just rolled her eyes.

'No, really – you were! Wasn't she, Lex?'

Alexa nodded enthusiastically, trying to wipe her mind free of depressing thoughts. 'The whole thing was brilliant,' she said. 'I especially loved the satnav scene on the way to Bethlehem.'

Leonie smiled bashfully. 'The kids wrote the script. I think they rather enjoyed casting me as the incompetent lorry driver.'

Alexa smiled.

'There's a pub at the bottom of the road. Really nice place – bit of a favourite with the staff.'

'Sounds good,' replied Kate.

'The only drawback is that it's also a favourite with the kids, too.'

Kate looked a little less keen. 'Reckon we can find a quiet corner?'

Leonie nodded confidently and smiled. 'They'll move as soon as they see a teacher coming.'

The pub was less crowded than they had imagined and while

Alexa and Kate argued over who would buy the first round, Leonie managed to secure them a table. Kate won the dispute on the grounds that she would be awarded her end-of-year bonus no matter what, whereas Alexa's was less certain. Alexa wasn't in a position to object; with the failure of her 'clean edition' stunt – and Kate didn't even know about that yet – her bonus was looking increasingly unlikely.

'So,' said Kate, sliding the drinks onto the table. 'Any budding Hollywood actors in the making?'

Leonie looked at her. 'At Langdale Comprehensive? You watched it. What do you think?'

Kate shrugged. 'I thought Jesus was pretty realistic.'

'Jesus was a doll.'

'Ah, yeah.' She grinned. 'Good point.'

'Was the . . .' Alexa was about to ask about the girl playing Mary, but she lost her nerve. She didn't want to get into another debate about the role her magazine played in the lives of young adults.

Kate and Leonie were looking at her, waiting.

'Sorry. Nothing.'

They were still looking at her.

Alexa tried to think of a diversion, but the question was growing in her mind as she stalled for time.

'The girl who played Mary . . . was she the same girl you mentioned – the one who came to you when . . . you know . . .'

Leonie leaned forward on her elbows and rubbed her eyes, looking suddenly sad. Alexa took this to mean that she'd guessed correctly, but was surprised to see that Leonie was shaking her head.

'No,' she said, sighing. 'Anna dropped out a week ago. That was Brooke, her understudy. Hence the problems with her knowing her lines.'

Kate frowned. 'She didn't seem too bad.'

'I guess not,' Leonie said vaguely. 'She wants to be an actress, would you believe.'

'Oh.' Kate grimaced. 'She wasn't *that* good.'

'Or a glamour model,' said Leonie, rolling her eyes.

Kate looked at her. 'What's wrong with that?'

Leonie groaned and took a sip of wine. '*Everything's* wrong with that.'

'It's her choice though, isn't it?' Kate pressed, clearly spoiling for a fight.

Alexa kept quiet. She didn't want to get involved – didn't want to end up in another conversation about the morality of the industry in which she worked. Besides, she was still thinking about the girl supposed to play Mary. The couple she had seen walking through the school gates hadn't been the troubled pair after all, which was reassuring, in a way. The blonde girl wasn't being pressured into sex by the acne-faced teenager. But what had happened to Anna? Alexa sensed that Leonie was purposefully digressing.

'Why did Anna drop out of the lead role?' she asked, when the debate finally ran out of steam.

Leonie went quiet again. She looked down at her lap.

'I shouldn't tell you,' she said. 'I should keep it confidential.'

Even Kate must have gauged the severity of the situation because she didn't try to object.

After several seconds, Leonie looked around the pub, presumably checking for colleagues or pupils. Then she leaned in, drawing Alexa and Kate towards her.

'She came to see me on the day she pulled out of the play and she hasn't been back to school since.'

'What happened?' Kate probed, unable to resist.

Reluctantly, Leonie told them. 'She had a row with her boyfriend. He was drunk, apparently. They were at a party – I think everyone was a bit messed up. Anyway, he trapped her in a room and forced himself on her. I think he felt as though everyone else was getting some and he wasn't. Poor girl. I don't even know whether she'll come back. They're in the same form; they sit in half their lessons together.'

Alexa remained silent. She couldn't think of anything to say. Even Kate was quiet.

Leonie picked up her drink and took a sip, looking at Kate and Alexa in turn.

'Sorry,' she said. 'I shouldn't have told you that. Don't say anything to anyone, obviously.'

Alexa nodded grimly. She certainly wasn't going to go discussing the matter.

'Well!' Kate looked up. 'That put a downer on things, didn't it? Shall we talk about something else? Lex, how's things going with you? Are you on track to launch your next app?'

Alexa didn't look up. She couldn't talk about any of the crass developments in her place of work after what Leonie had just said. Anyone could see that the two subjects were related – apart from Kate, perhaps. To talk about *Banter* in the face of such horrible news was like cracking a sick joke at a funeral.

'How did the boob-free edition go the other week?' asked Kate, innocuously.

Alexa looked at her, then Leonie, and sighed.

'Great,' she lied. 'It went really well.'

A glance was exchanged between Leonie and Kate.

'Is everything alright?' asked Leonie, cautiously.

'Yeah!' Alexa forced a smile. 'Everything's fine. Shall we . . . get some food?'

28

Alexa carved off a slab of pudding and doused it in custard on the way to her mouth. Then she stopped, replacing the spoon in her bowl and pushing the dessert away. She was obviously drunk. She didn't even like Christmas pudding.

A scream prompted Alexa to look up. Across the table, Specs was trying to lick Sienna's ear. Alexa smiled as the girl shook her head, gently pushing the junior writer away. Biscuit and Greg were challenging Paddy to an eating contest that involved downing bowls of pudding and custard with no cutlery. Alexa cringed as the junior writer emerged from the challenge, his eyes shining out from the dripping yellow wall of custard.

She looked away, grateful for Sienna's choice of venue. Zip Bar wasn't the type of place to care when its guests started behaving like untrained animals at the dinner table. In fact, it was ideal in every respect. The food was plentiful, the drinks were cheap and the music was loud enough to rule out any chance of a serious conversation. There was also a dance floor that encompassed the area in which they sat, making the whole place one big, cheesy nightclub.

Alexa turned her attention to the other end of the table, where Marcus and Louis were trying to engage a young waitress in conversation using some sort of prop – she couldn't focus for long enough to tell what it was. Jamie leaned sideways and whispered something in her ear.

'. . . big moment,' she heard. Then there was a sharp *ding ding ding*, right next to her other ear.

'Lads!' cried Derek, rising to his feet beside her. 'And laddesses,' he added with a dismissive laugh.

A hush fell, exposing the tinny beat of MC Hammer's 'U Can't Touch This' and the murmur of other less raucous tables nearby. Derek reached for his Santa hat and pulled it down over his oily brown hair.

'I hope you've been good boys this year . . .' He winked in Marcus' direction, to the sound of drunken laughter. 'Because the time has come for Secret Santa to award his presents! Ho ho ho!'

Alexa shuddered. She was drunk, but the alcohol did nothing to stem her sense of unease at the thought of the parcel in that bulging brown sack that bore her name. The fact that the gifts had been donated anonymously meant that her 'Santa' could be as offensive as he liked without having to worry about the consequences. Alexa couldn't even imagine what someone like Derek or Louis might pick for her.

Jamie shuffled sideways to give her more room. Alexa gave a grateful smile and retreated another couple of feet from the deputy editor. She had managed to get through the whole meal without confrontation from Derek. Admittedly, Derek had spent much of the past two hours shouting obscenities at Marcus and Louis relating to their trip to one of London's less salubrious night spots the previous week, but there was also another reason for the peaceful nature of their interaction tonight.

Derek's attitude towards Alexa had changed. In the last two weeks, there had not been a single altercation between them. Whereas once he had taken every opportunity to put Alexa up on a pedestal and knock her off it in front of the team, he now avoided confrontation altogether. In meetings, he would allow her to speak, sometimes even noting her suggestions and nodding. The inappropriate comments still escaped from time to time – like the one about women drivers last week and some stupid insinuation that housewives were happiest when bent over their kitchen units by passing tradesmen – but no longer were the remarks directed at Alexa. Since her gentle threat a fortnight ago, Derek had become almost demure in her presence.

'But first . . .' Derek looked around at the inebriated faces, clearly enjoying the limelight. 'My little elves have brought us some shots!'

Alexa followed his gaze and identified a line of shot glasses, half-buried beneath the debris in the middle of the table. Some were colourless and topped with a slice of lemon, the others dark brown, like glasses of crude oil. She felt ill.

'Take your pick!' ordered Derek. 'Tequila or Sambuca.'

Reluctantly, Alexa reached for a shot of tequila, holding out her thumb and forefinger out for Jamie to administer the salt.

'Merry Christmas!' cried Derek, pouring the Sambuca down his throat and slamming the empty glass on the table.

Alexa licked the salt, threw back the shot and bit into the lemon, sucking as hard as she could to mask the bitter taste of the alcohol. She felt it burning down her throat, mixing with the pre-dinner beers and the sickly red wine in her stomach. The walls of the room started wafting gently before her, like the walls of a circus tent. She closed her eyes and tried to focus on the words of Derek's speech.

'And the first one goes to . . . Paddy!'

Alexa opened her eyes to the sound of a table-top drum roll as the small, pink-wrapped parcel was handed down the table. The drum roll culminated in whoops and applause as Paddy revealed the cucumber eye mask – presumably a reference to his time at the Cheshire beauty spa earlier in the year. Alexa added her applause to the mix, feeling slightly sick and hoping that the next gift wouldn't be hers.

'And next . . .' Derek grinned stupidly at his audience. 'Sienna!'

Sienna smiled coyly, raising a hand to her blushing cheek as the gift was passed down, causing some intrigue along the way. It must have been half a metre in length and almost as thin as a pencil.

'Thanks, guys!' She ripped off the paper and stood up to demonstrate the gift in action, smacking the black, leather riding crop against Biscuit's backside and posing as Jamie leaned in to take a photo. 'How did you know my old one was wearing out?'

A raft of dirty remarks came from various parts of the table. Alexa's anxiety mounted as the distribution of gifts continued. Derek got away lightly with a razor, presumably intended as a hint for him to remove the growth on his face, and Louis looked genuinely pleased with his book of Spearmint Rhino vouchers. Riz was given a set of resistance bands for his biceps and was forced to demonstrate them in action for the camera, just as Biscuit opened the dirty jokes book that Alexa had picked out. Then Jamie's present was thrown down the table.

Alexa handed over the square, paper-like parcel and watched as the pictures editor put down his camera and made a tentative stab at the wrapping. Suddenly, it seemed, everyone was looking his way. As he pulled out the contents, Alexa could see that his hands were shaking.

'Ha ha,' he said, in a strangled voice. 'Very funny.'

Alexa watched, cringing as Jamie held up the magazines to reveal the gay pornography on the front.

'That's for the jumper you're wearing!' yelled someone.

'And the shoes!' added someone else.

Jamie smiled awkwardly and Alexa could see that his neck and face had turned a deep red. She looked enquiringly at Derek's sack, suddenly desperate for the spotlight to move off Jamie. It was clear to her now that nobody at *Banter* knew that he was gay. That was the ironic thing. They thought he was straight, which was why they found it so amusing to rib him about his dress sense and his taste in music. If they found out he had a boyfriend . . . Alexa baulked at the thought. They would eat him alive.

'Ms Long!' cried Derek, extracting a flat, floppy parcel and discarding the empty sack on the floor.

Alexa felt something lurch inside her. She had been secretly hoping that Sienna had forgotten to put her name in the hat or that her 'Santa' had omitted to buy her a present. She grasped the package and nodded in mock amusement at the wrapping paper, which was adorned with hundreds of very small, tessellating genitalia.

The tape came away easily in her hands and against her will, Alexa found herself pushing the paper to one side as she revealed, to much amusement, a black peephole bra and crotchless thong set.

Despite the alcohol, Alexa could feel her heart pounding as the wolf-whistles and shouting intensified around her. It wasn't her imagination; everyone was looking at her.

'Put 'em on!' cried Louis, from the other end of the table.

'On! On!' cried Marcus, looking around and encouraging others to join in.

Alexa froze, feeling the walls of the club swoop towards her and then quickly retreat, like tent walls blowing in a breeze. Her stomach seemed to be rejecting the toxic mix inside her and the chanting was making things worse.

'On! On!' went the chant, accompanied by the rhythmic thud of palms and cutlery against the table.

Alexa fingered the lacy fabric in her hands. The shouting was making her feel dizzy and the combination of alcohol and anxiety was turning her insides. She felt as though she might vomit any minute, but she knew that that would serve as no excuse to the boys. She had stick this out, to perform – to do as any one of them would do in the same situation. She had to put on the underwear.

'Alright!' she cried, waiting for the clamouring to die down.

The sickness abated a little and Alexa managed a smile. Slowly, with as much conviction as she could muster, she pushed back her chair and stepped into the small, lacy knickers, pulling them delicately over the top of her trousers and feeling grateful for her choice of outfit tonight. Kate's party dress had come a close second, but she had rejected it on the grounds that it showed too much leg. She was vaguely aware of the irony that she was now currently modelling a crotchless thong purchased by one of her colleagues.

Alexa reached for the bra, still feeling queasy but pressing on. She was very aware that the photos taken by the likes of Biscuit and Greg on their phones would probably find their way onto the internet at some point and could count against her in future roles – or even *this* role, given the potential for misuse by activists – but she also knew that there was no alternative. If she wanted to be a fully-fledged member of the *Banter* team, to lead them to success, then she had to act the part. Slowly, she picked up the peephole bra and fastened it around her chest, twisting it over her silk blouse.

It was a good fit, she was embarrassed to note. She didn't like the idea that one of her colleagues had sized up her breasts so accurately. Pulling the straps up over her shoulders, Alexa glanced up, offering a sly smile to those with camera phones. She was horrified to find Derek looking sideways at her, saying nothing, just appraising her with a slightly creepy smile on his face. Alexa dropped her eyes to the task in hand.

The bra looked ridiculous, of course, but that was the idea. On Sienna's suggestion, she performed a little spin on the spot for the benefit of those with phones. Jamie, she noted, was taking apart his camera – either as a distraction from his own shame or from hers, she didn't know. Either way, it was one less photographer to worry about.

Eventually, the cat-calls started to wane and attention returned to Derek, who was offering for someone to shave off his facial hair in return for the next round of shots. Alexa stumbled back into her chair and was embarrassed to find that it was already occupied. She started to clamber out of Riz's lap, trying to work out how she had ended up here, two seats along from hers. The spinning must have disorientated her.

'Oh, um . . . hi. Sorry.' She tried to push herself to her feet, but the ground seemed a long way down and she could feel the heat of Riz's arm along her back, which wasn't an altogether unpleasant sensation.

'Hello.' He smiled. 'This is unexpected.'

Alexa nodded, half-heartedly pushing herself to her feet again but distracted by the look on Riz's face. His dark, handsome eyes were boring straight into hers, quite intensely – as though he were searching for something in her expression. Alexa met his gaze, determined that this time, just once, she wouldn't revert to mindless babbling. She found herself wishing they were some-where else, away from the *Banter* Christmas do, away from their colleagues. Her gaze wandered to his perfectly chiselled, clean-shaven jaw and his dark complexion and then reverted to his eyes. Such gorgeous eyes. Alexa found herself fighting the urge to lean in and kiss him.

She jumped off his lap and looked away, suddenly appalled at her own thoughts.

'Sorry,' she said, stumbling backwards, away from the table. 'Wrong chair.'

Alexa blinked, trying to wipe the remains of the fantasy from her mind. What had she been *thinking*? She was obviously blind drunk. Alexa wandered off in the direction of the ladies', morti-fied yet distracted. She was struggling to separate the reality of what had just happened from the thoughts of what might have happened. The two scenes were blurring in her head. The muscular arm around her back was real, and his smile, and . . . had Riz been staring at her as though he wanted to kiss her, too?

Alexa stumbled into the ladies', taking stock of herself in the mirror under the bright, white lights. She was still wearing the peephole underwear over her outfit. She looked absurd. There was no way Riz could have been thinking about her in that way. She wrenched off the underwear and shoved it deep into the waste paper bin, splashing some cold water on her face. She still felt woozy, but no longer woozy enough to throw up. The shock of coming round from her daydream on Riz's lap had sobered her up a little.

Alexa stared at her flushed cheeks in the mirror, bracing herself for the rest of the night. She had no idea what time it was; it felt as though they'd been going for hours. She wasn't going to drink any more tonight. Since splitting up with Matt, Alexa had barely touched alcohol – she hadn't had time – and it seemed to be having a disproportionate effect on her body. Either that or she'd just drunk way too much. Water. That was what she needed. She dried her face and headed back into the club.

The lighting had been dimmed in her absence, leaving the dance floor and the corridor that led up to it in relative darkness. Alexa stopped for a moment, letting her eyes adjust as the door swung shut on the harsh, bright toilet lighting.

'Hel-*lo*,' said a male voice, with exaggerated intonation. Alexa squinted into the darkness and realised that the man walking towards her was someone exceedingly short. It had to be Derek.

'Didn't you like your peephole undies?' he asked, sending fumes of Sambuca wafting towards her.

'They weren't really my style,' she replied curtly. The darkness was making her feel dizzy again. She focused on a spot over Derek's shoulder, trying to find a point of reference and maintain her vertical position.

'Y'know, I've been thinking,' said Derek, moving closer.

'God help us,' Alexa replied, stepping back from the fumes. Her heel hit the wall and she realised that she was trapped between Derek and the gents'.

'I think,' said Derek, slowly, 'that you should do a shoot for *Banter*. A topless shoot.'

He leaned towards her, putting out an arm as he stumbled against the wall.

Alexa tried to shift sideways, but Derek's other arm blocked her way, his hand hitting the wall with a smack. She was trapped.

'I think you'd enjoy it. You could let your hair down a bit. You've got the figure for it, you know you have.'

Alexa froze. She could see his eyes now, beady and drunk, wandering up and down her body. She could feel his breath, too, hot and fast, on her chest. There were several things she wanted to say but she didn't dare say any of them. She couldn't move, for fear that it might bring their flesh closer together. Her heart was pounding.

'Why don't you do it?' he asked. Maybe he was standing on tip-toes, because his face was suddenly level with hers. 'You'd love it. See, I don't believe all this self-respect bollocks you preach in the office. You wanna get your kit off as much as the next girl. You wanna get on all fours and spread your legs, knowing that there's men all over the country jerking off to—'

All of a sudden, Derek's face was illuminated in white as the door to the gents' swung open.

Alexa looked sideways just in time to see the silhouette appear in the doorway, hesitating for a second and then hastening down the corridor, head down. She recognised the man's broad shoulders and closed her eyes for a second, knowing how the scene would have looked to Riz.

As quickly as he had approached, Derek stumbled off in the direction of the gents', mumbling something about 'fucking women'. Alexa blinked into the darkness, rooted to the spot, unable to move. She was no longer trapped against the wall, but her knees felt too weak to carry her and every muscle in her body was shaking.

After a couple of seconds, Alexa summoned the energy to leave the corridor and head back to the club. Running through her mind was a series of snapshots from the last few minutes.

She could still hear the echo of Derek's words. *You'd love it . . .*
You wanna get on all fours . . . Then the silhouette in the doorway.
She had to find Riz. She had to explain.

The dance floor was a confusing blur of bodies and shadows
and strobe lighting. Alexa traced random, desperate patterns
across it, looking left and right for a glimpse of his tall physique,
but there was no sign. She found Paddy by the DJ booth, but
he claimed not to have seen Riz since dinner. Biscuit and Greg
were by the bar, but they were so drunk they didn't understand
the question. Alexa raced off the dance floor and returned to
the area where they had eaten.

The table had been cleared to one side, with the chairs stacked
up alongside it and a large mound of clothing, bags, gifts and
general debris in a trail across the floor. Alexa looked about
hopelessly. She was about to head back to the dance floor when
she caught sight of two familiar faces, illuminated in the blue
glow of a camera display.

'Jamie?' Alexa shouted, above the din.

He looked up and raised a hand. His junior assistant gave a
little wave.

'Have you seen Riz?' she yelled.

'Seen what?'

'Riz!' she repeated, cupping her hand to his ear.

'Oh!' Jamie nodded. 'Yeah – he just left! Why?'

Alexa shrugged vaguely. 'Doesn't matter.'

As soon as Jamie's attention returned to the camera, Alexa
rummaged through the mound of belongings and drew out her
bag. The alcohol and adrenaline were mixing things up in her head,
but the only thing she felt certain about was that she had to explain
things to Riz. She couldn't let him leave before she had told him
the truth about what he had seen.

Scrambling up the two flights of steps, Alexa emerged at street
level, flustered and panting. There was a long line of people
outside the club, but Riz wasn't among them. The streets of Soho

were overflowing with suited revellers, looking for places to go, post-Christmas do. Alexa scanned the groups, trying to identify her colleague among them. He wasn't there.

Eventually, she gave up, reluctantly admitting that Riz must have picked up a cab. She thought about sending him an email, but this wasn't something that could be conveyed electronically – nor was it something she wanted to talk about in a form that could be forwarded on to others.

Alexa stuck out her hand and flagged down a cab for herself. She felt dizzy and sick, and it wasn't just the alcohol. It was the thought of what was to come.

29

The office was buzzing with pre-Christmas activity. In addition to the usual Thursday frenzy, there was the additional pressure of getting the first issue of the next year lined up, complete with end-of-year Real Girls Roundup, and the *Banter Anthology* – a hardback collection of favourites from the past seven years – ready for print before the break.

Alexa looked up and squinted at the features desk. She had been due to meet them ten minutes ago to discuss content for next month's first tablet edition. Neil was gulping down coffee as he sifted through page proofs, while his colleagues were taking his garbled feedback and rushing between desks like worker bees on speed. She decided to postpone the meeting.

On their way back to her screen, Alexa's eyes flitted to the tuft of greasy hair poking up above Derek's desk. A week had passed since the Christmas do and not a word had passed between them about what had happened. They had conversed on editorial matters, just as they always had done. Derek had remained civil towards her in his surly, resentful way, but there hadn't been so much as a glance that hinted at remorse for his actions. Alexa wondered whether he even remembered the incident.

She sent a cancellation note to the features team, still thinking about the situation with her deputy editor. She knew, as she had known all week, that it was her duty to make Derek realise that what he had done was unacceptable – that it was an act of sexual harassment. Alexa thought back to the moment she had realised she was trapped in the darkness and shuddered. She *wanted* Derek brought to justice, but she knew that the process of achieving that goal would be as painful for her as it would for him – probably more so. It was a repeat of the dilemma she had found herself in with the porn in her proofs. At best, she would have Derek convicted but find herself without a job and saddled with a reputation that would make it impossible to get another job. At worst, she would sacrifice her reputation, her career and her self-esteem for an accusation that could never be proved.

The option of just keeping quiet seemed increasingly appealing – especially given the likelihood that Derek had no recollection of events. If that was the case, then Alexa's preference was to keep it that way. She knew it was a cop-out, but at the back of her mind, she was secretly hoping that he had been so drunk he didn't remember what he had done.

There was, of course, one giant flaw in her plan. Even if Derek didn't remember the incident, there was someone else who did. Or rather, there was someone else who remembered something from the night, even if his recollection wasn't an accurate representation of what had happened. Alexa had spent the whole week trying to find a way to approach Riz about what he had seen, but there just never seemed to be a good time.

'Christmas post!' cried Paddy, stopping to adjust the elf costume that Biscuit had forced upon him as he dropped a pile of envelopes on her desk.

Alexa looked up to thank him but he was already lolloping back through the office. She wondered whether the lack of eye contact was significant. She couldn't help feeling that there had been a shift in attitude towards her this week. People were looking away, keeping quiet, avoiding contact. Perhaps they were just busy, or it might have been an after-effect of the nipple-free edition – or maybe just her paranoia – but it made her feel

263

uncomfortable. She worried that Derek had been spreading rumours about what had or hadn't happened in the club.

Most of the envelopes contained invoices. There was one from the mobile app developers, one from the freelance content editor working on the tablet edition, one from the modelling agency and . . . Alexa froze as she pulled out the next invoice. It wasn't an invoice at all. It was a flimsy postcard, like the type given away free in trendy bars. On its front was an image of a voluptuous blonde, her breasts spilling out of a low-cut, sparkly top either side of a vertical silver pole. In the bottom right-hand corner was a purple logo and a slogan written in a swirly font: *Playtime – the nation's favourite table dancing club.* Alexa could feel her pulse quicken. She flipped over the card to reveal densely-packed, child-like handwriting, covering its full width.

Dear Alexa, she read.

Just wanted to wish you a merry Christmas and to let you know that our offer still stands. Haven't heard from you since our shopping trip – my number is below, in case you've lost it. Give me a call sometime.

Merry Christmas, G.

P.S. A little festive story from the refuge: Brigita works as a dancer at Playtime. Last week one of her clients got drunk at a Christmas party and cut her face with a bottle. Perhaps next time we're on TV we can talk about how empowering it is for women to take their clothes off for strangers . . .

Alexa folded the card in two, then four, then eight and then hurled it into the bin. She knew that she shouldn't let these things get to her, but they did. Georgie's unwanted interjections were getting in the way of her plans. It wasn't that she believed in the link between *Banter* and all the horrendous case studies of misogyny that the girl dredged up; Alexa knew that the atrocities weren't the result of her publication's attitude towards women. But at the same time, she wasn't naïve enough to deny that the perpetrator of such acts *might* be the type of man who

264

also enjoyed flicking through *Banter*. Nevertheless, *Banter wasn't the cause.*

Alexa opened the final envelope, stacking the invoice on top of the others and trying to concentrate on the business plan on the screen. The resentment continued to weigh her down, her mind distracted by thoughts of Brigita and table dancers and drunk men at Christmas parties and . . . the scene with Derek in the club. She couldn't help making the connection. Yet again, Georgie seemed to have hit a nerve.

She looked down and realised that her phone was trilling away inside her bag.

'Hello?' she gabbled, grateful for the distraction.

'Hello, dear! Only me.'

Alexa pushed back her chair and hastened towards the lobby, feeling a plunging sense of unease. She was still working for an institution that her mother despised and she *still* hadn't told her mother about Matt.

'Are you at work?'

'Yes,' she replied, as civilly as she could, given the accusatory tone of the question.

'Oh. Well, I won't keep you. I just wanted to check on dates for Christmas, so I can sort out the beds – we've got quite a few guests staying, you see. I'm assuming you'll arrive on Christmas Eve and stay until the new year?'

'Mmm,' Alexa replied uncertainly. She had to tell her about Matt, *now,* before all the arrangements were made.

'Good. So, I was thinking of putting Auntie Jen in with Aunt Sue in the spare bedroom and then Rachel and Tim can have your room, so that would mean you and Matt could have the downstairs room and anyone else can stay in the lounge.'

'Um . . .' Alexa closed her eyes and leaned back on the metal panel that framed the lift. She wasn't ready for this.

'Of course, that's assuming Angie's lot don't stay – if they do, then maybe they can go downstairs, as they've got the baby.'

Alexa braced herself to speak.

'Or, we could always put them in the spare room and then Auntie Jen and Aunt Sue can—'

'It's alright, Mum,' said Alexa, cutting her off, mid-flow. 'I'll sleep in the lounge. Matt's not coming.'

'Oh?'

Alexa forced out the words. 'I'm not seeing him any more.'

'You're . . .' Alexa's mother took a couple of seconds to digest this information. 'You're not?' She sounded weak, all of a sudden.

'No,' Alexa replied softly. 'We split up a few weeks ago.'

Her explanation was deliberately vague so that her mother wouldn't have to know that it had all happened long before they had last spoken.

'Oh.'

Alexa could hear the disappointment in her mother's voice. She opened her eyes and let her head fall back against the metal, overcome by the familiar sense of shame. Her mother had approved of Matt. He was the one element in her life that she wholeheartedly endorsed, and Alexa had lost him. She had let her mother down again.

'It was . . . well, it just didn't seem to be working,' she explained. There was no point in admitting that it had been her obsession with *Banter* – with her career – that had driven them apart. That would open up a whole new set of arguments and I-told-you-sos.

'That's a shame,' said her mother, quietly.

'Mmm.' Alexa felt relieved that her mother didn't seem to want to seek out a reason or apportion blame. Maybe her mother understood something of what she had been through, she thought. Maybe she recognised how much Matt had meant to her – recognised that Alexa was sad enough already and didn't need anyone to rub it in.

'The lounge it is, then!' cried her mother with false jollity. 'Oh. I told you about the award, didn't I? Well, it turns out,' she went on without pausing for an answer, 'the winner will be announced over Christmas, so that's something to look forward to, isn't it?'

Alexa agreed, glad of the change of subject and aware, not for the first time, that her mother was longing to win this award. She suddenly understood what it felt like to wish for somebody else's success – and she did wish for her mother's success, despite the distance between them. It was harder than simply wanting something for yourself, because you had no control. She could almost understand why her mother had expressed such disappointment every time she hadn't quite made the grade. She had just been desperate for her daughter to succeed.

'Well, we'll see you on Christmas Eve, then.'

Alexa smiled, despite her mother's blatant false cheer. 'See you then. 'Bye, Mum.'

She returned to her desk to find Sienna leaning over it, looking at something on the screen and revealing a good proportion of the red, lacy knickers under her skirt.

'Have you got a catch-up in the diary?' she asked, straightening up. Several men got back to work.

Alexa checked her calendar and realised that she did in fact have a meeting with Sienna, to mark the end of her three-month probationary period working on Banter TV. She had completely forgotten to prepare for it – although, as it happened, very little preparation was required. Sienna had more than earned her promotion and pay rise.

'Do you have time?' she asked.

Sienna nodded. 'I think we should meet.'

Alexa led the way into the glass-walled meeting room, mildly amused by the tone of Sienna's response. She obviously knew she was in line for promotion.

'Well,' said Alexa, smiling reassuringly as the blonde settled in her seat. 'This won't take long. I've been really pleased with the work you've done on Banter TV. I'm also impressed with your

267

writing and . . .' She tried to think of a way to put it tactfully. 'Your general attitude around the office.' She gave a meaningful look, but couldn't tell whether Sienna clocked it. 'I'm pleased to say that you've earned yourself the pay rise we talked about and the new title of senior writer.'

Sienna's reaction was not one that Alexa had anticipated. She wasn't so much smiling as *laughing*. It was a coy laughter, as though Sienna knew something that Alexa didn't.

'Sorry,' said the girl, eventually. She tried to wipe the smile from her mouth but it seemed immovable. 'Sorry, it's . . . well, it's just as well, really.'

'What is?'

'The job. It's just as well I got the promotion, 'cause I told the guys at *Monsieur* it was a dead cert.'

Alexa looked at her, confused. 'What guys at *Monsieur*?'

Sienna's face suddenly straightened. 'I've got a new job,' she announced. 'On the news desk at *Monsieur*.'

Alexa said nothing for a moment. She shouldn't have been surprised, but she was. Sienna had always been on the lookout for her next move – Riz had warned her of that and it was evident in the way she behaved. She was a talented writer. Smutty, perhaps, but talented. She would do well at *Monsieur*.

'Congratulations,' she said, feeling suddenly overcome with a mixture of pride and sadness. There had been a time when she would have gladly seen the back of the surly PA, when her sluttish behaviour had overshadowed any benefits she brought to the team. But now Alexa saw her for what she was: a sassy young woman trying to climb the slippery ladder – much like her, in that respect. Sienna had her own ideas about how to climb it, but Alexa understood that now. She recognised the girl's assets – not just the visible ones – and she felt proud to have played a part in her ascent from PA to fully-fledged news writer. She didn't dare ask which assets Sienna had used to acquire herself the position on the *Monsieur* news desk – or whether there was any connection to the Facebook fiasco.

'So, I guess this is me handing in my notice,' said Sienna. Alexa thought she detected a hint of regret in her voice.

Alexa nodded, trying to think practically. 'Are you on one month's notice?'

'A week,' Sienna replied. 'Sorry.'

Alexa let out a little sigh. It was Christmas next week. They'd never be able to replace Sienna before the new year. In fact, maybe they'd never replace Sienna.

'Well,' she said as they rose from their seats. 'You'll be missed.'

Sienna gave her a sceptical look. 'Yeah, right.' She laid a hand against the door and then stopped and looked back at Alexa with a sly, sideways grin. 'Anyway,' she said. 'Sounds as though you're giving the lads plenty to get excited about, from what I've heard.'

She raised an eyebrow, letting her gaze linger on Alexa for a fraction of a second, and then flounced back into the office.

30

'What d'you mean by inexperienced?' asked Alexa, wearily. It was four o'clock on Christmas Eve; she wanted to go home.

'She's a school leaver,' the HR representative replied in a similar tone. 'She's only ever done summer jobs.'

'Summer jobs where?'

'Er . . .' There was a sound of rustling papers. 'Teddington Pies and Bakery, Nando's in Wimbledon . . . and Secrets, which is, um . . . a plus-size bra-packing factory.'

Alexa sighed. This was futile. Not a single one of the suggested replacements for Sienna was remotely suitable for the role.

'What about that internal transfer you mentioned?' she asked, trying to inject some optimism into her voice.

'She didn't like the idea of working for *Banter*.'

'Right.' Alexa dropped her pen on the blank piece of paper in front of her, conceding that the call was unlikely to yield anything useful. She wouldn't dwell on the candidate's reason for dismissing the role. 'Well,' she said, weakly. 'Keep looking, I guess.'

The woman snorted quietly. 'With respect, Alexa, I don't think there's much point. It's Christmas Day tomorrow. *Most* people have other things on their minds.'

Alexa ignored the dig. 'Fine,' she said, civilly. 'We'll pick up the search in the new year. But please don't give up. We have to find someone soon.'

'I understand,' the woman said curtly. 'Goodbye.'

'Merry Christmas to you too!' cried Alexa, to the dead line. She let the phone fall back into its cradle and sighed. There were plenty of things still on her to-do list, but it was looking as though they would have to wait until the new year. She had promised her parents she'd be home in time for dinner.

'Don't you have a home to go to?'

Alexa looked up. Jamie was standing, bag on shoulder, in the middle of the deserted office.

'Don't *you*?' she countered.

He smiled. 'I'm off there now.'

'Me too.' Alexa started to shut down her machine, looking around for any notes she might need for the break. She intended to use her laptop as an excuse for ducking out of family commitments if it all got too much. A week was a long time to spend with parents at twenty-nine.

She hauled her laptop bag onto one shoulder, smiling gratefully as Jamie leaned in and hooked the spare strap over her flailing arm. He looked away as she tried to catch his eye.

They walked to the lift together and stood in the lobby, waiting in what felt to Alexa like awkward silence.

'It's—'

'So—'

They were both speaking at once. They laughed, each motioning for the other to go first.

'No, go on.' Alexa conceded – mainly because she hadn't really had anything to say; she'd simply been planning to comment on the exceptional quietness of the building.

'I just . . .' Jamie stepped back, allowing Alexa to enter the lift first.

'You what?' she prompted, feeling a familiar nagging sensation at the back of her mind as she tried to guess what this was about. Two possibilities sprang to mind, and she didn't like either.

They started to descend.

'No, I was just . . . wondering about something.' Jamie looked at the lift floor.

The possibilities narrowed down to one in her mind. This clearly wasn't about Jamie and the homophobic Christmas present he'd been given by Secret Santa; this was about her.

'What?' she pressed, with trepidation.

'Well,' he said to the floor, 'I just wondered whether it was true, what I'd heard.'

They arrived at the ground floor, but Alexa couldn't move. Her worst fears were confirmed. There *were* rumours going around about what had happened at the Christmas do. She should have done something to stop them. Derek hadn't been too drunk to remember, after all. He was obviously spreading some warped version of events to anyone who cared to listen – which was everyone at *Banter*. Or worse, thought Alexa, maybe *Riz* was talking about what he had seen. Maybe he wasn't the trustworthy comrade she had assumed him to be.

'I'll take that as a no,' said Jamie, with a nervous laugh.

They stopped just inside the door. 'Yes – I mean, no. It's not true.' Alexa gulped. She felt sick at the thought of what was being said behind her back. Who was talking? What exactly were they saying? How many people knew?

'Oh.' Jamie nodded. 'Pity.'

Alexa looked at him, appalled at the implication. There was nothing remotely pitiable about the fact that the rumours were false.

'What d'you mean?'

'Well,' Jamie shrugged. 'It's been a while since we've had any proper juicy office flings.' He leaned in and smiled. 'Sienna aside, of course.'

Alexa just stared at him. Surely he didn't *want* her to be having a relationship with Derek? Gossip was one thing, but *Derek*? The thought of it made her feel ill. Surely Jamie, of all people, saw the deputy editor as the loathsome misogynist that he was?

'Oh, well.' Jamie pushed on the door, holding it open for Alexa to follow. 'I'm sure it will've blown over by the new year.'

Alexa slipped out into the darkness, in a daze. It was like being in one of those stressful, confusing nightmares where everything was out of your control and nobody else seemed to understand the problem. She raised a hand, suddenly wanting to get as far as she could from Senate House and Jamie and the rumours. Then something dawned on her.

'Sorry,' she said. 'Can you just . . . um, who did you think this "fling" involved?'

He looked perplexed. 'Only you and Riz. Why, were there more?'

Alexa just shook her head mutely. She found herself holding up a hand and wishing Jamie a Merry Christmas, then stumbling down the steps of Senate House and moving, on autopilot, towards the tube. Riz? *Riz?* How had that happened?

Slowly, she worked it out. This wasn't a case of Derek or Riz spreading rumours; it was something the lads had cobbled together for themselves. All they knew was that the sports editor had left the Christmas do early, followed shortly by Alexa, who, earlier in the night, had perched drunkenly on Riz's lap and had been last seen scouring the club for Riz. When questioned, Riz would have said nothing, maintaining his discretion in light of potential rumours about Alexa and Derek. Inadvertently, he had poured fuel on his own fire.

Alexa ploughed blindly through the crowds, trying to work out how she felt about this new revelation. It was reassuring to know that news of Derek's harassment hadn't translated into anything more sinister, but also . . . well, she didn't mind so much that the lads had cooked up an imaginary fling between Riz and herself. It was embarrassing – not to mention unfounded – but if she had to have an imaginary fling with someone, then of all the people in the office, Riz was not a bad option.

Alexa's jostled for a route into the heaving crowds of the tube station. She was almost at the bottom of the steps when she realised that her phone was ringing.

'Hello?' she yelled, turning and fighting her way back to ground level to get some reception.

'Hi, Alexa. It's Denise again, from HR. Good news: we've got you the perfect candidate for your editorial assistant role. She's called Emma, she's twenty-three, she's an English graduate from Brunel and she has two years' experience at Global Media. She comes straight from *Joy* magazine and she's keen to start ASAP.'

Alexa clamped the phone to her ear, wondering whether she'd misheard.

'Are you serious?' She found a gap in the flow of people just inside the station entrance and flattened herself against the wall. 'What's the catch?'

'No catch,' Denise replied proudly. 'She's after a challenge. I'll let you interview her, but I think she's a goer.'

Alexa thanked the HR rep and leaned back against the dirty, tiled station wall. *A challenge.* That wouldn't be a problem, she thought, smiling. She didn't want to get her hopes up too soon, but Alexa felt strangely excited by the prospect of the next four months.

31

'Well, that was nice, wasn't it? Everybody seems to be doing well.'

Alexa's mother threw the oven glove over her shoulder and bent down to pick up a stray mince pie from the carpet. The lounge was strewn with cups, plates, wine glasses, champagne flutes and leftover food from a three-day eating and drinking binge, every spare inch of floor space covered in makeshift seating and clutter, courtesy of the various family members who had descended upon Elm Rise in the last few days. Alexa couldn't help feeling relieved that the ordeal was over.

'Josh is a charming little fellow now, isn't he?'

Alexa exchanged a glance with her dad, who quickly shook his head and looked down at the floor. Clearly they weren't going to talk about the incident when the charming four-year-old had spat his Christmas cake out onto Aunt Sue's lap, or the point at which he had demanded to know why Auntie Jen didn't have a husband. Having spent much of her Christmas break somewhere between the kitchen and the lounge or upstairs, making beds, Alexa's mother had missed out on a few of the more fraught family moments.

'He liked his Christmas present,' Alexa remarked buoyantly, managing to keep a straight face as she pictured the boy careering around the house in the shimmering outfit that her parents had inadvertently bought him.

Her mother gave her a scalding look. 'Yes, well,' she said huffily, rounding on her husband. 'We know who's to blame for *that*.'

Alexa's dad shrugged helplessly. 'I told you, I thought it said *prince*; the SS looked like a size ... you know, XS or something.'

'Are you *blind*?' cried her mother, with unexpected venom. 'What sort of a prince outfit comes in lurid pink with a *tiara*? Honestly, John.'

'I didn't have my glasses on,' he explained quietly.

Alexa flashed him a sympathetic look, feeling guilty for stirring things up. Her mother was storming across the room, grabbing beanbags and piling them up by the door. She seemed tetchy now that the guests had gone. Two days of intensive feeding, fretting and festive joy had obviously taken its toll on her patience.

'Don't worry,' said Alexa, remembering something she had learned recently. 'There are too many stereotypes for young kids, anyway. That's why boys and girls turn out so different. Maybe you'll do him a favour by mixing things up a bit.'

Her mother stopped, beanbag in hand, and stared at her daughter.

'Boys and girls are *supposed* to be different,' she said, through gritted teeth. 'You should know. You're the one who works in *pornography*.' She sighed noisily and headed into the kitchen.

Alexa glanced at her dad, who stood, flattened against the wall in his wife's wake. He lifted his shoulders in a gesture of mutual ignorance, to which Alexa tried to respond, but she couldn't. She couldn't pretend she didn't understand what the fuss was about, because she did. She knew how her mother felt about her place of work. She ought to have known better than to come out with such a stupid, hypocritical line. It was stolen from Georgie Caraway, for God's sake – of course it was hypocritical. She knew that her relationship with her mother was a precarious one. They were treading a thin line, maintaining an outwardly peaceful relationship by avoiding contentious subjects and pretending that everything was fine, but the mere mention of gender stereotypes was enough to set fireworks flying. On Alexa's trigger, her mother's frayed nerves had caught light.

Alexa set about collecting the remaining cups from around the room, feeling annoyed at herself for being so thoughtless. On the surface, she and her mother had been getting on well since their conciliatory phone call. Like a fool, Alexa had taken this to mean that something had mellowed inside her mother. But it hadn't. Deep down, she was still the prudish, old-fashioned scout leader who saw children's soap operas as harmful to society. Alexa was cross with herself for letting her hopes get in the way of common sense.

Out of the corner of her eye, she saw her father move away from the wall, scratching his head for a couple of seconds before wandering out. She carried the mugs into the kitchen and slid them onto the draining board, retreating quickly and avoiding her mother's eye. She returned to the lounge and started collecting the balls of wrapping paper from around the room, feeling the aggravation and guilt rub together inside her. She should have thought.

Bundling the wrapping paper into the waste paper bin, Alexa crouched down, working her way along the trail of cake crumbs that Josh had trodden into the carpet and picking them out with her fingernails. In the kitchen, her father was whistling a tuneless rendition of 'O Come All Ye Faithful', clearly oblivious to the tension. Alexa wondered how he felt about her role at *Banter*. She had never actually asked. She imagined that he would take the side of her mother, for the sake of household peace and because he didn't have the energy to come up with his own opinions any more. But if she *forced* him to think . . . Alexa tried to picture her dad flicking through a copy of *Banter*. She couldn't help feeling that, deep down, he was liberal enough to see that it was just another magazine.

She crept into the kitchen, her hands filled with fruity crumbs. Her mother was washing wine glasses in the sink with what seemed like unnecessary vigour. Alexa watched anxiously, waiting for one to smash.

'Mum?' she said, quietly.

Her mother whipped round, sending soap suds flying across the kitchen. Her face was set in a deep frown.

'Can I just get to the bin?' With cupped hands, Alexa motioned for her mother to open the cupboard under the sink.

Her mother obliged, stepping back for Alexa to deposit her load, wine glass dripping onto the floor. Alexa was about to ask whether the beanbags needed cleaning or whether they could be put away as they were, but when she looked at her mother's face, the words deserted her. There was a crumpled look of despair where the frown had just been: she had tired, hollow eyes, a lined forehead and lips that were pressed together so tightly that they had lost all their colour. Alexa wondered whether her mother was about to cry.

She stood, looking at her mother, glancing down at the glass in her hand. It had stopped dripping now and Alexa wondered whether her mother had forgotten she was still holding it.

'Shall I . . .' She reached for the glass, not sure what else to do. In thirty years, she had never witnessed her mother crying.

'I'm sorry,' croaked her mother, falling back against the kitchen worktop. There were no tears, but her eyes looked red and she was clearly having difficulty controlling her breathing. 'Sorry I snapped,' she said, stiltedly.

Alexa took a step closer. She wanted to reach out and hold her mother – to squeeze her against her chest and to reassure her. She knew how it felt to be tired and irrational and angry; she had inherited those genes. But she couldn't. It was as though there was an invisible barrier around her mother. She had never been one of those smothering, hair-ruffling mothers; she wasn't the type to encourage physical contact. So Alexa stood, awkwardly, watching her mother try to stifle her emotions.

'I think I'm tired,' she explained, sniffing. 'I didn't mean it – about your job.'

Alexa leaned sideways against the kitchen surface, pulling off a sheet of kitchen roll and handing it to her mother.

'Yes, you did,' she said, softly.

Her mother pressed the absorbent paper against her face for a couple of seconds and then emerged, blinking at Alexa.

'It's alright,' said Alexa, feeling strangely emboldened by her new role as comforter. 'It's me who should be apologising. I know you don't approve of the magazine – I know you'd rather I didn't work there.'

'I just . . .' Her mother let out a quiet sigh. 'I just can't stand the idea of you in that place . . . with all those *images* . . .'

Alexa said nothing for a moment. She was glad that her mother hadn't ever been to the fifth floor of Senate House. If she had, she'd realise that the images were the least of Alexa's concerns.

'It's not how you think,' she said, truthfully. It was worse.

'Isn't it? I mean, how can that be? I've seen the magazine. I've seen those grotesque, insulting . . .'

She stopped, suddenly, looking out towards the hallway. Alexa found herself doing the same. She heard it too: the harsh trill of the phone.

They stood, frozen, for a moment, waiting for the thud of feet on the stairs to indicate that her father had taken the initiative. The phone continued to ring.

A moment later, Alexa reluctantly stepped aside to allow her mother to hurry into the hallway.

'Averley nine-two-eight?' she heard. Then there was silence. Then a gasp. Then more silence. Alexa crept to the kitchen doorway, peering out and trying to interpret the conversation by reading her mother's body language.

'Really?' Her mother gasped again. There were still no tears, Alexa noted.

After a few muted words of concurrence, Alexa heard the sound of the phone being put back in its cradle.

The footsteps were slower on her mother's return to the

kitchen. Alexa slipped away from the door, trying to prepare for anything. As she thought about what she had heard, something dawned on her. It suddenly made sense that her mother had been tetchy and emotional all day. It wasn't just Christmas exhaustion; she had been waiting for news.

'Well?' she asked as her mother stepped over the threshold.

Alexa needn't have asked. Her mother's face looked ten years younger than the one that had left the room. She was beaming like a little kid.

'That was the County Council,' she said, weakly. 'I won the Unsung Hero of the Year award.'

Alexa looked at her mother, feeling the emotion well up inside her as she abandoned her reservations and threw her arms recklessly around her mother's neck. She held on, feeling as though she might burst with pride at the thought of what her mother had done to deserve the award. Slowly, unexpectedly, she felt her mother's arms tighten around her shoulders and she held on, feeling a wave of relief pass over her as she squeezed even harder.

Her eyes were scrunched shut but behind them, Alexa could feel tears building up. She blinked, allowing them to spill out onto her sleeve as she gripped her mother's blouse. She knew that there was no comparison between what her mother had done in the last ten years and what she was trying to do at *Banter*, but it felt as though somehow, if she put everything she could into the next three months and made the very best of the opportunity, then her mother wouldn't be able to help feeling a tiny bit proud of her daughter, in the way that Alexa felt proud of her. Then one day, she resolved, she would do something as worthy as what her mother had done. She just had to get through the next three months.

32

Alexa swiped her finger across the glossy screen and eyed the visuals appraisingly. It was a lot of flesh to take in at once: legs, buttocks, cleavages, all smoothed and buffed to perfection by Jamie's team. She tapped on the interactive Girl Guide and clicked through to the New Year Babewatch teaser, finding herself face to face with a giant pair of breasts that belonged to the winner of the previous year's Real Girls Roundup.

She wondered briefly whether it might be too much of an eyeful for the reader, but decided to leave it be. This was the first edition of their tablet app and they wanted to make an impact. It wasn't enough that they would be the first lads' mag to launch; Alexa wanted them to be the first *and* the best, which meant upping the nipple count and ramming the pages full of girls. She understood that now and she was determined to use the insight to her advantage. *Banter* was going to blow *Diss* and the other lads' mags out of the water.

She followed the instructions on the screen and swiped her finger in a downward direction, in line with the zip of the girl's cat suit. The girl became naked except for a tiny, lacy thong. Alexa swiped upwards, smiling as the catsuit reappeared. Down, up. Down, up. She had a good feeling about this. It had potential. The content that filled the pages of *Banter* was ideally suited to the medium and if her analysis proved correct, the readership was exactly the type to own tablet devices and download apps.

As with the mobile launch, there was no guarantee of success, but it felt as though they were doing everything right. If *they* couldn't make a success of it, she thought, then nobody could. But they would. She would make sure that they would.

'Come on, just do it!' cried Marcus, prompting Alexa to look up.

Across the desk, some form of induction was taking place for Emma, the new editorial assistant who was replacing Sienna. Perhaps foolishly, Alexa had left her in the hands of Paddy to introduce her to the rest of the team. They seemed to have spent an inordinate amount of time on the news desk, she observed, much of which had involved Derek, for no apparent reason. He had taken to calling her 'Emsie' and was clearly enjoying the opportunity to recycle the same in-jokes that he had used on Sienna, regarding her 'assets' and her 'capacity'.

'Just a little suck, that's all.' Derek waggled his eyebrows in a way that was probably designed to appear seductive.

'Don't be ridiculous,' said the girl, tossing her head away from the large, black dildo that Marcus was waving in her face – the same toy that had appeared on Alexa's desk on her first day. 'I'm not going *near* that thing. I don't know where it's been.'

'Go on,' goaded Marcus, talking to the back of the girl's head. 'It's part of the initiation. You have to.'

Emma sighed wearily, looking up at her lanky guide. 'Paddy, shall we move on?'

Alexa smiled to herself as the new editorial assistant turned her back on the news desk and briskly followed Paddy over to features, leaving Marcus and Derek to slope back to their desks. Her qualifications and experience had only been part of the reason that Alexa had offered her the role. In fact, she probably would have got the job without knowing the first thing about editorial work, Alexa conceded. It was her attitude that had appealed. She had balls.

Emma's petite frame and pretty face were deceptive. That

had been one of the first things Alexa had noticed in the interview. She had dark hair that flicked out attractively around her shoulders and green, cat-like eyes that shone out from her olive complexion, but her personality was anything but delicate.

In the interview, having quickly ascertained that the girl was over-qualified for the role, Alexa had asked why she wasn't applying for the better-paid positions at other magazines. 'Because I want to show them,' she had replied, going on to explain that she was fed up with the all-female environment at *Joy* and didn't see why titles were edited almost exclusively by those of the same gender as their readership. Alexa had hired her almost on the spot.

It was also apparent that Emma held very different views to her predecessor on how best to progress her career. To the interview, she had worn a smart, high-cut blouse, suit trousers and flat shoes, an outfit not dissimilar to the one she had on today, although the blouse had been replaced with a loose-fitting, dark woollen top. She was stylish, but her style was the antithesis of Sienna's – which, Alexa supposed, might have been partly the appeal. They needed some fresh blood, someone who would shake the place up a little.

Alexa's attention returned to the iPad, swiping and tilting and tapping to test all the sophisticated visual effects. She was so impressed with the striptease function on the Brainy Banter feature that she didn't notice when somebody crept up behind her. With a flick of the wrist, the student's top was discarded, then her bra . . .

'Having fun?'

Alexa quickly dropped the device, feeling the heat rush to her face as Riz looked down at her.

'Hi,' she said, stiffly. 'I was just, er . . .'

He smiled. Then he looked down at the notes in his hand, as though remembering why he had come. 'Have you got a moment to go through the sports section of the app?'

'Yeah!' cried Alexa, with excessive cheerfulness. Cringing at her own awkwardness, she retrieved the abandoned device and shifted sideways to make room for Riz.

She flicked through the pages of the app, in search of the start of the sports section.

This was becoming a bit of a problem. The awkwardness wasn't simply a result of her inhibitions around good-looking men, or, in this case, the shame of being caught playing on the interactive striptease. It wasn't one-way, either. Alexa watched as Riz pulled up a chair and pulled up beside her, leaving an unusually large gap between them. He must have heard the rumours, too.

'So,' he said, leaning in and realising that he was still a long way away from the iPad between them. He drew closer, so that his knee touched Alexa's. They both pretended not to notice. 'I think this page is fine.'

Alexa nodded, her gaze fixed firmly on the muscular shoulders of the rugby player on the screen.

'But this one . . .' Riz flicked to the next page, which featured various quotes from footballers relating to their own extravagance. 'D'you think it needs to be more visual?'

Alexa nodded again, willing the blood to drain from her cheeks. 'Too much text,' she muttered, watching his fingers dextrously work their way through the interactive elements of the page. The back of his hands were so much darker than his palms.

'What do you think about this one?' he asked, looking sideways at her.

Alexa squinted at the sportsmen on the screen. She was thinking about the heat emanating from Riz's thigh, wondering how it was possible to feel it so intensely through two sets of trousers. 'It's a bit light, isn't it?' she offered.

'That's what I thought.' Riz nodded, jotting something down on a scrap of paper. The pen gave up on the second word. 'Sorry,' he said, looking around. 'D'you have . . .'

There was an awkward moment as they both reached for the same pen on the desk. Alexa was surprised by the roughness of his skin. Perhaps it was all the weights. Or the racket sports . . . She forced her attention back to the iPad.

Riz continued to critique the remaining pages of his section, explaining to Alexa why he thought this should be improved or that should be scrapped. Every statement was given an upward inflection, as though he was seeking Alexa's advice, but it was all Alexa could do to agree with him. She couldn't concentrate. It was worse, now that she knew about the rumours – as though they had something to be guilty about, which they didn't. There was nothing going on. There never would be. They were colleagues.

'Thanks, Boss.' Riz pushed the tablet back onto her desk and rose to his feet. 'Oh. Here.' He held out the pen.

Alexa grabbed it and swivelled hastily back to her screen, her heart hammering. She didn't mind the term 'Boss'. In fact, she quite liked it.

'Alexa?'

She looked up to find Emma, smiling efficiently at her empty desk. Clearly the induction tour was over.

'D'you have anything you want me to get going on?'

Derek's head shot up from behind his computer screen.

'I've got a few things you can *get going on*. Ha!' He looked over at the news desk, clearly hoping for some kind of reaction, having failed to elicit so much as a glance from the new assistant.

Alexa looked at Emma, trying to ignore the burning rage inside her. Derek was doing to Emma what he had tried to do to Alexa for the past five months. He was trying to undermine her. Alexa felt a stab of guilt as she remembered all the times she had let his harassment go unreported. She had set a precedent, allowing him to get away with it, and now Emma was suffering as a result.

'Alexa?' Emma was looking at her expectantly.

285

She blinked and started thinking through the long list of options. The Banter TV script had been cobbled together by a selection of unimaginative men and was in dire need of attention, the letters page needed looking at and there were several changes that needed to be made to the website copy. Alexa tried to decide on a priority. She sighed. Her phone was ringing.

'Shall I get that?' Emma asked keenly.

'Er . . . yes. Thanks.' Alexa was a bit taken aback; she wasn't used to having an assistant that actually assisted.

'. . . I'll just find out for you,' Emma told the caller in a sing-song tone. She pressed the handset against her shoulder and leaned forward, mouthing something at Alexa.

'What?' Alexa frowned.

'*Geor-gie Cara-way*,' Emma mouthed again.

Alexa pulled a face, suddenly even more grateful for Emma's intervention. She shook her head vigorously, just to clarify her response.

'I'm sorry. Alexa's in a meeting,' Emma explained sweetly. 'Can I take a message?'

Alexa couldn't hear the response. She watched, feeling the familiar sense of irritation grow inside her as she waited for the exchange to end. She had to warn her new assistant about Georgie Caraway.

The exchange didn't end. Alexa watched Emma's face, trying to interpret what was being said. Clearly Georgie was embarking upon one of her feminist monologues. After a minute or two, Emma looked up, her ear still glued to the phone, and pulled an exasperated expression in Alexa's direction. Alexa tried to indicate empathy. She didn't know what Georgie was saying, but she certainly didn't want her assistant to think that the activist was any friend of hers.

She watched anxiously as the one-sided conversation progressed, suddenly desperate for it to end. Eventually, Emma looked up and Alexa caught her eye, miming a throat-slitting gesture.

'Okay, thanks!' cried Emma. 'I'll take that on board. Bye, then!'

Alexa waited for the receiver to be replaced and then looked at her new assistant. 'What did she say?'

Emma pulled a disparaging look. 'Honestly? I'm not sure. It sounded like a load of bollocks to me.'

A smile crept across Alexa's face. She had a feeling that she and Emma were going to get along rather well.

33

'Okay!' The videographer clapped his hands and the studio was filled with a sudden silence. 'Thanks, girls, you're doing really well. Just a couple more and we'll be there.'

Alexa watched the eight self-conscious young women arrange themselves into a line against the wall, bending as instructed so that their pert, tanned buttocks were angled identically towards the camera.

'Lovely!' cried the energetic young man, giving a thumbs-up as he disappeared again behind his giant tripod.

They were shooting the quarter-final of the Girl-Next-Door contest, a text-vote that had run for the whole of December to decide who, out of the girls featured previously in *Banter*, was officially the sexiest. It was an annual contest, but this year's was bigger than any other – not just because the final round of voting would be open solely to readers of the inaugural tablet edition but because this time, readers were paying to vote. It was another of Alexa's initiatives that aimed to drive up revenue without increasing the cost base – at least, not by much. She had suggested paying the models for their time, but it transpired that they were willing to do it for their travel expenses alone.

Alexa couldn't help feeling secretly proud of the fact that the lure of an airbrushed appearance in *Banter* now had girls practically throwing themselves under the studio lights. Six months ago, *Banter* had been a dying magazine with a falling circulation and a reach that was shrinking by the minute. The girls wouldn't know it – maybe nobody outside of Senate would ever know it – but it was largely due to Alexa's initiatives that the magazine was now seen as such a big deal. She had built up the brand into something special.

'Lighting, can you just . . .' The videographer motioned for the spotlight to be moved down a little. 'That's it. I want buttocks that shine!'

There was a nervous titter from the girls, who continued to stand, shoulder to shoulder, in their identical, floss-like bikinis.

Alexa's attention was diverted for a moment by the crack of light that appeared in the doorway. A man crept into the studio. He was hunched over, like someone arriving late at the cinema, despite the fact that he was behind the camera and a long way from all the action. Alexa felt her heart sink as she realised that Derek was heading her way.

'How's it going?' he whispered, his eyes fixed on the line of girls.

'Fine,' she replied, wondering what he was doing here. The only reason she had come along was to ensure they had a sufficient mix of footage for the interactive features on the app. They had Jamie and the videographer; there was no need for any more editorial involvement. Had it been anyone else, she would have sent him packing, but unfortunately, Derek was senior enough to do what he liked and Alexa knew better than to call Derek's authority into question.

She shuffled sideways, leaving a large gap between them.

'Fuck me, this is a good line-up!' he hissed, closing in on Alexa and giving her a matey dig in the ribs. 'I think I'm getting horny!'

Alexa felt sick. She tilted her head to avoid the scent of red onion on Derek's breath, desperately trying to think of a suggestion for the videographer so that she could escape the man's inappropriate comments. Since returning to work after the break, this had become his speciality: making offensive remarks within

Alexa's earshot, under the breath so that nobody else could hear, in a tone that implied they had some sort of understanding. He was no longer outwardly aggressive towards her, but this, in a way, was worse. Alexa couldn't help wondering whether Derek had actually *meant* what he'd said in that darkened corridor in the club. She shuddered at the thought.

While the videographer was appraising his work, she thought of something. She rose from her seat and tapped him gently on the shoulder. 'Could we get them to take off their bikini tops? Maybe get them to . . . I dunno, fling them over their shoulder or something?'

The videographer squinted at the line of girls.

'I mean, not if you think it's too tacky.' Alexa backtracked a little. 'Whatever you think is best.'

'No such thing as too tacky.' He smiled. 'That could work, actually. As an interactive feature, were you thinking?'

Alexa shrugged. 'I just think we should show them taking their tops off, somehow.'

He nodded. 'You're right. Let's do it.'

Alexa stepped back as the videographer began to direct the girls in his calm, authoritative manner. She watched the girls obediently take off their tops and turn, as directed, to face the camera with their full, heavy breasts. This was definitely the way to go, she thought, imagining the finished product on the tablet, the flesh gleaming tantalisingly, enabling the user to zoom, scroll and play to his heart's content. *This* was what would send *Banter*'s circulation sky-rocketing.

Accidentally, Alexa caught Derek's eye as she looked away. He grabbed his crotch as though struggling to keep himself under control and then winked at Alexa. She looked away.

'Okay, great!' cried the videographer, when, after several attempts, he finally managed to get the girls to turn and then look at the camera in unison. 'Feel free to put your tops back on. We'll just do a few individual shots and then you'll be free to go.'

A few individual shots. Alexa looked down at the call sheet, hoping that none of the girls was bright enough to work out what was going on. This was the inevitable flaw in such a contest. With only one photo shoot and several rounds of voting, there would clearly be a smaller requirement for footage of girls who dropped out at an early stage – girls who, in this instance, would get no further than the quarter-finals. Having assessed a month's worth of voting data already, it was fairly clear to the team how successive rounds would pan out and therefore which girls wouldn't be featured again. Alexa watched as the cameraman shouted out the names of the prettiest, most voluptuous girls as though picking them at random.

She hung back in the shadows, avoiding Derek's eye and watching as two of the rejected models came tottering backstage in their high heels. One, a stunning brunette, was wearing a sarong over her bikini; the other, a blonde, had pulled on a tight pair of silver shorts and a pale pink boob tube.

'Where d'you get your boobs done?'

Alexa stared. She couldn't help it. Even now, after months of photo shoots and interviews, having come to terms with what *Banter* stood for as a magazine, she still found it odd to hear girls talk about their breasts in that way – like designer handbags or shoes.

The blonde just smiled. 'A place on Harley Street,' she replied. 'It cost me a fortune, but it's *so* worth it.'

'Yeah.' The other girl nodded. 'I could never go back to a 32B. No way. It just, like . . . well, it gives you confidence, innit?'

'Totally. It's empowering. I love it.' The blonde cupped her breasts in her hands and gave them an affectionate squeeze.

Alexa turned away. It was that word again. She couldn't hear it without thinking back to the TV debate. *One of the most dangerous myths of this century* – she could still hear Georgie's words in her head. *There's nothing empowering about being looked at like a piece of meat.* Alexa looked out at the shoot, trying to shake off the unwelcome memory by thinking about the additional revenue they would generate in the final rounds of voting, but it was no good. Her mind was stuck on Georgie Caraway and that fateful morning in White City.

Alexa closed her eyes and found herself imagining what the activist would say if she were here now – if she had witnessed that conversation between the girls. She would claim that the wannabe models were victims of an over-sexualised society driven by marketing campaigns and media that played on the girls' insecurities, persuading them that in order to be worth anything at all, they needed bigger breasts. She would no doubt claim that the surgically enhanced young women were being exploited by the very publications that had damaged their self-confidence in the first place and that *Banter* was one of the worst offenders. Alexa disagreed.

It was true that the girls were insecure. That was why they were here today. Alexa freely admitted that from *Banter*'s perspective, it was great that there were girls out there who were willing to go under the knife and then offer their assets for free to the magazine, but she wasn't going to take the blame for their insecurity. *Banter* was part of the solution, not the problem. It was a drastic way to fix one's self-esteem, but the fact was that these girls were transformed by shoots like this.

Alexa's phone started buzzing in her back pocket. She extracted it and squinted at the display, feeling instantly guilty. She hurried from the studio, trying to think of an excuse for not calling her parents back. The truth was that she simply hadn't had time. With only a week to go before the tablet launch, Alexa was struggling to fit in eating and sleeping around her work, let alone phone calls. She had lost track of the emails and voicemails from concerned friends, wondering why they hadn't heard from her in so long. She kept telling herself that it would calm down after the launch, but deep down, Alexa knew that post-launch would be even more stressful. The next three months, in fact, were going to be hell.

'Hi, Mum.'

'There you are! We were wondering what had happened.'

'I'm sorry.' Alexa rubbed her forehead. 'Lots on.'

'Oh. Are you still at work?'

'Yeah.' Alexa peered through the lobby glass to one of the small exterior windows. It was completely dark outside. She checked the time and realised that it was twenty past six. They must have spent longer than expected on the group shots. Instantly, Alexa's mind flipped to the stack of work on her desk upstairs. She shouldn't have stayed so long at the shoot.

'I won't keep you.' Surprisingly, there was no malice in her mother's voice, Alexa noted – only excitement. She smiled to herself, guessing what this was about. 'I just wanted to get a date in the diary. We've just heard back from the County Hall about my award. It's on Sunday 20th of April. Keep it free!'

Alexa felt a rush of warmth for her mother. It was good to hear her sounding so enthusiastic.

'Of course I will. Is the Mayor of Averley going to be there?'

'I don't know,' her mother replied bashfully. 'I'm sure it will be a very small affair, but . . .'

'I can't wait.'

After promising twice more to put the date in her diary, Alexa ended the call and headed back upstairs, duly blocking out the 20th of April in her phone as she went.

'Hi.' Emma looked up with a tired smile as she arrived at her desk. With the exception of Jamie, she was the only one left in the office. 'How was it?'

'Not bad.' Alexa nodded. 'It's still going on, actually – I left Derek down there.'

Emma lifted an eyebrow, saying nothing. Alexa suspected that the young assistant was beginning to form her own opinion of the deputy editor – an opinion not dissimilar to her own – but she wasn't going to try and influence it. From what Alexa had heard of their exchanges, Derek hadn't yet worked out that Emma was an altogether different type of girl to Sienna. He had taken to involving the news desk in lewd jokes relating to 'Emsie' and finding excuses to call her over to his desk, making comments that might have amused the old assistant – or at least, roused a titter of false laughter – but that certainly didn't amuse Emma.

'Oh. You missed a call.' Emma held out a Post-it note.

Alexa took it with a quick, grateful glance at the assistant's face. There were bags under her eyes that hadn't been there a week ago. She hoped it wasn't due to the late nights at *Banter*. What with the build-up to the tablet app launch and all the ongoing initiatives on top, there was a lot to take in – or rather, a lot to take on. She didn't want Emma to burn out.

Alexa looked at the note and let out a quiet groan.

'What did she want?'

Emma lifted her shoulders and shook her head. 'She was objecting about something in our New Year's Resolutions feature. I didn't really listen. Like you said, she does most of the talking.'

Alexa smiled. She had explained about the feminist campaigners after Georgie's first phone call. Since then, Emma had taken to fielding the calls – which, annoyingly for her, had become an almost daily occurrence. Alexa suspected it was causing some aggravation at Georgie's end, finding her communications inter-cepted by an unknown assistant, but the new arrangement suited Alexa fine.

'I think she wanted to catch you out by calling after six – she seemed pissed off that I was still on guard.'

'Well, I'm glad you were. Thanks.' Alexa screwed up the note and tossed it into the bin. 'Speaking of which, you should go home.'

Emma pulled a face at her computer screen. 'I've still got . . .'

'Can it wait 'til tomorrow?'

Emma rubbed her eyes, pulling at the skin around her temples. 'I guess.'

'So, go.'

Alexa waited for Emma to agree, then sat down at her desk and jiggled the mouse, waiting for the screen to come back to life. She wished *she* could dismiss herself for the night so easily. It was only a matter of weeks now until the final board presentation to the Americans in which she and Peterson would attempt to save the brand from extinction.

A lot hung on the success of the tablet edition, but Alexa knew that she couldn't rely on one initiative alone – especially not such an unpredictable one. The mobile app was still doing well and was on track to add a few million onto *Banter*'s top line, but it required constant marketing as there were now several competitive offerings out there. Banter TV had seen a decent uplift after an injection of new content and the new script-driven strategy, but there had been a serious dip since Sienna had left that Alexa was hoping Emma could rectify. It seemed as though there were too many things to fix and not enough time, but she *had* to fix them. She had to find the time.

'Oh!' Emma stopped on her way out. 'Sorry. I totally forgot. You and Riz were supposed to meet at half-five to catch up on the new sports section. He hung around for a bit but he had to dash – had to pick up his partner or something. I've rearranged for tomorrow at ten. Is that okay?'

Alexa looked up. She didn't know whether ten o'clock was okay or not. She couldn't concentrate. All of a sudden, her thoughts were eclipsed by the realisation that Riz had a 'partner'. What did that mean? He had a girlfriend? A *boyfriend*? Had she made the same mistake with Riz that she had done with Jamie? Alexa stared furiously at the reminder of her missed appointment on the screen, trying to convince herself that she didn't care either way. It didn't matter. It was no business of hers what relationships Riz had outside work.

Vaguely, Alexa nodded and bid her assistant good night. It did matter. She did care, because deep down, she knew that she had fancied Riz since her first day at *Banter*. She had let her lust grow with every sideways glance in every meeting – Jesus, she had even let herself fantasise about the groundless rumours that a bunch of ignorant lads had dreamed up on a drunken night out. Of *course* he had a girlfriend. It was so obvious, now that Emma had spelled it out. There had been so many clues along the way: that cryptic comment about a girlfriend during one of the early brainstorms; Riz's reference to more than one person moving into his new flat; his early exit from the Christmas do. All clues that Alexa had chosen to ignore.

She stared at the screen, depressed and surprised by the intensity of her disappointment. All this time, she had been bottling up her foolish desires, keeping them a secret from everyone – including herself. To think that she had imagined all that tension between them, when their fingers had . . . *No.* Alexa scrunched her eyes shut, forcing herself to stop remembering.

She had to move on. She had to forget about her childish crush – and that was all it was. Alexa dismissed the meeting reminder and navigated to the tablet launch document, forcing her thoughts away from the gorgeous brown eyes of her sports editor and his easy smile. She was the managing director, for God's sake. Of course she wasn't going to get involved with one of her staff.

34

Alexa let out a weary sigh and looked up. Paddy was lolloping towards her, brandishing a piece of paper.

'Cheer up!' he cried. 'It might never happen.'

Alexa straightened her posture and tried to smile, but as she did so, her face became distorted by a giant yawn.

'Thanks.' She reached for the sheet, which was a copy of the latest stats for the tablet app.

'It oughtta cheer you up,' said Paddy, grinning. 'We're close to a thousand downloads.'

Alexa squinted at the numbers and made another attempt at a smile. Paddy was right. The figures ought to have cheered her up. In the plan, she had accounted for two to three thousand downloads in their first week, and they were already halfway there after less than twelve hours. Alexa knew that she should have been thrilled by such early success, but she wasn't. She didn't feel thrilled or excited – she just felt exhausted. It was as though someone had drained the energy from her body, leaving her unable to feel anything at all.

She stared at the sheet, trying to engage her brain. She had consumed so much coffee and Red Bull that her thoughts were erratic and jumpy. It was partly the lack of sleep, too. Every night this week, she had been in the office when the cleaners came round at night. She was on first-name terms with the night security guard, who did his rounds of the building at some point in the early hours, and she couldn't remember the last time she had eaten anything cooked in something other than a microwave.

It wasn't that the other team members weren't pulling their weight. They'd been working late, too, but there was only so much that editorial staff could be expected to do when it came to making up for holes in marketing budgets and re-working financial models.

It reminded Alexa of her days at TDS. She hadn't been outside for a week, except to make the journey from her flat to the tube station in the morning darkness or to stumble down the steps of Senate House at night and fall into a cab. They were going through a cold spell, so colleagues said, but Alexa hadn't spent enough time outside to notice. It was February; she had about two months left on the magazine. All she could think about was the April board meeting.

In one sense, the targets still looked as distant as a speck on the horizon, but mathematically, Alexa knew that they could make it and mentally, she was not prepared to fail. They *had* to hit the targets. In her mind, the targets had become something of an obsession. Every waking hour was spent thinking about the various elements of her plan that was due to bring *Banter* back to life – and some of her sleeping ones, too.

The tablet edition had got off to a good start. Given the first day's downloads, there was definitely a chance that the new format could prove to be the cash cow she hoped it would be. But that was only one income stream and there were half a dozen that Alexa had to goad and caress into positive cash flow. It felt like juggling under duress. To drop one ball would be to sink the entire business and wash away any chance of future work with Senate – not to mention the twenty thousand pound bonus. To say that Alexa felt stressed would have been something of an understatement.

Alexa looked up to find that Paddy hadn't moved from his spot. She had no idea how long she'd been staring at the print-out, not taking anything in.

'Er . . .' He looked down at her, awkwardly. He was wringing his hands and glancing nervously across the office, which was deserted except for Jamie and Neil, who were working together on an edit in the far corner.

'How's the finger?' she asked, hoping to break the ice. A week ago, Paddy had been sent to write a feature entitled 'Britain's Angriest Hamster'. He had ended the day in Accident & Emergency.

'Getting there,' he replied, holding up the bandaged digit before scanning the office again as though he was worried that someone might overhear.

Alexa reached out and pulled up an empty chair. 'Here,' she said, motioning for him to sit down.

For a moment, it looked as though Paddy was about to make a run for it, but then he folded his gangly limbs into the chair and leaned sideways against the desk.

'It's about Emma,' he said, quietly.

Alexa nodded, trying to guess what he was about to say. Even through her exhaustion, she had noticed the bond that seemed to have developed between the two most junior members of the team. At lunch, they disappeared separately but always seemed to reappear within seconds of one another. Whenever Emma had a query, it would be Paddy who appeared at her desk with an answer.

'What is it?' Alexa prompted gently. She had visions of the young Irishman opening up about a secret crush and couldn't help thinking of her own silly aspirations that had been firmly put to rest the previous week. Paddy was frowning into his lap.

Eventually, he looked up.

'Look, I wouldn't normally say anything. Not if it was me, you know?'

Alexa nodded encouragingly. She had no idea what he was talking about.

'I mean, banter's banter, and that's fine . . . it is *Banter*, after all, right?'

Alexa nodded again, still lost.

'But sometimes, it's not just banter.' Paddy's nostrils flared angrily. When he spoke again, his voice sounded firmer, more resolute. 'It's like . . . they *touch* her and say things . . . I mean, if she was Sienna or someone like that, then fine, but she's not, you know? I think it's getting to her.' Paddy's voice dropped again. 'I'd say something to the lads, but . . .'

But the lads would rip you apart, thought Alexa, closing her eyes and suddenly realising what Paddy was saying to her. He was trying to highlight a problem that she should have noticed – should have done something about, long before now. He had left it until this moment to tell her because he'd been hoping she would step in of her own accord. But she hadn't stepped in. She had buried herself in launch plans and board presentations and pretended it wasn't an issue.

The truth was that she *had* noticed the way in which certain members of the team were treating the new assistant. She had witnessed Louis' attempts to slap her backside as she bent over to refill the printer. She had seen the way Derek talked to her and heard the dirty jokes featuring 'Emsie' that he and Marcus liked to share. She had observed it all and done nothing. Why? Because she'd been too preoccupied with her own personal battles. Selfishly, she had just hoped that Emma was tough enough to give as good as she got, to put up with it as Sienna had done.

Alexa was wracked with guilt. Even *she* struggled in the sea of testosterone that filled the *Banter* office and she had authority on her side. Emma was tough, but no self-respecting twenty-three-year-old would be equipped to deal with that.

The urge to bury her face in her hands and simply apologise, over and over again, was almost overwhelming, but Alexa knew that she couldn't reveal her remorse. She was Paddy's boss' boss' boss; it was her job to remain assertive and in control at all times.

'Of course,' she said calmly, with a look that she hoped would convey her sincerity. 'Leave it with me.'

Paddy started to rise to his feet. He didn't look convinced.

'I won't mention your name,' Alexa assured him. 'Obviously.'

He gave a tentative smile. 'Cool.'

'Thanks for letting me know.'

Alexa gave a little nod of appreciation and watched as the gawky young man swung his bag over one shoulder and headed for the exit. She knew from the tone of his voice and the look on his face that Paddy wasn't counting on her to do anything about Emma's plight. Why would he? She hadn't supported any of the juniors in the past. Alexa's mind went from blankness to sudden emotional overdrive, overcome suddenly by shame and self-loathing. True, she hadn't had cause to get involved until now, but *this* . . . it had been staring her in the face for weeks. She sighed. She had to do something. Next week. As soon as she got the chance, she would talk to the lads. Derek was the ringleader. If he stopped the baiting, then everyone would. She resolved to take him aside as soon as she got the chance.

Alexa blinked at the screen, trying to focus on the overflowing inbox in front of her. There were several messages from Terry Peterson's PA about the board meeting in April and a number of 'urgent' alerts from the app developers that had been superseded by impatient phone calls. She scanned them, too tired and too depressed to even decide on which ones to delete. There were personal emails in there, too. Alexa tried to recall the last time she had caught up with her parents or friends. It must have been over a week ago, but she couldn't remember when, or who it was with, or what had been said.

Drowning in guilt at her own self-absorption, Alexa picked out the personal messages, one by one, starting with the oldest.

From: Leonie Hatton
Subject: Happy new year
Hey Lex,
Where've you been? How was your Christmas? Wanna meet up some time? It's been ages.
xL
PS Did you hear, Kate's seeing her boss?! Some Clark Kent type, apparently.

Alexa stared at the title line: *Happy new year*. It was absurd. They were so close; they had known everything there was to know about one another for the past twenty-five years, and yet they hadn't met up since before Christmas.

Maybe that was it, thought Alexa, wearily. They *had* known everything there was to know about one another, but maybe they didn't any more. Something had come between them in recent months and Alexa had a feeling she knew what it was. She felt a rush of remorse. It was the same feeling that had swept over her when Paddy had prompted her about Emma. It was the same problem. Her work was getting in the way of the bigger picture.

She scrolled through the messages, holding off on her reply in case she had missed more than one from her friend and because, in truth, she didn't know how to reply. Another email caught her eye.

From: John Harris
Subject: Shhh
Alexa
Don't tell your mother, but there are plans afoot for a big celebration in the village on the afternoon of her prize ceremony. No firm itinerary yet, but we're thinking of

302

booking the village hall for the afternoon/evening or maybe using the house. Make sure you keep it free.
DAD

Alexa smiled. She loved the occasional emails she got from her father. There were no kisses and no words of affection – it was always the same, standard greeting, the same formal tone and the customary, capitalised sign-off. That was just the way her dad was. But between the lines, Alexa knew, there was warmth. The idea of her father helping to organise a surprise party for her mother (bearing in mind it was her mother that did all the organising in both of their lives) was almost enough to reduce Alexa to tears. She blinked and closed the email. She was obviously tired.

From: Kate Kidson
To: Leonie Hatton; Alexa Harris
Subject: All over
Hey you two,
Fancy drinks? Was gonna invite you to our company drinks next Thurs, but not sure I'll go now as I just split up with Seb so it's a bit awkward in the office at the mo! Maybe we cd go out that night instead?
Lex – read lots of press for your tablet app. Gd luck with launch!
Kx

Alexa closed the email and realised that the next one – sent only minutes after the time stamp on Kate's – was a reply from Leonie.

From: Leonie Hatton
To: Kate Kidson; Alexa Harris
Subject: Re: All over
Oh no!
How did that happen? Are you OK? I might be around next Thurs – will let you know. We're looking after the school

dog so it depends on Piers' parents' evening (not kidding –
it's like having a child!)
Lex, are you receiving . . .?
xL

Alexa scanned through the remaining emails to make sure she
hadn't missed any more in the chain, which she hadn't – unless
Kate and Leonie had continued the conversation without her,
which was a possibility. She wouldn't blame them if they had.
Alexa felt terrible; she had ignored a week's worth of missed calls
and emails from her friends. It was just fortunate that Kate took
her break-ups in her stride. She hit Reply All and hastily typed
out a message.

From: Alexa Harris
To: Leonie Hatton; Kate Kidson
Subject: Re: Re: All over
Hey,
I'm so sorry! Been totally swamped with the launch etc. No
excuse, I know.
Kate, hope you're OK. I'm sure the office is a more
interesting place now, at least??
Let's meet up! Are you still around on Thurs? If so, we're
having a night out on Banter to celebrate the app launch.
You'd both be v welcome – free drinks all night, if that's
any incentive. Otherwise, maybe the week after?
Sorry again for the lack of contact. Counting down the
weeks now . . .
Lex x

Alexa read through her message, lingering on the invitation
to Thursday's drinks. She ran the cursor along it, preparing to
get rid of it altogether. She could imagine Kate fitting in fine
with the *Banter* team – surprising the lads with her sharp tongue
and her sassy, post-feminist attitude. She was like an older, more
confident version of Emma – in fact, they would probably get

along well. But Leonie . . . Alexa tried to picture her teacher friend amid the inebriated *Banter* boys. It would be a disaster. Leonie would be appalled at their outwardly chauvinist attitude and would end the night even more convinced than she already was that her friend was working for the devil's magazine. But then, she couldn't just invite Kate and she couldn't *not* invite Kate. Before she had a chance to change her mind, Alexa pressed Send and returned to her inbox. She would just have to hope that Leonie's dog-sitting would get in the way of the *Banter* night out.

A new email appeared on her screen.

From: Margaret Harris
Subject: 20th April
Hello dear,
I meant to ask, will you be bringing a +1 to the award ceremony on the 20th? We've asked for four tickets, but I thought I'd better check, just in case. We can always ask Auntie Jen.
Lots of love,
Mum x

Alexa sighed, too tired to feel anything but a sense of lonely despondency. *No, there would be no plus one.* There had been nobody since Matt – not even the frisson that she had imaginatively conjured up in her head. Auntie Jen would end up being her pseudo date to the big event, just as she had for Alexa's dad's retirement do and Josh's christening before that.

She re-read the message and cringed. Even by email, her mother had the ability to convey disappointment – at least, that was how it seemed. Maybe the lack of sleep was making her over-sensitive, Alexa thought. She considered typing a reply, but suddenly the effort required seemed too much. It was time to go home. Alexa made a cursory attempt at clearing her desk and then closed down her files. As she did, three emails popped into her inbox.

From: Kate Kidson
To: Alexa Harris; Leonie Hatton
Subject: Re: Re: Re: All over
Free drinks on Banter? I'M IN. Where & when?
See you Thurs!
Kx

Alexa quickly opened the next message and found herself smiling.

From: Leonie Hatton
To: Alexa Harris; Kate Kidson
Subject: Re: Re: Re: Re: All over
She lives!
Sorry, I'm not around Thurs after all – dog duties. Have fun though and let's not leave it another two months this time, eh?
xL

The smile of relief was still on Alexa's face when she opened the last email. It was an update from Terry Peterson's PA on the April board meeting.

From: Jenny Pankhurst
To: Alexa Harris
Subject: Travel arrangements for Apr board mtg
Hi Alexa,
Please find attached your itinerary for the April board mtg in New York. Note that due to the early start on the Monday, your outbound flight leaves from London Heathrow at 3pm on the Sunday and arrives at Newark at 6pm, so you'll need to be at the airport for 1pm latest.
Best,
Jenny

Alexa closed the email and shut down the application. She was about to log off when a dark cloud of anxiety descended upon her. Re-opening the programme, Alexa clicked on Jenny's email again and stared at the text, suddenly engulfed by a sickly, stifling panic.

The board meeting was on Monday, April 21st. Her flight was on the day of her mother's prize-giving.

35

'Cheers!' yelled Kate, above the din.

Alexa smiled and lifted her glass to meet her friend's. The wine spilled out over the top and sloshed onto the table between them, but neither Kate nor Alexa cared. Every item of furniture in Scorpion bar bore the scars of a hundred raucous, rowdy nights and besides, the drinks were being paid for by Senate Media. The tablet app had achieved eight thousand downloads in its first week, exceeding expectations by a factor of four, and tonight was a night of celebration. Alexa could feel the latent caffeine in her system, mixing with the wine and the cheap champagne that Derek had forced down everybody's throats at 4 p.m.. She felt shattered, but she was determined to enjoy the night.

She watched as Kate tipped back her head and returned the glass to the table with drunken panache.

'That's to Norfolk sex,' she said. At least, that was what Alexa heard. Deafening rock music was pumping from a wall-size speaker right next to her ear.

'What?' she yelled, frowning.

'That's to your success,' mouthed Kate, raising her glass again and taking another swig.

Alexa smiled, shifting in her seat so that her ear was no longer directly in line with the speaker. The bar was an interesting choice on Emma's part. Its music was a peculiar mixture of techno and rock and the grey, low-hanging ceiling reminded Alexa a little of an underground car park. Still, it was clearly a popular hangout for media types and it seemed to have the lads' vote of approval. Unusually for an after-work bar, there were a good number of attractive females dotted about the place and most importantly, there was a four-for-two deal on shots.

On Kate's suggestion, they abandoned their seats by the speaker and headed for the amorphous mass of drunken *Banter* employees. Greg was entertaining some of the junior lads with a trick that involved a spoon, a drink and a cigarette lighter, while Derek – who had finally removed the four months' worth of prickly growth from his face – was regaling the news team with tales of his latest conquest. At the edge of the group, Louis had Emma trapped between the wall and the back of a chair and was gesticulating slowly, in what looked like a very poorly-concealed attempt to touch her breasts. Alexa shuddered as the assistant politely stepped aside. She had to do something. Tonight.

Kate nudged her, gawping at the drifting, drunken lads. 'You should've invited me along months ago.'

Alexa smiled, wondering whether Kate would be saying the same thing after a few more hours in her inebriated colleagues' company.

'Who's that?' Kate nodded approvingly at a nearby bunch of writers.

Alexa followed her gaze and deduced that Kate was referring to the scruffy young jokes editor.

'His name's Biscuit,' she said.

'Biscuit?' Kate laughed as though she'd misheard.

Alexa nodded at the sleek-haired management consultant, hoping her scathing expression would say it all. Unfortunately, Kate didn't appear the least bit put off. She gazed out again in the direction of the dishevelled young man, whose T-shirt was half-tucked into his jeans – accidentally, Alexa suspected – and whose ragged locks looked as though they'd been cut with gardening shears. Even when Biscuit started hopping from foot to foot, tickling his own armpits like a deranged chimpanzee, Kate simply smiled, looking at Alexa as though her mind was made up.

'He is *cute*,' she declared.

Alexa pulled a face. 'If you say so.'

Kate rolled her eyes. 'You don't know how lucky you are. Most of my colleagues are either tucked up in bed with the *FT* by now or they're still in the office because they can't think of what else to do.'

Alexa gave a sardonic smile. Kate was right; the management consultant stereotype held true. But unfortunately, so did the stereotype for her industry. Lads' mag editors were every bit as laddish and shallow as the rest of the world liked to imagine. At least, most of them were.

'Any time you want a life-swap . . .' Kate raised an eyebrow.

Alexa laughed. 'You're on. As long as you promise to hit my targets.'

Kate looked up at the ceiling, pretending to consider the idea. 'Actually . . . maybe not.'

They finished their drinks and headed to the bar for another round. A cloud of uncertainty descended on Alexa at the thought of her targets – or more specifically, the date on which she was due to present her achievements versus the targets. Now, in addition to the challenge of hitting the damn things, there was the additional complication of her outbound flight clashing with her mother's award ceremony. She had put in an urgent request with Peterson's PA to get the board meeting moved from the 21st, or as a last resort, to put her on the red-eye flight that got into New York at 8 a.m., but knowing how inflexible the Americans were known to be, Alexa wasn't at all confident about her chances. She couldn't bear the idea of missing her mother's big day.

'Seriously,' said Kate, turning to Alexa as their bodies were rammed up against one another in the rabble around the bar. 'You should be really proud.'

'Of that lot?' Alexa jerked her head in the direction of her colleagues, assuming Kate's mind was still on the life-swap idea.

'No. Of what you've achieved.'

Alexa shook her head. 'I haven't achieved it yet.'

Kate looked at her for a moment, eyes narrowed. She knew as well as Alexa that while the mobile app and the tablet edition were adding significantly to *Banter*'s top line, they still had a long way to go.

'You will, though.' She smiled knowingly. 'You will.'

Alexa hung back while her friend waved the tab card at the barman and tried to strike a deal on the cost of two bottles of wine. It was good to see Kate. She was one of the few people in the world who understood what she was trying to achieve *and* had faith in her ability to achieve it. Alexa tried to remember when they had last met up. She realised that it had been Leonie's nativity play, back in December. She recoiled at her own self-absorption. The last time she had seen her best friends had been over two months ago.

Observing Kate's negotiation with the barman, Alexa couldn't help wondering how different tonight might have been if Leonie had made it along. She would never have admitted it to anyone, but she was secretly glad that her old school friend had been unable to come – not because she didn't want to see her but because some people just weren't meant to mix, and she had a feeling that Leonie and Derek fell into that category. Leonie and Marcus. Leonie and Louis . . . in fact, Leonie would find most of the news team abhorrent.

'*Voilà*,' said Kate, coming away from the bar with two bottles of red wine, two fresh glasses and a broad grin.

Alexa relieved her of the glasses. 'You do realise we're not picking up the tab?'

Kate shrugged. 'I like a challenge.'

311

Alexa quickly followed in her wake as she elbowed her way through the masses. They eventually found themselves back at the table next to the speaker. Alexa was about to suggest moving the bottles to a surface that wasn't vibrating in time with the music, when she felt someone tap her on the shoulder. She turned to find herself looking down on a head of soft, peroxide blonde curls. Sienna's Bambi eyes smiled up at her through thick, fake lashes.

'Hello,' she mouthed, grinning up at her old boss.

For a moment, Alexa hesitated, not sure how to greet her. Then she leaned in and hugged the girl.

'I didn't think you'd come,' she said, withdrawing from their embrace. She had invited Sienna along tonight, partly because she felt the ex-editorial assistant deserved to be a part of the celebration, having played a small role in the development of the tablet edition, but also because she had wanted to see how the girl was doing.

'Why wouldn't I?' Sienna asked, coyly.

Alexa smiled. Her old assistant had lost none of her sexy allure. Sienna's plump, glossy lips were still set in that familiar pout and her poise was exactly the same. But something had changed. Alexa studied her ex-colleague for a moment and suddenly realised what it was. Sienna was wearing a blouse that buttoned all the way to the top. Admittedly, the peach-coloured, satin fabric fell heavily across her uplifted breasts, leaving little to the imagination, but the fact remained, *there was no cleavage on display*. In addition, she was wearing a pencil skirt that went all the way down to her knees and low-slung pumps that must have been half the height of her usual stilettos.

'You look . . . great,' said Alexa, doing her best to convey sincerity without sounding patronising.

'Yeah, well.' Sienna gave a bashful smile. 'New horizons, new wardrobe.'

Alexa glanced sideways, intending to introduce Sienna and

312

Kate, but Kate had wandered off, taking with her one of the bottles of wine and a glass. She turned back to Sienna.

'How's it going at *Monsieur*?'

Sienna tilted her head to one side. 'Early days. It's good to be writing stuff that's not fake sexual fantasies, but . . .' She shrugged, looking over her shoulder at the increasingly inebriated group of lads. 'I miss all this.'

Alexa could see that Sienna's attention had already drifted to the human pyramid that was being erected under Derek's drunken guidance.

'Go on,' she prompted. 'Looks like they need someone lightweight on top.'

Sienna looked at her. 'Who are *you* calling a lightweight?' she asked, tossing her blonde mane as she turned to the group, waiting for someone to notice her.

Inevitably, the human pyramid quickly crumbled as Derek caught sight of his one-time assistant and others followed his gaze, scrambling clumsily to their feet. Alexa watched as Sienna sashayed up to the deputy editor, maintaining her cool as he yelped with boyish delight, making minimal effort to return his embrace. Fairly soon, the others joined in with cat-calls and old in-jokes. It was rather brilliant, watching Sienna handle it all – turning the jokes around on the boys and making it known that she was no longer their bitch. Alexa couldn't help glancing at Emma, who had escaped Louis' clutches and was perched on the sidelines, watching, and wondering whether she was taking tips from her transformed predecessor.

The guilt reared its head again as Alexa stood, knowing that almost a week had passed since she had promised to do something about Emma's harassment and that she had done nothing. She waited for Derek to finish miming an imaginary, ass-slapping sex scene to Marcus and took a purposeful step towards him.

'Hi,' she said, raising her glass in what she hoped was a vaguely matey fashion.

'Sorry.' He looked at her, eyes wide, raising a hand to his mouth as though recognising that he had done something wrong.

'What for?'

Derek re-enacted the ass-slapping moment in accelerated form. 'For offending you. I presume you're here to tell me off?'

Alexa just shook her head.

'Ah . . .' Derek gave a dirty smile and pressed his face up against hers. 'I see,' he slurred. 'Like a bit of ass-slapping then, do you?'

Alexa sighed, wondering whether it was even worth broaching the subject of Emma's torment, given the state of the deputy editor. Then she realised that she was just looking for excuses. She had to confront him.

'I came to ask a favour,' she said, maintaining their close proximity despite the stench of vodka on Derek's breath.

'Oh yeah?' he replied, with a wink. 'Sexual, is it?'

Alexa looked at him, stony-faced. 'It's about Emma,' she said.

'Sexual, then.'

'That's the point. Derek, you've got to stop treating her like some sort of sex object. She's an editorial assistant and our PA; not a toy.'

'*What?*' Derek screwed up his face, looking outraged. 'That's bollocks.'

'It's not, Derek. I've seen how you behave – you and half of the team. You talk to her as though—'

'No!' He shook his head. 'I mean it's bollocks that we can't treat her like that. It's *Banter*, for fuck's sake. It comes with the territory. If she can't hack a few dirty jokes, she shouldn't have taken the job, should she?'

Alexa stared at him. 'Are you saying it's in Emma's job description to be verbally abused and sexually harassed by her colleagues?'

Derek rolled his eyes. 'Jesus Christ, Legs. What's wrong with you? It's not "harassment".' He made exaggerated quotation marks in the air. 'She loves it. She can't get enough of it with me and the lads.'

'Derek, listen—'

'No. *You* listen. I've been at *Banter* since you were in a fucking baby-grow. *I* know how to run an editorial team and if it means a few little jokes about the size of a girl's tits or—'

'Derek!' Alexa squared up to him, shouting above the combined din of his words and the techno music. 'It's not *little jokes*. It's harassment. Okay? You have to make it stop or we'll be left with no editorial assistant and a lawsuit on our hands. And if you don't, you know exactly what I'll do.' She looked him in the eye, waiting for a sign of comprehension.

After a couple of seconds, there was a brief nod of the head. Alexa turned on her heel and walked off, her pulse still racing. She was so enraged by Derek's pathetic, outdated, ignorant stance that she almost failed to notice the scene playing out in the corner of the bar, by the speaker.

Sitting shoulder to shoulder, sharing the remains of a bottle of red wine and attracting a growing number of onlookers, were Biscuit and Kate. Kate's lips were stained purple and her cheeks were flushed, but there was a sparkle in her eye that Alexa recognised: the sparkle of an oncoming conquest.

Alexa turned and headed for the bar, wondering what she had done by inviting her friend along tonight. It felt very much as though she had opened up a whole new can of worms for the editorial team.

36

Alexa couldn't help looking up as the ginger head of hair loomed over the desk opposite.

'Emma, I was wondering whether you'd be so kind as to circulate this article to the rest of the news team?'

Marcus placed the page, which looked to be a clipping from this week's edition of *Diss*, on the assistant's desk and then took a generous step backwards, putting at least a metre between them.

Alexa caught Emma's expression and gave her a sympathetic roll of the eyes. It had been like this for over a week – ever since her conversation with Derek the previous Thursday. The lads had clearly elected to take her advice to the extreme and now avoided all forms of contact with the editorial assistant except those that were absolutely necessary, addressing her in an overly-polite, formal manner that had left Emma looking confused and suspicious until Alexa had taken her aside and explained. It was better than sexual harassment, she figured, but it still wasn't fair.

Emma dealt with the situation in her usual swift, efficient manner, allowing Alexa to return to the presentation on her screen. It was only a matter of weeks before the big presentation in New York. She still hadn't heard back from Peterson's PA on the potential for rearranging the board meeting, despite repeated reminders. Alexa picked up the phone. If Jenny failed to pick up, she decided, she would storm into the management office and stage a sit-in until she got a reply.

'Terry Peterson's line, Jenny speaking?'

'Oh, hi. It's Alexa. From *Banter*.' Alexa quickly composed herself; she had been fully expecting the PA's voicemail.

'Ah. Hi, Alexa.' Jenny's voice quickly changed from breezy to stutteringly awkward. 'I got your emails.'

All six of them? Alexa nearly replied. *And the voicemails?* She wanted to believe that Jenny had made every effort to shift the board meeting, but she couldn't help feeling sceptical.

'Unfortunately, no luck.' Jenny's tone was clinically sympathetic, like that of a nurse administering the same bad news that she gave out every day. 'It was near-on impossible to find a time that everyone could do, you see. There's no way we can rearrange it now.'

Alexa crumpled inside. She *had* to be there for her mother's award ceremony. It was the one day in the whole year that she couldn't miss. There had to be a way.

'What about flights?' she asked. 'I know there was an overnight one that got into New York at around eight?'

'No good,' replied Jenny, in the same tone. 'The offices are in midtown Manhattan. Even if the flight lands on time then you're looking at ten or eleven o'clock by the time you get in. You can't make them wait.'

Alexa sighed. She knew that Jenny was right. It was a fact: you couldn't make the Americans wait.

'Is there *anything* we can do?' Alexa didn't really know what she was asking; there was nothing that anybody could do except to wish for a miracle, like a localised earthquake in midtown Manhattan or the existence of a diary clash that nobody had spotted until now.

'I'm sorry,' said Jenny, her voice softening a little. 'If anything changes, I'll let you know.'

Alexa sighed. 'Thanks.'

She hung up the phone and stared for several seconds at the skeletal slide on her screen. She had to tell her parents. She had to break it to them that she wouldn't be there on the 20th. With the guilt weighing heavily inside her, she reached for her phone and headed for the lobby.

Unusually, it was her father who answered.

'Hi, Dad. It's me.'

'Oh, hello.'

There was a pause. Alexa's dad had never been overly effusive on the phone.

'How's things?' she asked, trying to warm him up.

'Not too bad.'

Alexa pictured him, standing in the hallway by the door, scratching his head and forgetting that with a cordless phone, it was possible to move through the house while talking. 'Your mother's just out getting some string for the Cub Scouts, later.'

'String? She's tying them up, is she?' Alexa laughed at her own joke, even though it wasn't funny.

Her dad chuckled. A silence fell. Alexa drew a breath and forced herself to stop stalling.

'Dad,' she said. 'Something's come up.'

'What sort of thing?' He sounded worried. Alexa felt bad. *Work* had come up, that was all. It wasn't anything to worry about, per se. Only the consequences mattered.

'I'm really sorry but I'm not going to be able to come to Mum's award ceremony on the 20th.' The words tumbled out in quick succession.

'What d'you mean? What's happened?'

'No – no, it's nothing like that. It's, um . . . I'm sorry. It's only . . .' Alexa pushed the words out. 'It's a meeting. It sounds pathetic, I know. I wouldn't usually pull out of something so important for a meeting, but the thing is, this is *the* meeting that determines whether I've done my job . . . whether the

magazine stays alive or whether they kill it off. I've tried everything. If there was something I could do, then–'

'Okay, calm down.' Her father's voice was low and steady again
– the voice of reason. 'You've got a meeting on the *Sunday*?'

'It's on the Monday at 9 a.m., but the only flight that gets in
on time is on the Sunday afternoon and I've asked them to move
the meeting or get another—'

'Flights? Where is this meeting?'

'Oh.' Alexa realised she had neglected the critical piece of
information. 'It's in New York.'

'Ah.' Alexa pictured her father nodding. 'I see.'

There was another silence. Alexa tried to think of something
to say that would redeem her.

'I guess we could celebrate separately, the next weekend?' she
suggested, meekly.

Her father didn't reply. He wasn't deliberately trying to make
her feel guilty, Alexa knew that. He was probably just working
things out in his head. Perhaps he was trying to devise a solution
to enable her to attend. Unfortunately, Alexa knew that there
was no solution. This was simply an improbable but immovable
clash.

'I suppose we can, yes.' Her father seemed to be resigning
himself to the conclusion that Alexa had already drawn. 'You'll
be missed at the village party.'

Alexa felt another sharp tug on her conscience. It was the
village party that mattered, really. The award ceremony would
be prestigious and fancy, with the mayor and all his cronies
giving out gold-plated awards, but that wasn't the place where
her mother could bask in the warmth and admiration of all the
people who mattered: the parents and friends and co-helpers
and kids from the village groups.

'I'm so sorry, Dad.'

'Oh, it's not your fault,' he said, with a sigh. 'These things
happen.'

'It's just the worst possible timing.'

'It is. Don't worry.' He gave a half-hearted chuckle. 'I'll save you some cake!'

Alexa laughed softly, but she knew that neither of them was laughing inside.

'Will you tell Mum, or . . .'

'I'll tell her.'

Alexa breathed a sigh of relief. It wasn't the idea of breaking the news to her mother that worried her; it was the thought of hearing her mother's reaction. She knew exactly how it would go. There would be a flippant, dismissive remark – 'Oh, never mind!' – and then, at intervals throughout the rest of their conversation, little digs that revealed the true extent of her disappointment.

'Thanks, Dad.' Alexa closed her eyes, wishing there was a better way of conveying her gratitude.

'Good luck with it all.'

'See you soon.'

Alexa switched off the phone and leaned back against the wall, feeling like a coward. This wasn't the first time she had avoided confronting her mother. For three months, she had lied about where she was working – or rather, omitted to tell them the truth – and then, when they had discovered her dirty secret in the worst way possible, instead of coming clean and explaining her reasons, Alexa had simply stopped talking to them altogether. And now, yet again she was prioritising her work over family commitments and letting her father take on the task of telling her mother.

She sighed, thinking about how different things might have been if she had made different decisions along the way. She could have told her parents about the new role as soon as she took it on – or even sought their advice before she accepted the role. She could have talked them through her plans and explained why she was doing what she was doing. She could have held firm and told Peterson she *couldn't* fly out on the 20th of April.

Alexa opened her eyes as the lift doors slid open. No, she couldn't have done that. The board meeting was the one obligation she couldn't turn down.

'Are you waiting?'

Alexa looked up and realised that Paddy, buckling under the weight of a giant silver soda-stream, was one-handedly holding the lift for her.

'Oh. Sorry. No . . .' She tucked her phone away and followed the junior writer into the office.

The phone buzzed as she made her way back to her desk. Despite her mood, the message prompted a reluctant smile.

It's official!
We R an item.
Kxx

It was unlike Kate to send unsolicited texts during the working day. Alexa glanced over at Biscuit, who was clambering onto the window sill, trying to secure a poster of the world's hairiest man onto the blind. They certainly were an unlikely couple, thought Alexa. To her knowledge, Kate had never dated anyone who didn't in some way work in finance, and as far as she knew, Biscuit was in his mid-twenties. She thought about Kate's three-week record and gave it until the weekend.

'Alexa! *Alexa!*' Emma was half-sitting, half-standing at her desk, looking over her shoulder. There was something in her tone that set Alexa's heart racing.

'Look.' Emma pushed back her chair and motioned for Alexa to step in and read what was on her screen.

Alexa bent down. A browser was open on the BBC homepage, displaying a grainy image of a young black girl alongside the headline, GANG OF FOUR RAPES GIRL AND UPLOADS VIDEO TO APP. Alexa felt a wave of nausea rise up inside her. She forced herself to read the text.

A GANG of teenage boys from South London drugged and raped a fifteen-year-old girl and then posted a film of the events leading up to the attack on the popular mobile phone app, *My Girlfriend*.

On Saturday, 26 February, Letitia Chinwe was walking home from school when four young men asked her to follow them into a nearby flat. In what is believed to be part of a gang initiation, the four men raped Chinwe repeatedly, taking turns to record the ordeal on a mobile device. It is not yet known whether the youths, aged between sixteen and twenty-two, were previously known to Chinwe.

The six-minute ordeal was filmed in its entirety and the first minute, in which the girl was forced to undress, was uploaded to the *My Girlfriend* app. It was this mobile footage that led police to the youths, who were arrested at the South London property and later charged with multiple counts of rape.

Alexa stopped reading. She felt as though she was about to vomit. Her eyes roamed the office, unseeing. She tried to think rationally about what to do but repulsive images were filling her mind, blocking out her capacity to reason.

'How . . .' was all she managed.

'A friend forwarded it,' Emma said quietly. She looked pale and anxious.

At the back of her mind, Alexa knew there were more questions she needed to ask, like what exactly the 'events leading up to the attack' entailed and why the moderators had failed to notice anything suspicious and how the press had got hold of the story before they even knew about it and whether the app was still live and what they needed to do to cooperate with police, but all she could do was stare into space, picturing the fifteen-year-old's ordeal and the unthinkable events that had led up to it, driven, in part, by *her initiative*.

'Fucking kids.'

Derek's voice sounded distant, although he was standing right next to Emma, looking at the headline over her shoulder. Alexa heard him mutter something about the age limit on the app, but she wasn't really listening. She couldn't concentrate on anything. It felt as though she was wearing ear muffs. Everything seemed very far away.

'Are you okay?' she heard someone ask after a while – maybe seconds, maybe minutes.

Blindly, Alexa felt her way back to her desk and collapsed in her chair. She should have foreseen this. Anybody could have anticipated the app's potential for misuse. It was only a matter of time – Alexa saw that now. Too late. Leonie had warned her. Even Neil had voiced reservations. She had ignored all the warnings because the app had looked like an easy win: a bold, new offering that would reinforce the brand and bring in some extra cash. How short-sighted. How selfish. How *stupid*.

Alexa took a deep breath and let it out in a long, uneven sigh. She didn't care what Derek said; they were at fault here, age limit or no age limit. If the youths hadn't had the option of uploading their footage to the app, perhaps they wouldn't have gone so far. Perhaps they wouldn't have even accosted the girl. Perhaps . . .

Alexa closed her eyes. There was no point in thinking about what might have been. What was done was done. The news was out. Her app – and by definition, its creator – was implicated in the crime. Alexa was partly responsible for the rape of a fifteen-year-old girl.

37

'*It's another one,*' hissed Emma, cupping her hand over the mouth-piece. '*A London paper. What shall I say? The usual?*'

Wearily, Alexa nodded. She felt bad for her PA. Fielding calls from aggressive journalists and incensed activists was not supposed to be part of her role.

'Hi, no, she's not available to take your call right now,' Emma recited down the phone, not even bothering to inject any energy into her voice. 'I can tell you that *Banter* has temporarily withdrawn the mobile app from service and is cooperating fully with police enquiries.'

Alexa tried to ignore it, but her brain seemed to be prioritising Emma's words over the numbers swimming about on the screen in front of her.

'No, no firm date as yet. Yes. Suspended until further notice.'

Emma politely shrugged off the caller and turned to the stack of proofs on her desk, which, Alexa noted, had hardly dropped in height since she'd arrived at her desk eight hours earlier. Alexa wondered whether it was worth getting a temp in to handle the calls. She kept thinking it would all die down – that the media would find another story, the activists would move onto another cause – but after three days, it was showing no sign of abating. The date of the hearing for the alleged young rapists had been set for early May and it seemed that interest was shifting from the youths to the mechanism by which their crime had been committed, broadcast and, ultimately, uncovered. *Banter*'s mobile app was centre-stage again, for all the wrong reasons.

The official line was that *Banter* had 'withdrawn the mobile app from use', but that wasn't strictly true. The regulatory bodies had been swift to step in and eliminate any chance of the same thing happening again and it had been the industry watchdogs, not *Banter*, who had initiated the temporary suspension of the app. They hadn't stopped there, either. To Derek's immense delight, *Diss* had seen its equivalent mobile app withdrawn, alongside several similar offerings. Alexa wasn't even sure that the apps would ever be allowed back onto the market. In fact, secretly she was willing the regulators to ban them for good. That was the ironic thing. In the last three days, she had realised that she didn't *want* her app to go live again. It should never have been let loose in the first place. She wanted *My Girlfriend*, *Voyeur* and all the others like it outlawed once and for all.

Alexa sighed, propping her head on her hands. The rape incident had clouded her view of the world. It was as though she was seeing everything through a grey lens: the app, the magazine, her role, her targets, her future . . . . She felt like a disgrace to mankind – or to *woman*kind, as Georgie had pointed out. Of course, Georgie had called. She had made several attempts to speak with Alexa, along with other campaigners from other women's charities that Alexa had never even heard of. Thankfully, Emma had been there to intercept. But it wasn't the phone calls from angry protesters that bothered Alexa. What bothered her was the reaction of the people who mattered: Kate, Leonie and her parents.

It wasn't as though they had been openly aggressive towards her; they had all remained calm as they had dispensed their disappointment. But that was the worst part. They weren't angry, like the protesters – they were ashamed. Alexa thought back to her conversation with Leonie, torturing herself by remembering the softness with which she had delivered her words. *It was bound to happen*. Alexa knew that the phrase wasn't meant as a form of consolation; it was a reminder. Leonie had warned her that something like this might happen, months ago, when the app was just an idea, yet Alexa had ignored her, bulldozing her way towards the April targets, determined that nothing should stand in her way.

Her mother was less shrewd in her response. She had simply sighed despairingly, asking Alexa the same question again and again: why? Why had she got involved with such a despicable magazine? Why had she launched such an app? Why hadn't she stopped to think? Alexa hadn't had any answers – only apologies.

Alexa shuddered as she recalled the first phone call she had taken after the news had broken. Of all the people she knew, Kate was the one who seemed to understand best what she did for a living and what drove her to do it. Yet even Kate seemed disappointed. Kate, who had wholeheartedly endorsed the mobile app when it had looked to represent a lucrative revenue stream, had turned around and shaken her head at Alexa, asking why more safeguards hadn't been put in place to prevent such a thing from happening. Naïvely, Alexa had picked up the phone, hoping for some form of consolation. Instead, she had found herself drowning in shame.

Alexa looked up and realised that Emma was talking to her.

'. . . late? Only it's been a bit of a long day.'

'Sorry.' Alexa blinked and refocused on the assistant's pretty face. 'What did you say?'

'I was just wondering whether I could clock off in a bit.'

'Of course,' Alexa replied quickly, feeling even more ashamed. She ought to have noticed the dark hollows around her assistant's eyes – ought to have registered the exhaustion in her voice. 'I'm sorry – I should've said. Just put the phone to voicemail. Go and get an early night. You look as though you need one.'

Emma smiled gratefully and glanced over her shoulder to where Paddy was packing leftover toys from Red Nose Day into his bag.

Alexa waved the two juniors goodbye and slumped back in her chair, letting her eyes glaze over as the screensaver kicked in. Peterson wanted the financial summary on his desk by the morning. She sighed. All her motivation had gone.

'You okay?'

Alexa looked up, attempting to arrange her features into some sort of smile. Then she realised who it was and looked away, embarrassed. 'Yeah, fine.'

Riz had his gym bag slung over one shoulder, but he didn't seem to be in a hurry to leave. Alexa felt the blood slowly creep to her face. It was the first sign of emotion she had experienced in days and it wasn't a good one. No matter how hard she tried, she couldn't shake off the embarrassment of her imagined pseudo-affair with Riz.

'You don't look it.' Riz smiled.

'Thanks.' Alexa could feel the heat radiating from her face. She was all too aware of her red-rimmed eyes and her pasty – and now blotchy – complexion.

'When did you last eat?' he asked.

Alexa shrugged. Eating had become one of those background tasks that just happened without involving any conscious thought. The sandwich bar across the road now knew Alexa by name and she, in turn, knew their menu off by heart. Meals had given way to grazing; when her stomach felt empty, Alexa grabbed another sandwich. She honestly couldn't remember the last hot meal she had eaten.

'Fancy a pizza?'

Instinctively, Alexa shook her head, despite the prick of excitement piercing through her fatigue at the idea that maybe, just maybe, *Riz was asking her to dinner*. She didn't have time for a pizza and she definitely didn't have time to be distracted by more fantasies involving Riz. She needed to get her head straight, finish the financials and go to bed.

'I was supposed to be playing squash, but my partner just

cancelled on me.' Riz swivelled sideways to reveal a racket handle, sticking out of his sports bag.

Alexa was about to explain the urgency of the financial summary behind her screensaver when something occurred to her.

'Your partner,' she said, before she had properly worked out what she was going to say. 'Is that . . .'

'John. Mate from uni.'

'Right.' Alexa nodded.

'Been playing together nearly ten years. God, that's depressing, isn't it?' He grimaced. 'Ten years . . .'

Alexa forced a little laugh. She couldn't think of a way to ask the question. What she wanted to know was whether Riz had a 'partner' as well as a squash partner, or whether she had got hold of entirely the wrong end of the stick two months ago.

'Is that who you live with?' she tried, remembering the reference to the other person in Riz's new flat.

Riz frowned. 'I live on my own. Tried sharing with my old flat mate, Mark, but it's a small place, you know . . . two blokes, one bathroom . . .' He pulled a face.

Alexa nodded vaguely. There were so many things going through her head that it was difficult to concentrate, but it did seem to be looking more and more likely that there was no 'partner' in Riz's life. *In which case* . . . Alexa tortured herself by thinking back to the time they had worked together at her desk, their thighs touching, the moment his fingers had brushed hers.

'So?' He was looking at her, one eyebrow raised.

Alexa smiled, despite everything.

'Have you ever been to the Dean Street Pizzeria?'

Alexa shook her head.

'You haven't lived.' He tipped his head towards the door. 'Come on. You look like you need a proper meal.'

After a moment's hesitation, Alexa abandoned the financial summary, muttering something about finishing it off later. Even as she said the words, she knew it wasn't going to happen. She'd have to come in early tomorrow. Or hell, she'd have to miss the deadline. What could Peterson do? She wasn't even sure she wanted to present the over-inflated numbers, now that her eyes had been opened to what lay behind them. For the first time in days, Alexa felt alive. Tired, but alive.

By mutual consent, they left the office one after another, Riz holding the door for Alexa as though they just happened to be departing at the same time. Alexa wondered whether Riz was aware of the rumours that had travelled the office in the week after the Christmas do. She felt a little lurch of anticipation as they stood side by side in the lift. Nothing would happen, of course. It couldn't; they were colleagues. Things were complicated enough in her life without having a romantic involvement with one of her editors. But still, it was exciting to imagine what Derek might say if he saw them out in Soho together. Or Marcus. Or Louis . . .

The proprietor of the Dean Street Pizzeria was a small Italian man with a thick head of curly grey hair and a kindly smile. He greeted Riz with a firm handshake and stepped back with overt admiration as Riz introduced Alexa.

'*I know*,' Riz muttered under his breath as they were shown to a table for two at the back of the restaurant. '*I come here too often.*'

Alexa smiled. On the table between them was an unlit candle stuffed into a bulbous, glass bottle that was coated in so many layers of wax that it was impossible to tell what colour the glass had once been. She couldn't remember the last time she'd been to a real, Italian-run pizzeria. It must have been before Matt. Matt held the view that pizza was a modern form of peasant food: cheap, basic and unhealthy. He was probably right, but frankly, she didn't care. Matt could inflict his snobbish, rich-boy attitude on somebody else; right now she was looking forward to her quattro formaggi with extra cheese. Looking back, she wasn't even sure why she had been so besotted with Matt, or so distraught when it had all ended. Their opinions had differed on so many fronts and they had had almost nothing in common.

Riz gently closed his menu and looked up as the proprietor appeared at their table. Then he turned to Alexa.

'What colour wine?'

She thought for a second. Matt had never asked her that. He had always made the decision for her, according to what they were eating – or rather, what he was eating.

'White would be nice,' she replied, smiling.

Riz and the wizened old man discussed the various options, consulting Alexa on her exact preferences for sweetness and flavour and eventually plumping for the house white, which came highly recommended by the restaurateur. As he turned to leave with their order, he suddenly whipped back round and, with an apologetic flourish, leaned in and lit the candle between them.

'Sorry,' Riz muttered, as his friend swept back into the kitchens. 'I think he thinks . . .'

Alexa blushed. 'Yeah.'

They lapsed into silence. Alexa was grateful for the hubbub around them, masking their lack of conversation.

'So.' Riz straightened up, looking right at her as though unaware of any awkwardness between them. 'You've only got a few weeks left at *Banter*?'

Alexa nodded. At one point in her ongoing dialogue with Peterson, the chief executive had hinted at the possibility of extending her contract beyond April, to keep the new initiatives flowing. Nothing had been said on that front for several weeks now. Alexa was glad; she didn't think she wanted to work for the brand any more. It wasn't that she had made a conscious decision, exactly, it was more that she didn't feel sure about anything any more. The last few days had cast a dark shadow over her work and Alexa was finding it harder and harder to justify being there. She did wonder what it meant for the initiatives, though. Would the tablet edition go on to bring in the revenues without her? Would the mobile app be reinstated? She hoped not. Even though the mobile revenue was necessary to enable them to hit their April targets – and even then, only just – she was fully prepared to turn down her bonus if it meant never again seeing a situation like the one last week.

'What's up?'

Alexa busied herself tasting the wine that the proprietor had brought over, swilling it around in her glass, taking a tentative sip and eventually giving the nod of approval, very aware of Riz's eyes, tracking her every movement. The black cloud had descended again. Every time she allowed her thoughts to wander, they drifted to the same dark corner of her mind.

'I just . . .' Alexa shrugged. She wasn't sure whether she wanted to admit her feelings of guilt to a colleague. 'Nothing.'

Riz continued to look at her over the rim of his untouched glass of wine.

'You've made a real difference,' he said, eventually. 'I don't know if you can tell, from where you sit, but *Banter*'s a very different place to the one it was a year ago.'

Alexa smiled sardonically. 'A better place?' she asked. It was ironic that Riz had taken her silence to imply that she felt she had underachieved in her role. The reality was that she had overachieved.

Riz was frowning. 'Much better. Jesus Christ – a year ago, we were just a struggling lads' mag in a crowded market. Our readers were dropping like flies. We were in a bad way. To be honest, I was waiting for the board to give us our marching orders.'

Alexa looked away, wishing she could tell Riz how close to the truth he was.

'But now . . . well, we've got the tablet edition, a new TV station, a—'

'An app that's used to record gang rapes,' Alexa put in, unable to stop herself. She looked down at her cutlery, embarrassed. She hadn't meant for the conversation to go this way.

Riz slowly lowered the wine glass from his lips.

'Are you . . . do you blame *yourself* for that?'

Alexa closed her eyes for a second, trying to decide how to answer. They were at a fork in the road and she was driving; she could either guide them back onto safer ground by lying or she could tell the truth and steer them straight into a debate about the morality of what they did for a living.

'Yes,' said Alexa. 'I do.'

'Wh . . .' Riz appeared to be lost for words.

'I launched it,' she said, simply. 'If I hadn't, then maybe that poor girl wouldn't have—'

'*What?*' Riz shook his head, leaning back as the pizzas were delivered to their table but maintaining eye contact with Alexa as though he couldn't believe what he was hearing. The proprietor tried to distract him with an offer of his home-made chilli sauce but Riz ignored him completely as he stared at Alexa.

'You actually think that?' he asked, when the Italian had wandered off, looking a bit put-out.

Alexa nodded.

'That's ridiculous. You know that?'

'Why?' she challenged. It felt odd, opening up such a heavy topic with someone she had only ever talked to about work and football – odd, but not unpleasant. Riz was probably the only man in the office with whom Alexa felt she could share her insecurities without having them ridiculed.

'Because . . .' He lifted his shoulders. 'It's not your fault, what happened. Those kids would've done what they did, whether or not they had an app to upload to.'

'Maybe,' said Alexa. 'But maybe not. It might have been the prospect of uploading it that pushed them to do it.'

Riz was looking at her as though she was crazy. 'It *might* have been,' he said. 'But even if that were the case, then you're still not to blame.'

'Why not?'

'Well, it's like blaming . . . I don't know, the manufacturers of light bulbs for global warming. Or shops, for causing people to get into debt. You put things out there, but you're not responsible for how they get used.'

Alexa carved her pizza into ever smaller divisions, thinking for a moment about Riz's argument. It was a neat way of looking at things – one that effectively absolved her and the rest of the team of any wrongdoing. It was convenient, but it wasn't right.

'Sorry,' she said, taking a bite. 'I don't buy it. We have to take responsibility.'

Riz shook his head. His brow was set in a permanent frown and he looked more serious than she had ever seen him in the office. 'Seriously, Alexa. It's no more your fault than the regulators', for letting the app pass all their criteria. Or the app developers', for building it.'

The regulators. Alexa hadn't factored them into her thinking. In a sense, Riz was right. They were the last line of defence; they were there to catch problems like this before they happened.

'Look at YouTube,' said Riz, waiting to catch her eye. 'D'you think they take responsibility for every piece of footage that goes up?'

Alexa shrugged uncertainly. There was, she admitted, a small possibility that she had been too hasty to rush forward and shoulder the blame. Perhaps she ought to have shared it, at least. Riz was right to some extent, in that she hadn't single-handedly launched the app. He was right, too, about YouTube. Alexa tried to imagine herself in the shoes of the YouTube founder, whoever that was. Would she accept responsibility for every piece of footage that went onto the site? Probably not. But would she feel bad every time the website was used in a harmful or abusive way? Yes. Just as she felt bad for the part her app had played in that teenage girl's ordeal.

'The thing is,' said Riz, leaning in, 'you've got to credit the reader with a bit of intelligence. The majority of *Banter* fans aren't members of gangs that rape little girls. They get it. They use it properly. It's a bit of fun. With every successful product, you're going to get a few who abuse it. But you can't be held to account for what they go on to do.'

Alexa fingered the cold, clear stem of her wine glass, weighing up the points for and against. It was refreshing to hear someone so adamantly deny that she was to blame for what had happened, but there were so many sides to the argument and she wasn't going to spend the rest of the evening discussing them.

'Maybe,' she conceded. 'Anyway. I think you owe your Italian friend an apology.' She nodded towards the proprietor, who was fawning over the table near the window. 'You just turned down his home-made chilli sauce without even noticing.'

'Oh,' he said, smiling. 'I noticed.'

Alexa looked at him, confused.

'The last time I tried Dante's home-made chilli sauce, I couldn't taste anything for a fortnight – and he won't take no for an answer.'

Alexa laughed. To her relief, Riz quickly moved on to the subject of how he had originally stumbled upon the pizzeria, which took them on to the aborted night out with the news team that had preceded his discovery, which led them to Marcus' and Louis' shared passion for frequenting gentlemen's clubs and, eventually, to the subject of Derek's recent fling with a 32FF stripper.

The wine was slipping down easily and Alexa was starting to feel the familiar urge to open up more than she usually would.

'He did go a bit quiet on that front,' said Riz, pensively. 'I guess it didn't last. Hardly surprising. In fact, the surprise is that he managed to snare her in the first place.'

Alexa tipped back her glass. She was fully aware that she ought to keep her mouth shut and think of another topic, but the idea of telling Riz the truth about Derek's 'relationship' was just too appealing.

'Derek never actually—'

'Shall we—'

They were both talking at once.

'Go on.'

'No, you first.'

Alexa looked down at the empty bottle between them. She knew it was wrong to tell Riz. She knew she'd had too much to drink. She was aware, deep down, that if news got out about her practical joke and the deputy editor found out that she had spilled the beans, she would lose her leverage over him. But then, her contract came to an end in a month. And besides, Riz was trustworthy.

'Derek never actually went out with the stripper,' she said.

'Really?' Riz didn't seem very surprised. 'Was it all in his head?'

'Well, sort of.' Alexa caught his eye. 'He did actually believe he was going out with her, though.'

'He was deluded?'

Alexa thought of a way to put it. 'He had some assistance in his delusion.'

Riz began to smile. 'Alexa Harris,' he said, slowly, 'did *you* assist in the deputy editor's delusion?'

Alexa drew out her phone. A grin was spreading across her face. 'Just a few texts and emails,' she explained. 'And a date.'

'A date? How did you engineer that?'

She slipped the phone across the table, showing Riz the photo and switching on an expression of false empathy. 'She never turned up.'

Riz stared at the photo, shaking his head.

'Brilliant,' he declared, smiling with suppressed excitement. 'That is *brilliant*. Am I allowed to share the news with selected members of the team?'

Alexa looked at him through narrowed eyes. 'Maybe wait 'til I leave,' she said. 'I'll email it to you.'

A waiter cleared away their empty plates and tried to entice them with the dessert menu. Alexa shook her head, suddenly feeling very drunk.

'I should go,' she said.

Riz didn't object; he just nodded and asked the waiter for the bill.

Alexa found herself foraging in her bag for her purse, wondering whether she would regret what she'd done in the morning. This was the problem with white wine. It went straight to her head – or more specifically, to her tongue. She shouldn't have told Riz about the trick she'd played on Derek. Nor should she have confided in him about her reservations over the app. She was nearly thirty; she ought to have learned by now to keep her mouth shut.

'Hey.' Riz held up a hand as she finally extracted the purse from a bundle of print-offs that had been lurking there all week. 'I'll pay.'

Alexa tilted her head to one side. 'I should pay,' she replied. 'I'm the managing director.'

He raised an eyebrow. 'And I'm the man.'

'That's a bit sexist, isn't it?'

'You're the one trying to pull rank.'

The waiter reappeared with the bill, placing it on Riz's side of the table. He snatched it up with a victorious smile.

'You work for *Banter*, remember?' He pulled out a card from his wallet and pressed it against the saucer, handing it to a passing waiter. 'Girls shouldn't pay the bills.'

Alexa watched with a look of mock annoyance as Riz dealt with the payment, forbidding her to even contribute to the tip.

'Sure you don't fancy a drink?'

Alexa rose to her feet and found herself reaching for the back of the chair. Her legs felt weak and the floor seemed to be moving beneath her feet. She looked up at Riz's handsome face and thought about what might happen if they went for a drink. It appealed, more than ever, but the fact remained, they were colleagues. For the next month, she had to avoid mistakes like that.

'Early start tomorrow,' she said, apologetically.

Riz slung his bag over his shoulder. 'I'll walk you to the tube.'

They waved goodbye to the troop of Italian serving staff and headed out onto the streets of Soho. It was a warm, almost spring-like evening. Wooden tables and chairs littered the pavements of Old Compton Street and a noisy chatter filled the air. A thought entered Alexa's head. She tried to push it out, but it lingered, growing and growing until she felt as though she might explode if it didn't come out.

'Riz?'

He turned to her as they walked.

Alexa tried again to put the thought to the back of her mind, but it was almost on her lips now – there was no way she could put it away.

'Did you hear . . . the rumours? Before Christmas?'

It was the wine talking again, Alexa knew that, but she couldn't seem to do anything about it. Riz slowed almost to a halt. They were somewhere near Chinatown, walking down a side street that ran past the back of a theatre. Alexa watched him, waiting for some kind of a response.

'Yeah,' he said, eventually. 'Yeah, I did hear something.' He stopped and looked at her, his eyes glistening in the orange glow of a street lamp.

'About . . .?' She looked away, unable to finish the question in case they were talking at cross purposes.

'About us.' He said, nodding.

Alexa's heart was pounding. She looked up at his handsome, half-lit face just in time to work out what was about to happen.

She felt his stubble, first – like warm sand against her chin.

Then his arms reached around to the small of her back and pulled her firmly towards him. Riz's lips crushed hers and she could feel his fingers work their way up her spine.

Alexa knew that the right thing to do was to step away and to state, firmly but politely, that she couldn't get involved with one of her editors. But the knowledge didn't translate into action. She couldn't push him away because her arms were wrapped tightly around his shoulders and Alexa's muscles didn't seem to be following her instructions.

She ran a hand up to his short, dark hair and kissed him harder, enjoying the taste of his mouth. The fact that they were only a few blocks away from the Senate Media office, that at any point, one of their colleagues could wander out of a bar and catch them like this seemed no deterrent at all; it just added to the excitement.

Riz took a step backwards towards the wall, taking Alexa with him and pulling her tight to his chest. She made one last, half-hearted attempt at breaking away, but they were locked together, arms and hands entangled in each other's clothing and hair. She closed her eyes and accepted defeat. For once in her life, Alexa was abandoning the world of rules and challenges and targets and allowing herself to be free.

38

Peterson assessed the page of numbers in front of him, his brow deeply creased.

'. . . seems rather high,' he was saying. 'Can we do anything about that?'

Alexa looked up. She had completely lost track of what they were discussing.

'Sorry, which particular . . .?' She leaned across his desk, trying to identify the figure on the print-off that looked awry.

'Headcount,' he said, as though she was hard of hearing. 'Can we reduce it at all?'

'Ah, right.' Alexa nodded assertively. This wasn't the first time she had had to ask Peterson to repeat himself this morning. For the past two days, in fact, she had found her attention drifting – and always to the same place in her mind. 'Well, I did a quick audit with the section editors to check that none of the staff on our books could be made to go freelance. I'm afraid I think the team is as lean as it can be.'

Peterson gave a pensive nod. Alexa found herself thinking back to the circuit of the office she had conducted the previous morning – the morning after *that night*. Her conversation with Riz had been awkward and brief. Alexa had suggested going into the board room, but Riz was running late for a meeting so he had offered her a chair at his desk. Because they were talking about staff and salaries, Alexa had been forced to talk in a hushed whisper, which meant putting her face so close to his that she could feel his breath on her cheek. She had a feeling that neither of them had been fully focused on the question of headcount reduction.

Peterson stroked his clean-shaven chin, his eyes narrowed in scrutiny.

That had been the full extent of their communication since the kiss – or rather, kiss*es*. Alexa allowed herself a quick flashback to the moment she and Riz had finally pulled apart, then almost immediately fallen into another hard embrace. They had said nothing to one another afterwards – no words, at least. Riz had caught her eye and held her gaze for a moment as though conveying some sort of subliminal message; then by silent agreement they had started walking towards Leicester Square, hand in hand.

'. . . come back to cost-cutting later, if we're not happy with the revenues.'

Alexa blinked and returned to the room. *This* was why she had tried to avoid starting relationships at work. Even before they started, they caused trouble. This was an important meeting; she had to stay focused. It was her last chance to discuss the content of what she would be presenting to the Americans in four days' time. What happened today would dictate what would happen in New York, which would determine whether *Banter* survived as a brand. It would also determine whether Alexa would be awarded her twenty thousand pound bonus. She mirrored Peterson's actions as he slid the financials to one side and flipped over the first few slides of the deck.

Despite the indifference she had felt towards her position two days previously, Alexa had regained some of her resolve to impress the Americans at the meeting next week. It wasn't a complete change of heart – she still felt appalled and disgusted at the role her magazine had played in the rape of the fifteen-year-old girl – but as the date drew nearer, she had found herself rationalising the more unsavoury elements of her job and focusing on the bigger picture – the business. Riz had made a good case. It wasn't *Banter*'s fault that there was a market out there and it wasn't *Banter*'s fault that, occasionally, some depraved member of society fell into that market. She didn't feel proud, but at the same time she didn't see the point in letting the *Banter* brand collapse.

'Can we cut all this brand nonsense?' said Peterson, striking through several pages in quick succession. 'I don't think the Americans will give two hoots what we've done to boost recognition or improve engagement. They'll just want to see the numbers.'

Alexa watched anxiously as Peterson whipped the slides from the pack.

'Don't you think . . .' She tried to come up with a tactful way of disputing his thoughts. 'Maybe we should give them an idea of how far we've come, you know – how loyal our readers have become?'

Peterson continued to turn the pages as though only vaguely aware she was speaking.

'This can stay,' he said, stabbing his finger against the chart that showed the reduction in their legal bill following Alexa's policy on celebrity quotations. 'They'll like that.'

Reluctantly, Alexa nodded. Peterson was better acquainted than she was with the Americans' way of thinking. He probably knew best.

'Now,' he said, clasping his hands together and leaning over the most important slide in the deck. It was the graph of monthly revenues for the year, in comparison with Alexa's targets. '*This* is what they'll be interested in.'

Peterson's hands slid against one another as he stared intently at the numbers. Then suddenly, the sliding stopped. He looked up.

'What's happened here? I thought you said we were on track to hit the fifty-four million?'

Alexa met his eye. She had been expecting this reaction. 'I took out the forecasts for the mobile app,' she explained.

Peterson frowned. 'It's only a *temporary* suspension. You only need to allow a dip for the next couple of months or so.' He sketched a new line on his version of the chart, adding hatching across the months of March and April.

'I think,' she said, 'to be prudent, we should assume it's not going live again.'

'What?' Peterson frowned. 'Why ever not? I thought the regulators were just putting on a show. No need to worry.'

'I think, even if the regulators do clear us to go live again, we should think carefully about whether we re-launch the app. We might have to consider building a new one.'

'But . . . we've paid for the development of this one! It's here, in the cap-ex! We've got to get our money's worth out of this, Alexa. *You* were the one who proposed it. I suggest you put the forecast back onto this chart or the Americans will wonder what the hell you've been playing at.'

There was belligerence in Peterson's voice but Alexa wanted to make her point.

'With respect, Terry, I don't think the Americans know the extent of the damage caused by our involvement in the rape of that girl.'

'No, quite right. I hope you're not planning to put in a slide about *that*?'

Alexa sighed. She had foreseen this argument, although not the extent of Peterson's wrath. She had known that he would push for an unrealistic forecast that made *Banter* look healthy to the Americans, ignoring the potential damage that re-launching the app could do – to the brand but also to society. Her conscience hadn't allowed her to assume that the app would ever see the light of day again.

'No,' she said calmly. 'But I think we should warn them that this revenue stream is in jeopardy. We shouldn't count on it.'

342

'Right,' he said, aggressively. 'So how do you propose we make up the extra three million to hit our target?'

'We won't,' she replied. 'Without the app revenue, we won't hit our target.'

Peterson leaned forward on the desk, tilting his head to one side, his eyes boring straight into hers.

'Exactly,' he growled. 'Which is why we're *not going to tell them about the problems we've been having with the app.*'

Alexa exhaled, saying nothing. She knew when to walk away from an argument.

'Fine,' she said, softly. 'I suggest that you talk them through that particular slide.'

'Fine,' he replied, with venom. 'It will be my pleasure. Honestly, Alexa, anyone would think you didn't *want* your bonus.'

Alexa didn't reply. They flicked through the remaining slides to the sound of Peterson's heavy, nasal breathing. Eventually, the chief executive flipped over the final page and looked up.

'Well, I'm happy if you are.' He flashed her a loaded smile.

Alexa nodded briefly and rose from her seat.

'Don't forget to add in that revenue line,' he called, as she left. 'We *have* to hit fifty-four million.'

Alexa didn't look back. She let the door fall shut and hurried through the management offices, looking straight ahead. In a week's time, she would be touting the *My Girlfriend* app to the board of Senate Media as though it was the best thing since sliced bread. She felt like an unscrupulous, fraudulent bitch.

39

Alexa hoisted the rucksack onto her shoulder and glanced vaguely at the discarded suits that littered the hallway. She couldn't think straight. Her mind was filled with an intense, all-consuming paranoia.

She took a deep breath, trying to feed some oxygen to her stifled brain. She hadn't slept at all last night. She had made the mistake of running through the presentation one last time on her laptop before going to bed. The next six hours had been spent wide awake, worrying about all the things she had to remember to say and all the things she really didn't want to be saying.

Peterson had remained adamant that the Americans weren't to know the full extent of the damage caused by the *My Girlfriend* app, or its potential for further misuse. He intended to talk as though the re-launch was imminent and that the revenue stream coming from the app was assured – that they were on track to hit the fifty-four million target by the end of the year. Alexa had never felt less comfortable about anything in her life.

With a final, fleeting glance around the flat, Alexa headed out, letting the door slam behind her. Outside, a light drizzle was filling the air – not falling, exactly, just hanging, as though unable to make up its mind what to do. Alexa squinted at the line of parked cars, struggling to identify the company cab.

'Ms Harris?' The steamed-up window of an estate car opposite opened to reveal a ruddy-faced driver with a friendly smile. On her nod, he rolled out of his cab, threw her rucksack into the boot and bustled back to his seat.

'Lovely day for it,' he remarked, pulling out of the space and joining the slow-moving West London traffic.

Alexa gave a brief, sardonic nod and let her head fall back against the plastic headrest. Her brain was tired but restless, churning through the same thoughts that had plagued her all night. If she went along with Peterson's plan, she would not only be setting the *Banter* team up for a giant fall at the end of the year, but she would be signing them up for another go with the *My Girlfriend* app – something she simply couldn't do. But then, to speak out about the app would be to undermine the UK chief executive in front of the American board, ruling out any chance of survival for the magazine, along with her chances of future work – and of course, her twenty thousand pound bonus.

'Where're you off to?' asked the driver.

'Heathrow,' she replied, distractedly.

He grinned at her in the rear-view mirror and rolled his eyes. 'I know that,' he said. 'I mean, where're you *heading*, from Heathrow?'

'Oh.' Alexa gave a nervous laugh. 'New York.'

'Ah.' The driver nodded. 'The Big Apple.'

Alexa looked away, feeling a fresh wave of anxiety engulf her as she pictured the boardroom in midtown Manhattan, imagining the row of clean-shaven faces that would be sitting, listening to her desperate plea to save the brand. She had researched the directors' profiles on the intranet the previous week. There were eight, in total – all of them men. Brent Dearman, the marketing director, and Randy Taverner, chief operating officer, were the only two she recognised, having liaised with them over the re-launch of *Hers* the previous year. The others were complete unknowns.

The driver put his foot down as they came off a roundabout

and headed onto the motorway, humming quietly to himself. Alexa wiped a patch in the steam and looked out at the drab, grey tower blocks looming out of the mist.

They passed a sign to Heathrow. The driver's face reappeared in the rear-view mirror.

'Got your passport?' He winked.

Alexa's hand went instinctively to her pocket. She could feel the slender, plastic-bound book through the fabric of her coat but she drew it out all the same, just to be sure. As she did so, a piece of folded-up paper fell out onto her lap. Alexa could feel her heart rate quicken. She grabbed the leaflet and screwed it into a tiny ball, looking around for a bin. There was no bin. Reluctantly, she stuffed it back into the pocket and tried to block the memory of the protest from her mind.

'. . . never forget that time!' The cabbie laughed. He was telling some kind of story. 'She was only eighteen – it was her first time away from home, see. I think she just got carried away with all the bikinis and little dresses – she forgot the one important thing!'

Alexa nodded obligingly. She was trying to listen, but her thoughts were elsewhere. The leaflet's strap-line was emblazoned on her mind, despite her attempts to block it out. *ABUSE STARTS WITH LADS' MAGS.* That had been her second-ever encounter with Georgie Caraway, after the TV debate. Alexa remembered the look of belligerence on the campaigner's face as she'd handed her the leaflet. '*With respect, Alexa, I don't think I'm the one who needs help . . .*' The rage coursed through Alexa's veins as the memory crystallised.

'. . . driving home, double-speed, turning the house upside-down and then getting back into the car!' The taxi driver was wrapped up in his own memories.

Alexa closed her eyes, unable to shift her thoughts. As the cabbie went on, something began to dawn on Alexa. It wasn't rage that she felt – at least, not rage directed at the feminists.

She was angry at *herself*. She was ashamed of herself. The rape incident had brought it home to Alexa how off-kilter her thinking had been in the beginning. She had blindly assumed that any form of nudity that passed the regulators' approval was an opportunity for *Banter*; she hadn't stopped to think about the real impact it would have. It was the same with the magazine as a whole. *She hadn't stopped to think.*

Reaching into her pocket, Alexa felt around for the screwed-up ball of paper. Slowly, she drew it out again, flattening it against her knee. The woman's face stared back at her from the crumpled page: bruised, cut and bleeding. On the back of the leaflet was some text that told of how the young woman, whose name was Tatiana, had been trafficked from Romania and forced into a life of prostitution by a pimp who kept her locked up and allowed clients to beat her. Alexa stopped reading and flipped over the leaflet, feeling sick.

She looked out of the window but there was nothing to see. The sights were all in her head: the young Romanian being punched until her face bled; the fifteen-year-old girl being gang raped; the kid at Leonie's school being coerced into sex by her boyfriend. The bile rose up from her stomach and she swallowed it back down. She hadn't even asked Leonie how the girl was – whether she had made it back into school. She hadn't even *seen* Leonie in months.

'She was panicking, I can tell you . . .'

Alexa nodded mutely. Her mind were flicking between the image of Tatiana's swollen face and that of Derek's familiar, gleeful grin as he and Marcus headed off to the strip club at the end of the night. For months, she had persuaded herself that there was no connection. She had convinced herself – with the help of Riz and the other members of the team who had some semblance of a conscience – that the misogynistic, homophobic machismo that pervaded the office had no bearing on the plight of women like Tatiana. They had held firm in the belief that the magazine was the symptom, not the cause. But that wasn't true. Alexa saw that now. *It wasn't true.*

She was involved in an enterprise that made its money from denigrating women in a way that had far-reaching effects. Her best friends were ashamed of her. That said something, didn't it? Surely that was her cue to change something, when a woman like Kate started frowning on her actions. But she couldn't – or at least, she hadn't felt able to until now. So much depended on her staying at *Banter*, helping it to struggle to its feet. There was a brand at stake, a business – not to mention people's jobs. Besides, this was *her* job. She was good at what she did and from the inside, it hadn't looked as though she was doing anything wrong.

'. . . said she'd get a minicab to the airport, but I said no. I mean, I didn't really have *time* to drive her there – I was late as it was. But she's my daughter, y'know? I'd do anything for me daughter.'

Alexa looked up. Something in what the cab driver had said set her thoughts on another path. *She* was somebody's daughter. Her parents would do anything for *her*. They had done, all through her life. They had paid for her swimming lessons, taught her to canoe, helped with her homework, given her lifts to parties, driven her up to university . . . . They had made sacrifices to enable her to get the most out of life. And in return, what had she done? *What was she doing, flying to New York on the biggest day of her mother's life?*

Alexa's thoughts flitted between this question and the one that had been troubling her for weeks, ever since the rape of Letitia Chinwe. *What was she doing, helping the* Banter *brand to survive?* In a panic, she joined up the two trains of thought and realised that she did have another option. It was a frightening one that meant abandoning all of her self-imposed rules and any chance of 'success' as she knew it. She could walk out, right now, and go to her parents' party instead of the board meeting.

She leaned forward and checked the time. It was half-past twelve. Her mother would have received her award by now. She and her father would be on their way back to Averley, with Auntie Jen and Aunt Sue – her father driving slowly, so as to give the local residents time to arrive at the house for the surprise party. Alexa thought about her own contribution to the proceedings and closed her eyes, crumpling with guilt. She had sent flowers. That was it. On the most important day of her mother's life, she had sent a bunch of flowers.

Alexa fingered the leaflet in her hand and made up her mind.

'Excuse me,' she said, catching the driver's eye. For the first time in nine turbulent months, she felt utterly sure about something. 'I'm sorry. Change of plan. Can you take me to Surrey?'

The cabbie frowned. 'What did you say?'

Alexa repeated herself. Adrenaline started to displace some the guilt and the shame as she realised the enormity of what she was doing. She wasn't going to New York. She wasn't going to stand up in front of the Americans and tell them how to make more money from the exploitation of women like Tatiana. She wasn't going to prevent the demise of the magazine and she wasn't going to put her targets ahead of her family and friends any longer.

The driver looked bewildered but he didn't question his instruction. Once Alexa was sure they were past Heathrow and heading for the M25, she pulled out her phone and called Peterson. His voicemail kicked in immediately.

'Hi,' she said, mentally scrambling to compose her message. 'It's Alexa. Um, look. I can't make the board meeting in New York. I know it's short notice, but . . . there's something more important I have to do. A family thing.' She realised this might sound melodramatic and hastily added a clarification. 'It's nothing bad,' she explained. 'It's just . . . well, it's more important. I'm sorry.' Alexa tried to think of what else she needed to say. She had plenty more to tell Peterson, but that could wait until they were face to face. She pulled the phone from her ear and ended the call.

The driver raised an eyebrow at her in the mirror, inviting an explanation, but Alexa just smiled and looked out of the window. The mist was clearing, she noticed. There were other things she noticed, too – like the straightness of the trees either side of the road and the signs to the zoo and the little purple flowers growing along the middle of the central reservation.

The traffic was surprisingly light for a weekend and Alexa could feel her anticipation mount as the motorway gave way to A-roads, then B-roads, which eventually led to the sleepy village of Averley. It was particularly sleepy today, Alexa noted, smiling as they pulled into Elm Rise.

'This it?' The driver twisted round in his seat, clearly angling for more information.

Alexa directed him to number twelve and squinted at the front door of her parents' house. The sun was beginning to shine through the wisps of cloud, casting dappled shadows through the wisteria around the door. Alexa frowned. She had expected to see signs of life inside. The plan was for one of the neighbours to let everybody in while her parents were at the ceremony, but the house looked deserted.

'Yeah,' she replied, vaguely. She wondered whether her father might have changed the plan. He wouldn't have bothered to tell her, knowing that she'd be on her way to New York. Alexa thought about calling him, but then she saw it: a twitch of the net curtain in the lounge. It was only slight, but it was enough to reveal something colourful on the other side. Balloons.

'Yeah,' said Alexa, more firmly. 'This is it.'

She thanked the driver as he held out her rucksack. As she did so, something dawned on her. The cab had been paid for by Senate Media.

She foraged for her wallet. 'I should settle up, as I didn't go to . . .'

The cabbie was shaking his head. 'No need,' he said, grinning. 'I'll just tell them I dropped you at Heathrow.'

The smile spread slowly across Alexa's face.

'You have a good time with the family.' He raised a hand and slipped back into his cab, tooting the horn as he went.

Alexa stood for a moment in the spot where the taxi had dropped her, looking at the familiar, pebbledash exterior of her parents' home – *her* home, for two thirds of her life. It was only when her cousin, Angie, opened the door and hissed for her to come inside that she realised her parents' car had just turned into the street.

The initial commotion lasted several minutes: party-poppers, hooters, screams, whoops, cries of delight from Alexa's mother, bashful looks from her father, who was clearly delighted that his plan had come off successfully. There must have been nearly a hundred people in the house, Alexa estimated. Her mother had touched the lives of a hundred people – probably more, if you counted all the children who weren't here. Alexa sat on the stairs, waiting for the revellers to disperse and feeling unexpectedly emotional.

After a while, despite the protests, Alexa's mother fought her way into the kitchen, clearly unable to hand over the organisation entirely. Alexa rose to her feet and crept down the stairs. She stood in the doorway, watching as the troop of helpers gradually found other jobs elsewhere; then, when her mother was alone in the kitchen, she made her appearance.

'Hi, Mum.'

Her mother instinctively passed her a quiche dish and then froze, staring at Alexa.

'I thought . . .'

Alexa smiled. 'I was supposed to be. But I came here instead. Congratulations, Mum.'

Her mother let the quiche dish slide onto the kitchen table, her eyes not leaving her daughter's. She stepped forward and hugged Alexa, squeezing her hard across the shoulders. They stayed like that for a long time, as though making up for all the missed hugs of the last thirty years. When they parted, Alexa wasn't sure, but she thought her mother might have been welling up.

'Right, quiche!' she said, turning away and wiping her eye with the corner of the oven glove. 'Let's get them sliced and served, shall we?'

Alexa nodded, smiling through her own tears as her mother got back to what she did best. She had been to so many of her mother's parties, but it felt as though this was the first one she was actually attending, in person. She sliced the quiches and transferred them onto a plate as instructed, carrying them into the lounge with a smile that stayed with her until the end of the night.

40

Alexa knocked on the door and waited for a couple of seconds, rehearsing her lines one last time in her head. Hearing nothing from the other side, she took a deep breath and marched in.

To her surprise, Peterson was smiling. He was sat behind his desk, hands clasped neatly together, wearing the exact same expression that Alexa remembered from their meeting ten months ago, when he had offered her the position at *Banter*.

'Good afternoon.' Peterson nodded towards the chair.

Hesitantly, Alexa took a seat, trying to work things out. This was not the reaction she had expected from a man who had been let down at less than twenty-four hours' notice for one of the most important meetings of the year.

'So,' he said, eyes twinkling.

Alexa assumed this to be her cue to explain herself. She summoned her opening lines from her short-term memory, wondering whether this aura of calm might be a precursor to the extreme rage that people spoke of. She had never experienced Peterson's infamous temper, but she imagined he might be the type to start eerily placid, like a volcano about to erupt.

'You probably want to know what happened on Monday?'

It was put as more of a statement than a question. Alexa found herself nodding. This was unnerving. Where were the angry questions about her non-appearance? Where was her chance to explain, once and for all, why she was walking out on the *Banter* brand?

'Well.' Peterson rubbed his clasped hands together, still smiling. 'As it happens, it all went rather well.'

Alexa nodded meekly, letting go of her theory that the chief executive was about to explode. He seemed genuinely pleased with himself.

'They love what we've done with the brand over the last nine months and they seemed reasonably confident about the forecasts. We – as the Americans say – are *back in business*.'

We, Alexa noted, trying to rein in all the questions in her head. One particular question jumped to the front of her mind. 'So . . . what did they say about the mobile app?'

Peterson looked down at his hands, his smile briefly faltering. 'There was a discussion,' he said. 'I didn't go into detail, but it was generally agreed that our forecasts look realistic, assuming the app re-launches in the next month or so.'

Which it won't, Alexa nearly replied. She hesitated, trying to determine whether it was worth opening up this argument again. It was too late, she concluded. The Americans had bought Peterson's lies now; they were expecting great things from the app. It would be up to Derek and the rest of the team to argue with the regulators to get the app reinstated and frankly, Alexa didn't fancy their chances. Either way, there was nothing she could say now to change things. She would just have to watch from afar as her own vile initiative ran its course.

'So *Banter* lives to see another day,' he declared proudly.

Alexa nodded.

Peterson looked at her, his head cocked to one side. He was clearly perplexed by her lack of enthusiasm. Alexa wondered whether now might be her chance to tell him why she was walking away from the brand. She tried to think of a way to begin.

'Ah,' said Peterson, nodding as though he found something mildly amusing. 'I know what you're thinking.'

Alexa doubted it. She waited for his explanation nonetheless.

'Your bonus.' He pulled up his chair and leaned towards her across the desk. The smile lingered on his lips, although his eyes had narrowed to conjecturing slits.

Alexa stared, unable to speak. She was astonished that there was even any mention of a bonus. After all, she had neglected to turn up to the key board meeting and she had failed to deliver revenue streams that guaranteed fifty-four million by the end of the year – although, of course, the Americans didn't know that. She found herself holding her breath as she waited for Peterson's next words.

'Now, you were expecting twenty, were you not, on the under-standing that we hit the fifty-four million mark?'

Alexa nodded mutely.

'I've been pushing for the full amount, of course, but because of the uncertainty over the mobile app . . .' Peterson grimaced, as though the involvement of their app in the gang rape was a minor inconvenience. 'We've settled on a split payment. Ten percent now, the rest at the end of the year, if and when the forecasts are proved to be correct.'

Alexa let out the lungful of air, unable to hold it in any longer. She felt confused and guilty. Of course, the forecasts would never be achieved; they were just over-inflated figments of Peterson's imagination, so there was no chance of Alexa being paid the majority of the bonus. But ten percent of twenty thousand was still two thousand pounds and the principle was still the same. She was being rewarded for helping Banter to stumble to its feet. Alexa looked away. It was like taking blood money. She couldn't accept it.

'I know it's disappointing,' said Peterson, condescendingly, 'but that really is the best we can hope for, given the circumstances.'

Alexa couldn't meet his eye. She didn't know what to do. It

would be hypocritical to accept the money. She despised everything that *Banter* stood for. It might have taken her nine months to realise it, but now that she did, she had to draw a line – to walk away. She couldn't profit any more from the magazine's success.

'Oh!' Peterson gasped, looking suddenly mortified. 'I should have asked. I'm sorry. Is everything alright with the family?'

Alexa closed her eyes for a moment, trying to think. This was all going wrong. It wasn't meant to be happening like this. She had explained in her voicemail that the 'family thing' wasn't anything bad, but Peterson had got hold of the wrong end of the stick. Now, instead of standing up to the chief executive and boldly explaining her reasons for walking out on the brand, Alexa was faced with fending off his misplaced sympathy and turning down two thousand pounds of his money.

'It's fine,' she said, trying to remember some of the feisty lines she had intended to use in her explanatory speech. 'There was actually nothing—'

Peterson raised a hand, stopping her, mid-flow. 'No need to explain,' he said, with a kindly smile.

Alexa opened her mouth to protest, but as she did so, something occurred to her. There was absolutely no point in protesting. Peterson was too insensitive to understand her explanations. He would never see the merit in her U-turn. He cared only about circulation and profit; he had no interest in morality. There was nothing to be gained by enraging the chief executive. If she just kept quiet, she could take the two thousand pounds and donate it to Georgie's charity. In fact, that was a good idea. Alexa looked up at Peterson and matched his smile. She would give the money to REACT.

'It's been a bumpy few months, hasn't it?' Peterson looked across at her, the twinkle returning to his eye.

Alexa wondered where he was going with this. Peterson wasn't one for abstract reflection.

'As you know,' he said, 'I'm very pleased with your achievements at *Banter*.'

She watched him, carefully. His expression seemed suspiciously warm, considering the circumstances.

'I think you proved a lot of people wrong – not least, the Americans.'

An alarm bell started ringing in Alexa's head. She had heard these words before.

'I'm thinking,' he said, eyes narrowed, 'you might be able to help us out on something else.'

Alexa stared. She couldn't believe it. Peterson was asking her back. In her mind, she had walked out on *Banter*, walked out on Senate Media. This meeting was simply a courtesy call to end relations on a cordial note. Clearly Peterson had a very different idea of where they stood.

He swivelled in his chair and looked up at the array of framed magazine covers on the wall above him.

'*Teenz*,' he declared, stretching his solid frame and pointing.

Alexa followed his gaze and then looked away, feeling suddenly disgusted by the sight of all the flesh spilling off the cover of *Banter*, next to the magazine she was supposed to be looking at.

'It's the same old story,' said Peterson, woefully. 'Falling circulation, falling ad revenue, too much competition . . . it would be a similar arrangement to your last two assignments.'

Alexa could hear the chief executive talking about day rates and contracts, but she wasn't listening properly. She was wondering how she might have felt if she had never taken on the job at *Banter* – if this meeting had happened nine months ago and she had come straight from her role at *Hers*. Would the bare breasts up there have offended her? Would she have made the connection between the pornographic poses and all the cases of misogyny and violence against women? Would she have had the same awakening that she'd had at *Banter* – the realisation that there was more to life than the pursuit of targets?

357

'Of course, you'll need to think about it.' Peterson's kindly gaze returned to Alexa.

Alexa nodded vaguely. There were so many things she could have said. She could have explained to Peterson that she was done throwing all of her energy into something that ultimately boiled down to money. She could have pointed at the cover of *Banter* and educated him on the effect that such publications had on the wider society. She could have told him that as chief executive, *he* had a duty to think more about the bigger picture and less about the bottom line of his sinking media empire. But instead, Alexa rose to her feet in silence and left the room, not even stopping to bid him goodbye.

She passed through the management office in a daze. Fragments of her conversation with Peterson kept popping back into her head, triggering more thoughts about what might have been and what could potentially be, if she allowed it.

Alexa stepped into the lift, aware that in all likelihood, this would be the last time she set foot in Senate House. As the realisation permeated her brain, a sudden impulse gripped her to press '5' and head up to the *Banter* floor. She hadn't expected to leave in such a hurry. While it was true that she wouldn't miss the general atmosphere on the fifth floor, or the attitudes of certain members of the team, there were some people – and one in particular – to whom she would have liked to say a proper goodbye.

Alexa held a hand out to keep the lift doors from closing, the fingers of her other hand wavering between '5' and 'G'. It was Riz she cared about. Emma, Jamie, Neil, Paddy, Biscuit . . . they would be missed, but they'd be fine with a farewell email. In fact, given the apparent strength of Kate's relationship with the jokes editor, Alexa suspected she might have another means of keeping in touch with her ex-colleagues. But Riz . . .

A woman in high heels clacked her way down the corridor from the management office.

'You going up or down?' she asked.

Alexa opened her mouth to reply. She and Riz had barely spoken since that night. Alexa had been so busy pulling together the board presentation that she hadn't really given him a chance – and besides, she had been so determined to live by her own stupid rules and not mix business with pleasure, she had probably put him off for good. What was she planning to say to him? What was she hoping to achieve by entering the office of the magazine she had left behind?

'Down,' she said, stepping aside for the woman to join her.

Under pressure, going back suddenly seemed like an absurd thing to want to do. She had drawn a line. She was no longer associated with *Banter*. There was no point in hanging around the offices, hoping to catch a glimpse of a man who had probably already forgotten her anyway.

Alexa stepped into the bright April sunshine, thinking about what she would do to end the uncertainty. She would send a note to the team from her personal email address, she decided, which would allow Riz to contact her if he wanted to. That way, she wouldn't have to face the shame of outright rejection. It was silly to get hung up over someone she knew so little about, she told herself. It was just a kiss.

Alexa wandered through Soho, pushing her thoughts back to Peterson's proposition and the larger question of what she was going to do next. She couldn't help thinking that if it hadn't been for her experience at *Banter*, she would have jumped at the chance to rejuvenate *Teenz*. It was a brilliant opportunity within a global media business – and of course, there was a great salary. But her latest turnaround project for Senate Media had left a bitter taste in her mouth and the idea of taking on another just didn't appeal. *Banter* had changed the way she saw magazines – in fact, it had changed her views on media as a whole. It suddenly seemed like a grubby, unethical, manipulative industry that served no benefit to society as a whole. She felt a vibration inside her bag and reached inside, grabbing her phone.

It was an unknown number. Alexa's heart lurched. The office phone came up as 'unknown'. Maybe the team had been told about her departure and Riz was calling to see if . . . Alexa picked up the call, shoving her childish hopes to the back of her mind.

'Alexa speaking?'

'Hi, Alexa.' It was a woman with an American accent. 'My name's Sheryl. I'm calling from a company called Pixelate. I don't suppose you've heard of us, but we make e-magazines and tablet editions for various US charities looking to digitise the content of their newsletters. We're a small business, but we're looking to expand to the UK in the next few months and . . . well, we've seen the work you've been doing at Senate and we were wondering whether you'd be interested in helping to run our UK operation.'

'Um . . .' Alexa faltered, not sure what to ask first.

'We can't offer a huge salary,' Sheryl clarified. 'Like I said, we're a small outfit and we work only for charities, so the margin's pretty slim. But I can promise that the work is very rewarding and often quite a challenge. I was told that you like a good challenge.'

'Wh . . .' Alexa stuttered, her mind bursting with unanswered questions. 'Who told you that?'

'Georgie Caraway,' Sheryl replied. 'She tells me you might be looking for something new. Is that right?'

A reluctant smile crept across Alexa's face. 'Yes,' she said. 'I guess it is.'

Alexa took down the woman's details, thinking about Georgie and her various appearances over the past six months. She had become such a regular, obstinate feature in Alexa's life, causing such disruption and so much angst that Alexa had become instinctively dismissive of her cause. In fact, she now realised, the campaigners' cause was aligned with her own. She agreed with much of what they were trying to achieve. She still couldn't condone the techniques they had employed to get her to change her mind, but she saw now why they acted as they had. Ironically, she *had* changed her mind, although it wasn't down to the poster campaigns or the stalking or the aggressive phone calls.

Alexa put down the phone, resolving to write out a cheque for two thousand pounds as soon as she banked her bonus.

41

Alexa watched anxiously as her friend reached for the remote control and switched off the television.

'Well,' said Leonie, hoisting her legs up onto the sofa and giving a conclusive sigh. 'I guess that's all you can hope for.'

Alexa couldn't meet her eye – not just because hers were filling with tears but because she couldn't cope with any more of Leonie's compassion. She didn't deserve it.

They had been watching the outcome of the trial for the four youths accused of raping Letitia Chinwe. The ringleaders, aged twenty and twenty-two, had pleaded guilty and each received nine-year sentences. The two teenagers, aged just sixteen and seventeen, had also pleaded guilty and had been awarded indeterminate detention orders with no option of parole for four years. Alexa felt hollow – as though someone had reached into her gut and scooped out her insides.

The trial had had more of an effect on her than she had anticipated. Hearing the names of the kids involved and listening to the reporter's quote from the victim's statement made it suddenly seem very personal. Alexa knew it was irrational; she hadn't met Letitia Chinwe and never would. She wasn't directly involved in the case. Yet she felt involved. At the back of her mind, as she had listened to the fifteen-year-old's statement about how she could no longer leave her house, how she didn't feel comfortable with her friends any more, how she was afraid to go to school . . . Alexa felt as though *she* should have been sentenced, alongside the four young men. She couldn't help believing that if the mobile app hadn't existed in the first place and if magazines like *Banter* weren't perpetuating this culture of aggression, then maybe the whole ordeal might have been avoided.

Alexa looked out of the window, focusing on the tiny, white-clad bodies running around the school cricket pitch. She tried to blink back the tears, but as she did so, she heard the cushions shift beside her and felt the warmth of Leonie's arm along the back of her neck. She blinked again and let the tears spill out onto her cheeks. Guilt and wretchedness coursed through her as she turned and buried her face in Leonie's shoulder.

'I'm sorry,' she said, into the fabric of Leonie's top.

Leonie rubbed her back. 'It's okay.'

Alexa pulled away, just enough to see her friend's face, which was set in a grim smile.

'No.' She scrunched her eyes shut, trying to compose herself. 'I mean . . .' She opened them again and looked at Leonie. 'I'm *sorry*. For being so . . .' She lifted her shoulders, unable to choose between all the words running through her head. *Selfish. Thoughtless. Pig-headed. Ungrateful. Self-serving . . .*'

'Don't be,' said Leonie, shaking her head. 'At least you've seen sense.'

Alexa let out a shaky sigh. She deserved to hear *I told you so*. She deserved to be berated by Leonie – deserved never to have the benefit of her friendship again. But Leonie was offering her another chance. Alexa couldn't think of adequate words to express her gratitude, so she leaned into Leonie's open arms and squeezed her slender frame.

Leonie emerged, smiling.

'Cup of tea?' she asked.

Alexa gave an enthusiastic nod and wiped the tears from her

eyes. She followed Leonie into the kitchen, wondering how she had managed to veer so far from the good advice her friend had been offering all along.

They waited for the kettle to boil, looking out over the vast, striped lawn that flanked the tree-lined driveway of the school.

'Piers wants to move,' Leonie said, vacantly.

'What?' Alexa frowned. Leonie and Piers were currently enjoying rent-free accommodation in the landscaped surroundings of King Charles'. 'Why?'

Leonie lifted her shoulders. 'He finds it claustrophobic, living among his pupils. He wants to rent a place nearby.'

'But . . .' Alexa was about to point out the obvious fact that a flat in Dulwich would set them back at least a thousand pounds a month, but she didn't have the heart. Leonie would have done the sums; that was why she looked so disheartened.

'I can sort of see what he means,' Leonie conceded. 'It is a bit intense, seeing the boys and the other teachers the whole time, never completely getting away from work, but . . .'

The kettle clicked, prompting Leonie back into action. She poured the hot water into the mugs, giving them each a vigorous stir. Alexa grabbed the milk from the fridge and passed it across, wishing she could help in some way. She knew that Leonie would never allow Piers to pay more than half of the rent, despite the fact that she earned half of what her boyfriend took home each month and she had none of Daddy's money to fall back on, as he did.

'Here.' Leonie held out a mug of steaming tea.

As they settled back down on the sofa, Alexa felt her phone vibrate with an email. She pulled it out with the intention of turning it off, but then stopped, noting the name of the sender. It was Riz.

'What's up?' asked Leonie.

'Um . . .' Alexa realised that her hand was trembling. She clicked on the email and felt something plunge inside her. It was nothing – just a brief, two-line message that consisted of a link to a website. There was no mention of their kiss – of 'them'.

Hey Boss, I presume you've seen this?
http://www.medianewsuk.co.uk/end-of-an-era.htm

'It's . . .' Alexa clicked on the link, not sure she wanted to explain everything to Leonie. In context, now that she effectively had it in writing from Riz that nothing was ever going to happen between them, there seemed little point. 'An ex-colleague,' she explained.

She clicked on the link, waiting for the page to load.

Leonie leaned over, intrigued.

Alexa was about to offer an explanation for her trembling hands when the page appeared on the screen and she read the headline. *END OF AN ERA AS BANTER CLOSES FOR BUSINESS.* She tried to swallow but her throat felt dry.

'Oh my God,' said Leonie, reading it over her shoulder.

Alexa squinted at the tiny words on the screen, feeling a strange mixture of excitement and horror as she read the article.

Senate Media's £50m men's magazine, *Banter*, closed today after launching nearly eight years ago to great acclaim in the publishing world.

The news comes after the UK's largest lads' mag increased its circulation by twenty percent in the last quarter and launched a string of successful digital initiatives aimed at young men, including the controversial mobile app, *My Girlfriend*, which was banned by regulators last week amid controversy over its use in the rape of Letitia Chinwe earlier this year. *Banter* representatives refuse to comment on the possible link between the removal of the app and the demise of the brand.

'Senate UK chief executive, Terry Peterson, broke the news to staff last week,' an insider told Media News UK. 'Apparently the decision has been made for financial reasons.' It is thought that the death sentence was prescribed by parent company, Senate

Media Inc., after many months of deliberation over whether to keep the unprofitable title afloat.

Senate stated that it had 'reluctantly' taken the decision to close the brand but had not ruled out a future revival in the form of 'one shot' publications or special tablet editions. The last official issue of *Banter* magazine went out on Tuesday 6th May. Its closure will affect twenty-four staff.

Alexa handed the phone to Leonie and sat, cradling her cup of tea and staring at the coffee table. She couldn't work out how she felt. It wasn't as though the news had come as a surprise; she had expected the regulators to pull the mobile app. She had known that without the app, the magazine wouldn't hit its targets and would therefore be seen as an unnecessary drain on resources by the Americans. She just hadn't expected it to happen so soon.

'Wow,' Leonie gasped, returning Alexa's phone. 'The end of an era.'

Alexa mirrored her half-smile. She knew that in principle, this was a good thing. Ultimately, it was the best result all round. Like a star, the magazine had burned so brightly, brought so much attention upon itself that it had imploded. It had brought *itself* to its knees. But there was one line in the article that made Alexa's stomach turn. The last line. She quickly returned to the email and replied to Riz.

I'm sorry, she typed. *What will you do? What will everyone do?*

She slid the phone onto the coffee table and took a sip of tea. She could feel Leonie's gaze on the side of her face.

'I guess this rules out the job at the teen magazine?'

'I don't know.' Alexa smiled. 'But I wouldn't have taken it anyway.'

Leonie raised an eyebrow. 'So, you're accepting the other one?'

She nodded.

'With the measly salary?'

She nodded again. 'I start on Monday.'

'Wow, Lex. That *is* a new leaf.'

Alexa laughed. 'I'm trying.'

Leonie started to drink her tea and then looked up as though suddenly remembering something. 'Ah!' she said, wiping a splash of tea from her lap. 'In which case . . .'

Alexa watched as her friend slowly placed the mug back on the table and turned to face her.

'Would you consider allowing a very sweet, prize-winning English literature student to do an internship at your firm?'

Alexa felt suddenly emotional again. She didn't need to ask Leonie whether this was Anna, the girl who had been forced into having sex with her boyfriend – who, she now knew, had made it back into the classroom and was doing fine.

'It would be an honour,' she replied.

They sipped their tea, conversation wandering from Alexa's new job to Leonie's class to her imminent flat-hunt at which point, Piers came in, dressed in grass-stained cricket whites and a baseball cap.

'I should go,' said Alexa, greeting Piers with a peck on the cheek and taking the mugs back to the kitchen.

Piers disappeared to get changed, leaving Alexa and Leonie to hug goodbye. Alexa held on, digging her fingers into Leonie's back, wanting her friend to know the strength of her shame and her gratitude. As they stood, clamped together in the doorway, a buzzing sound could be heard from somewhere nearby. Two vibrations, it turned out.

They both pulled out their phones and smiled. Kate had been made director at TDS. *PS*, said the message, *am still seeing Biscuit – 5 weeks and counting!*

They laughed. Alexa tucked her phone away, preparing to bid Leonie a final farewell, when her phone buzzed again with an email. She opened it, in case it was an update from Riz. When she saw the name of the sender, she nearly slipped the phone back into her pocket but her curiosity got the better of her.

Hi Lex,
  Thanks for the cheque, but no thanks. I'm guessing you've read the media news today? We don't want your money. We never did, actually. We wanted someone to bring Banter down from inside and while I realise you never intended to be that person, it looks as though you've done exactly that – in fact, you've done more than we ever could have hoped for. I'm returning the cheque to your home address.
  Good luck with the new job.
  Georgie

'What is it?'

Alexa absent-mindedly passed Leonie the phone, buying herself some time while she tried to straighten out her thoughts. 'It's from the girl who followed us around Mothercare,' she explained.

It was ironic. For months, she had resisted Georgie Caraway's campaigns, rationalising her own behaviour, making excuses for the magazine, and now the end result was the best thing that any anti-lads' mag campaigner could have wished for.

Leonie handed back the phone. 'You were offering them your bonus cheque?'

Alexa nodded, feeling uncomfortable. She hadn't expected REACT to turn down the money. The transfer had come through from Senate and Alexa had expected the money to go straight out again when the activists cashed the cheque. Now, they were refusing to do so and it felt as though she was sitting on dirty money. The two thousand pounds had been obtained through unethical practices. She didn't want it.

'Leonie, might you . . .'

Leonie shook her head firmly. She knew what Alexa was about to ask.

'I can't keep it,' Alexa explained. 'I want to get rid of it. And you need the cash, with this new flat.'

Leonie gave a pained expression. Alexa returned it with one of her own. She knew that Leonie was proud, but this was no ordinary handout. She *had* to get rid of the money, somehow. If Leonie wouldn't take it then she'd find a charity that would, but given the support Leonie had offered over the past nine months, it seemed fitting that she should be the recipient. Alexa knew that she needed it.

'Please . . .?'

Leonie shrugged helplessly, looking at the ground. Slowly, her expression melted into a hesitant smile. 'Well, it's not as if you ever listen to my protests, anyway.'

Alexa grinned back at her.

'I'll listen to you next time, I promise.'

Epilogue

It seemed that the collapse of *Banter* hadn't had the devastating impact on the team that Alexa had feared. Within a fortnight of Peterson's announcement, nearly all of the twenty-four members of staff had found other positions.

Derek moved across to the only remaining lads' mag in circulation, *Diss*, whose mobile app *Voyeur* had been shut down alongside *My Girlfriend*. Rumour had it, Global Media was looking to conduct a similar cull of its under-performing titles to the one recently undertaken by Senate, but in the meantime, Derek continues to live out his power trip by entertaining a dwindling number of teenage boys with his chauvinist fantasies.

Marcus made an internal move and took a small demotion to became a senior news writer on *Monsieur*, where, in a cruel twist of fate, Sienna had worked her way up to the position of news editor, making her Marcus' boss. Louis also applied for the same position but was turned down, making him the only member of the *Banter* team unable to find work.

Neil opted to take some time out of his career, looking after his children while his wife took on a full-time role in post-production. Biscuit went down a similar route, only without the children. Kate's director salary made it unnecessary for him to find work immediately.

Paddy got an assistant editor role at *Adventure* magazine,

where he continues to be sent to far-flung parts of the country to be set unachievable challenges. Emma moved across with him, her role being to set the challenges.

Jamie turned his airbrushing skills to the thighs and torsos of American catwalk models, taking on the position of art director at *Runway* magazine and Riz became football editor of *SPORT* magazine.

Alexa scrolled to the bottom of the email, smiling as she re-read the last line.

PS I get two tickets to all the Premiership games. Can I tempt you? If you promise to avoid disagreements over the offside rule, that is?

Read on for an exclusive interview with Polly Courtney

Q&A with Polly

Leonie offers Alexa sound advice, but Alexa ignores it and does her own thing. Why?

Leonie and Alexa grew up together. They are close, but over the years they have developed very different perspectives on life, which is one of the reasons why Lex goes against Leonie's advice. She thinks she knows better – not because she is arrogant but because she is so blinded by her own ambition that she can't see that from Leonie's point of view, her intentions seem way out of line.

The extent of their friendship is only revealed when it all goes wrong and Leonie's warnings start to ring true. Instead of turning her back on Alexa and saying 'I told you so', Leonie says nothing, waiting for her friend to see the error of her ways. Alexa comes round, eventually, and by the end of the book she is mortified that she went her own way for so long. That's what friendship is all about: unconditional amity and forgiveness.

You have worked in media; did you exaggerate the office scenes or is life on a lads' mag really like that?

I have worked in media but never directly for a lads' mag. I know people who have, though, and I tried very hard to reflect their experiences in the book. Men like Derek really do exist – I've met them – but I was careful to make sure that not all of the characters were stereotypical chauvinists because that wouldn't be fair.

A friend of mine who works in the civil service read an early draft of the book and kept pulling me up on various points. *Are you serious?* she asked. She couldn't believe that Alexa's colleagues would get away with what she considered to be sexual harassment. But I guess that's the point; one person's sexual harassment is another person's banter.

Having worked in various male-dominated workplaces, I'm intrigued by the different attitudes towards this type of treatment of women. Was Alexa subjected to bullying, or was it just harmless fun?

Georgie is a feisty character. Why does Alexa refuse to see her point of view?

I don't think it's a point-blank refusal on Alexa's part; it's more that Georgie's opinions don't fit with what she is trying to do. Alexa has rationalised her intentions in her own mind and Georgie's crusade goes against everything she is working towards.

Georgie doesn't give up easily though and I think it is partly her regular, ballsy appearances that start to wear Alexa down, making her think about the wider context of what she is doing. Fundamentally, Alexa is not a bad person; she doesn't want to abandon her morals for the sake of her work but the thrill of the challenge overcomes her – that is, until Georgie's points start to hit home.

There are several incidents throughout the book in which Alexa considers going to the authorities, but decides against it every time. Why?

This was a question that played on my mind as I wrote the book. There was as much turmoil in my head as there was in Alexa's when she opened the proofs to find the hidden porn and then again, when she was thinking about Derek's actions at the Christmas party.

I asked myself what I would do in the same situation and I

honestly couldn't be sure. This is the dilemma that faces so many women in the workplace. They are effectively choosing between justice and their careers – with no guarantee of justice ever being done. It's no wonder that so many opt to keep quiet, as Alexa did.

I have a confession to make on this front. As a young investment banker in the early stages of writing my first novel, I sent a letter to a national newspaper in response to a lawsuit by a female investment banker about her treatment at the bank. The letter was entitled "The City is no place for cry-babies" and my attitude was that the woman in question should have kept her complaints to herself so as not to deter employers from hiring women. I now see that whilst the antics to which the victim was subjected (shouts of 'you stink', raspberry-blowing, staring) seemed like harmless banter, they no doubt formed part of a relentless campaign that gradually wore away at the woman's self-esteem.

It is rare for victims to speak out and make public their persecution, but for those who do, I have a newfound respect. I wish I had never written that letter.

How do *you* see lads' mags and their role in society?
My opinions changed during the process of researching and writing the book. I started off thinking that the *Banter* office would serve as a light-hearted, amusing backdrop for a novel and that any objections to the lads' mag culture were simply overreactions. But when I spoke to those who were protesting, particularly the women at OBJECT, I began to see that they had some valid points.

Sex *is* becoming ingrained in our – and our children's – lives. Women *are* increasingly seen as objects, not people. We *don't* have equality in many workplaces.

Like Alexa, I now believe that lads' mags have a detrimental effect on our society and I predict (and hope) that they have a limited time left on our newsagents' shelves.